P9-CJE-966

Acclaim for
THE DEATH OF THE
NECROMANCER

"Wells continues to demonstrate an impressive gift
for creating finely detailed fantasy worlds rife with
many-layered intrigues and immensely
personable characters."
Publishers Weekly

"A seamless blend of fantasy, history, magic and
mystery. This is the kind of world that you come to
believe exists, somewhere; a place you leave
only reluctantly."
Sean Russell

"Wells never fails to intrigue, amuse, and fascinate
with her imaginative world, wonderful characters,
and expert grasp of narrative style. I highly
recommend *anything* by Martha Wells—and I wish
she wrote faster!"
Jennifer Roberson

"A chillingly convincing tale that will entrap
genre readers."
Booklist

"Splendid plotting and characters . . .
Thoroughly engaging."
Kirkus Reviews

"An enchanting blend of detection and sorcery, it
features a memorable cast of characters and a wealth
of 'period' detail. Highly recommended."
Library Journal

"A thoroughly entertaining high adventure."
Locus

THE DEATH OF THE
NECROMANCER

MARTHA WELLS

AVON · EOS

To Matthew Bialer

AVON BOOKS, INC.
1350 Avenue of the Americas
New York, New York 10019

Copyright © 1998 by Martha Wells
Excerpt from *Signal to Noise* copyright © 1998 by Eric S. Nylund
Excerpt from *The Death of the Necromancer* copyright © 1998 by Martha Wells
Excerpt from *Scent of Magic* copyright © 1998 by Andre Norton
Excerpt from *The Gilded Chain* copyright © 1998 by Dave Duncan
Excerpt from *Krondor the Betrayal* copyright © 1998 by Raymond E. Feist
Excerpt from *Mission Child* copyright © 1998 by Maureen F. McHugh
Excerpt from *Avalanche Soldier* copyright © 1999 by Susan R. Matthews
Cover art by Jean Pierre Targete
Inside back cover author photo by Troyce Wilson
Library of Congress Catalog Card Number: 98-11917
ISBN: 0-380-78814-4
www.avonbooks.com/eos

First Avon Eos Paperback Printing: July 1999
First Avon Eos Hardcover Printing: July 1998

AVON EOS TRADEMARK REG. U.S. PAT. OFF. AND IN OTHER COUNTRIES,
MARCA REGISTRADA, HECHO EN U.S.A.

Printed in the U.S.A.

WCD 10 9 8 7 6 5 4 3 2 1

1

The most nerve-racking commissions, Madeline thought, were the ones that required going in through the front door. This front door was simply more imposing than most.

Lit by gray moonlight, the monumental facade of Mondollot House loomed over her, studded with lighted windows. High above the street the pediment was a passionately carved relief of the hosts of Heaven and Hell locked in battle, the shrouds of doomed saints and the veils of the angels flying like banners or hanging down to drape gracefully over the stone canopies of the upper windows. A quartet of musicians played from an open balcony somewhere above, entertaining the guests as they arrived. Glass sconces around the doorway had been an unfortunate modern addition; the flicker and peculiar color of gaslight made it look as if the door was meant to be the mouth of Hell itself. *Not a serendipitous choice, but the Duchess of Mondollot has never been singled out for restraint or taste*, Madeline thought, but kept an ironic smile to herself.

Despite the frosty night air and the chill wind off the river, there were other guests milling around on the wide marble portico, admiring the famous pediment. Madeline tucked her hands more firmly into her muff and shivered, partly from the cold, partly from anticipation. Her coachman received his instructions and urged the horses away, and her escort Captain Reynard Morane strolled back to her. She saw the flakes of snow on the shoulders of his caped greatcoat, and hoped the weather held until later tonight, at least. *One disaster at a time*, she thought, with an impatient shake of her head. *Let's just get inside the place first.*

Reynard extended an arm to her. "Ready, m'dear?"

She took it with a faint smile. "Very ready, sir."

They joined the crowd of other guests milling toward the entrance.

The tall doors stood open, light and warmth spilling out onto the scuffed paving stones. A servant stood to either side, wearing the knee breeches and silver braided coats of old style livery. The man taking the invitations wore the dark swallowtail coat of fashionable evening dress. *I don't imagine this is the butler*, Madeline thought grimly. Reynard handed over their invitation and she held her breath as the man opened the linen-paper envelope.

She had come by it honestly, though if she had needed to she could have gone to the finest forger in the city: an old man nearly blind, who worked in a dank cellar off the Philosopher's Cross. But she could sense something stirring in the eaves overhead, in the dimness high above the reach of the gas lamps. Madeline did not look up and if Reynard was aware of it he betrayed no reaction. Their informant had said a familiar of the sorcerer who protected the house would guard the door, an old and powerful familiar to spy out any magical devices brought in by the guests. Madeline clutched her reticule more tightly, though none of the objects in it were magical. If it were searched, there was no way a sorcerer of any competence whatsoever could fail to recognize what they were for.

"Captain Morane and Madame Denare," the man said. "Welcome." He handed the invitation off to one of the footmen and bowed them in.

They were ushered into the vestibule where servants appeared to collect Madeline's fur-trimmed paletot and muff and Reynard's greatcoat, cane and top hat. A demure maid was suddenly kneeling at Madeline's feet, brushing away a few traces of gravel that had adhered to the hem of her satin skirts, using a little silver brush and pan specially designed for the purpose. Madeline took Reynard's arm again and they passed through the entryway into the noisy crush of the main reception area.

Even with the carpets covered by linen drapers and the more delicate furniture removed, the hall was opulent. Gilded cherubs peered down at the milling guests from the heavy carved molding and the ceilings were frescoed with ships sailing along the western coast. They joined the crowd ascending the double staircases and passed through the doors at the top and into the ballroom.

Beeswax, Madeline thought. *They must have been at the floors all night.* Beeswax, and sandalwood and patchouli, and sweat, heavy in the air. Sweat from the warm presence of so many finely-clothed bodies, and sweat from fear. It was all so familiar. She realized she was digging her gloved nails into Reynard's arm in a death grip, and forced her fingers to unclench. He patted her hand distractedly, surveying the room.

The first dance had already started and couples swirled across the floor. The ballroom was large even for a house this size, with draped windows leading out onto balconies along the right hand side and doors allowing access to card rooms, refreshment and retiring rooms along the left. Across the back was a clever arrangement of potted winter roses, screening four musicians already hard at work on the cornet, piano, violin, and cello. The room was lit by a multitude of chandeliers burning expensive wax candles, because the vapors from gas were thought to ruin fine fabrics.

Madeline saw the Duchess of Mondollot herself, leading out the Count of . . . *of something*, she thought, distractedly. *I can't keep them straight anymore.* It wasn't the nobility they had to be wary of, but the sorcerers. There were three of them standing against the far wall, older gentlemen in dark swallowtail coats, wearing jeweled presentation medals from Lodun. One of them wore a ruby brooch and sash of the Order of Fontainon, but

even without it Madeline would have known him. He
was Rahene Fallier, the court sorcerer. There would be
women sorcerers here too, more dangerous and difficult
to spot because they would not be wearing presentation
medals or orders with their ball gowns. And the university at Lodun had only allowed women students for the
past ten years. Any female sorcerers present would be
only a little older than Madeline herself.

She nodded to a few acquaintances in the crowd and
she knew others recognized her; she had played the
Madwoman in *Isle of Stars* to packed houses all last
season. That wouldn't affect their plans, since everyone
of any wealth or repute in Vienne and the surrounding
countryside would be in this house at some time tonight.
And of course, someone was bound to recognize Reynard. . . .

"Morane." The unpleasantly sharp voice was almost
at Madeline's left ear. She snapped her fan at the speaker
and lifted an eyebrow in annoyance. He took the hint
and stepped back, still glowering at Reynard, and said,
"I didn't think you showed yourself in polite society,
Morane." The speaker was about her own age, wearing
dress regimentals of one of the cavalry brigades, a lieutenant from his insignia. *The Queen's Eighth*, Madeline
realized. *Ah. Reynard's old brigade.*

"Is this polite society?" Reynard asked. He stroked
his mustache and eyed the speaker with some amusement. "By God, man, it can't be. You're here."

There was a contemptuous edge to the younger man's
smile. "Yes, I'm here. I suppose you have an invitation." It was too brittle for good-natured banter. There
were two other men behind the lieutenant, one in regimentals, the other in civilian dress, both watching intently. "But you always were good at wiggling in where
you weren't wanted."

Easily, Reynard said, "You should know, my boy."

They hadn't drawn the eye of anyone else in the noisy
crowd yet, but it was only a matter of time. Madeline
hesitated for a heartbeat—she hadn't meant them to become conspicuous in this way, but it was a ready-made

diversion—then said, "You'll excuse me a moment, my dear."

"All for the best, my dear. This would probably bore you." Reynard gave her all his attention, turning toward her, kissing her hand, acting the perfect escort. The young lieutenant nodded to her, somewhat uncomfortably, and as Madeline turned away without acknowledging him, she heard Reynard ask casually, "Run away from any battles lately?"

Once away she moved along the periphery of the dancers, heading for the doors in the left hand wall. A lady alone in the ballroom, without a male escort or other ladies as companions, would be remarked on. A lady moving briskly toward the retiring rooms would be assumed to require a maid's assistance in some delicate matter and be politely ignored. Once past the retiring rooms, a lady alone would be assumed to be on her way to a private tryst, and also be politely ignored.

She passed through one of the doorways leading off the ballroom and down the hall. It was quiet and the lamps had been turned low, the light sparking off the mirrors, the polished surfaces of the spindly-legged console tables and the porcelain vases stuffed with out-of-season flowers. For such a luxury the duchess had her own forcing-houses; the gold flowers Madeline wore in her aigrette and on her corsage were fabric, in deference to the season. She passed a room with a partly open door, catching a glimpse of a young maid kneeling to pin up the torn hem of an even younger girl's gown, heard a woman speak sharply in frustration. Past another door where she could hear male voices in conversation and a woman's low laugh. Madeline's evening slippers were noiseless on the polished wood floor and no one came out.

She was in the old wing of the house now. The long hall became a bridge over cold silent rooms thirty feet down and the heavy stone walls were covered by tapestry or thin veneers of exotic wood instead of lathe and plaster. There were banners and weapons from long-ago wars, still stained with rust and blood, and ancient family portraits dark with the accumulation of years of smoke and dust. Other halls branched off, some leading to even older sections of the house, others to odd little cul-de-sacs lit by windows with an unexpected view of the street or the surrounding buildings. Music and voices from the ballroom grew further and further away, as if she was at the bottom of a great cavern, hearing echoes from the living surface.

She chose the third staircase she passed, knowing the servants would still be busy toward the front of the house. She caught up her skirts—black gauze with dull gold stripes over black satin and ideal for melding into shadows—and quietly ascended. She gained the third floor without trouble but going up to the fourth passed a footman on his way down. He stepped to the wall to let her have the railing, his head bowed in respect and an effort not to see who she was, ghosting about Mondollot House and obviously on her way to an indiscreet meeting. He would remember her later, but there was no help for it.

The hall at the landing was high and narrower than the others, barely ten feet across. There were more twists and turns to find her way through, stairways that only went up half a floor, and dead ends, but she had committed a map of the house to memory in preparation for this and so far it seemed accurate.

Madeline found the door she wanted and carefully tested the handle. It was unlocked. She frowned. One of Nicholas Valiarde's rules was that if one was handed good fortune one should first stop to ask the price, because there usually was a price. She eased the door open, saw the room beyond lit only by reflected moonlight from undraped windows. With a cautious glance up and down the corridor, she pushed it open enough to see the whole room. Book-filled cases, chimney piece of carved marble with a caryatid-supported mantle, tapestry-back chairs, pier glasses, and old sideboard heavy with family plate. A deal table supporting a metal strongbox. *Now we'll see*, she thought. She took a candle from the holder on the nearest table, lit it from the gas sconce in the hall, then slipped inside and closed the door behind her.

The undraped windows worried her. This side of the house faced Ducal Court Street and anyone below could see the room was occupied. Madeline hoped none of the Duchess's more alert servants stepped outside for a pipe or a breath of air and happened to look up. She went to the table and upended her reticule next to the solid square shape of the strongbox. Selecting the items she needed out of the litter of scent vials, jewelry she had decided not to wear, and a faded string of Aderassi luck-beads, she set aside snippets of chicory and thistle, a toadstone, and a paper screw containing salt.

Their sorcerer-advisor had said that the ward that protected Mondollot House from intrusion was an old and powerful one. Destroying it would take much effort and be a waste of a good spell. Circumventing it temporarily would be easier and far less likely to attract notice, since wards were invisible to anyone except a sorcerer using gascoign powder in his eyes or the new Aether-Glasses invented by the Parscian wizard Negretti. The toadstone itself held the necessary spell, dormant and harmless, and in its current state invisible to the familiar who guarded the main doors. The salt sprinkled on it would act as a catalyst and the special properties of the herbs would fuel it. Once all were placed in the influence of the ward's key object, the ward would withdraw to the very top of the house. When the potency of the salt wore off, it would simply slip back into place, probably before their night's work had been discovered. Madeline took her lock picks out of their silken case and turned to the strongbox.

There was no lock. She felt the scratches on the hasp and knew there had been a lock here recently, a heavy one, but it was nowhere to be seen. *Damn. I have a not-so-good feeling about this.* She lifted the flat metal lid.

Inside should be the object that tied the incorporeal ward to the corporeal bulk of Mondollot House. Careful spying and a few bribes had led them to expect not a stone as was more common, but a ceramic object, perhaps a ball, of great delicacy and age.

On a velvet cushion in the bottom of the strongbox were the crushed remnants of something once delicate and beautiful as well as powerful, nothing left now but fine white powder and fragments of cerulean blue. Madeline gave vent to an unladylike curse and slammed the lid down. *Some bastard's been here before us.*

"There's nothing here," Mother Hebra whispered. She crouched in the brick rubble at the base of the barred gate, hands outstretched. She smiled and nodded to herself. "Aye, not a peep of a nasty old sorcerer's ward. She must've done it."

"She's somewhat early," Nicholas muttered, tucking away his pocketwatch. "But better that than late." Tools clanked as the others scrambled forward and he reached down to help the old woman up and out of the way.

The oil lamps flickered in the damp cold air, the only light in the brick-lined tunnel. They had removed the layer of bricks blocking the old passage into Mondollot House's cellars, but Mother Hebra had stopped them before they could touch the rusted iron of the gate, wanting to test to see if it was within the outer perimeter of the ward that protected the house. Nicholas could sense nothing unusual about the gate, but he wasn't willing to ignore the old witch's advice. Some household wards were designed to frighten potential intruders, others to trap them, and he was no sorcerer to know the difference.

The tunnel was surprisingly clean and for all its dampness the stale air was free of any stench. Most inhabitants of Vienne, if they thought of the tunnels beneath the city at all, thought of them as filthy adjuncts to the sewers, fit for nothing human. Few knew of the access passages to the new underground rail system, which had to be kept clear and relatively dry for the train workmen.

Crack and Cusard attacked the bars with hacksaws and Nicholas winced at the first high-pitched scrape. They were too far below street level to draw the attention of anyone passing above; he hoped the sound wasn't echoing up through the house's cellars, alerting the watchmen posted on the upper levels.

Mother Hebra tugged at his coat sleeve. She was half Nicholas's height, a walking bundle of dirty rags with only a tuft of gray hair and a pair of bright brown eyes to prove there was anything within. "So you don't forget later. . . ."

"Oh, I wouldn't forget you, my dear." He produced two silver coins and put them in the withered little hand she extended. As a witch, she wasn't much, but it was really her discretion he was paying for. The hand disappeared back into her rags and the whole bundle shook, apparently with joy at being paid.

Cusard had cut through several bars already and Crack was almost finished with his side. "Rusted through, mostly," Cusard commented, and Crack grunted agreement.

"Not surprising; it's much older than this tunnel," Nicholas said. The passage had once led to another Great House, torn down years past to make way for Ducal Court Street, which stretched not too many feet above their heads.

The last bar gave way, and Cusard and Crack straightened to lift the gate out of the way. Nicholas said, "You can go now, Mother."

The prompt payment had won her loyalty. "Nay, I'll wait." The bundle of rags settled against the wall.

Crack set his end of the gate down and turned to regard Mother Hebra critically. He was a lean, predatory figure, his shoulders permanently stooped from a term at hard labor at the city prison. His eyes were colorless and opaque. The magistrates had called him a born killer, an animal entirely without human feeling. Nicholas had found that to be somewhat of an exaggeration, but knew that if Crack thought Hebra meant to betray them he would act without hesitation. The little witch hissed at him, and Crack turned away.

Nicholas stepped over the rubble and into the lowest cellar of Mondollot House.

There was no new red brick here. Their lamps revealed walls of rough-cut stone, the ceiling arched with thick pillars to support the weight of the structure above. A patina of dust covered everything and the air was dank and stale.

Nicholas led the way toward the far wall, the lamp held high. Obtaining the plans for this house, stored in a chest of moldering family papers at the Mondollot estate in Upper Bannot, had been the hardest part of this particular scheme so far. They were not the original plans, which would have long since turned to dust, but a builder's copy made only fifty years ago. Nicholas only hoped the good Duchess hadn't seen fit to renovate her upper cellars since then.

They reached a narrow stair that curved up the wall, vanishing into darkness at the edge of their lamplight. Crack shouldered past Nicholas to take the lead and Nicholas didn't protest. Whether Crack had sensed something wrong or was merely being cautious, he had learned not to ignore the man's instincts.

The stairs climbed about thirty feet up the wall, to a narrow landing with a wooden ironbound door. A small portal in the center revealed that it would open into a dark empty space of indeterminate size, lit only by the ghost of reflected light coming from a door or another stairwell on the far wall. Nicholas held the lamp steady so Cusard could work at the lock with his picks. As the door groaned and swung open, Crack stepped forward to take the lead again. Nicholas stopped him. "Is something wrong?"

Crack hesitated. The flicker of lamplight made it even harder than usual to read his expression. His face was sallow and the harsh lines around his mouth and eyes had been drawn there by pain and circumstance rather than age. He wasn't much older than Nicholas's thirty years, but he could have easily passed for twice that. "Maybe," he said finally. "Don't feel right."

And that's the most we'll have out of him, Nicholas thought. He said, "Go on then, but remember, don't kill anyone."

Crack acknowledged that with an annoyed wave and slipped through the door.

"Him and his feelings," Cusard said, glancing around the shadowed cellar and shivering theatrically. He was an older man, thin and with a roguish cast of feature that was misleading—he was the nicest thief that Nicholas had ever met. He was a confidence man by vocation and far more used to plying his trade in the busy streets than to practicing his cracksman's skills underground. "It don't half worry you, especially when he don't have the words he needs to tell what he does think is wrong."

Nicholas absentmindedly agreed. He was wondering if Madeline and Reynard had managed to leave the house yet. If Madeline had been discovered interfering with the ward. . . . *If Madeline had been discovered, we would surely know by now.* He pushed the worry to the back of his mind; Madeline was quite capable of taking care of herself.

Crack appeared at the gap in the doorway, whispering, "All clear. Come on."

Nicholas turned his lamp down to a bare flicker of flame, handed it to Cusard, and slipped through the door.

Hesitating a moment for his eyes to adjust, he could see the room was vast and high-ceilinged, lined by huge rotund shapes. Old wooden tuns for wine, or possibly water, if the house had no well. Probably empty now. He moved forward, following the almost weightless scrape of Crack's boots on the dusty stone. The faint light from the opposite end of the chamber came from a partly open door. He saw Crack's shadow pass through the door without hesitating and hurried after him.

Reaching it, he stopped, frowning. The heavy lock on the thick plank door had been ripped out and hung by a few distended screws. *What in blazes. . . .* Nicholas wondered. It was certainly beyond Crack's strength. Then he saw that the lock had been torn out from the other side, by someone or something already within the cellar room. The angle of the distended metal allowed no other conclusion. *That is hardly encouraging.*

Nicholas stepped through the door and found himself

at their goal. A long low cellar, modernized with brick-lined walls and gas sconces. One sconce was still lit, revealing man-high vaults in the walls, each crammed with stacked crates, metal chests, or barrels. Except for the one only ten paces away, which was filled with the bulk of a heavy safe.

The single lamp also revealed Crack, standing and watching Nicholas thoughtfully, and the dead man stretched at his feet.

Nicholas raised an eyebrow and came further into the room. There were two other bodies sprawled on the stone flags just past the safe.

Crack said, "I didn't do it."

"I know you didn't." Engineering Crack's escape from the Vienne prison had been one of the first acts of Nicholas's adult criminal career; he knew Crack wouldn't lie to him. Nicholas sat on his heels for a closer look at the first corpse. Startled, he realized the red effusion around the man's head wasn't merely blood but brain matter. The skull had been smashed in by a powerful blow. Behind him, Cusard swore in a low voice.

Exonerated, Crack crouched down to examine his find. The dead man's suit was plain and dark, probably the uniform of a hired watchman, and the coat was streaked with blood and the filthy muck from the floor of the cellar. Crack pointed to the pistol still tucked into the man's waistband and Nicholas asked, "Are they all like this?"

Crack nodded. "Except one's had his throat torn out."

"Someone's been before us!" Cusard whispered.

"Safe ain't touched," Crack disagreed. "No sign of anyone. Got something else to show you, though."

Nicholas pulled off his glove to touch the back of the dead man's neck, then wiped his hand on his trousers. The body was cold, but the cellar air was damp and chill, so it really meant little. He didn't hesitate. "Cusard, begin on the safe, if you please. And don't disturb the bodies." He got to his feet to follow Crack.

Cusard stared. "We going on with it then?"

"We didn't come all this way for naught," Nicholas said, and followed Crack to the other end of the cellar.

Nicholas took one of the lamps, though he didn't turn the flame up; Crack didn't seem to need the light. Finding his way unerringly, he went to the end of the long cellar, passing all the boxes and bales that contained the stored wealth of the Mondollot family, and rounded a corner.

Nicholas's eyes were well-adjusted to the dark and he saw the faint light ahead. Not pure yellow firelight, or greasy gaslight, but a dim white radiance, almost like moonglow. It came from an arched doorway, cut into a wall that was formed of old cut stone. There had been a door barring it once, a heavy wooden door of oak that had hardened over time to the strength of iron, that was now torn off its hinges. Nicholas tried to shift it; it was as heavy as stone. "In here," Crack said, and Nicholas stepped through the arch.

The radiance came from ghost-lichen growing in the groined ceiling. There was just enough of it to illuminate a small chamber, empty except for a long stone slab. Nicholas turned the flame of the lamp up slowly, exposing more of the room. The walls were slick with moisture and the air stale. He moved to the slab and ran his hand across the top, examining the result on his gloved fingers. The stone there was relatively free of dust and the oily moisture, yet the sides of the slab were as dirty as the walls and floor.

He lifted the lamp and bent down, trying to get a better angle. *Yes, there was something here.* Its outline was roughly square. Oblong. *A box, perhaps*, he thought. *Coffin-sized, at least*.

He glanced up at Crack, who was watching intently. Nicholas said, "Someone entered the cellar, by a route yet undetermined, stumbled on the guards, or was stumbled on by them, possibly when he broke the lock on the older cellar to search it. Our intruder killed to prevent discovery, which is usually the act of a desperate and foolish person." It was Nicholas's belief that murder was almost always the result of poor planning. There were so many ways of making people do what you wanted other than killing them. "Then he found this room, broke down the door with a rather disturbing degree of strength, removed something that had lain here undisturbed for years, and retired, probably the same way he entered."

Crack nodded, satisfied. "He ain't here no more. I'll go bank on that."

"It's a pity." And now it was doubly important to leave no trace of their presence. *If I'm going to be hanged for murder, I'd prefer it to be a murder I actually committed.* Nicholas consulted his watch in the lamplight, then tucked it away again. "Cusard should be almost finished with the safe. You go back for the others and start moving the goods out. I want to look around here a little more." There were six other men waiting up in the tunnel, whose help was necessary if they were to transport the gold quickly. Crack, Cusard, and Lamane, who was Cusard's second in command, were the only ones who knew him as Nicholas Valiarde. To Mother Hebra and the others hired only for this job, he was Donatien, a shadowy figure of the Vienne underworld who paid well for this sort of work and punished indiscretion just as thoroughly.

Crack nodded and stepped to the door. Hesitating, he said again, "I'll go bank he's not here no more. . . ."

"But you would appreciate it if I exercised the strictest caution," Nicholas finished for him. "Thank you."

Crack vanished into the darkness and Nicholas stooped to examine the floor. The filth and moisture on the pitted stone revealed footmarks nicely. He found the tracks of his own boots, and Crack's, noting that the first time his henchman had approached the room he had come only to the threshold. In the distance he could hear the others, muted exclamations as the new arrivals saw the dead men, the rumble of Crack's voice, a restrained expression of triumph from everyone as Cusard opened the safe. But there were no footmarks left by their hypothetical intruder. Kneeling to make a more careful survey, and ruining the rough fabric of his workman's coat and breeches against the slimy stone in the process, Nicholas found three scuffles he couldn't positively attribute to either Crack or himself, but that was all. He sat up on his heels, annoyed. He was willing to swear his analysis of the room was correct. There was no mistaking that some object had been removed from the plinth, and recently.

Something that had lain in this room for years, in silence, with the ethereal glow of the ghost-lichen gently illuminating it.

He got to his feet, meaning to go back to the guards' corpses and examine the floor around them more thoroughly, if the others hadn't already obliterated any traces when carrying out the Duchess's stock of gold.

He stepped past the ruined door and something caught his eye. He turned his head sharply toward the opposite end of the corridor, where it curved away from the vaults and into the older wine-cellars. Something white fluttered at the end of that corridor, distinct against the shadows. Nicholas turned up the lamp, drawing breath to shout for Crack—an instant later the breath was knocked out of him.

It moved toward him faster than thought and between the first glimpse of it and his next heartbeat it was on him. A tremendous blow struck him flat on his back and the creature was on top of him. Eyes, bulging because the flesh around them had withered away, stared at him in black hate out of a face gray as dead meat. It bared teeth like an animal's, long and curving. It was wrapped in a once-white shroud, now filthy and tattered. Nicholas jammed his forearm up into its face, felt the teeth tearing through his sleeve. He had kept his grip on the lantern, though the glass had broken and the oil was burning his hand. He swung it toward the thing's head with terror-inspired strength.

Whether it was the blow or the touch of burning oil, it shrieked and tore itself away. The oil had set the sleeve of Nicholas's coat afire; he rolled over, crushing the flames out against the damp stone.

Crack, Cusard, and Lamane were suddenly clustered

around him. Nicholas tried to speak, choked on the lung-
ful of smoke he had inhaled, and finally gasped, "After
him."

Crack bolted immediately down the dark corridor. Cusard and Lamane stared at Nicholas, then at each other.
"Not you," Nicholas said to Cusard. "Take charge of
the others. Get them out of here with the gold."

"Aye," Cusard said in relief and scrambled up to run
back to the others. Lamane swore but helped Nicholas
to his feet.

Cradling his burned left hand, Nicholas stumbled after
Crack. Lamane had a lamp and a pistol; Crack had gone
after the thing empty-handed and in the dark.

"Why are we following it?" Lamane whispered.

"We have to find out what it is."

"It's a ghoul."

"It's not a ghoul," Nicholas insisted. "It wasn't human."

"Then it's fay," Lamane muttered. "We need a sorcerer."

Vienne had been overrun by the Unseelie Court over
a hundred years ago, in the time of Queen Ravenna, but
as far as the superstitious minds of most city people were
concerned, it might as well have happened yesterday.
"If it's a fay, you have iron," Nicholas said, indicating
the pistol.

"That's true," Lamane agreed, encouraged. "Fast as
it was, though, it's miles away by now."

Perhaps, Nicholas thought. Whether it had actually
moved that quickly, or it had afflicted him with some
sort of paralysis he couldn't tell; his mind's eye seemed
to have captured an image of it careening off the corridor
wall as it charged him, which might indicate that its
movement toward him hadn't been as instantaneous as
it had seemed.

This was the lowest level of the Mondollot wine-
cellars. The lamplight revealed cask after cask of old
vintages, some covered by dust and cobwebs, others obviously newly tapped. Nicholas remembered that there
was one of the largest balls of the fashionable season

going on not too many feet above their heads, and while a large supply had undoubtedly already been hauled upstairs, servants could be sent for more casks at any moment. He could not afford to pursue this.

They found Crack waiting for them at the far wall, near a pile of broken bricks and stone. Nicholas took the lamp from Lamane and lifted it high. Something had torn its way through the wall, pushing out the older foundation stone and the brick veneer. The passage beyond was narrow, choked by dust and filth. Nicholas grimaced. From the smell it led straight to the sewer.

"That's where he came in." Crack offered his opinion. "And that's where he went out."

"Ghouls in the sewers," Nicholas muttered. "Perhaps I should complain to the aldermen." He shook his head. He had wasted enough time on this already. "Come, gentlemen, we have a small fortune waiting for us."

Still inwardly cursing, Madeline took a different stairway down to the second floor. They had planned this for months; it was incredible that someone else would scheme to enter Mondollot House on the same night. *No*, she thought suddenly. *Not incredible.* On every other night this place was guarded like the fortress it was. But tonight hundreds of people would be allowed in and she couldn't be the only one who knew of a good forger. This was an ideal time for a robbery and someone else had seized the opportunity.

She reached the ballroom and forced herself to calmly stroll along the periphery, scanning the dancers and the men gathered along the walls for Reynard. He would expect her back by now and be where she could easily find him. He wouldn't have joined a card game or. . . . *Left*, she thought, with a wry twist of her mouth. *Unless he had to. Unless he got into a fistfight with a certain young lieutenant and was asked to leave.* He would not be able to insist on waiting for her, not knowing where she was in the house or if she had finished with the ward. *Damn.* But with the ward gone, it would be possible to slip out unnoticed, if she could get down to the first floor. . . .

Madeline saw the Duchess of Mondollot then, a distinguished and lovely matron in pearls and a gown of cream satin, heading directly toward her. She stepped behind the inadequate shelter of a tall flower-filled vase and in desperation shielded her face with her fan, pretending to be screening herself from the lecherous view of an innocent group of older gentlemen standing across from her.

But the Duchess passed Madeline without a glance, and in her relief she found herself closely studying the man trailing in the older woman's wake.

He was odd enough to catch anyone's attention in this company. His dark beard was unkempt and though his evening dress was of fine quality it was disarrayed, as if he cared nothing for appearances. And why come to the Duchess of Mondollot's ball, if one cared nothing for appearances? He was shorter than Madeline and his skin appeared pale and unhealthy even for late winter. His eyes glanced over her as he hurried after the Duchess, and they were wild, and perhaps a little mad.

There was something about him that clearly said "underworld," though in the criminal, not the mythological sense, and Madeline found herself turning to follow him without closely considering her motives.

The Duchess strode down the hall, accompanied also, Madeline now had leisure to notice, by a younger woman whom Madeline knew was a niece and by a tall footman. The Duchess turned into one of the salons and the others followed; Madeline moved past, careful not to glance in after them, her eyes fixed further down the hall as if she were expecting to meet someone. She reached the next closed door, grasped the handle and swung it opened confidently, ready to be apologetic and flustered if it was already occupied.

It was empty, though a fire burned on the hearth and a firescreen was in place, shielding the couches and chairs gathered near it in readiness for ball guests who desired private conversation or other amusements. Madeline closed the door behind her carefully and locked it. All these rooms on this side of the corridor were part of a long suite of salons and there were connecting panel doors to the room the Duchess had entered.

The doors were of light wood, meant to swing open wide and interconnect the rooms for large evening gatherings. Madeline knelt beside them, her satin and gauze skirts whispering, and with utmost care, eased the latch open.

She was careful not to push the door and the air in the room swung it open just enough to give her a view of the other room's carpet, and a thin slice of tulip-bordered wallpaper and carved wainscotting.

The Duchess was saying, "It's an unusual request."

"Mine is an unusual profession." That must be the odd man. His voice made Madeline grimace in distaste; it was insinuating and suggestive somehow, and reminded her of a barker at a thousand-veils peep show. No wonder the Duchess had called her niece and a footman to accompany her.

"I've dealt with spiritualists before," the Duchess continued, "though you seem to think I have not. None required a lock of the departed one's hair to seek contact."

Madeline felt a flicker of disappointment. Spiritualism and speaking to the dead were all the rage among the nobility and the monied classes now, though in years past it would have been feared as necromancy. It certainly explained the man's strange demeanor.

She started to ease away from the door but with fury in his voice the spiritualist said, "I am no ordinary medium, your grace. What I offer is contact of a more intimate, lasting nature. But to establish that contact I require something from the body of the deceased. A lock of hair is merely the most common item."

Necromancy indeed, Madeline thought. She had studied magic in her youth, when her family had still hoped she might demonstrate some talent for it. She hadn't been the best student, but something about this pricked her memory.

"You require a lock of hair, and your fee," the Duchess said, and her voice held contempt.

"Of course," the man said, but the fee was clearly an afterthought.

"Aunt, this is ridiculous. Send him away." The niece, bored and faintly disgusted with the subject.

"No," the Duchess said slowly. Her voice changed, quickened with real interest. "If you can do as you say . . . there seems no harm in trying. . . ."

I wouldn't be too sure of that, Madeline thought, though she couldn't explain her uneasiness with the whole idea, even to herself.

"I have a lock of my son's hair. He was killed in the Parscian colony of Sambra. If you could contact him—"

"Your son, not your husband?" The spiritualist was exasperated.

"What does it matter to you whom I wish to contact, as long as your fee is paid?" The Duchess sounded startled. "I would double it if I was pleased; I'm not counted stingy," she added.

"But your husband would be the more proper one to contact first, surely?" The man's tone was meant to be wheedling, but he couldn't disguise his impatience.

"I don't wish to speak to my husband again, alive or dead or in any state between," the Duchess snapped. "And I don't understand what it could possibly matter to you who—"

"Enough," the man said, sounding disgusted himself. "Consider my offer withdrawn, your grace. And the consequences are your own concern." Madeline clearly heard the hall door slam.

The Duchess was silent a moment, probably stunned. "I suppose I'll never know what that was about. Bonsard, make sure that man is conducted out."

"Yes, my lady."

I'd do more than that, Madeline thought. *I'd summon my sorcerer, and make sure my wards were properly set, and lock away any relics of my dead relatives. That man was mad, and he wanted something.* But it wasn't her concern. She eased away from the door, waited a moment, then slipped out into the hall.

The safe had yielded to Cusard's ministrations and proved to hold nearly sixty small gold bars, each stamped with the royal seal of Bisra. Nicholas's men had already packed them on the sledges they had brought and started back down the tunnel under Cusard's direction when Nicholas, Crack and Lamane caught up to them.

Nicholas motioned them to keep moving, lifting one of the heavy bars with his good hand to examine the crest. The Duchess of Mondollot maintained a trading business with one of the old merchant families of Bisra, Ile-Rien's long-time enemy to the south. This fact was little known and in the interest of keeping it that way, the Duchess did not store her gold in the Bank Royal of Vienne, which Nicholas knew from experience was much harder to break into. The Bank would also have expected the great lady to pay taxes, something her aristocratic mind couldn't countenance.

Mother Hebra clucked at his burns and made him wrap his scarf around his injured hand. Lamane was telling the others something about the sewers being infested with ghouls and in such a nice part of the city, too.

"What do you make of it?" Cusard asked Nicholas, when they had reached the street access of the maintenance tunnel, which opened up behind a public stable across Ducal Court Street from Mondollot House. The other men were handing up bars of gold to be stored in the compartment under the empty bed of the waiting cart. The street boys posted as lookouts worked for Cusard and thus for Nicholas too, as did the man who ran the stables.

"I don't know." Nicholas waited for the men to finish, then started up the bent metal ladder. The cold wind hit him as he climbed out of the manhole, the chill biting into his burns, making him catch his breath. The horses stamped, restless in the cold. The night was quiet and the men's hushed voices, the distant music from Mondollot House, and the clank of soft metal against wood as the gold was packed away in the special compartment under the wagon bed, seemed oddly loud. "But I'll swear it removed something from that room Crack found," he said as Cusard emerged.

Cusard said, "Well, I don't much like it. It was such a sweet little job of work, otherwise."

Someone brought Nicholas his greatcoat from the cart and he shrugged into it gratefully. "I don't either, that you can be sure of." The wagon had been loaded and he wanted to look for Reynard and Madeline. He told Cusard, "Take the others and get home; we'll draw attention standing here."

The driver snapped the reins and the wagon moved off. Nicholas walked back down the alley toward Ducal Court Street. A layer of dirty ice and a light dusting of snow made the streets and alleys passable; usually they were so choked with mud and waste water that pedestrians had to stay on the promenades or use the stepping stones provided for street crossings. He realized Crack was following him. He smiled to himself and said aloud, "All right. It didn't go at all well the last time I sent you away, did it? But no more ghoul-hunting tonight."

At the mouth of the alley, Nicholas paused to remove the small hairpieces that lengthened his sideburns and changed the shape of his mustache and short beard, and rubbed the traces of glue off his cheeks. The touches of gray in his dark hair would have to be washed out. He never appeared as Donatien except in disguise: if any of the men who had participated on one of these jobs recognized him as Nicholas Valiarde it could be ruinous. Maintaining the masquerade wasn't much of a hardship; in many ways he had been practicing deception for most of his life and at this point it came easily to him.

He buttoned and belted his greatcoat, took the collapsible top hat and cane from one of the pockets, and tugged a doeskin glove onto his uninjured hand. With the other hand in his pocket and the coat concealing everything but his boots and gaiters, he was only a gentleman out for a stroll, a somewhat disreputable servant in tow.

He paused across the wide expanse of street from Mondollot House, as if admiring the lighted façade. Footmen stood ready at the door, waiting to hand down late arrivals or assist those making an early night of it. Nicholas moved on, passing down the length of the large house. Then he spotted their coach, standing at the corner under a gas street lamp, and then Reynard Morane waiting near it. Nicholas crossed to him, Crack a few paces behind.

"Nic. . . ." Reynard stepped down from the promenade to meet them. He was a big man with red hair and a cavalryman's loose-limbed stride. He took a close look at Nicholas. "Trouble?"

"Things became somewhat rough. Where's Madeline?"

"That's the problem. I had the opportunity to provide a diversion for her but it went too well, so to speak, and I found myself asked to leave with no chance to retrieve her."

"Hmm." Hands on hips, Nicholas considered the façade of the Great House. For most women of fashionable society, getting out of the place unnoticed would have been an impossible task, but Madeline had studied tumbling and acrobatics for the more active roles in the theater and she wouldn't necessarily need a ground floor exit. "Let's go around the side."

Mondollot House was flanked by shopping promenades and smaller courts leading to other Great Houses and it was possible to circle the place entirely. The shops were closed, except for one busy cabaret set far back under the arcade, and all was quiet. There were no entrances on the first floor of the house except for an occasional heavily barred carriage or servants' door. The terraces and balconies of the upper floors were all later additions: originally these houses had been impenetrable fortresses, frivolous decoration confined to the rooftops and gables.

They made one circuit, almost back to Ducal Court

Street, then retraced their steps. Reaching the far side, Nicholas saw the panel doors on a second floor terrace fly open, emitting light, music, and Madeline.

"You're late, my dear," Reynard called softly to her, "we've been looking everywhere for you."

"Oh, be quiet." Madeline shut the doors behind her. "I've had to leave my best paletot behind because of you."

"We can afford to buy you another, believe me," Nicholas told her, concealing his relief. He should know her abilities too well by now to worry much about her safety, but it had been a disturbing night. "And it's well earned, too."

Madeline gathered her delicate skirts and swung over the low balustrade, using the scrollwork as a ladder, and dropped to land in a low snowdrift just as Nicholas and Reynard scrambled forward to catch her. She straightened and shook her skirts out, and Nicholas hastened to wrap his coat around her. She said, "Not so well earned. I didn't have a chance to distract the ward because someone had beaten me to it."

"Ah." Nicholas nodded, thoughtful. "Of course. I'm not surprised."

"He never is," Reynard said in a tone of mock complaint. "Let's discuss it somewhere else."

2

*When they were sheltered from the wind inside the well-*upholstered coach, Nicholas had Madeline tell her part of the incident and gave the others his description of the unexpected encounter in the Duchess's vaults.

Reynard swore softly. "Do you suppose someone sent it after you, Nic? You know we have old acquaintances that wouldn't mind seeing you dead."

"I thought of that." Nicholas shook his head. The coach jolted along the uneven stones of the street, making the tassels on the patent leather window shades dance. "But I'm certain it took something out of that room Crack found. A room which isn't on any of the house plans that we were able to obtain, either. I think that was why the creature was there. It was only as an afterthought that it tried to kill me."

Madeline tucked the woolen lap rug more firmly around her. "And the key for the house ward had already been destroyed. I think it was that awful little man who wanted a lock of the late Duke's hair. What sort of spiritualist asks for something like that? It's too much like necromancy."

What sort of spiritualist indeed? Nicholas thought. "I wonder why the creature was still there? It was already in the wine vault; it didn't have to attack me to escape. If it successfully removed something from that room, why was it coming back?"

"For the gold?" Madeline suggested thoughtfully.

"Though that isn't exactly common knowledge."

Nicholas had deduced the gold's existence from investigation of the Duchess's trading concerns. Someone else might have done so as well, but. . . . "Possibly," he said. *Possible, but perhaps not probable.*

Reynard leaned forward. "What's that muck on your arm?"

Nicholas had given his greatcoat to Madeline and was making do with one of the lap rugs. In the musty darkness of the coach, the sleeves of his workman's coat bore a green-tinged stain that faintly glowed. Nicholas frowned. At first glance it looked like ghost-lichen, but he couldn't remember brushing against the walls of the room where it had grown so profusely. He remembered the ghoul's fingers, strong as iron bands, gripping him there, and the way it had shone with a dim unhealthy radiance in the dark cellar. "I believe it's a memento from the ghoul." It made him want to return to Mondollot House to make an examination of the corpses of the three watchmen in darkness, to see if their clothing had the same residue. He didn't imagine Madeline and Reynard would be amenable to that suggestion.

When the coach stopped outside the fashionable Hotel Biamonte where Reynard kept rooms, Nicholas said, "I suppose you're going out to celebrate."

"I would be mad not to," Reynard replied, standing on the snow-dusted promenade and adjusting his gloves. Behind him the doors and fogged windows of the hotel spilled light and warmth, music and the laughter of the *demi monde*.

Worried, Madeline added, "Take care."

He leaned back into the coach to take her hand and drop a kiss on the palm. "My dear, if I was careful I would not have been cashiered out of the Guard and we would never have met. Which would have been unfortunate." He tipped his hat to them and Nicholas smiled and pulled the coach door closed.

He tapped his stick against the ceiling to signal the driver, and Madeline said, "I worry about him. Those bucks at Mondollot House were holding grudges."

"They may talk, but they won't act. If they were in his regiment they know what Reynard is like with sword and pistol. He can take care of himself."

"I wish I could say the same of you," she said, her voice dry.

Nicholas drew her close, inside the circle of his arms. "Why my dear, I'm the most dangerous man in Ile-Rien, its provinces, and all the Parscian Empire combined."

"So they say." But she said no more on the subject, and their thoughts quickly turned to other things.

It was a relatively short ride to Coldcourt, which stood in one of the less fashionable quarters just outside the old city wall.

They drew up in the carriage way and Nicholas helped Madeline out as Crack jumped down from the box.

This was the house that had been Nicholas's first real home. The walls were thick natural stone, built to withstand the Vienne winter. It was only three stories at its tallest, sprawling and asymmetrical, and boasted three towers, one square and two round, all with useless ornamental crenelations and embellishments in the style known as the Grotesque. It was ugly and unfashionable, and not terribly comfortable, but it was home and Nicholas would never give it up.

Sarasate the butler opened the door for them as the coachman drove the horses around to the stables in the back and they gratefully entered the house.

Coldcourt was also as drafty as its name implied, but the spacious hall felt warm and welcoming after the chilly night. The straight-backed chairs along the walls and the sideboard were well-used, though still in fine condition, relics of the time when Nicholas's foster father had lived here. The carpets and hangings were new, though in a restrained style in keeping with the rest of the house, and they had only had gas lighting laid on in the main rooms on the first two floors and the kitchen. Nicholas didn't like vulgar display and Madeline's taste was even more particular than his. Still, the plaster above the dark wainscotting was looking a little dingy and he supposed they might afford to have it redone now.

Madeline headed immediately toward the stairs; Nicholas supposed her patience with delicate and cumbersome evening dress had reached its limit and she was going to change. His own progress was more leisurely. His ribs ached from the encounter with the ghoul, or whatever it had been, and he felt singed and three times his age. He shed coat and makeshift bandages as he crossed the hall and told Sarasate, "Warm brandy. Hot coffee. And Mr. Crack will be staying the night, so if his usual room could be prepared, and a meal. . . . If Andrea hasn't gone to bed?"

"He thought you might want something after such a late night, sir, so he prepared a bit of veal in aspic and a chestnut souffle."

"Perfect." Sarasate and the coachman Devis were the only Coldcourt servants who knew anything about Nicholas's activities as Donatien. Sarasate had been at Coldcourt for at least thirty years; Devis was Cusard's oldest son and almost as reliable as Crack. Nicholas saw the butler collecting the ghoul-stained coat with an expression of distaste, and added, "That coat's ruined, but don't dispose of it. I may need it later." That was Sarasate's one fault as a butler—he understood nothing about the sometimes vital information that could be gleaned from objects that otherwise appeared to be rubbish.

Nicholas went to the last door at the end of the hall and unlocked it with the key attached to his watch chain. The room was chill and dark and he spent a moment lighting the branch of candles on the table. There were gas sconces on the yellowed plaster walls, but gas fumes could damage oil paint, and it was very important that the work of art in this room not be altered in the slightest degree.

The flickering light of the candles gradually revealed the painting on the far wall. It was a large canvas, almost six feet long and four feet wide, set in a narrow gilt frame. It was a copy of a work by Emile Avenne called *The Scribe*, which purported to be a depiction of harem life in an eastern land. It showed two robed women lounging on a couch while an aged scholar turned the pages of a book for them. Nicholas knew the scene came from nowhere but the artist's imagination. Experts had long maintained that the styles and colors of the tiles on the floor and walls, the detail of the fretted screens and the textiles draping the couches were not common designs known in Parscia, Bukar, or even far Akandu. But it was a subtle, masterful work and the colors were rich and wonderful.

The original hung on the wall of the library at Pompiene, Count Rive Montesq's Great House. Nicholas had sold the painting to the Count, who had affected to believe that he was doing a favor for the foster son of the man whose work he had once sponsored. Nicholas's public persona was that of an art importer and he used his inheritance from Edouard to act as a patron to several young artists of notable talent. He was more of a patron than most people realized, having once anonymously retrieved some paintings stolen from the public gallery at the old Bishop's Palace and punished the offending thieves severely. He didn't believe in stealing art.

Nicholas dropped into the velvet upholstered armchair which had been carefully placed at the best point for viewing the work and propped his feet on the footstool. In the long dead language of Old Rienish, he said carefully, "Beauty is truth."

The colors in the painting brightened, slowly enough at first that it might have been a trick of the eye. They took on a soft glow, obvious enough for the watcher to tell this was no trick, or at least not a natural one. The painting then became transparent, as if it had turned into a window opening onto the next room. Except the room that it revealed was half the city away, though it appeared just as solid as if one could reach out and touch it.

That room was dark now, just a little faint light from an open door revealing bookcases, the edge of a framed watercolor, and a marble bust of Count Montesqsculpted by Bargentere. Nicholas glanced at the clock on his own mantel. It was late and he hadn't expected anyone to be about. Again in Old Rienish, he said, "Memory is a dream."

That scene faded, became washed in darkness, then formed another image.

The artist who had painted this work had known only that he was copying an Avenne for Nicholas's own home. He had believed that the paints he was using were special only in that they were the same mixtures Avenne had used, necessary to duplicate the marvelous soft colors of the original. This was true, but the paints had been personally mixed by Arisilde Damal, the greatest sorcerer in Ile-Rien, and there was even more sorcery woven into the frame and canvas.

The library appeared again, this time in daylight, the curtains drawn back at the windows and a parlormaid cleaning out the grate. That image ran its course, followed by views of other servants coming into the room on various errands, and once a man Nicholas recognized as Batherat, one of Montesq's Vienne solicitors, evidently coming to pick up a letter left for him on the desk.

The beauty of the painting as a magical device was that if Montesq had a sorcerer in to search his home for evidence of magical spying, as he had twice done in the past, the painting on his library wall would be revealed as what it was—only so much canvas, paint, and wood. The magic was all contained in the copy of it.

Montesq had believed the purchase of the original painting a cruel, private joke, an amusing favor for the family of a man he had caused to be killed. But cruel, private jokes were the ones most apt to turn on the joker.

Nicholas sat up suddenly, hearing a voice he would have known anywhere.

The painting now revealed the library at night, lit by only one gas sconce. Nicholas cursed under his breath. It was too dim to read the clock on the library wall, so he couldn't tell what time this had taken place, except that it must be earlier this evening. Count Montesq sat at the desk, his face half shadowed. Nicholas's memory filled in the details. The Count was an older man, old enough to be Nicholas's father, with graying dark hair and a handsome face that was fast becoming fleshy due to too much high living.

The solicitor Batherat was standing in front of the desk, a nervous crease between his brows. Any other man of consequence in Ile-Rien would have invited his solicitor to sit down, but though Montesq was charming to his equals and betters, and in public showed admirable condescension to those beneath him, in private his servants and employees were terrified of him. In a tone completely devoid of threat, Montesq said, "I'm glad you finally succeeded. I was becoming impatient."

Nicholas frowned in annoyance. They must be continuing a conversation begun out in the hall and he didn't anticipate gleaning much information from this exchange. If Montesq killed Batherat, of course, it would certainly be worth watching. The solicitor held his calm admirably and replied, "I assure you, my lord, nothing has been left to chance."

"I hope you are correct." Montesq's soft voice was almost diffident, something that Nicholas had learned from long observation meant that a dangerous anger was building.

When Nicholas had first put together his organization, it had been necessary to free Cusard and Lamane and several others whose assistance he desired from their prior obligations to the man who considered himself the uncrowned king of criminal activity in the Riverside slums. This individual had been reluctant to give up their services, so it had ended with Nicholas putting a bullet in his head. The man had been a murderer several times over, an extortionist, a panderer, and addicted to various sexual perversions that would have startled even Reynard, but he was the rankest amateur at villainy compared to Rive Montesq.

The Count stood and circled around the desk to stop within a pace of Batherat. He didn't speak, but the solicitor blinked sudden sweat from his eyes and said, "I'm certain, my lord."

Montesq smiled and clapped Batherat on the shoulder in a fashion that might be taken for amiable comradeship by a less informed observer. He said only, "I hope your certainty is not misplaced."

Montesq walked out, leaving the door open behind him. Batherat closed his eyes a moment in relief, then followed.

That was the last image the painting had absorbed and now the scene faded as it returned to its quiescent state, becoming merely a static window on some foreign household. Nicholas sighed and ran his hands through his hair wearily. *Nothing of note. Well, we can't expect miracles every day.* Twice the painting had revealed pertinent details of the Count's plans. Montesq moved among the financial worlds of Vienne and the other prominent capitals, bribing and blackmailing or using more violent means to take what he wanted, but he was careful enough to preserve his reputation so he was still received at court and in all the best homes.

But not for much longer, Nicholas thought, his smile thin and ice cold. *Not for much longer.*

He got to his feet and stretched, then blew out the candles and locked the door carefully behind him.

As Nicholas was crossing the central foyer to the stairs there was a tap on the front door. He stopped with one hand on the bannister. It was too late for respectable callers, and the not-so-respectable callers on legitimate business wouldn't come here at all. Sarasate hesitated, looking to him for instruction. Crack reappeared in the archway to the other wing, so Nicholas leaned against the newel post, folded his arms, and said, "See who that is, would you?"

The butler swung the heavy portal open and a man stepped into the foyer without waiting for an invitation. He was lean and gaunt and over his formal evening dress he was wearing a cape and opera hat. The gaslight above the door gave his long features and slightly protuberant eyes a sinister cast, but Nicholas knew it did that to everyone. The man was ignoring Sarasate and looking around the hall as if he was at a public amusement.

Piqued, Nicholas said, "It's late for casual callers, especially those I'm unacquainted with. Would you mind turning around and going back the way you came?"

The man focused on him and instead moved further into the hall. "Are you the owner of this house?"

One would assume it, since I'm standing here in my shirtsleeves, Nicholas thought. His first inclination was that this was some curiosity seeker; it had been years since his foster father's death, but the notoriety of the trial still drew those with morbid hobbies. People with a more conventional interest in the old man's work also came, but they were usually more polite and presented themselves during the day, often with letters of introduction from foreign universities. This visitor's appearance—his cravat was a dirty gray and the pale skin above it unwashed, his dark beard was unkempt and his cape was so ostentatious it would have looked out of place on anyone but a March Baron at a royal opera performance for the Queen's Birthday—suggested the former. "I'm the owner," Nicholas admitted tiredly. "Why? Is it interfering with your progress through the neighborhood?"

"I have business with you, if you are Nicholas Valiarde."

"Ah. It can't wait until tomorrow?" Nicholas twisted the crystal ornament on top of the newel post, a signal to Sarasate to summon the servants more experienced at dealing with unwelcome guests. The butler shut the door, turned the key and pocketed it, and glided away. Crack knew the signal too and came noiselessly into the room.

"It is urgent to both of us."

The man's eyes jerked upward suddenly, to the top of the stairs, and Nicholas saw Madeline stood there now. A gold-brocaded dressing gown billowed around her and she had taken the dark length of her hair down. She came down the stairs slowly, deliberately, as elegant and outré as a dark nymph in a romantic painting. Nicholas smiled to himself. An actress born, Madeline could never resist an audience.

The man brought his gaze back down to Nicholas and said, "I would like to speak to you in private."

"I never speak to anyone in private," Nicholas countered. The butler reappeared and Nicholas gestured casually to him. "Sarasate, show our guest into the front salon. Don't bother having a fire laid, he won't be staying long."

Sarasate led their unwelcome visitor away and Madeline stopped Nicholas with a hand on his sleeve. In a low whisper, she said, "That's the man who spoke to the Duchess tonight."

"I thought it likely from your description." Nicholas nodded. "He may have recognized you. Did he know you were listening?"

"He couldn't have. Not without everyone knowing." She hesitated, added, "At least that's what I thought."

He offered her his arm and together they followed their guest into the front salon, a small reception room off the hall.

The walls were lined with bookcases as the room served as an adjunct to the library, housing the volumes that Nicholas found less use for. The carpet had been fine once, but it was old now and the edges were threadbare. There were a few upholstered chairs scattered about and one armchair at the round table that served as a desk. The stone hearth was cold and Nicholas waited for Sarasate to finish lighting the candlelamps and withdraw. Crack had followed them in and as the butler left he drew the door closed.

Their visitor stood in the center of the room. Nicholas dropped into the armchair and propped his boots on the table. Madeline leaned gracefully on the back of his chair and he said, "What was it you wanted to discuss?"

The man drew off his gloves. His hands were pale but work-roughened. He said, "Earlier tonight you entered the lower cellars of Mondollot House and sought to remove something. I was curious as to your reason for this."

Nicholas allowed himself no outward reaction, though the shock of that statement made the back of his neck prickle. He felt Madeline's hands tense on his chair, but she said nothing. Crack's eyes were on him, intent and waiting with perfect calm for a signal. Nicholas didn't give it; he wanted to know who else knew this man was here and more importantly, who had sent him. He said, "Really, sir, you astound me. I've been at the theater this evening and can produce half a dozen witnesses to that effect."

"I'm not from the authorities and I care nothing for witnesses." The man took a slow step forward and the candlelight revealed more of his gaunt features. The shadows hollowed his cheeks and made his strange eyes sink back into their deep sockets.

How appropriate for a spiritualist, Nicholas thought, *he looks half dead himself.* "Then who are you?"

"I am called Doctor Octave, but perhaps it is more important who you are." The man laid his hat and stick on the polished surface of the table. Nicholas wondered if he had refused Sarasate's attempt to relieve him of them or if the butler had simply not bothered, assuming that the unwelcome visitor was not going to survive long enough to appreciate the discourtesy. Octave smiled, revealing very bad teeth, and said, "You are Nicholas Valiarde, at one time the ward of the late Doctor Edouard Viller, the renowned metaphysician."

"He was not a metaphysician, he was a natural philosopher," Nicholas corrected gently, keeping any hint of impatience from his voice. It had occurred to him that this might very well be Sebastion Ronsarde in one of his famous or infamous disguises, but now he dismissed the thought. Ronsarde and the rest of the Prefecture knew him only as Donatien, a name without a face, responsible for some of the most daring crimes in Ile-Rien and probably for a good deal more. If Ronsarde had known enough to ask Donatien if he was Nicholas Valiarde, he would have asked it in one of the tiny interrogation cells under the Vienne Prefecture and not in Nicholas's own salon. Besides, Ronsarde's disguises were exaggerated by rumors spread by penny sheet writers who were unable to fathom the notion that the most effective Prefecture investigator in the city solved his cases by mental acuity rather than sorcery or other flashy tricks. Nicholas exchanged a thoughtful look with Madeline before saying, "And Doctor Viller was also a criminal, according to the Crown's investigators who executed him. Is that your reason for accusing me of—"

Octave interrupted, "A criminal whose name was later cleared—"

"Posthumously. He may have appreciated the distinction from the afterworld but those he left behind did not." Edouard had been executed for necromancy, even though he had not been a sorcerer. The court had found his experiments to be a dangerous mix of natural philosophy and magic, but that wasn't what had condemned him. Was this a clumsy blackmail attempt or was the man trying the same game he had played with the Duchess, and suggesting Nicholas pay him some exorbitant sum to speak to Edouard Viller? *Ridiculous. If Edouard wanted to communicate from the grave he was quite capable of finding some method for accomplishing it himself.* Nicholas couldn't decide how much he thought the man knew about him, his plans. Did he know about Reynard or the others? Was he an amateur or a professional?

Octave's lips twisted, almost petulantly. He looked away, as if examining the contents of the room—the leatherbound books, the milky glass torcheres, a landscape by Caderan that badly needed to be cleaned, and Crack, unmoving, barely seeming to breathe, like a watchful statue.

Nicholas spread his hands. "What is this about, Doctor? Are you accusing me of something?" Behind him he sensed Madeline shift impatiently. He knew she didn't think he should give Octave this chance to escape. *I want answers first. Such as what he wanted in Mondollot House and what that creature was and if he was the one who sent it.* Finding things out was the second driving force of Nicholas's life. "There are criminal penalties for making false accusations."

Octave was growing impatient. He said, "I submit

that it is you who are the criminal, Valiarde, and that you entered the Mondollot House cellars tonight—"

Nicholas had slipped off his scarf to give himself a prop to fiddle with and now pretended to be more interested in its woolen folds than in his visitor. "I submit that you, Doctor Octave, are mad, and furthermore, if I did enter someone's cellar it is none of your business." He lifted his gaze to Octave's dark, slightly demented eyes and thought with resigned disgust, *an amateur.* "I also submit that the only way you can know this is if you, or your agent, were also there. I suggest you think carefully before you make any further accusations."

Octave merely asked, "You still own Doctor Viller's apparatus? Is any of it here?"

Nicholas felt another chill. *He does know too much.* "Again, you show too much curiosity for your own good, Doctor. I suggest you go, while you still can. If you have some complaint to make against me, or some suspicion of criminal activity on my part, you may take yourself to the Prefecture and bore them with it."

Octave smiled. "Then it is here."

Nicholas stood. "Doctor, you have gone too far—"

Crack, catching the change in tone, took a step forward. Octave reached for the walking stick still lying on the table, as if he meant to go. The gesture was entirely casual; if Nicholas hadn't already been on the alert he would never have seen the spark of blue spell light that flickered from Octave's hand as he touched the cane.

Nicholas was already gripping the edge of the heavy round table; with one swift effort he lifted and shoved it over. It crashed into Octave and sent the man staggering back.

Light flickered in the room, jagged blue light bouncing from wall to wall like ball lightning. Octave staggered to his feet, his stick swinging back to point toward Nicholas. He felt a wave of heat and saw spellfire crackle along the length of polished wood, preparing itself for another explosive burst. Crack was moving toward Octave, but Madeline shouted, "Get back!"

Nicholas ducked, as a shot exploded behind him. Oc-

tave fell backward on the carpet and the blue lightning
flared once and vanished with a sharp crackle.

Nicholas looked at Madeline. She stepped forward,
holding a small double-action revolver carefully and
frowning down at the corpse. He said, "I wondered what
you were waiting for."

"You were in my line of fire, dear," she said, preoccupied. "But look."

Nicholas turned. Octave's body was melting, dissolving into a gray powdery substance that flowed like fine
hourglass sand. His clothes were collapsing into it, the
substance flowing out sleeves and collar and pants legs
to pool on the faded carpet.

The door was wrenched open, causing Crack to jump
and reach for his pistol again, but it was Sarasate and
the two footmen, Devis the coachman, and the others
who guarded Coldcourt gathered there. Their exclamations and questions died as they saw the body and everyone watched the spectacle in silence.

Finally there was nothing left but the clothing and the
gray sand. Nicholas and Crack stepped forward but Madeline cautioned, "Don't touch it."

"Do you know what it is?" Nicholas asked her. Madeline had some knowledge of sorcery and witchcraft,
but she usually didn't like to display it.

"Not exactly." She drew the skirts of her robe off
the floor carefully and came to stand next to him. "My
studies were a long time ago. But I know the principle.
It's a golem, a simulacrum, constructed for a certain task
and animated by some token . . . probably that walking
stick."

The stick lay near the body. Crack nudged it thoughtfully with the toe of his boot but there was no reaction.

"We should fold the whole mess up in the carpet,
take it out to the back garden and burn it," Madeline
continued.

"We will," Nicholas assured her. "After we take a
sample and go through its pockets. Sarasate, send someone for my work gloves, please. The thick leather ones."

"Nicholas, dear," Madeline said, her brows drawing

together in annoyance, "I didn't say it was dangerous for the pleasure of hearing myself speak."

"I'll take great care, I promise, but since we can't ask our visitor any more questions, this is the only way we can find out who sent him."

Madeline seemed unconvinced. She added, "Besides, if whoever sent it had any sense at all, there won't be anything in its pockets."

She was right but Nicholas never ignored the possibility that his opponent had overlooked something. Even the best went wrong; the trick was to be ready when it happened. Sarasate brought the gloves and Nicholas searched the clothing methodically, but found nothing other than a battered and much folded invitation to the Duchess of Mondollot's ball, tucked into the inside pocket of the frock coat. More to himself than to the others, Nicholas muttered, "It could be a forgery, but spiritualism is popular enough now that he may have been invited as a curiosity." A close comparison to Madeline's invitation note should decide it.

Madeline had taken a seat in the armchair, her legs curled up under her dressing gown. The other servants had gone to check the grounds for more intruders and to prepare a pyre for the carpet and their late visitor. Only Crack had stayed behind, watching worriedly.

"It didn't come in a coach, did it?" Madeline asked suddenly. "How did it follow us?"

"It didn't, apparently." Nicholas nodded to Crack, who shifted uneasily and explained, "Devis saw it walk up the road to the drive when he was coming back from the stables."

"So someone dropped it off earlier and it waited until it saw us arrive," she said thoughtfully. "I wonder, was that Octave at the ball tonight or was it this thing? No, that can't be right. The ward would have detected it, or the familiar above the doorway. It has the invitation, but the real Octave must have given the creature his outer clothes, and forgotten to take the invitation away."

"True." Nicholas was taking a sample of the gray powder, scooping it carefully into a glass vial. Crack came over to help secure the stopper with a bit of wire. "We'll take this when we visit Arisilde tomorrow and see what he makes of it."

"If he's of any help." Madeline rubbed her face tiredly. "There's no telling what state he's in."

Nicholas rested his arms on his knees. His back was aching and it had been a long night. "He's got to be of some help. Someone is taking an alarming sort of interest in us." He took the vial of powder back from Crack and set it on the table. It caught the candlelight as if it were more diamond dust than sand, but the reflection it gave off was the blue of Octave's spell light. "A very alarming sort of interest, indeed."

3

Nicholas gave Madeline his arm as she stepped down
from their coach. She smothered an unladylike yawn,
glanced around the street, and winced. Nicholas couldn't
agree more. The Philosopher's Cross was not a pleasant
prospect so early in the morning. Under the cold dawn
light, with its customarily colorful inhabitants still abed,
the place resembled nothing so much as a theater after
a long night's performance: empty of magic, with all the
tawdry underpinnings of the stage exposed, and the hall
cluttered with trash left behind by the audience.

It was called the Philosopher's Cross because two
great thoroughfares met here: the Street of Flowers and
the Saints Procession Boulevard. The Street of Flowers
ran all the way up to the Palace wall and down to the
river, to intersect with Riverside Way, and the Boulevard
connected the Carina Gate and the Old City Gate, at
opposite ends of Vienne's sprawl. It had once been the
only street that bisected the city, uninterrupted by canals
or masses of decaying slums, failing to suddenly dead
end into a tiny alley, but the building projects of the last
century had added a new bridge across the river and cut
six new streets through crumbling neighborhoods.

Nicholas signaled their coachman to wait and Crack
climbed down from the box to accompany them. It was
barely after sunrise and the few people who were stirring
were well-bundled against the early morning cold and
hurrying to their destinations. The remains of stone stalls

under the promenades revealed there had once been a
great market here, but the area had long since given way
to cabarets, coffeehouses, mazes of small alleys and decaying buildings. Some were ancient structures with a
certain fallen grandeur, solidly built with chipped and
weathered statuary along their gables. Others were new
slapdash affairs of cheap brick, leaning slightly as if they
meant to topple at any moment. All were darkened with
soot and smoke. When the sun was well up, the streets
would be crowded not only with old women hawking
everything from herbals to hats, but with the beggars,
musicians, lunatics, poor sorcerers, witches, artists, and
gypsies that the area was famous for.

Crack went a short distance down the filthy alley and
opened the door there. Nicholas and Madeline followed
more slowly, picking their way carefully through the
muck. There was no one watching the tenement's entrance; the stool in the tiny cupboard where the concierge would normally sit was empty, though the litter
of apple cores and crumpled penny sheets around it
showed the abandonment was only temporary. The
cramped and dirty stairs were lit only by a shattered
skylight, visible as a dim circle of light several stories
up.

Madeline's mouth twisted wryly. "Poor Arisilde. But
I suppose most of the time he doesn't notice."

Nicholas didn't comment. She was probably right and
the reason why had been a nagging worry for some time.
Arisilde Damal was undoubtedly the most powerful sorcerer for hire in Ile-Rien and he had the added distinction of often failing to remember what he had been hired
for, so if he was caught and questioned his evidence
would be next to useless. But Arisilde had been on a
one-way journey for some years now and Nicholas knew
it was only a matter of time before he arrived at his
destination. With Crack going ahead to scout the way,
they climbed the stairs.

They reached the narrow landing at the top floor and
Crack knocked on the door for the garret apartment. The
fact that the door was so readily available was a good

sign and indicated that Arisilde was receiving callers. If he had been indisposed the portal would have been far more elusive.

There was the sound of what might be furniture being shifted within, then the door was opened by the sorcerer's ancient Parscian servant. The man was wearing faded tribal robes and a convincingly evil leer. When he recognized Crack, he dropped the leer and waved them in. Crack stepped aside to wait for them on the landing; he trusted Arisilde, as Nicholas did, but after last night extra caution was called for.

They went down a dingy low-ceilinged little hall and into a long room. The far wall was covered with windows, some draped with patchy patterned velvets and others bare to the dreary sky. In the yellowed ceiling were two small iron-rimmed domes, each a multipaned skylight. Faded carpets covered the floor and there were piles of books and stray papers, jugs, glass vials, bags and little ceramic containers crowding every available surface. There were plants too, herbs growing out of various bottles and jars and more exotic vines that climbed the walls and twined up into the skylights. The room was warm and the air thick with the smell of must and foliage.

The most powerful sorcerer in the city, perhaps in all Ile-Rien, was seated in an armchair with stuffing leaking out of the cushions, gazing up at them with vaguely benevolent eyes. His hair was entirely white and tied back from a face that revealed his youth. Nicholas said, "Hello, Arisilde."

The Parscian was clearing a chair for Madeline by shifting the papers stacked on it to the floor. Arisilde smiled dreamily and said, "How very good to see you both. I hope your father is well, Nicholas?"

"Very well, Arisilde. He sends you his regards." As a talented student at Lodun, Arisilde had been part of the cadre of intellectuals who had surrounded Edouard Viller, and had collaborated with him on some of his greatest work. He had also been present at Edouard's execution, but Arisilde's hold on present reality had never been too firm and his dissipations over the past years had weakened it greatly.

"And the lovely Madeline. How is your grandmother, my dear?"

Madeline looked taken aback. Nicholas was surprised himself, though he didn't allow it to show. Madeline was nothing if not reticent about her family and her past; he hadn't known she had a grandmother still living. If, considering who was asking the question, the woman was still living. An odd expression on her face, Madeline managed to reply, "She's quite well, thank you, Arisilde."

The sorcerer smiled up at Nicholas again. His eyes were violet and had once held a lively intelligence. Now their only expression was one of vague contentment and the pupils were so small they resembled pinpricks. He said, "I hope you didn't come for anything important."

Nicholas had to close his eyes briefly, summoning patience and controlling the desire to swear violently. Arisilde must have forgotten about the Duchess's ball last night and their plan for her Bisran gold, even though he had been the one to investigate the house's sorcerous defenses and discover how to circumvent its ward. Nevertheless, Nicholas stepped forward, drawing out a swatch cut from the coat that had taken the brunt of the ghoul's attack and a glass vial containing a portion of the golem's remains. "This first. I wanted you to look at these and tell me what you thought." Among the clutter on the little table at the sorcerer's elbow were two opium pipes, an old fashioned tinderbox, a thin iron bodkin fixed in a handle, and a small brass lamp. There was also a bowl of strawberries so soaked with ether that the stink of it in the air burned Nicholas's throat. They had been lucky to find Arisilde even this coherent.

"Ahh." Arisilde's long white fingers touched the fabric gently. "How very strange." He took the vial and held it up to catch the candlelight. "Someone's made a golem. A nasty one, too."

"It came to my home and behaved rather mysteriously,'' Nicholas said, hoping to engage the sorcerer's curiosity.

But the light in Arisilde's eyes was already fading. He lowered the vial slowly, setting it aside. ''I'll get to it soon, I promise.''

Nicholas sighed inwardly and said only, ''Thank you, Arisilde.'' There was no point in arguing; Arisilde would either do it or not and that was that. Nicholas had held back other samples to take to practitioners whose talents were lesser but more reliable, but he had hoped to get Arisilde's opinion. He hesitated now, wondering whether he should broach the topic of the gold at all. *This was for Edouard, Ari. You could have remembered it. He was a father to you as well.* He said, ''Do you remember what we were going to discuss today, Ari? I've got the gold stamped with the Bisran Imperial seal, and the forged documents are finally ready. Do you remember you were going to help me place them in Count Montesq's Great House?''

''Montesq.'' Arisilde's violet eyes darkened. In an entirely different voice, he said, ''I remember Montesq.''

Nicholas watched him intently. If destroying Count Montesq, the man who had destroyed Edouard Viller, would help bring Ari out of his daze, then it was doubly worth the risk. He said, ''Yes, Montesq. Do you remember the plan we discussed?''

''That, yes, I've been working on that. Very powerful protective wards on that Great House. Found that out when I tried to burn it down, years ago, didn't I? Must be careful, mustn't leave a trace, going in or coming out. That's it, isn't it? We put the Bisran gold and the papers there, then tell the Prefecture, and Montesq is executed for treason.'' Arisilde looked pleased. The dangerous light had faded and he sounded more like himself. Nicholas didn't find it an improvement.

''That's vaguely it.'' Nicholas turned to Madeline for assistance, but Arisilde said, frowning, ''While I'm thinking of it, you are looking into these goings-on, aren't you?''

''What goings-on?''

"Oh, you know, everyone is talking about it." The sorcerer waved a languid hand unhelpfully. Fortunately the servant understood the gesture and fetched a folded paper from one of the piles of debris and brought it to Nicholas. "Yes, he's right, it's in the front page of that," Arisilde explained.

It was the *Review of the Day*, the only one of the penny sheet dailies, other than the *Court Record* or the *Lodun Literary Comment*, that was occasionally anything more than rabble-rousing nonsense. The title of the piece taking up most of the front page was "Strange Occurrence in Octagon Court."

It described a young girl called Jeal Meule, who had apparently disappeared as she walked home from her work at a dressmaker's. The strangest part of the "strange occurrence" seemed to be that the girl had vanished twice. She hadn't returned home from work and her mother had canvassed the neighbors searching for her, in greater and greater anxiety as the evening wore on. Yet some children and old people who inhabited Octagon Court during the day had reported speaking to Jeal the next afternoon. They said the girl had seemed to be in a state of terror and that no one could persuade her to go home. Some had seen Jeal speak to an old woman of vague description and after that the girl had vanished for good. The dress she had been wearing had been found in the stretch of park land between the western expanse of the old city wall and the gas factory. *And everyone knows what that means*, Nicholas thought grimly. The family's only hope was that the body would be caught in the water gates and discovered before it washed out of the city.

The penny sheet writer had tried to link the unfortunate event to the disappearance of three children from Selse Street, a poorer neighborhood on the far side of the city from Octagon Court. The children had been seen speaking to an old woman of roughly the same vague description before they had vanished without a trace.

Madeline had come to look and was reading over Nicholas's shoulder. She said, "It's terrible, but it's fairly common, Arisilde. If the man stays in the city, they'll hunt him down soon enough.''

"The man?" Arisilde's brows rose.

"The person who lured the children away," she explained. "It's a man dressed as an old woman, obviously."

"Ahh. I see. Are you looking into it then, Madeline?"

Nicholas folded the paper. The date indicated it was several days old. "The Prefecture is looking into it, Arisilde. People who do that sort of thing are usually mad as well as clumsy. He'll make a mistake and they'll catch him easily."

"Oh, well, then. But. . . .'' Arisilde frowned, his violet eyes fixed on some faraway point.

"Yes?" Nicholas asked, trying to keep the impatience out of his voice. It was possible Arisilde had seen something in the smeared print that he and Madeline had missed.

"Nothing." The dreamy look was back. "Would you like to stay for coffee? It's a delicacy in Parscia, you know, and Isham is wonderful with it."

As they went down the stairs later, Madeline said, "Sometimes I think Arisilde believes you work for the Prefecture, like Ronsarde."

"He might," Nicholas admitted. "He knew that as a boy I admired Ronsarde. If he thinks Edouard's alive, then he might think anything."

The coach took them next to a street near the southern river docks, where all the various river cargo lines had their offices and tall warehouses with steeply-pitched barrel roofs clustered behind the smaller buildings.

They had speculated about Octave's motives and possible accomplices or employers on the drive from the Philosopher's Cross, but it hadn't done them much good. *We need facts to speculate*, Nicholas thought, *and facts are something we're woefully short of.* "I want to find Octave again before he finds us," he was saying as the coach drew up at the end of the street. "I sent a message to Reynard this morning asking him to try to get some word of the man. If Octave really is a spiritualist." He opened the coach door and stepped down. The street was moderately busy with mid-morning traffic: horse-drawn vans and lighter passenger coaches trundled past and men of business and shoremen crossed by along the promenade. The breeze carried the smell of the river, alternately fresh and foul, and brought to mind again the missing girl Jeal Meule, and her probable fate.

"And the Duchess accepted him as such," Madeline pointed out as she stepped down from the coach and took his arm, "or he wouldn't have been invited last night, and he certainly wouldn't have been able to speak privately to her."

Nicholas signalled the coach to continue. Devis and Crack would take it to its customary spot in the stables around the corner and then Crack would join them in the warehouse. He said, "Granted, but if he is talking to dead relatives for the aristocracy, his name should at least be mentioned in some of the circles Reynard still has entrance to. We haven't been much in society lately; that's probably why we hadn't heard something of him before." Nicholas had decided long ago not to risk entertaining at Coldcourt and he had no desire to maintain another house merely for partygiving. Fortunately, among the few members of fashionable society that he maintained contact with, this reticence was ascribed to his sensitivity about Edouard Viller's death. Keeping a low profile also helped him maintain the Donatien persona, which was essential to his plans for Montesq.

"We should go to the theater tonight, then," Madeline said. "We can make more inquiries there. And besides, Valeria Dacine is performing *Arantha* and it should be marvelous."

They turned into the alley that led past the importers and cargo lines and down to the back entrance of a warehouse that was owned by Nicholas under the name of Ringard Alscen. Nicholas unlocked the deceptively strong door and they passed inside.

He had other strongholds, because he didn't believe

in putting everything in one place, but this was by far the largest. The others were spread throughout the city and Madeline was the only one besides himself who knew the location of them all.

The door opened into an office where shelves stuffed with ledgers lined the walls and two men were playing cards on a battered trunk under the light of a hanging oil lamp, just like the offices of all the other warehouses along the street. But one of these men was Lamane and the other was one of Cusard's sons. They both stood at Madeline's presence.

Nicholas asked, "Is Cusard here?"

"Oh, aye," Lamane replied. "He hasn't stirred. He says it makes him nervous, and he just has to sit there, looking at it."

"Does he?" Nicholas smiled. "In a while he will be spending it, or at least part of it. I think he'll like that better."

They chuckled and Nicholas and Madeline went on through the inner door into the main part of the warehouse.

This was a massive chamber, several stories in height, with a vaulted ceiling that had been augmented by iron girders at some later date. Daylight entered through narrow windows high up in the walls and lanterns made pools of brighter light at intervals.

They crossed the stone-flagged floor between rows of trunks, crates, and barrels. The warehouse did real business for at least two of the smaller cargo lines along the river. Some of the things stored here were for businesses Nicholas owned under other names, though he was careful to keep Valiarde Imports from having any connection with this place. There were men working at the far end, loading a wagon that had pulled up to one of the large panel doors, and Nicholas spotted Crack among them, still keeping watch.

Nicholas stopped to unlock a door at the opposite end and they went through into a much smaller area. There were crates stacked here, too, and shelves lining the walls and locked glass-fronted cabinets. There was also a safe about waist high, square and forbidding, which held nothing more exciting than the receipts from the warehouse's honest clients.

Cusard glanced up from the clerk's desk and tipped his cap to them.

"Any problems?" Nicholas asked.

"Not a one. Want to see it?"

Nicholas smiled. "I've seen it. Last night, remember?"

"M'lady hasn't seen it." Cusard winked at Madeline. "Want to see it?"

Madeline took a seat, laying aside her parasol and slipping off her gloves. "Yes, I want to see it."

"Very well." Nicholas surrendered, going to lean against the mantel. "But don't become attached—it's not staying long."

Cusard knelt and slid the braided rug aside—the rug was pure window dressing; this particular safe hole was hidden better than mere human ingenuity could manage—and pressed his palm flat against one of the smooth fieldstone blocks that composed the floor. A small section of the blocks seemed to ripple, not like a trick of the light, but as if the stone itself had become suddenly liquid.

It was one of Arisilde's old spells, cast before he had begun his retreat into opium. Nicholas knew there was not one sorcerer in a thousand who would have been able to tell that the spell was here, let alone to break it. Arisilde had explained something of the principle: the blocks were still the same fieldstone, but the spell caused them to change their "state" from solidity to something more malleable. It was set to respond only to Nicholas, Madeline, and Cusard. Reynard knew of its location but had claimed at the time to be too unreliable to be trusted with a key to the money box.

"Keep watch for a man calling himself Doctor Octave," Nicholas told Cusard while they waited. He described the man in detail, including the style of clothing the golem had worn. "He's probably a sorcerer, possibly a deadly one. And he seems to know somewhat more than is comfortable about us.''

Cusard looked properly taken aback. ''Don't that ruin my mood,'' he muttered. ''I'll make sure the others are warned.''

The section of stone was sinking down and rippling sideways, running like water to vanish under the more permanent blocks. Revealed was a compartment lined with mortar, now filled with the small gold bars.

''Forty-seven of them,'' Cusard said, with great satisfaction. ''That's what, fifty thousand gold royals?'' He fetched out a bar and handed it to Madeline.

Her arm sagged from the unexpected weight as she accepted it. ''I didn't realize it was so heavy.''

''I also want you to pay everyone involved the bonus we discussed,'' Nicholas said. There was a penny sheet, *Review of the Day* again, lying on a nearby table, and his eyes were irresistibly drawn to it. He picked it up and scanned the contents.

''Today?'' Cusard asked. ''Before we're finished?''

''We're finished with their part.''

Cusard hesitated, looking from Nicholas, who was now engrossed in the penny sheet, to Madeline, who was smiling enigmatically and hefting the small bar. He asked, ''Is this one of those I'm not going to want to know about, and wish I didn't know once I do?''

Nicholas turned a page and didn't answer. Madeline handed Cusard back the bar, and said, a little ruefully, ''It's most likely, yes.''

''When did you get this, Cusard?''

''The pamphlet? My wife carries that about.'' Madame Cusard made lunch for all the men who worked in the warehouse and came in daily to clean the offices. It was important that Madame Cusard be seen by her neighbors to work, to help explain the presence of the generous funds that fed and clothed her and all the little Cusards.

''What is it?'' Madeline asked.

''They found a body in the river. Washed up in the watergates.''

Cusard snorted. "That's worth putting in a pamphlet? Happens every day."

"Not the missing girl Arisilde was interested in?" Madeline said, her brows drawing together.

"No, not her. A young man. Not identified as yet."

"And . . . ?"

"And," Nicholas read, " 'Attention was called to the ghastly occurrence when the gatekeepers spied a spectral glow under the surface in the vicinity of the water gate. When the working men drew near, the glow vanished. Upon further investigation, they discovered the young person's corpse.' "

"A spectral glow?" Madeline frowned. "You're thinking of last night. That stuff that was on your coat."

"What stuff?" Cusard demanded.

"When that creature attacked me in the cellar, it left a residue on my clothing," Nicholas explained, preoccupied. "Once I was away from torchlight, in the darkness of the coach, the glow was plain to see."

Madeline stood and came over to take the paper. "When they drew near the glow disappeared," she muttered. "This happened last night. They were carrying lanterns, of course."

"It bears looking into," Nicholas said, taking back the penny sheet and folding it. He smiled at Madeline. "You didn't have any plans for the afternoon, did you?"

"Sometimes I wonder about you," Madeline said. Her scalp itched under her cap.

"Why do you say that?" Nicholas seemed honestly surprised. They were standing in a corridor beneath the Saints Crossing Morgue, at the ironbound door that was the entrance to the lower levels, and he had just sounded the bellpull for admittance. Nicholas was dressed in a plain dark suit, with the short top hat and caped coat affected by professional men. He wore spectacles and Madeline had used a theatrical powder to tint his hair and beard gray. He carried a surgeon's bag. Madeline wore a plain dark dress with a white apron and had tucked all her hair away under a white cap. She had skillfully used makeup to change the long lines of her face from elegant to gaunt and to narrow her wide dark eyes. The floor of the hall was wet and filthy and the plaster was dank and smelled of carbolic.

"I think you'll do anything for curiosity's sake."

"I'm trying to establish foundation for a hypothesis."

"You're curious."

"That's what I said."

Madeline sighed and supposed it was her own fault for not voicing any real objections. There was no danger in coming here like this; Nicholas was adept at assuming different personas and she had faith in her makeup and her own acting ability. But she could think of better things to do with her afternoons than look at drowned young men. They would be starting rehearsals at the Elegante about now, she remembered, and then tried to put it out of her mind.

There was a thunk from the heavy door and the sound of bolts being pulled back, then it was opened by a man with thinning brown hair wearing an apron over his suit. He said, "Ah, Doctor . . . ?"

"Doctor Rouas, and my nurse."

Madeline dropped a little curtsey, keeping her eyes downcast. The other man ignored her, which was the attitude most physicians took with nurses and what made it such an effective disguise, almost as good as making oneself look like an article of furniture. He said, "You're here for our latest unfortunate from the river? It's this way."

He motioned them through and locked the door after them, coming forward to lead the way down. This hall was stone and stank even more strongly of carbolic. Madeline knew the heavy door and the size of the locking bolts were not current precautions, but holdovers from when this place had been part of the dungeons of the old prison that had once stood on this site.

The doctor led them down the hall, past ancient archways filled in with brick and modern wooden doors. Finally they turned a corner into a wide chamber with something of both the laboratory and the butcher shop about it. There were shelves containing chemical apparatus and surgical equipment. There was also an air that led one to expect chains, torture devices, and screaming captives. *Perhaps it's only the weight of the past*, Madeline thought. Or her imagination.

In the center of the room was a steel operating table and atop that a limp form wrapped in burlap. There was another doctor present just now, an older man, with gray in his receding hair and in his neatly-trimmed mustache and beard. He was washing his hands in the basin against the wall, his sleeves rolled up and his coat hanging on a peg nearby. He glanced up at them, his expression open and friendly. *There is something familiar about that face*, Madeline thought. He said, "I'm just going."

"Doctor Rouas, this is Doctor Halle," their guide said.

"Ah." The older man dried his hands hastily and came forward to shake hands with Nicholas. He nodded pleasantly to Madeline and this gesture of uncommon politeness on his part she almost met with a blank stare. She recovered herself in time to smile shyly and duck her head, but her mind was reeling. Doctor Halle. Of course she knew that face. Only once before had she seen it at such close range: two years ago at Upper Bannot when Ronsarde had almost uncovered their plot to steal the jewels in the Risais ancestral vault. This man was Doctor Cyran Halle, the good friend and colleague of Inspector Ronsarde.

She had been in disguise then, and far more thorough a disguise than she was wearing now. The other times she had seen him had been at a distance and in innocuous circumstances: the theater, the grill room at Lusaude's, in a crowd outside the Prefecture. He couldn't be suspicious and indeed, he didn't seem so, but Madeline became acutely aware of a nervous flutter in the pit of her stomach.

With an expression of easy goodwill, Nicholas said, "Doctor Halle, I'm familiar with your work. It's an honor to meet you."

"Thank you." Halle appeared honestly pleased with the compliment. He nodded toward the body as he rolled his sleeves down. "You're here to make an examination?"

"No, I'm to attempt an identification only. One of my patients has a son who's gone missing—though the rest of the family believes him to have run away on his own. The mother isn't well and I agreed to come here in her place."

"A sad duty." There was real sympathy in Halle's voice. He put on his coat and took his bag from the stained table. "I'll be out of your way, then. Pleasure meeting you, Doctor, and you, young lady."

Madeline had to remind herself that this man was dangerous to them, even if he did have impeccable manners and was as genial as a favorite uncle. *If he knew who we were*, she thought, *if he knew Nicholas was Donatien, the man Ronsarde has been searching for all this time. . . .*

Nicholas had moved up to the slab and turned the burlap sheet back. Madeline caught sight of a face, hardly recognizable as human, discolored as if it was some nightmare creature of the fay. Nicholas said, "He resembles the boy slightly, but I don't believe it's him." He shook his head, frowning. "I'd rather be absolutely sure. . . . Has his clothing been saved?"

"Yes, it has. Doctor Halle advised us to do so." The other doctor turned to open one of the cabinets and as he rummaged through its contents, Madeline took the opportunity to glare at Nicholas with a mixture of annoyance and exasperation.

He frowned at her. He hated to break character in the middle of a performance and normally so did she, but it wasn't every day that one encountered one's second most deadly opponent.

The doctor returned with a metal bucket, which he upended on the table. "There's not much left," he admitted. "Fragments of a shirt and trousers, the rags of a coat. No shoes. Nothing in the pockets, of course."

Nicholas used a pencil from the workbench to fastidiously poke through the damp stinking collection. "No, you're right, that's not much help." He tossed the pencil away and took the doctor's elbow, turning him back toward the body on the slab. "I take it you noticed these marks on his arms? What is your opinion on them?"

With the other physician's attention engaged, Madeline slipped a pair of sewing scissors out of her sleeve and quickly cut fragments from the torn and bedraggled coat and trousers. She folded the pieces in her handkerchief and tucked it away in the pocket of her apron, then turned back to the two men.

Nicholas took their leave shortly after that and within moments they were back out in the dank corridor on the other side of the ironbound door.

"Interesting that Ronsarde is taking notice of this," Nicholas said in an undertone. "He must have sent Halle—the man doesn't stir a foot from his house unless Ronsarde sends him."

Madeline wouldn't have put it that way; she had always found Cyran Halle the least objectionable one of the pair, but Nicholas had never forgiven the doctor for describing some of Donatien's activities as "the products of an hysterical and badly disturbed mind" in a letter to the current head of the city Prefecture. "Interesting? Is that the word for it?" she asked dryly.

"My dear, he suspected nothing."

They were nearing the stairs up into the main part of the building and Madeline was prevented from answering.

The dingy corridors on the ground floor were far more crowded and it was almost impassable near the public area. Here one of the walls was a glazed partition, behind which stood two rows of black marble tables, inclined toward the glass wall and each cooled by a constant stream of water. They held the bodies of the most recent unidentified dead, usually lost souls found on the street or pulled from the river. Each was left three or four days, in the hope that persons who were missing relatives or friends might come and claim them. Over half the corpses found in the city were eventually claimed this way, but Nicholas had told her that many were probably identified incorrectly. It was just too difficult for the bereaved to recognize even close relations under these circumstances.

They had expected to see the drowned boy on display, but had been told that they could find him in the examination room instead. Madeline wondered if it was Doctor Halle who had saved the nameless young man from this fate. As Nicholas forged a path through the crowd for her, she could see that few of the people here looked as if they were searching for loved ones; most of them looked remarkably like well-dressed tourists, drawn here by the grotesque nature of the display.

Once they were outside in the late afternoon light and relatively fresh air of the street, Madeline had decided it was useless to argue. The day had grown warmer and the morning clouds had given way to brilliant blue sky, incongruous after the morgue. The nights would still be cold, but the snow last night had probably been the last of the season and winter was in its death throes. She asked, "What were you saying about the marks on the boy's arms?"

"They were shackle galls. He was obviously held prisoner before he was killed."

"Killed, and not accidently drowned? It does happen, you know."

"Not in this case. His throat was torn out. It could have happened after death, if something in the river attacked the corpse, but Halle didn't think so. He had left some case notes for them on the table and I managed to glance over the first page."

Madeline considered that, frowning. They had to walk two streets over, to where their coach was waiting for them. Nicholas hadn't wanted it to wait in front of the building so that no one would associate it with the ordinary medical doctor and his nondescript nurse, and she was glad of it. Meeting Cyran Halle wasn't the same as running into Sebastion Ronsarde, but it was far too close a brush with the famous Inspector for her comfort. "Well, do you think this boy was killed by the same creature, or same sort of creature, that attacked you under Mondollot House?''

"I won't know that until I have the substance on the corpse's clothes examined and compared to the substance on my coat. I wish Arisilde. . . . But there's no help for that."

"I could see there was something on the clothes other than river sludge; it was a sort of silvery grease. If it is the same, what does that tell us?"

"At this point, not much."

Nicholas leaned back in his seat, resigning himself to waiting. From the height of their private box he could watch the crowd swarming into the stalls below. Reynard was late, but then lateness at the theater was eminently fashionable. Nicholas had never managed to catch the habit of it himself. He had spent the first twelve years of his life in the Riverside slums, among decaying tenements and human misery, before Edouard Viller had taken him in. He still found the theater a delight.

Nicholas glanced at Madeline and smiled. She was watching the activity around the stage below with a jeweled lorgnette. She had started as a member of the chorus in the opera five years ago, working her way up to last season, when she had taken a leading role at the Elegante. It was only because of Nicholas's plans for destroying Count Montesq that she hadn't accepted a role for this season.

Members of the *demi monde* had wondered why a fashionable young actress had taken up with a restrained and often reclusive art importer, no matter how wealthy he was. Nicholas still wasn't sure he knew, either. His original plans had never included Madeline at all.

Three years ago he had sought her acquaintance on impulse, after seeing her several times in her first ingenue role. Before he knew it he was helping her extricate herself from a tangle involving a rather predatory lord who habitually stalked young actresses. Though by the time Nicholas had arrived, the only help Madeline had really required was instruction in the little known art of artistically arranging a body to make its injuries look self-inflicted. After making certain the lord's death would appear to be suicide, Nicholas had taken Madeline back to Coldcourt. At some point during their first night together, he had been shocked to discover that he had not only told her about his identity as Donatien, but blurted out his entire life story as well. He had told her things that only Edouard, or Nicholas's long dead mother, had known. It hadn't just been a haze of lust clouding his brain; he had never had that kind of rapport with anyone before, never felt that kind of bond. He had certainly never expected to find instant camaraderie with a country girl, self-educated and come to Vienne to be an actress.

But Madeline had more than native wit. She had had no intention of staying in the chorus and had prepared for a career in classical theater by reading every new play she could get her hands on and studying the history behind the old period pieces. She had taught herself to speak and read Aderassi so she could take roles in the opera if she had to, but her real goal was the dramas and comedies played out on the stages of the big theaters of the fashionable district.

This theater was the Tragedian, one of the newest in the city. The wide sweep of the stage was lit by gas jets and the walls were delicately molded in white, pale yellow, and gold. The overstuffed seats in the boxes were stamped velvet of an inky blue, matching the plush seats of the stalls, and the curtains were yellow silk brocaded with flowers.

The curtain around the door was swept aside and Reynard appeared. He said, "Did you know the opera is absolutely full of thugs?"

"Well, there is a Bisran composer there," Nicholas said. Anticipating the request, he started to pour Reynard a glass of wine from the bottle breathing on the little table nearby.

Reynard leaned down to kiss Madeline's hand and dropped into the nearest chair. "Besides him. The place is stuffed with thugs from the Gamethon Club and they're blowing whistles, of all things. Of course, it doesn't help that the damn Bisran is crouched up on the stage, giving alternate signals to the orchestra. It's driving the conductor mad.'' Reynard was dressed much as Nicholas was, in black trousers, tailed coat, and straw-colored gloves appropriate for the theater. Reynard's black satin vest only had three buttons as was *de rigueur* for someone who carried themselves as a bit of a dandy and Nicholas's buttoned further up the chest, exposing less of his starched shirtfront, as befit his persona as a young though staid businessman.

Madeline lowered the lorgnette in alarm. ''If someone blows a whistle during *Arantha*, I'll have him killed.''

''My dear, I would be devastated if you did not demand the favor of dispatching such an undiscriminating character from me personally. But to continue, the reason I went to the opera was to speak to someone about your Doctor Octave.''

''I'm relieved,'' Nicholas said. ''Go on.''

''Octave appeared on the scene in just the past month, but he's already done circles at three or four homes of the *beau monde*—not the sort of places I could get invitations to, mind.'' Reynard leaned forward. ''Apparently, at one of the first of these exhibitions, the host hired a real sorcerer, from Lodun, to watch and to certify that Octave was not a sorcerer himself and that he was not performing any sort of spell. That's what made his reputation.''

''That's odd.'' Nicholas shook his head. ''There's a sorcerer in this business somewhere.'' He had taken steps through acquaintances in the Philosopher's Cross to meet with a spiritualist who might have an insider's view of Octave's activities, but real spiritualists were apparently elusive beasts and it would take a day or so to arrange the meeting.

''What do people say about him?'' Madeline asked Reynard. ''Are they afraid of him?''

''Not that I could tell. I spoke to several people and they all thought him a bit odd, but that's fairly normal for someone in his business. Though the people I ques-

tioned were friends of friends, you understand, not anyone who had been at one of these circles. But tomorrow
night Octave is descending far enough in society to pre-
side at a spiritual evening at Captain Everset's house.
Everset used to be invited to court, but then there was
that gambling scandal with the son of the Viscount Rale,
so he's a member of the fringe at best, now. He's stark
raving wealthy, though, which keeps him in company.
The circle is being held at that new place of his a few
miles outside the city proper. I managed to bump into
him at the opera and coaxed an overnight invitation out
of him.''

"Was it his idea to invite Doctor Octave for a circle?'' Nicholas asked. "If we're going to walk into the
good doctor's lair, I'd like to have a little more fore-
warning than this.''

"No, it was his wife's idea. From what I've heard,
she's merely bored, sick of Everset, and trying to be
fashionable.'' Reynard appeared to consider the matter
seriously. "Everset is flighty, and not terribly clever.
Not the type to be involved with this, I'd think.'' He
sipped the wine and held the glass up to the light. "He's
invited me along to liven things up, but I wouldn't have
the man on a bet.''

"Very good.'' Nicholas nodded to himself. "That
should do nicely. I'll come along as your valet.''

"Good.'' Reynard downed the last of his wine. "It'll
be fun.''

"It won't.''

"And what do I do?'' Madeline asked, her voice caus-
tic. She lowered the lorgnette to eye them critically.
"Stay at Coldcourt and roll bandages?''

"But my dear, if Nicholas and I are killed, who else
can we depend upon to avenge us?''

Madeline gave him a withering look and said, "What
if he recognizes you? He knew Nicholas, he might know
you as well.''

Reynard shrugged philosophically and made a gesture
of turning the query over to Nicholas, who said, "That's
a chance we have to take. Octave wanted something at

Mondollot House and he was afraid that we had some-how discovered what it was. We have to find out how he knows about us.'' Madeline was right; spiritualists catered to people who knew nothing about real sorcery. Most were tricksters, fakes for the most part who couldn't attract a ghost in the most haunted house in the city. But speaking to the dead was dangerously close to necromancy.

Necromancy was primarily a magic of divination, of the revealing of secret information through converse with spirits and the dead. There were plenty of simple and harmless necromantic spells, such as those for iden-tifying thieves, or recovering lost objects or people, that did not require the spilling of human blood. There were scarcely any apprentice sorcerers at Lodun, at least not when Nicholas had been studying at the medical college there, who had not used a simple necromantic spell to derive hidden knowledge from visions conjured in a mir-ror or a swordblade. The more powerful spells did re-quire the use of a corpse, or the parts of a corpse, or a human death, and the whole branch of magic had been outlawed in Ile-Rien for two hundred years or more. If any of the spiritualists had really been necromancers they would have found themselves on the wrong side of a prison wall long before now. That they were ignored by both the law courts and the sorcerers of Lodun showed how powerless they really were. Why would a sorcerer capable of making a golem bother posing as a spiritualist?

Nicholas turned his own glass to the light, watching the blood red sparkle. His hand still ached from the oil burns, though they hadn't blistered. *You don't have time for this*, he reminded himself. Octave was distracting him from the destruction of Count Rive Montesq, his real goal. Montesq had caused Edouard Viller's death, as surely as if he had personally fired a bullet into the gentle scholar's head, by making it appear that Edouard was experimenting with necromancy. Nicholas still didn't know the full story; he had been away finishing his education at Lodun when it had happened and

Edouard had said only that he had regretted accepting Montesq as a patron and that he had discovered him to be dishonest. The only explanation Nicholas could arrive at was that Edouard had learned something about Montesq that the Count found dangerous. What that was, Nicholas had been unable to discover and Edouard had refused to tell anyone anything about his work during the last months of his life.

Nicholas had managed to convince himself that the why didn't matter; Montesq had done it and he was going to pay for it.

But Nicholas couldn't simply ignore Octave. *He knows we were in the Mondollot House cellars. If he also knows about the Duchess's Bisran-stamped gold, then we can't use it to frame Montesq.* And he couldn't afford to ignore the danger. *Octave could send another golem tonight, even,* he thought.

The house lights dimmed and the noise of the crowd swelled in anticipation before levelling off somewhat. It would never quite cease, but the performances of the actors and actresses in this play were absorbing enough that it would stay a background hum and not rise to drown out the dialogue entirely.

Any more discussion among themselves now, however, would cause Madeline to become agitated. And besides, Nicholas wanted to see the play himself. He said, "We'll work out the details at dinner tonight."

4

*The late afternoon air was chill, but Nicholas had low-*ered the shades on the coach windows so he and Reynard could view the approach to Gabrill House. The wide packed-dirt road led up through a stand of trees toward a triumphal arch, perhaps fifty feet high and wide enough for four coaches to pass through side by side. As they drew nearer Nicholas could see the stones were weathered and faded as if the thing was a relic of some long forgotten age. He knew it had been built no more than ten years ago.

"Strange choice for a garden ornament, isn't it?" Reynard said.

"If you find that odd, wait till you get inside. This place was built by a wealthy widow from Umberwald. She had two grown sons, neither of whom she allowed to inherit. She had smaller homes built for them—one on either side of the main building." Constructing opulent houses outside the city wall had become all the rage in the past few decades and they had passed many such, of varying degrees of size and wealth, along the way. It allowed for large gardens and the dirt roads out here were wider and tended to have better drainage than the ancient boulevards within the city proper. "Before Everset bought it last year the owners were selling tickets for people to come out and look at it."

"Yes, I'd heard that." Reynard adjusted the set of his gloves as their coach turned off the road and passed under the arch. "You're not a sorcerer, Nicholas. What do you intend to do if this Octave takes exception to your presence with something more than another golem?"

Nicholas smiled. "Only you would ask that question as we are actually driving up to the house where Octave is." Two paved carriage ways led toward the house from the entry arch, splitting off to bridge a sunken garden where they glimpsed the tops of tall stands of exotic foliage. The house had been built backwards, so the facade facing them was a large colonnaded oval, which in other homes of this design would have given on to the back garden. But the architect had planned it well and the graceful columned portico had a mound of natural rock at its base, connecting it to the grotto of the sunken garden their carriage was passing over and giving the whole front of the large house the look of an ancient temple in ruins.

"Oh, I've no sense of self-preservation," Reynard replied easily. "That's what I depend on you for."

"I suppose we should have brought Madeline, then, because that's what I depend on her for. But even your reputation wouldn't support a female valet."

"I don't know about that." Eyeing Nicholas thoughtfully, Reynard said, "Seriously. What if Octave resents your intrusion?"

"Seriously, I only mean to observe Octave. For now," Nicholas said. There had been no disturbances at Coldcourt or at any of his other headquarters last night, though several of his henchmen had kept watch with firearms just in case.

The hooves of the horses clopped on stone as the carriage passed under an arched opening to the right of the portico and into a well-lit stone-walled passage. They were going through the ground floor of the house itself now. One of the flaws in the backward-facing design was that this was the only practical way to reach the carriage entrance.

The passage opened out into the cool air and late afternoon sun again and their coach pulled up in the semicircular carriage court, overlooked by the elegant pillars of the back façade of the house.

Reynard collected his hat and stick. "We're on." He nodded to Nicholas. "Good luck. And don't embarrass me, my good fellow."

"If you'll do me the same favor," Nicholas murmured. A footman was already running to open the coach door. "Reputation of the firm, you know."

"Of course."

As Reynard stepped down a man appeared between the carved set of double doors and came down the steps toward him. *Our host, Deran Everset,* Nicholas thought, *and he looks quite as dissipated as Reynard said he would.*

Everset's clothes were foppish in the extreme, his waistcoat patterned with a loud design and his cravat tied in an elaborate way that seemed to interfere with any attempt to move his head and his lanky frame wasn't well suited to the fashion. He was pale, with a long face and limp blond hair, and he was consulting a jeweled watch on a chain. "My God, you're late," he said, by way of greeting. "And since when have you kept a coach?"

"It's on loan," Reynard said, "from a very, very dear friend of mine." He clapped Everset on the shoulder, turning him back toward the house. "I hope you have a wild night planned for us."

"None of this was my idea...." their host protested, the rest of his answer lost as the two men passed inside.

Nicholas stepped out of the coach himself. He stretched, keeping one eye on the doorway into the house as a real valet would, in case a butler appeared. "Can we take down the baggage?" he asked the waiting footman.

"Yes, your man's the last guest to arrive, so there's no hurry." The man scuffed one polished shoe against the clean-swept stones of the court, obviously bored. The house livery was dark green, with gold piping on the coat. "Need a hand?"

Crack, dressed as a coach outrider, had hopped down

from the box. "No," Nicholas told the footman. "Thanks the same, though."

There was stabling for the horses and coaches built into the walls of the court. Some of the carriage doors still stood open and Nicholas counted at least three town coaches. Reynard had wangled the invitation so quickly there had been no opportunity to find out about the other guests. A terrace ran along the top of the wall; he could see urns of potted flowers and benches facing out into the rest of the garden. He knew the elevated terrace extended out from the back of the carriage court, crossing over the garden to reach a small elevated pavilion built to resemble a classical temple. It was isolated from the main house, but easily reached along the terrace by guests in evening clothes; if they meant to hold the circle anywhere else, Nicholas would eat his hat.

He took Reynard's single case as Devis handed it down and exchanged a nod with Crack. Crack and Devis would be quartered out here with the coach for the night and would probably be too closely watched to slip out and be of any help to him. Hopefully, he wouldn't need them.

The footman led him up the steps and through the open doors. Nicholas caught sight of an airy high-ceilinged vestibule, floored in what was probably imitation marble with the classical theme continued in frescoes with nymphs and graces that climbed the walls above a grand staircase. The footman showed him a servants' door and Nicholas climbed a narrow plain staircase up two floors, hoping this would provide him an early opportunity to scout around.

But as soon as he reached the top he almost walked into one of the upstairs maids, who directed him to the chamber assigned to Reynard.

The room was well-appointed and the eccentricity of the rest of the house hadn't been extended to the bedrooms, or at least not the guest bedrooms. Heavy damask draperies of pale yellow framed the windows, matching the ivory silk panelled walls and the cushions and covers on the couches, overstuffed chairs, and the delicate little tables. The bed hangings made up for this restraint with embroidered garlands, silk blooms, and a crown of ostrich feathers.

Nicholas had never employed a valet himself and was able to unpack Reynard's case with speed and efficiency. While the guests were at dinner, maids would be in and out of the rooms, freshening flowers, filling the basin, and making sure the sheets were aired, and he didn't want the room to look out of the ordinary. Finishing up, he took out his pocket watch—a cheap one, without any ornament, that he kept for this sort of disguise—and gauged the time he had until Reynard came up to dress for dinner. That would be an ideal opportunity to get an initial report on the other guests and whether Octave was present in the house yet. The more information he had to act on, the better.

He slipped out into the hall and quietly shut the door behind him. It was quiet, except for the faint hiss of gaslights inside their porcelain globes and muted voices echoing up the grand stairwell. He moved down the hall, quietly but purposefully, and without furtive caution. In a house of this size, with as many servants as this one had, and with the additional confusion of an overnight party, anyone who looked as if he knew where he was going was not too likely to be questioned.

He found the servants' stair at the far end of the corridor and went down it quickly, coming out in a narrow low-ceilinged hall that ran toward the back of the house. As he passed an open door someone called out, "Wait, there, whose are you?"

Nicholas stopped obediently. It was a pantry, a small room lined with glassfronted cabinets, with china and silver plate gleaming inside. The man who had addressed him was gray-haired and stout, dressed in a dark suit and clutching a bundle of keys. *The butler, obviously*, Nicholas thought. There was a woman in the room too, a respectable-looking matron in a gray gown and an apron. Nicholas said, "Captain Morane's, sir."

"Ah, go on, then." The butler turned back to the agitated woman in the flour-dusted apron. "No, tell Listeri that's my final word."

"No, you tell him! I'm sick of his Aderassi chatter and you can—"

Without even having to deliver his carefully prepared excuse concerning gloves left behind in the carriage, Nicholas reached the arch at the end of the passage and the argument was lost in the greater clatter of the kitchen. The stove was a monolithic monument stretching across the far wall, copper fish kettles steaming on the burners. A long plank table was weighed down with molds, baking trays for meringues, and stone dishes for pies. Dressers standing against the brick-lined walls held the plain china and an array of silver pots for chocolate and coffee.

The cook, sweating under his white cap, slammed a pot on the range and shouted an amazing Aderassi profanity. From the hearth an aproned woman turning spitted capons over a sheet metal scallop shouted, "What do you know about it, you dirty Foreigner!" The door in the far wall banged open to admit two scullery maids struggling with a tub of water. Nicholas hastened to help them guide it in and deposit it on the tiles near the table, then left them to join their colleague in battle. He escaped through another pantry and out the door into the kitchen garden.

He made his way down a dirt path, past geometrically laid out beds for melons, cabbages, endives, and wooden racks for climbing vegetables. The wall to his left was lined with skeletal pear trees and bordered on the carriage court. There was a wooden door, a back entrance to the stables, but it was fortunately closed. On his right, over the top of the garden wall, he could see the side of one of the two outbuildings the widow had constructed for her sons. The gray stones were overgrown with climbing vines, but it looked as well-kept as the main house. Both were probably used for extra guest and servants' quarters.

He reached the trellised gate in the back wall and opened it to enter the garden proper. He hesitated, taking his bearings. This was dangerous territory; he could explain his presence in the carriage court and the kitchen garden. Any servant except a gardener would be forbidden this area.

It seemed deserted. Rambling roses, quince trees, and willows obscured the walls that ran down to terminate in a slight dip and another high wall. Tangled greenery that would flower in the spring hung out of the beds and threatened the cobbled pathways and a fountain with a nymph trapped in winter-dry vines played near the center.

Nicholas trotted the length of the wall, over which he could see the carved balusters of the terrace enclosure. At the end of the garden the terrace formed a wide square platform. Overgrown brush screened him from the house now, and he was able to dig fingers and boot tips into the cracks in the rough stone wall. He hauled himself up and slung one leg over the balustrade, hoping the moss stains wouldn't show too badly on his dark clothes.

The temple was in the center of the platform. It was a simple design, an open circle of columns supporting a carved entablature. The stones were artificially weathered, as the triumphal arch was, giving the little place a look of aged dignity. A fine wooden table had been placed in the center, surrounded by eight chairs.

The great spreading mass of several oak trees, each large as a small hillock and far older than the house itself, blocked the view on three sides of the platform, and the only clear line-of-sight was straight down the connecting stone bridge to the carriage court terrace and the back of the main house. Huge flower urns and classical statues of various faunal gods around the edges of the platform provided some cover, but the little temple would be clearly visible to anyone standing on the further terrace. No one seemed to be out and Nicholas left the sheltering statuary and approached the temple cautiously.

He crouched to examine the underside of the table for wires, or mechanical or magical devices. There seemed to be none, and no secret compartments either. The table was also heavy and sturdy, impossible for a clever spiritualist to rock with his boot tips, which was one of the more common tricks. He moved on to the chairs, checking underneath them and palpating the seat cushions. Next was the temple itself.

Finally he had searched as much of the place as he was able to without a ladder and he went to sit in the concealing shadow of an oversized urn. It was getting late and darkness was gathering in pools under the winter-stripped trees and in the thorny brush. No preparations had been made for the kind of show people such as Captain Everset and his lady would expect for their money.

Is that really a surprise? Nicholas asked himself. *You know Octave has real power, or at least access to real power.* If he had found the table prepared with flash-powder and false bottomed drawers, it would only have obscured the issue further. He would simply have to wait and see what he could discover during the circle.

Nicholas made it safely back to the room to find Reynard already dressing for dinner.

"There you are," Reynard said. He was tying his cravat in front of the mirror. "I was beginning to wonder. Did you find anything?"

"No, as I expected. Is Octave here? Who are the other guests?"

"I didn't see Octave. Madame Everset talked about him as if she expected him to descend on us out of the ether at any moment, though. Whether that means he's in the house now or not, I couldn't tell you." Reynard swore, tore the cravat off and discarded it over his shoulder, selecting a fresh one out of the open drawer. Nicholas caught the bit of cloth before it could flutter to the floor and put it away. Reynard continued, "As to the other guests, they're what you'd expect. Amelind Danyell, the half-mad one who's been dangling after what's his name, the unpleasant poet who's an opium addict—"

"Algretto?"

"That's it. He's here too, of course, and he's brought his wife along to play off Danyell. There's also Danyell's escort, a pimply-faced bit who has propositioned me twice already and I'm old enough to be his father, for God's sake. There's Vearde and his current mistress, Ilian Isolde the opera singer, and of course Count Belennier, who couldn't get invited to a salon party on a sinking ship since he was caught in that Naissance Court scandal."

Reynard was about to ruin another cravat. Nicholas impatiently stopped him, turned him around and finished tying it himself. The company was uniformly scandalous, but then no one would have invited Reynard to any other kind of occasion. He had gained a reputation for casual behavior before he had taken an officer's commission in the Guard, but the worst scandal by far was the one that had lost him that commission and made him Count Montesq's enemy.

Reynard had been conducting an affair with a younger officer, a member of a noble family, at the same time as the young man was also seeking an engagement with a young woman of an even nobler and far more wealthy family. Montesq's solicitor Devril, who had a second career as a blackmailer, had managed to buy an incriminating letter written by the young man to Reynard, which had been stolen out of Reynard's kit when their regiment was stationed on the Tethari peninsula. The young man had paid the blackmail at first, paid it until he had exhausted his personal funds, but Devril's demands had continued until finally, on the day before the wedding, Devril had made the letter public through intermediaries. The scandal and the pressures of his position and, possibly, the belief that Reynard had given the letter to Devril himself, worked on an excitable temperament, and the young man had killed himself. Reynard had returned to Vienne shortly thereafter to find his friend dead and most of the *beau monde* of the belief that Reynard had driven him to suicide. The feeling against him was so high his commanding officer had trumped up some charges against him in order to cashier him out of the Guard.

The part of the story that no one else but Nicholas and Madeline knew entirely was that Reynard had tracked down the unscrupulous batman who had stolen the letter and killed him after extracting Devril's identity. Montesq's men had discovered that Reynard was on Devril's trail and planned to eliminate him, but Nicholas had been following the situation as well and managed to contact Reynard and warn him. Together they had rid the world of the blackmailing solicitor Devril, and Reynard had worked with Nicholas ever since.

Nicholas finished tying the cravat and Reynard examined the result in the mirror carefully. "You did that well. Did they teach it at Lodun when you were there?"

"They teach everything at Lodun." The other guests were familiar names, except for one. "Vearde, do you know him by sight?"

"Yes, I've met him on several occasions. Just an acquaintance, though." Reynard turned to regard him quizzically, with a hint of a smile. "You think he's really Ronsarde in disguise?"

"No, I do not think that." Damn Reynard for being so astute, anyway. Nicholas didn't want to seem like a nervous fool, but Ronsarde was the one enemy he wasn't completely confident that he could outwit. He put away Reynard's old suit, knowing a real valet would never leave clothing on the floor. Well, maybe Reynard's valet might, but it would excite comment among the other servants and he didn't want to call attention to himself. "We did see Halle at the morgue, you know."

"When you went to look at that drowned boy? I thought Madeline said there was no connection to Octave?"

"Not yet." He hadn't heard back from the practitioners he had given the samples to. He would probably have to go to Arisilde again himself and remind him. "There were only eight chairs around the table."

"Well, Everset said he wouldn't be joining us for Octave's little show. I assume some of the others have also made their excuses. Do you think that matters terribly?''

"No.'' Nicholas considered a moment. "Do you think Everset will be suspicious that you haven't made an excuse?''

"I've mentioned that I haven't seen one of the things yet and I'm curious. That should do it. No one in this group is going to suspect anyone of anything except sneaking off to debauch on the sly.''

"You're right, of course.'' Nicholas had learned early that one of the chief problems in deception was the tendency to try to overexplain one's actions. The truth was that people did the oddest things for the most inconsequential reasons and elaborate justifications only made one look guilty.

Like most parvenu households, the Eversets had paid a great deal for an excellent Aderassi chef and since they had no real taste, had managed to hire only a mediocre one. Nicholas watched the chaos from the safety of the kitchen doorway, with one or two of the other upstairs servants who were malingering now that the guests were settled. Earlier, from the shelter of the stables, they had all watched Octave's coach arrive. The spiritualist had brought no baggage and no one to accompany him except the coach driver.

The chef Listeri carried on dinner preparations as if the kitchen were a besieged citadel that would inevitably fall to superior force and this entailed a great deal of banging, breakage, and profanity toward the scullery maids. It made Nicholas all the more grateful for his own dignified Andrea, who had never thrown a tantrum in his life.

He shook his head over the choice of an inferior grade of wine for a sauce, then left his indolent pose in the doorway and made his way toward the dining room. Nicholas had made it a point to see all the servants brought in by the guests and to make sure that they were all, as far as he could tell, what they appeared to be. Crack had orders to do the same with the coachmen and outriders quartered in the stables and Nicholas knew if

his henchman had discovered anything suspicious he
would have found a way to send word by now. It was
only the guests he was worried about.

It proved impossible to get close enough to the dining
room to overhear the conversation. The only possibility
was a small anteroom used by the butler to marshall the
footmen who were serving the courses and it was always
occupied. Nicholas grudgingly returned to his position
in the kitchen, where Listeri seemed about to succumb
to a seizure.

Not that casual conversation over the plates was likely
to provide much illumination, though Nicholas knew
that Algretto the poet was associated with Count Rive
Montesq. Last month Nicholas had been at Contera's
with Reynard and Madeline, when the Count had come
in with a large party that had included Algretto. There
was nothing particularly damning in that. Algretto's current popularity made him a much sought-after guest with
all levels of society.

But after a time Nicholas had become aware of the
particular attention being directed at them from the
neighborhood of Montesq's party. It might be due to
Madeline's presence; as a feted actress she often drew
attention. Or it might be due to Reynard, who tended to
draw his own share of notice.

"We're being observed, my dears," Reynard had
said. "Out of jealousy, it's obvious." He had betrayed
absolutely no discomfort; Reynard loved challenges.

Madeline had laughed and lifted her glass to him as
if he had said something extremely witty and cutting
about the people watching them. "God," she murmured,
"I must have a guilty conscience. I'm afraid he knows."

She meant Montesq, who was straightening the black
opal studs on his cuffs as he leaned over to speak to one
of the women in his entourage. Just that day Nicholas
had obtained the rest of the builder's plans for Montesq's Great House, which they would need to plant the
Duchess of Mondollot's incriminating Bisran gold.
"Guilty?" he said, raising his own glass.

"Not guilty, precisely. An occupied conscience, perhaps.'' She touched her hair ornament in a gesture of flirtation and without moving her lips, said, ''He's coming over here.''

Out of the corner of his eye Nicholas had seen Montesq excuse himself to his party and stand. ''He knows nothing,'' he said.

''And that's Enora Ragele with him,'' Madeline added, in a more audible voice. ''The woman's such a whore.''

''Now Madeline, you sound like an actress,'' Reynard chided her gently.

The exchange had been for Montesq's benefit. The Count reached their table on the tail end of Reynard's comment and Nicholas stood to shake hands with him.

''It's been a long time, Valiarde. I had thought you left the country,'' Montesq said, easily. He looked every inch the noble of Ile-Rien, from the sober cut of his tail coat to the impeccable grooming of his oiled hair and closely trimmed beard. His smile didn't reach his flat black eyes.

''I'm not much in society, my lord.'' Nicholas turned to introduce Madeline and Reynard. The knife-edge of tension that went through him when Montesq formally kissed Madeline's hand surprised him, but it was made up for as he watched the Count pretend he had never heard of Reynard Morane before. *Though he probably loses track of the people he orders his men to kill; there are so many of them.*

The introductions done, Montesq turned back to Nicholas. ''Edouard Viller was a great loss to philosophy, Valiarde. I'm sure Lodun feels his absence.''

''We all feel his absence,'' Nicholas said quietly. He was finding that being offered condolences, even long after the fact, by his foster-father's murderer was an almost enjoyable experience. The fact that Montesq had not yet tired of his grotesque private jokes was a sign of weakness. *He isn't aware who the joke is on—yet.*

Montesq's face betrayed nothing. He said, ''You are still an art importer?''

''Yes, I am.'' Nicholas made his expression one of

polite interest. Montesq might be fishing, though he couldn't think for what.

"Really, and I thought my company was considered scandalous by the *beau monde*." The speaker was the poet Algretto, who had come up behind Montesq. He looked as if he had just rolled out of bed, his clothes disordered and his cravat hanging loose around his neck, his blond curls in disarray. The poet had given this same impression every time Nicholas had seen him so he strongly suspected it was a deliberate affectation. "Take care, my lord, this is almost too much."

Nicholas barely managed to conceal his amusement. There was no mistaking what Algretto was referring to. As an attempt to please his patron it backfired badly; Montesq's connection to his blackmailing solicitor had almost been exposed during the incident that had won Reynard the shame of the *beau monde*, and from the Count's expression he obviously remembered it with no fondness either.

"True," Reynard said to the poet, his voice amused. "Your company should be scandalous enough. Any more would be a surfeit of riches."

Algretto started to speak but then glanced at Montesq. He must have read impatience in the set of his patron's jaw, because he contented himself with an ironic bow, as if acknowledging the hit. Montesq smiled, too well-bred to acknowledge the coarseness of the *demi monde* he had found himself surrounded by, and said, "My agent will contact your men of business, Valiarde."

"Of course." Nicholas smiled, gently.

When Montesq had taken his leave and gone back to his table, Madeline said seriously, "Sometimes your self-control frightens me."

"Thank you," Nicholas said, lifting his glass to her, not that he thought she had meant it as a compliment.

"I thought you were as subtle as a ground adder myself," Reynard commented dryly. "What did I miss?"

"If I had been too obliging, he would have become suspicious." Nicholas swirled the contents of his wine glass. "He knows I hate him. He just doesn't realize to what extent I've acted on it."

"So he was testing you," Reynard said thoughtfully.

Madeline idly shredded a flower petal from the table decoration. "I wonder why."

Nicholas had smiled, with a razor edge that was anything but gentle. "Perhaps he has an occupied conscience."

Algretto was a connection to Montesq, but not to Octave. And it was Octave's appearance on the scene, in the middle of the plan to destroy Montesq, a culmination of years of effort, that worried Nicholas the most. The chef Listeri suddenly became aware of his audience and flung a pot at the wall near the doorway, causing Nicholas and the other servants to hastily scramble for cover, and brought Nicholas's thoughts abruptly back to his current role.

After dinner had been served, the apparently chronic confusion in the servants' hall allowed Nicholas to fortify himself with a bowl of gamey stew before slipping out of the house to take up a position near the circle.

Colored lamps had been hung at strategic intervals throughout the formal garden, making the trip out to the platform somewhat more interesting, but he managed it without incident. Once there he scouted the area for any other watchers before climbing up to the balustrade again. A glass candlelamp had been placed in the center of the table and more lamps had been hung from some of the pillars. The shadows among the statuary at the edges of the platform were even darker for these yellow beacons, so he retired behind the large urn with some confidence.

It was cold, though Nicholas had taken the precaution of bringing dark gloves and a scarf to wrap around his throat. The wind had died down since earlier in the day and the quiet of the night was the heavy silence of the country. Nicholas was even able to hear a late carriage go down the road in front of the house, passing Gabrill's triumphal arch and continuing on toward the even grander parks further away from the city.

Not long after, the doors to the terrace from the main house opened and he heard talk and laughter. Lamps had been lit along the bridge of the terrace and he was able to see the guests making their way toward the temple platform.

Amelind Danyell was in front, her shoulders bare in a gown better suited to a warm salon, escorted by a young man not quite her height with a waistcoat of such startling pattern Nicholas could make it out even in lamplight at this distance. At her other side was Count Belennier, who seemed to be paying Danyell more attention than was quite necessary for a woman who already had one male arm to steady her. Behind them he recognized Algretto, the flamboyant poet, who had come out in his shirtsleeves, possibly in an attempt to encourage an attack of tubercle that would make him even more attractive to women like Danyell. He had given his arm to Madame Everset, his hostess, who had bundled up in a paletot and wrapped a scarf around her head, showing far more sense than most of the others present. Possibly she was more interested in the circle itself than she was in being seen to have it by these people. Nicholas wondered if Octave had solicited some relic of a dead relative from her for tonight.

Behind them was Algretto's long-suffering wife, a rather plain woman in a dress of muted color under a long shawl, escorted by Reynard. He was paying her all the courteous attention due a lady of her station, despite attempts from the more boisterous members of the party to distract him. Nicholas smiled to himself. Reynard, despite his protests to the contrary, was a gentleman to his bones.

Behind them trailed Octave.

He wore a plain dark suit, without the ostentatious opera cape this time. If he had recognized Reynard, he might have given some sign by now. The man they had encountered at Coldcourt the night before would have, Nicholas thought, but there was no knowing how closely the golem's personality had matched the real Octave's.

He seemed to be the last member of the party. Everset had already told Reynard he intended to stay behind. Vearde must have opted out as well and as an opera singer Ilian Isolde could not afford to expose her throat to the night air.

The first group reached the temple and Amelind Danyell called out gaily, "Does it matter where we sit, my dear?"

Madame Everset glanced back at Octave, but he gave her no indication, one way or the other. She answered, "No, dear, it doesn't matter."

Two footmen were stationed a short distance down the terrace to answer any calls for service. The guests found seats with a great deal of shuffling back and forth and some subtle jockeying for position on Belennier's part. Octave reached the temple and stood framed in the entrance, a slight contemptuous smile on his pale face. His appearance was subtly disreputable: frayed cuffs, a cravat that was distinctly gray in the lamplight. Nicholas wondered whether the effect was intentional. Octave stroked his unkempt beard and stared at the people around the table.

It wasn't until everyone was seated that he came forward into the temple. Most of the guests seemed to regard him as a hired entertainer; they chatted among themselves, Belennier flirting with Danyell, Danyell punishing Algretto with subtle jibes for ignoring her, Algretto parrying with a faintly superior smile, and Danyell's young escort fighting for some sort of notice from someone. Crouching in the darkness behind the solid bulk of the urn, cold and damp seeping up through his boots from the stone flags, Nicholas was still reminded of why he didn't much care for society. It had its own predators, just like the streets of Riverside, but they dealt their blows with words, gestures, expressions. Here there were no allies, only enemies, and yet everyone conducted themselves as though they were the dearest of companions. Nicholas hadn't been oblivious to it, but he had felt as if it all took place on another plane of existence which he could view but not interact with. Not that anyone in his right mind would wish to. He preferred the world where enemies were enemies and war was war, and the blows cut to the bone.

Madame Everset was torn between attending her guests and keeping one eye on Octave; it was obvious she was anxious for the circle to start. Reynard was keeping one eye on Octave also, but in a far more subtle fashion, while carrying on a light conversation with Madame Algretto.

Madame Everset, her voice pitched a little too high from anxiety, said abruptly, "Do we begin, Doctor?"

The others looked toward her, some startled, some amused.

Octave said, "We begin, Madame." He was standing behind his empty chair now, facing the others, his back to the wide gap between the pillars that marked the entrance to the temple.

Algretto, probably resenting the sudden cessation of attention from himself, drawled, "I, personally, am an unbeliever in this sort of fantasy, Doctor. Do you really propose to make our good hostess's late brother appear among us?"

Madame Everset winced and Nicholas made the mental note, *discover the history of the dead brother.* Her face was white in the lamplight and the skin beneath her eyes bruised by fatigue. Nicholas had assumed any signs of strain were due to being married to Captain Everset; now it was obvious Madame had other concerns. It seemed less and less as if she had sought Octave out simply for the societal coup of holding a circle at a salon party. He wondered if perhaps Octave had sought her out, instead.

The doctor said, "Belief is unnecessary." His voice was almost the same as the golem's, perhaps a trifle lower in pitch. Nicholas reminded himself again that this might be an entirely different person from the golem he had met. Its reactions were nothing to judge the real man by.

"Is it?" Algretto smiled, prepared to enjoy baiting

Octave and plaguing his obviously anxious hostess. "I thought it essential to this sort of . . . enterprise."

"Your thought was inaccurate." Octave was unruffled. He was in his own element and confident. He had his hand in the pocket of his frock coat and there was something about his stance that was not quite natural. Nicholas might have suspected a pistol, but somehow he didn't think Octave would carry a weapon. Or not that sort of weapon.

Algretto was not accustomed to being parried with such unconcern. Eyes narrowed, he said, "If you would care to word it thus. Your tone is insulting, Doctor. Though what you are a doctor of, exactly, has never been specified."

Madame Algretto sighed audibly, Amelind Danyell tittered, and Belennier looked bored. Madame Everset tried to interject, saying, "Really, I'm sure no harm was—"

"Really, Algretto," Reynard said, managing to sound as if the subject both amused and wearied him. "Poetry is your field of expertise. Why don't you stick with that and let the good doctor carry on?"

Algretto's eyes went hooded. There was nothing of outright insult in the words, but Reynard was a master of insinuation. The poet said, "I hadn't thought you were the type to be interested in poetry, or this spirit nonsense, Morane."

"Oh, I don't know poetry, but I know what I like."

"Then why are you here?"

"I'm here because I was invited. I often am, you know. Everset and I are the dearest of friends. Why are you here?"

Octave was obviously enjoying the confrontation, a smile playing about his pale lips. Belennier said, "Really, gentlemen, surely it's not—"

Watching his opponent intently, Algretto said, "Perhaps to lend a badly needed air of artistic integrity to the proceedings. But I suppose, after hearing what is said of you, you are unfamiliar with the subject of integrity."

"Perhaps," Reynard agreed, smiling gently. "After

hearing about your performance of your latest epic at Countess Averae's literary evening, I think you might be better qualified to lend advice on monkey posturing.''

Algretto came to his feet with a curse, knocking back his chair.

With reflexes honed by years of dueling, Reynard stood just as abruptly, his elbow knocking Doctor Octave's arm and sending the spiritualist stumbling back a step. In an unconscious gesture to keep his balance, Octave's hand came out of his pocket.

Nicholas was smiling to himself, thinking, *good old Reynard*, when Octave's hand came up and he saw the object the spiritualist was clutching. There was only time for a moment's glimpse, before Octave hurriedly stuffed it back into concealment. Reynard was saying to Algretto, ''Sorry, old fellow, didn't realize you'd take it personally. My apologies.''

Algretto was hardly appeased but it would have been the worst manners to refuse the offered apology. He managed to nod grudgingly and sit down as Reynard gravely excused himself to Octave for jostling him and took his own seat again.

Nicholas's smile had died. The object had appeared to be a metallic ball. It had looked very much like one of the models of Edouard Viller's apparatus, except it was much smaller.

It can't be, he told himself. *The others were destroyed.* He had seen the Crown Investigators smash them to bits himself. It had been Edouard's last experiment in combining natural philosophy and magic, begun from a desire to communicate with his dead wife, whom Nicholas knew only as a portrait in the main salon at Coldcourt. By itself, a device for speaking to the dead, whether it worked or not, was not necromancy. But Count Montesq had made it appear as though Edouard had murdered a woman in an attempt to perform magic, fulfilling the legal definition of necromancy. And when the court had discovered what the device had been meant to do, Edouard had looked all the more guilty.

But how had Octave gotten his hands on one of the

devices? Every bit of Edouard's surviving work, his notes, his journals, the last intact models of the apparatus, everything the Crown hadn't burned was at Coldcourt. Nicholas cursed silently. *Perhaps there was some sort of prototype we never knew about.* Arisilde Damal would know, if anyone would. He had worked most closely with Edouard in the initial studies at Lodun. The only alternative was that Octave had somehow re-created that work and had developed the same theories independently.

If he hadn't, if he had somehow stolen Edouard's research. . . . *He won't need a device to speak to the dead,* Nicholas thought. *He will do it quite comfortably from his own grave.* He would rather have seen all of Edouard's work burned by the Crown than let Octave use it for some filthy trick.

Octave had recovered his composure as the other members of the party resettled themselves. He nodded at the still sullen Algretto and said, "To answer the original question, I am a doctor of the spirit, good sir. Any student of sorcery will tell you of the etheric plane. It is possible to use the ether to reach the souls that dwell beyond it, who were once part of our world. To communicate with them. To bring them—temporarily—back to the living. Now. . . ."

Octave let the silence grow, until the only sound was the wind moving gently through the oaks. His eyes seemed to go blank, then roll up into his head. A tremor passed over him and he moaned softly.

Theatrics, Nicholas thought in disgust. *And not very good theatrics at that.* Octave must still be rattled from Reynard's near-battle with Algretto. He wasn't the only one who found the performance less than convincing. He could see an expression of quite open skepticism on Madame Algretto's refined features. But if the spiritualist was using a device that Edouard had had some hand in making, he was playing with power indeed.

A sudden loud rasp startled everyone. Someone gasped. The rasping noise came again and Nicholas realized it was the sound of wood scraping painfully against stone. Then he noticed what the others had already seen—the heavy wooden table was rotating, slowly, ponderously, rotating.

Algretto said, "It's a trick."

Reynard pushed back from the table to look beneath it. Nicholas writhed inwardly, wishing he had thought of a way to make himself a member of the party, now entitled to jump up and examine the table for himself. Reynard said, "It's not a trick. He's not touching it." He scraped at something with one boot. "And there are splinters on the pavement."

"Then it's sorcery." Algretto smiled. "Such a thing wouldn't even amuse the market crowds, Doctor. Though I can see why you found this way of earning your bread more amenable than working as a hedgewitch in the Philosopher's Cross."

The lamps all flickered once and simultaneously, as if a hand had briefly lowered over the flame of each. Without dropping his pose of rapt concentration, Octave said, "Believe what you wish. I am the key that unlocks all doors between our world and the next."

"Necromancy," Madame Algretto said clearly, "is punishable by death, aptly enough." Her hands hovered over the still moving table, not quite touching it. That she was beginning to find the proceedings distasteful was obvious.

"But not before the party is over, I hope," said Amelind Danyell slyly.

A trace of irritation in his voice, Octave said, "This is not necromancy, not ghost summoning or grave robbing. This is communication of the highest form."

"This is a table moving," Algretto pointed out, rather cogently Nicholas had to admit. "We've seen nothing but—"

Octave held up a hand for silence. Behind him there was a man standing framed between the pillars of the temple entrance. Nicholas caught his breath. He had glanced in that direction a bare instant before and there had been nothing there.

The man was young, dressed in a naval officer's uniform. Nicholas stared hard, trying to memorize details.

The others were silent, those facing the other direction whipping around in their chairs to see. Even the table had stopped its halting clockwise progress. Madame Everset came to her feet without conscious volition, as if she had levitated out of her chair. Octave didn't turn, but he had abandoned his apparently trance-like state and was watching her with avid attention.

It isn't a projection from a picture-lantern, was Nicholas's first thought. Its eyes were moving. Bloodshot, as if from salt water or lack of sleep, its eyes went from face to face around the table. It might be an illusion: sorcerous illusions could move, speak. Arisilde was capable of illusions that even seemed solid to the touch. It might be a living accomplice but he didn't see how a man could have gotten past the servants stationed down the terrace without being remarked.

Madame Everset tried to speak and failed, then managed to gasp, "Justane. . . ."

Or how Octave acquired an accomplice Madame Everset would recognize as her brother, Nicholas thought.

Then Octave murmured, "Ask him, Madame. You remember our agreement."

Reynard started, his gaze jerking away from the apparition to Octave, and Nicholas knew he wasn't the only one to hear those discreet words. None of the others seemed to take notice.

Madame Everset nodded, swayed as if she meant to faint, but said, "Justane, your ship. Where did it go down?"

The young man's searching eyes found her. His face was not corpse white, Nicholas noted, but tanned and reddened from the sun. Somehow he found that point more convincing than anything else. The apparition licked its lips, said, "Off the southern coast of Parscia, the straits of Kasha-triy." His voice was low and hoarse. "But Lise. . . ."

He was gone. There was no gradual fade, no dissolve into mist. He was gone and it was as quick as a door slamming between one world and the next. Madame Everset screamed, "Justane!"

In the suddenly vast silence of the night there was one sound. It was the click, click, click of a man's bootheels on stone.

Nicholas felt himself seized by something, some invisible force that seemed to stop his heart, to freeze the breath in his lungs. It was very like the moment when the ghoul had rushed him in the Mondollot cellars and he had been momentarily trapped, powerless to move. He wondered if he had made a fatal miscalculation in coming here tonight.

At first nothing was visible. Then the shadows between the lamps resolved into a dark figure walking at an even, unhurried pace up the bridge of the terrace toward the temple. Nicholas squinted, trying to see the man's face, and realized he was shivering; the normal dank chill of a late winter night had suddenly turned bitter cold. It was as if the temple platform was made of ice and his hands burned with cold inside his gloves. Something scraped across the roof of the temple, as if the wind had dragged a tree branch against it. Nicholas managed to move, jerking his head to stare up at the deeply shadowed edge of the roof. There were no trees overhanging the temple.

He looked at Octave.

The spiritualist was staring with grim concentration at the table. He hadn't turned to look at the approaching figure but something told Nicholas he was more aware of it than any of them. Octave wet his lips nervously and muttered, "Not yet, not yet. . . ."

That worried Nicholas more than anything. *Good God, the man can contact the dead, and he doesn't know what he's toying with.* The figure was drawing inexorably closer. Nicholas tried to recognize it, to study its features, anything to understand what was happening, but something seemed to obscure its face. Even though he should be able to see it clearly at this distance his eyes seemed to slide away when he tried to focus on its features. He concentrated harder, knowing that Arisilde had told him it was a way to penetrate the most clever of sorcerous illusions, but it didn't seem to work. The constriction in his chest and his heart pounding like a train engine didn't help, either.

The figure was two paces from the temple entrance. It stopped. Nicholas caught a glimpse of dark clothing, the swirl of a garment, a cloak or coat. Then it was gone.

Nicholas found himself gripping the balustrade and trembling. The members of the circle still sat or stood like statues, like carvings of yellowed marble in the candlelight.

In the breathless silence, Octave said, "We are finished, Madame." He bowed briefly to Madame Everset and walked out of the temple and down the terrace.

Madame Everset tried to protest, but her legs seemed to give way and she sagged, gripping her chair for support. Belennier jumped up to grasp her arm and Algretto said, "Get her to the house—"

"Wait," Reynard interrupted. He called out, "Footman! Get down here with a lamp!"

He's thinking of our underground ghoul, Nicholas thought. And the scraping across the temple roof. He leaned back against the balustrade until he almost tumbled headfirst backward over it, but saw nothing. With the shadows moving across the weathered stone, there might be any number of ghouls crouched up there.

A confused footman brought another lamp and Reynard snatched it from him and moved back down the terrace, holding it high, trying to see if there was anything waiting for them on that roof. Nicholas could see he was questioning the footman, though he couldn't hear the low-voiced inquiry; the man shook his head as he answered.

Reynard said, "All right, bring her out this way."

The others didn't question him. Even the irrepressible Amelind Danyell was gripping Algretto's arm and shivering. Madame Algretto had gone to Madame Everset's side; their hostess seemed to have recovered a little, though she was obviously dazed and shaken. With Belennier's assistance she stood and the entire party made for the terrace.

It was more than time for Nicholas to go as well. If Everset had any sense he would turn half the household out to search the gardens and the surrounding area. If Nicholas hurried, he might manage to be one of the searchers. He climbed over the balustrade and dropped the rest of the way down, landing somewhat noisily in piled leaves and an unfortunate bush.

His own descent was so noisy that he almost didn't hear the corresponding crash of dried twigs and leaves from the nearest of the ancient oaks. He tried to fling himself toward cover, stumbled and fell sprawling. A few feet away something dropped to the packed dirt beneath the tree, stumbled, and caught itself on one of the massive lower branches.

There was just enough light to see it had the outline of a man, dressed in a scarf and a hunter's coat. Startled out of all thought, Nicholas automatically said, "Pardon me, but—" at the same time it said, "Sorry, I—"

They both stopped, staring at each other in astonished and somewhat embarrassed silence. Then the other man said, "Good day to you," and bolted for the outer garden wall.

Nicholas scrambled to his feet and stumbled toward the relative safety of the kitchen garden, cursing under his breath. He knew that voice. He remembered it from ten years ago at Edouard's trial, testifying in the witness box, so calm, so confident, so damning. He remembered it from the Crown Hearing that had rescinded the conviction months too late to save Edouard's life, equally calm, despite the deadly mistake it was admitting. He remembered it from all the close calls, the other trials, when he had been carefully in disguise.

He had spoken to Inspector Ronsarde before, but this was the first time since he was a young man barely out of Lodun that he had used his own voice.

In all the confusion Nicholas managed to get into the formal areas of the house. Servants were running everywhere, and it was easy to look as if he had been summoned.

The guests were gathered in the largest salon, the one with enormous bay windows in the front of the house, that overlooked the grotto and the sunken garden and the triumphal arch, all lit by colored lamps now and as strange in that light as something out of Fayre.

The room was yellow—yellow brocaded fabric on the walls, the firescreen, yellow silk upholstery on the scattered couches and chairs, yellow gowns on the nymphs in the woodland scene in the painted medallion on the high ceiling—and guests and servants were scattered throughout. Madame Everset was draped on a divan like a dead woman, her pale features blue-tinged from shock. A maid hovered over her, trying to persuade her to sip a glass of brandy. Everset stood nearby, ineffectual and bewildered.

Reynard was saying, "Dammit, man, you've got to turn the servants out to search."

Algretto was pacing impatiently. Danyell was collapsed on a sofa but still the center of a little whirl of activity, with her escort and the opera singer Isolde and a small cluster of maids in anxious attendance. Belennier seemed to be describing what had occurred to a tall, dark man who must be Vearde. One of the tables bore wine glasses and a scatter of cards from an interrupted game. As evidence for how Vearde, Everset, and Isolde had occupied themselves while the others were at the circle, Nicholas couldn't accept it at face value. He would have to pry more information out of the servants in their remaining time here. He wasn't willing to dismiss the notion of accomplices, not yet.

Octave was nowhere to be seen.

Everset shook his head, baffled. "Why? Search for what?"

Reynard stared. "For accomplices, of course. The weasel frightened your wife out of her wits, you've got to find out if those . . . if those men were what they seemed to be or compatriots of Octave's."

Reynard, Nicholas thought wryly, *you've been keep-*

*ing company with me too long and it's beginning to
show.*

"What's the point? The bastard's leaving with his fee.
They're bringing his coach round in the court."

"Leaving already?" Algretto said, turning back toward them and unexpectedly siding with Reynard.
"That's damned suspicious, Everset. You ought to detain him at least until you've had a chance to inventory
the plate."

. . . *Coach round the court.* Nicholas was already
slipping out of the room. He found the nearest servants'
door and bolted up the stairs to the third floor, digging
in an inside coat pocket for notepaper. In the guest room
he scribbled a line hastily and stuffed it in the pocket of
Reynard's spare coat, then he was dashing back down
the stairs.

He made his way to the front of the house, cutting
through the formal rooms since anyone of note was gathered in the salon. He reached a conservatory with a wall
that was formed entirely of glass panes in a wrought iron
framework, lit only by moonlight now and looking out
on the grotto and the sunken garden. He ducked around
cane furniture and stands and racks of potted flowers,
boot soles skidding on the tile floor. Down the steps to
the lower part of the room where a fountain played under
a draping of water lilies. Yes, there was a door here for
the gardeners.

He unlocked it and stepped out into the chill night air,
closing it carefully behind him. He was at the very front
of the house, at the head of a stone path cluttered with
wind-driven leaves that ran along the edge of the sunken
garden and toward the triumphal arch. The stone of the
grotto entrance was to his right, the archway that led
under the house and to the carriage court to his left. He
needed to be on the opposite side.

A brief scramble over the rock left him glad of his
gloves. It was made of dark-painted concrete and not
much softened by time. He was too near the side of the
house to be seen from the windows in the salon; there
was a possibility someone would spot the unorthodox

method that he planned to depart in, but it would be too late for them to do anything about it and he would probably be taken for one of Octave's hypothetical accomplices. Nicholas climbed down the side of the grotto entrance and took up a position flat against the wall next to the exit archway for the carriage court.

He had only been there a few moments, barely long enough to calm his breath, when he heard quiet footsteps in the carriage passage. He sank back against the wall, into the thick shadows.

A man stepped out of the passage, stood for a moment in the light from the lamp above the archway, then turned suddenly and looked right at Nicholas. It was Crack.

His henchman swore under his breath. Nicholas smiled and whispered, "I was here first."

Crack slid into the decorative hedge bordering the path. A moment later his apparently disembodied voice said, "Ain't I your bodyguard? Ain't that my job?"

"Two of us hanging onto the back of the coach would be noticed. On my own I'll be taken for a groom." Nicholas was only fortunate that Octave kept a private vehicle. Hire coaches often had a harrow installed beneath the groom's step, to keep children and anyone else from snatching free rides. A private coach wouldn't be equipped with that deterrent. "And I doubt even Reynard could conceal two servants abandoning him in the middle of the night. And someone has to keep an eye on him."

Crack snorted, possibly at the idea that Reynard needed guarding.

"And more importantly," Nicholas added, allowing a hint of steel into his voice, "because I said so."

Crack had a tidy mind and tended to dislike it when others questioned Nicholas's orders. The implication that he was guilty of this himself seemed to subdue him. One of the bushes trembled and there was some low muttering, but no further outright objections.

Hooves clopped on the pavement, echoing down the

passage. Nicholas moved closer to the edge of the arch and braced himself.

Two pairs of harnessed chestnut horses, then the side of Octave's dark coach whipped past. The window shade was down. The coach had slowed to navigate the passage but it was still travelling at a good clip; knowing he couldn't afford to miss, Nicholas took a step forward as it passed and then leapt.

He caught the rail the grooms used to hold on and in another instant his feet found the small platform. Clinging to the handhold, he looked back up at the salon window. No astonished figures were outlined there. He had made his leap unnoticed.

A whip snapped and the coach accelerated as it passed under the arch and reached the road. Gabrill House receded rapidly behind.

5

Trees rose up on either side of the road, turning it into a dark canyon, but Octave's coach barely slowed. This was far too fast a pace for night travel, even with a moon. The lamps at either side of the driver's box swayed, the frame shuddered as the wheels struck holes, and Nicholas huddled against the back, trying to keep a solid grip on the outrider's handle. Fortunately the coach was a sizable one and he wasn't large enough to make the vehicle draw heavy behind; the chances of reaching the city unnoticed by the driver were good.

Trees gave way to manicured hedges, garden fronts empty and ominous under the moonlight. Greater and lesser houses stood on either side of the road, some still lit for late night guests, others closed and dark. The coach slowed for nothing, even when they passed other traffic; somehow the driver managed to keep his vehicle upright and out of the ditches.

He had to slow as they neared the old city wall. The road grew narrower, buildings clustered more closely to it and each other, and there were more obstacles to dodge. The wall materialized out of night mist and shadow suddenly, as if it were forming itself out of the ground and growing larger as they drew nearer. Gaslights and lamps from a nearby brandy house threw wild shadows on the ancient stone, each weather-stained block larger than the coach Nicholas clung to. Then they were through the immense gates and under the shadow of the old square towers and cobblestones clattered under the horses' hooves as they turned down Saints Procession Boulevard.

There was still heavy traffic on the boulevard, even this late at night. The crested coaches of the nobility jostled the smaller vehicles of the merely well-to-do and the little hire cabriolets fought for space to pass. The promenades on either side of the wide street were almost choked with pedestrians at times and the tree-lined verge down the center was often just as crowded; there were a number of theaters on this end of the city and the shows had let out not long ago. Nicholas stood more upright, casual and relaxed, as a groom huddled against the back of the coach and hanging on for dear life was sure to draw attention. They turned off the boulevard and down a narrower, less frequented street. The houses were dark here, huge structures that blotted out much of the moonlight, as though they were driving down a steep-sided canyon. Nicholas thought the driver was avoiding the theater traffic but the coach didn't take any of the cross streets that roughly paralleled the boulevard.

Gas street lamps grew less and less frequent and Nicholas wondered if they were taking this street all the way down to Riverside Way.

It was one of the oldest neighborhoods in the city and had once been the bankers' district, but now it was a notorious thieves' kitchen. *For a nondescript address Octave couldn't have chosen better*, Nicholas thought, smiling. *Even the Prefecture doesn't enjoy coming down here.*

The buildings were high and narrow, stretching up four and five stories to peaked garrets. Shadows concealed the entrances to courts though Nicholas knew most of them were impassable from trash and filth. The street lamps, tall iron poles topped by ornate grillwork, had disappeared altogether and were replaced by oil lamps and torches, usually above the entrances to penny theaters or cheap brandy shops and cabarets. Crowds gathered around the lighted fronts of these establishments, laughing, calling out to friends, breaking off in apparently amiable groups that suddenly tumbled into fistfights. There were more ordinary businesses here: cafes, tanneries, and dye shops, but from a nighttime view the place looked like nothing but a den of iniquity.

The coachman took the sharp corner too abruptly and Nicholas lost his footing on the platform, his legs swaying dangerously out from the coach before he managed to haul himself up again. *The driver must have felt that*, he thought, shaking his head to keep the hair out of his eyes. The coach springs weren't good enough to conceal what must have been an odd shift in the balance of the vehicle. *Perhaps he isn't the observant sort.*

But one of the revellers on the corner staggered toward the street and called out helpfully, "Hey, there, skite! Slow down, you almost lost your groom."

Oh, hell. Nicholas closed his eyes briefly. *He didn't hear that.* The coach lurched under him, abruptly gaining speed as it barrelled dangerously down the dark street. *No, he heard it all right,* he thought grimly.

The coach swayed sharply to the right, then again to the left. Nicholas clung tightly, glad of the gloves protecting his sweat-slick hands. Occupied with keeping a grip on the fast-moving vehicle, he didn't see the next corner until the coach took it at an alarming rate of speed.

His feet slipped and he slammed against the back of the coach. He felt his legs strike the left wheel and hauled himself up desperately before he became tangled in the spokes. He barely found his footing again when the coach careened around another corner.

He had to get off the damn thing. Nicholas leaned out dangerously, getting a glimpse of what they were heading into. He saw the rows of buildings seem to come to an abrupt end not far ahead and suddenly recognized the street. They were on Riverside Way again and about to cross the river.

The buildings fell away behind them and a chill wind swept over him as they broke out into the open. Across the black chasm of the river he could see the lights of the far bank, the docks and warehouses of the shipping district. The coach barrelled down a steep incline in the road and the lip of an ancient stone bridge appeared in the erratic light of the lamps.

Nicholas braced himself. The coach hit the bottom of the incline with a crash of springs and abused wood and he leapt into darkness. The breath was knocked out of him as he struck the ground, landing on the grassy verge instead of the stone roadway more by luck than design. He rolled into a foul-smelling muddy flat, gasping for breath.

He propped himself up, shaking his head to clear his senses. The coach had stopped at the top of the bridge above him, the horses trembling with exertion, their sides steaming in the cool air. The coachman was climbing from the box as the side door swung open.

His eyes accustomed to the torchlit streets, Nicholas was almost blind in the heavy dark along the river. He scrambled down the bank until he felt the ground crumbling under his hands. There must be a drop-off here where the dirt had eroded away though he could see little but moonlight limning the water below. The coachman was lifting one of the coach lamps out of its holder and would be down here in moments.

Nicholas ripped off his already torn coat and flung it over the edge of the drop-off, then rolled sideways to leave as little intelligible imprint in the wet ground as possible. He reached a more solid surface covered with patchy grass and struggled upright, groping his way toward the arch of the bridge.

Above him the light bobbed, suggesting the coachman had started down the steep bank, following his progress through the disturbed mud and dirt. Nicholas worked his way under the low stone arch, blundering into pockets of stinking mud and bruising himself on broken bricks and metal debris. Cursing silently, he slid down and managed to fetch up against the first support pillar and crouched against it, waiting.

He heard their footsteps over the lapping of the water and the distant hum from the busy neighborhood. Their lamp appeared and Nicholas edged quietly around to the far side of the pillar. The light shifted erratically as the coachman investigated, then a voice said, "I think he fell over here. There's a bit of cloth caught on a bramble down there—looks fresh."

"You think." It was Octave's voice. "You didn't think. It would have been better to summon a constable than to draw attention with that ridiculous display."

"If he's dead, then he can't follow us," the coachman muttered, sullen.

Octave said, "If he's dead," and Nicholas heard grass rustle as footsteps retreated up the bank. In another moment, the lamp and coachman followed.

Nicholas let out his breath. He listened to the coach make an awkward turn on the bridge, then head back up the incline at a more sedate pace. He gave them time to get up the slope, then climbed back to the road.

He paused there, his breath misting in the cold damp air, and saw the coach passing between houses. He grimaced, then started to run up the sloping road after it. This night's work was not turning out exactly as he had hoped.

Fortunately, the coach kept to a more restrained pace as the coachman tried to make it look like a completely different vehicle from the one that had just torn so violently through the neighborhood. Nicholas kept to the side of the street, dodging in and out of groups of noisy revellers, staying out of the infrequent pools of lamplight. Hatless, coatless, and with his good servant's clothes muddy and torn, he looked as if he fit in among the crowd and no one accosted him.

He kept up the whole distance down Riverside Way and through two turns onto shorter cross streets but after a long straight stretch he began to fall back. The coach turned left down another intersecting street and Nicholas put on a burst of speed to reach the corner, his lungs aching. This was Gabard Lane, even narrower and more crowded than the other streets of this warren. The coach forged its way through at a good pace but was stopped at the end of the street by a cart that was trying to make a late delivery and had managed to strew barrels down the middle of the lane.

Nicholas leaned against an alley wall, breathless, while the coachman shouted, the carter threatened and spectators took sides. They were near the edge of the Riverside Way area, almost on the border of the Garbardin Quarter. It was run down too, but not as gone to hell as its nearest neighbors.

The carter summoned his helpers out of the nearest brandy house and the barrels were removed. Nicholas pushed off from the wall, his brief respite over.

The coach turned at the end of the lane and Nicholas reached the corner only to stop short and fall back against the wall.

The coach had halted in front of a large building that had more the look of a fortress than a private home. It was several stories tall, with towers sprouting from the pitched roof. It was a Great House, a very old one, fallen on hard times as the neighborhood around it had decayed. As Nicholas watched, the doors of the carriage entrance swung slowly open and the coach passed inside. The windows on the upper floors were apparently lightless behind their heavy shutters and the house had a deserted look.

Nicholas knew little about this particular area, though he was far too familiar with its immediate neighbor Riverside. He stepped around the corner, moving casually down the street toward the only source of light—a small brandy house operating out of what appeared to be the old stable of another Great House, long ago torn down for tenements.

The front wall was open to the street, revealing a high-raftered interior packed with people, noise, and smoke. Outside a few regulars were loitering and an old man was serving patrons who didn't care to fight their way in from an open barrel.

"It's a penny for a drink, unless you don't got your own cup, then it's two," he said wearily, as Nicholas sat down on an overturned trough.

"It's two," Nicholas answered, tossing the coins

over. The old man caught them and passed him a cup.

He took a cautious sip and managed not to wince. It burned all the way down his throat, with a faint aftertaste of kerosene. It brought back a host of disagreeable memories, of the one tiny room he and his mother had occupied in a tenement unpleasantly similar to those throwing their shadows over the street now.

The old man was still watching him. The only other patrons nearby were passed out entirely, huddled up against the wall of the old stable or staring vacantly into space. Nicholas was in no mood to fence. He said, "Whose house is that?"

"I saw you watching it." The old man grinned, caught Nicholas's expression, and added hastily, "There's nothing there. Just old people. Nothing to steal."

"Their name?"

"Valent. It's Valent House, or it used to be. Just old people live there."

Nicholas tossed him another penny and stood. He started to dump the brandy in the street but instead handed it off to the most conscious of the huddled figures and walked away.

He went to the opposite corner which intersected a street where late night coach and wagon traffic still travelled and several raucous establishments spilled customers into the gutters. He went down it a short distance until he found an alley that led between two high, featureless brick walls back in the direction of Valent House.

He followed it with difficulty, finding his way past one dead end and two other intersecting passages, and finally came out into a carriage court that had been orphaned by the demolition of its original owner: none of the structures crowding close around opened on it and it was piled high with rubbish. There were windows looking down on it but all were closed or darkened; this entire side of the street seemed completely deserted. Nicholas fought his way through debris, bruising his shin on a broken dog-cart axle in the process, and reached the far wall.

He climbed it in a shower of loose bits of mortar and looked over the top into a dingy little court that had once been a garden, now choked with weeds and long abandoned. Looking up, he saw the outline of gables against the dark sky and knew this was the back of Valent House. The windows in the upper floors were all securely boarded shut and there were, of course, none in the ground floor and only a single door to allow access. He struggled over the top of the wall and dropped softly down into the remains of a flower bed. The shadow of the house blotted out much of the moonlight and he had to feel for the steps and then the door. He tried the handle cautiously and found it securely locked and far too solid to force. He cursed it silently and stood back to look up at the house again. There was not a hint of light or sound from within, but these walls were thick, and one or a few people, moving quietly and with hand lamps, would not be noticeable from outside.

More searching turned up an alley that led off the garden court and back to the street at the front of the house. There seemed no other ground floor entrances but the garden door and the front, which he was not quite fool enough to try.

Nicholas had prepared tonight to pose as a manservant, not act as a housebreaker. He needed to send a message to Cusard. This meant a walk back to Riverside and his older haunts, where he could find a reliable messenger among the street boys who worked for the old thief.

He made his way back to the noisy side street with some difficulty and paused at the corner, to look toward Valent House again. Octave might think the night's work was over, but Nicholas knew it was just beginning.

In a thieves' kitchen in Riverside, Nicholas found a street boy who worked occasionally for Lamane and who could take a message to Cusard. It would be an hour at least until Cusard could receive it and respond, so he used the time to walk back up to Saints Procession Boulevard where there was an office of the Martine-Viendo Wire which stayed open all night, mainly for the convenience of the foreign embassies in the district that began across the street. There he sent a telegram to be delivered to Madeline at Coldcourt.

Both messages were cryptic and not readily to be understood by anyone who might intercept them. The message to Madeline had said only "E's storeroom—ascertain security of inventory." He might have waited on that until he could do it himself, but he was impatient and if Octave had found a way to get to Edouard's research without alerting them, he wanted to know as soon as possible.

He caught a hire cabriolet on the boulevard and took it as far back down to Gabard Lane as the driver was willing to go and walked the rest of the way. He waited on the upper corner, comfortably out of sight of the street where Valent House lay, stamping his feet against the cold. He would have liked to keep watch on the house but wasn't so dead to common sense as that—Octave would be suspicious at best after the performance on the riverbank.

Fortunately there were few prostitutes working this street and most were easily fended off. The district seemed to be quieting a little as the night wore on, but he had to keep moving to avoid suspicion. The ostler's wagon with Cusard on the box was a welcome sight. Even more welcome were Reynard and Crack, who climbed down as soon as the wagon was reined in at the curb.

"How did you make it here?" Nicholas asked.

"After I found your note, I made my excuses and got the hell away," Reynard explained. He had changed out of his evening clothes and with the somewhat battered greatcoat he wore, looked sufficiently enough like someone who would be riding in an ostler's wagon in this part of the city. "We went to the warehouse to see if you'd gone back there and met Cusard." He glanced around the street. "Lovely neighborhood."

"I brought these." Cusard finished tying off his reins and pulled a leather satchel out from under the bench. He handed it down to Nicholas. "Everything there we might need. I checked it myself. Who's staying with the wagon?"

"You are," Nicholas said, taking the satchel. "Did you remember the oil?"

"Of course I remembered the oil." Cusard was affronted at being left behind. "I'm the only official cracksman here and I taught you everything you know. It was a lie, the charge they laid against him." He gestured at Crack, who rolled his eyes in annoyance.

"I know that," Nicholas said with asperity. "I'll work the doors myself. Someone has to wait with the wagon and he'll have to keep sharp in this patch. You think on that." In another moment, Nicholas reflected, he would be speaking entirely in backstreet Vienne thieves' cant. This night was bringing his past back to him in unpleasant detail.

"All right, all right, have your own way, that's the young for you." Cusard gave in with poor grace. He handed Crack a dark lantern and Nicholas waited impatiently as it was lit.

"What happened to the coach?" Reynard asked as they started down the street.

"The driver realized I was on the back and I had to jump off and follow on foot." He led them to the corner and took Crack by the shoulder, pointing out the dark bulk of Valent House. "Octave drove into the carriage door of that house. See if you can tell if he's still there."

Crack slipped around the corner. Nicholas leaned back against the wall, feeling through the contents of the satchel Cusard had brought him.

"Your note was incoherent, by the way," Reynard said, regarding him thoughtfully. "What did you see at the circle that I didn't?"

"That item that you so adeptly forced him to reveal."

"Yes?"

"Edouard's last work. Did you ever know what it was?" Nicholas hadn't known Reynard then and he was well aware his friend had had his own troubles at that time.

"Not really." Reynard shrugged. "I heard rumors, none of which made much sense."

Nicholas suspected Reynard was exercising tact, something he only did with close friends. The rumors at the time had been explicit and damning. "It was a mechanical device that would allow someone who had no sorcerous ability to direct sorcerous power, in a limited fashion."

"Ah. That would tend to explain some of the events at the circle, wouldn't it?"

"Yes. It took the help of a sorcerer to make it work at first. That's why Edouard and I lived at Lodun for so long. He worked on it with Arisilde for a time." He looked back at Reynard. "When one of the devices is completed, it's in the form of a metal sphere, like the one Octave had."

"I see why you chased him over half the city. But how did he get his hands on Viller's work? Didn't the Crown have it destroyed?"

"We managed to get to Lodun before the Crown did. The University authorities weren't amenable to having a scholar's property seized, and their resistance gave me enough time to remove most of the important papers—" Nicholas realized he was saying far more than he had meant to. The conversation was moving away from the security of the bare facts of Edouard's work and the events surrounding his trial and into the dangerous ground of his own actions, thoughts, and feelings at that nightmarish time. He looked away up the street and added only, "I couldn't save anything from the workroom he kept in Vienne where he was arrested." In the last months of his life, Edouard had moved his experiments from Coldcourt to a hired studio on Breakwater Street in Vienne. It had been an odd thing for him to do, since previously he had worked only at his home or his quarters in Lodun. The Prosecution at the trial had made much of this, suggesting that Edouard was trying to hide his activities from his family and servants.

One morning Edouard had unlocked the studio to find a woman, very obviously and messily dead, on the table in his workroom. His reaction had been to run out into the street, shouting for help—not the act of a guilty man, as his counsel had pointed out. She had been a beggar woman who sold charms and flowers on the street and the Prosecution gave evidence that Edouard had been seen to give her money, suggesting this was how he had lured her into his rooms. Edouard was found guilty of trying to use her death to power his magical device and had been executed only a week later.

Nicholas had learned later that Inspector Ronsarde had never been happy with the case. Six months after Edouard's death the Inspector had penetrated the deception and discovered that the woman had been murdered by a local thug named Ruebene. Ruebene had been killed when the Prefecture attempted to arrest him, leaving Edouard's name cleared, but the Crown investigation had gone no further. Nicholas had taken up where Ronsarde left off, working for months until he found the link to Edouard's old patron Count Montesq. The evidence was poor and since the chief witness was one of Montesq's lower-class mistresses who had been present when the Count had hired Ruebene, and who was then dying of syphilis, he knew it would never go to court. Besides, Montesq couldn't be accused of necromancy, only of hiring the death of a beggar.

Nicholas wanted him to suffer far more than that. He took a deep breath and made himself think of the present and not the past. "I don't know how Octave could have gotten his hands on any of it. And I don't think I can make myself believe he was able to duplicate Edouard's work from his own inspiration."

"No," Reynard agreed. "He didn't seem the inspired type, if you know what I mean. I think I detected an air of the professional confidence man about him."

"That wouldn't surprise me." Reluctantly, Nicholas added, "And we have another worry. Ronsarde was at Gabrill House tonight."

Reynard was badly startled. "That's not funny."

"I'm not joking. He was in the garden, watching the circle. I spotted him as I was leaving. He saw me, too, of course, but not close enough to recognize, considering it's been years since he's seen me without a disguise of some sort." Nicholas had avoided contact with Ronsarde after the trial, at first because he had been planning to kill him, later because he was building the Donatien persona.

"Damn." Reynard folded his arms. "That could complicate everything enormously."

"I'm well aware of that." Nicholas's expression was sour. "If he realizes you're connected with Donatien, that's going to give him the answers to more than a few mysteries." Reynard had been the inside man for several of their early jewel robberies, when they had needed operating funds for the campaigns against Montesq. "But at the moment he has no reason to suspect Donatien's involvement."

Reynard wasn't ready to let it drop. "But what if he saw the sphere? He'll recognize it just as you did. That will give him every reason to suspect the involvement of a member of the Viller family. And if he connects you with Donatien. . . ."

"We have to assume he did see it, and did know it for Edouard's work. He could be led straight to us." The walls of the tenements around them seemed to be closing in and Nicholas told himself this was shadow and imagination. He took another look toward Valent House and saw Crack coming back up the street. "We'll just have to get to Octave first, and remove the evidence."

Reynard shrugged philosophically, apparently satisfied with letting the problem rest there. Nicholas wished he could be so sanguine.

Reaching them, Crack said, "There's an alley with slatted windows looking into the stable. No horses, no coach. Been there recently, though."

Nicholas swore, resisting the urge to kick the foundation of the nearest wall. "He knows we're after him.

I don't know if he realized it was me on the coach, but he knows someone is after him.''

"He's cautious." Reynard scratched his beard thoughtfully. "The house is still worth looking at."

Nicholas agreed. Nothing was keeping him out of that house. "Yes, he had to leave in a hurry, if he wasn't just visiting someone. There may be something left behind. Let's try that door I found earlier."

They went down the quiet street, keeping a wary eye on the brandy house in the old stable, the only possible source of interference. But the patrons who had crowded it earlier seemed to have retired and even the old man serving from the barrel had retreated inside. Several bundled forms were still stretched out on the walk in front but they seemed dead to the world and disinclined to interfere.

They reached the corner of the house and turned down the narrow alley that led directly to the garden court, Crack in the lead. As they made their way across the dry overgrown grass, Reynard swore softly and stopped to scrape something off his boot.

Nicholas followed Crack up the steps to the door he had tried earlier and in the muted light of the dark lantern examined it cautiously. It was solid mahogany and barely weathered at all. "New," he whispered. "And in the last month."

Crack nodded agreement, taking the lantern as Nicholas fished a leather tool case out of the satchel. He selected a bit and fitted it to a small steel brace, then knelt on the step to work near the keyhole.

Frequent application from a small bottle of oil kept the drilling reasonably quiet. He could hear nothing but their own breathing and an occasional fidget from Reynard. The house might have been empty.

It took almost thirty separate holes and the better part of an hour before Nicholas could wrench out the lock and push the heavy door open.

Crack handed back the lantern and slipped in first, Nicholas and Reynard following. The air smelled of damp and rats and something even more foul, as though meat had spoiled and been left to rot somewhere inside.

They crept down a short hall, the lantern illuminating fragments of rooms, the wire mesh meat safe of a servery, once-white tiles coated with dust and filth, an open and empty coal bin. Crack pushed silently through a door at the end of the hall, then leaned back to motion Nicholas to shut the slide on the lantern entirely. He complied, then followed his henchman through the door, Reynard behind him.

They were in the central foyer. Some light was entering through the cracked glass windows above the deep shadow of the front entrance and Nicholas could tell that this had once been a very fine house. The staircase had a grand elegant sweep, splitting into two midway up its length to lead into the separate wings. Torn and rotting fabric that had once been draperies still clung to the walls and paper and paint had peeled away in the damp. If people were living here, as the old man had said, they must carve out a miserable existence in one or two rooms, probably on the ground floor. The rest of the place was like a tomb.

Crack whispered, "No one's here. No one alive."

Nicholas glanced at him in surprise, supposing he was succumbing to a heretofore unexpressed religious streak. Then Reynard said softly, "You smell it too, hey? I can't tell where it's coming from; seems to be everywhere."

"Smell what?" Nicholas asked, puzzled. "The rats?"

Reynard's mouth twisted, not in amusement. "You've never spent a long period of time in a war—or a prison. That's not rats."

Nicholas accepted the statement without argument; he was beginning to realize just what it was they might find here. He said, "Crack, look for the cellar door. We'll search this floor first."

Crack vanished into the gloom and Nicholas and Reynard turned toward the doors off the entrance hall. The first had been a reception room. Nicholas raised the slide again and lifted the lantern, revealing spiderwebs like lace stretching from the ornate cornice and floral frieze

out to the broken remnants of the chandeliers. The carpet
had been worn to rags and he could clearly see that it
and the heavy layer of dust on the floor had been recently disturbed. What was once a fine table still stood
in the center of the room, its surface long ruined by
damp, but not as heavily covered in filth as it should
have been.

Reynard called softly from another doorway, "Signs
of life, here."

It was a library. The walls were lined with empty
shelves and the floor was bare, but a large secretaire
stood against one wall, with a straight-backed chair
nearby.

Nicholas went to it, holding the lamp close to examine
the scarred surface. There was hardly any dust at all and
the lamp that stood on the shelf above was still half-
filled with oil. The drawers were standing open and one
had been pulled all the way out onto the floor.

"Left in a hurry," Reynard commented softly.

They searched the desk without having to discuss it,
each taking one side. Nicholas found nothing but broken
pens, an empty ink bottle, and a deserted mouse nest,
and Reynard's haul wasn't nearly so promising. Nicholas pulled out the other drawers and crouched down to
reach further back into the cabinet, disturbing a flurry of
spiders and something that skittered noisily away. He
was rewarded when his hand brushed paper.

"There's something back here," he muttered.

"Hopefully not a rat."

"Someone pulled out that drawer," Nicholas argued,
"because something was stuck and he didn't want to
leave it." It felt like a sheaf of torn paper fragments,
wedged into a crack.

"Or because he was in a hurry and clumsy."

"Well, that too." The paper gave way without tearing
and he was able to withdraw his arm. In the dim light,
he could see the scraps were covered with handwriting.
He reached for the lamp, just as Crack's voice came
from the doorway.

"Found something."

"Found what?" Reynard asked, as Nicholas stood and shoved the paper fragments into his vest pocket.

"What you thought," Crack elaborated and vanished back into the hall. Reynard turned to Nicholas, brow raised, for a translation.

"The not-rats," Nicholas explained, already moving toward the door.

Crack led them to an alcove under the staircase. Going down, they found themselves in a hall with bare plaster walls, with various closed doors leading off it, probably to such places as the stillroom, the wine storage, the butler's pantry, and the bedrooms for the upper servants. Crack turned right and opened a door. The smell warned Nicholas what to expect. It had grown stronger as they neared this room and as the door swung open he nearly gagged. Crack took the lantern out of Nicholas's hand, knocked the slide all the way up and held it high.

In the center of the room a makeshift table had been fashioned out of planks and overturned tubs. Stretched across the planks was the corpse of a man. The chest and abdomen had been ripped open, the ribs pried back. Most of the organs had been removed and were littering the flagstoned floor, along with a great quantity of blood and other bodily fluids. The entrails were still attached but had been pulled out and were dangling to the floor.

Nicholas heard himself say, "I wasn't expecting this."

"There's more," Crack said, his soft raspy voice grimly matter-of-fact. "But this is the worst. That room there, closest to the stairs, I checked it first. There's a hole knocked in the back wall with six of 'em crammed in it."

Reynard turned to him, aghast. "Six?"

"Kids," Crack added. He looked at Nicholas earnestly. "There's more, I know there is. I could find 'em all for you if you need it."

"That won't be necessary just at the moment." Nicholas was staring at the carnage. Whether Crack had sensed it on a visceral level, or observed signs that led him to that conclusion, he knew it was true. Bile was rising in his throat and he had to turn away for a moment and rest his head against the doorframe. Reynard stepped down the hall a few paces and stayed there, cursing under his breath.

Nicholas forced himself to turn back and look at the room again. He had, for a time, trained in the physician's college at Lodun, though he had given up the courses after Edouard died. He could recognize a dissection when he saw it, and this was not one. This was a vivisection.

He made himself take a step further into the room, confirming the theory. There was no reason to tie down a corpse and the man's wrists and ankles, practically the only intact flesh still left on the body, bore terrible galls from straining against the bonds. One of the eyes had been gouged out and the face cut and disfigured. *He wasn't alive through much of it*, Nicholas told himself. *He couldn't have been.* But the moments the victim had lived through had been terrible enough.

He looked down at the debris on the floor. The remains were that of more than one person.

He almost turned and walked out of the room then, certain he was going to be ill. Nothing had ever affected him this way before. He was not squeamish: anatomical studies, the morgue, or the surgeries he had watched had never disturbed him. This was different. This was foul in a way almost past comprehension. He knew what Crack was seeing here, why the other man was so certain they would find more corpses if they searched. This was not something one did once. This was a crescendo, worked up to with time and much experimentation.

Nicholas forced himself to look around the room again and this time saw something else. The whitewashed plaster on the walls, where it wasn't stained with blood or some other fluid, was melted.

"What the hell...." he said softly, so intrigued by the anomaly he almost forgot the butchery around him. He stepped to the wall nearest the door, where he could reach it without having to move anything aside or step into a puddle, and probed the affected area. It was not only the plaster that was melted, but the wood beneath it. It was fused, the two disparate materials running together, forming glassy textured lumps. Nicholas swore again. This was something he had learned at Lodun too, but not in the medical college. This was something sorcerous; the result, perhaps, of uncontrolled power.

He should search for more telltale signs of sorcery, but he found himself suddenly unable to turn and look at the rest of the room again. He stepped out and nodded to Crack, who dimmed the lantern again and pulled the door shut.

They climbed the stairs and once back in the hall Reynard turned immediately to the passage that led outside.

Nicholas caught his arm. "We still have to search the rest of the house. We can come back tomorrow to investigate further, but we have to make sure there's no one still hiding here."

Reynard hesitated. He was badly disturbed and doing his best to conceal it. "Yes," he said finally. "You're right. Let's finish it."

They split up to make quicker work of it. Crack had already scouted the basement, which seemed to contain nothing but the bodies and the instruments that had been used to torture and kill. They found repeated evidence that the house had been inhabited and recently. The ground floor was barren, except in the kitchen which still showed signs of meals prepared and eaten at the deal table. Stores of candles, lamp oil, and various foodstuffs had been left behind. The dust and dirt coating the remaining carpets took footprints easily, though it didn't hold enough of the shape to make identification of the type of shoe possible.

On the second floor Nicholas found a bedroom that had seen recent use and a search of the drawers and cupboards in the remaining furniture turned up a slim stack of notebooks, covered with elegant, spidery handwriting. He fell on those eagerly, but as he flipped through them they seemed to be nothing but verbatim notes out of a book of sorcerous instruction. It was mildly encouraging that the type of sorcery discussed was necromancy. That was patently obvious from the first page, which went on about all the uses of dried human skin. It was the type of notes a student would make, from a book he was allowed to use but not remove from a master's library. Nicholas took the notebooks anyway and found nothing more of use.

In the last room at the far end of the left hand wing, the now familiar smell of mortal decay stopped Nicholas in the doorway. It was a bedroom, more completely furnished than the others he had searched. His eyes went to the dressing table, where brushes and combs and a few cut glass bottles stood under a heavy layer of dust. He moved reluctantly to the heavily curtained bed and drew back one of the tattered drapes.

This, at least, was peaceful death. An old woman lay on the counterpane, dressed in a faded gown of a style out of fashion for twenty years, her feet in delicately beaded slippers. Her eyes were closed and her arms folded on her breast. Her flesh was deeply sunken and decayed; she must have lain like that for a year or more.

He let the drape fall back. It was unlikely the usurpers of her house had ever known she was there. He hoped that last loyal servant, who had dressed her in her best and laid her body out and drawn the bedcurtains, had followed those actions with packing her things and locking the door behind her, and had not lingered to become part of the collection in the basement.

Nicholas kept them searching as long as he could, but with only the three of them and lamplight, there was only so much they could do. Finally, Reynard collared him.

"Nic, there is nothing more we can do tonight. We need a medical doctor, and a sorcerer, and enough men to look in every cabinet, cubby, and mousehole in this house. Besides, you aren't going to find a message scrawled in blood on a wall that says, 'I did this come find me at such and such address' no matter how hard you look. Leave it for now. We can come back in the morning with help."

Nicholas looked around at the silent hall and the disturbed dust hanging in the damp air. Finally he said, "You're right, let's go."

They left the house by the garden door. Nicholas was hoping the outside air, remarkably clean and fresh after the fetid humors inside, would revive him, but he didn't get two paces down the broken path before he found himself braced against the garden wall, being messily sick.

When he straightened up he saw Crack had gone ahead, probably to scout the street. Reynard was waiting for him, arms folded, staring at the silent house.

Still leaning weakly against the wall, unable to help himself, Nicholas said, "It doesn't make sense. What does this have to do with spirit circles? You heard him ask Madame Everset's brother about his ship. It was so obvious that he was after the cargo, probably valuable if they were coming out of a Parscian port. He was after hidden wealth, not. . . . What does this have to do with it?"

Reynard looked back at him, frowning. "But you thought he had something to do with those disappearances, that boy you went to look at in the morgue?"

"There was evidence, I couldn't discount it, but I thought it would turn out to be some sort of coincidence. This doesn't make sense."

"Madness doesn't have to make sense." Reynard turned away from the house and took Nicholas's arm. "Let's get away from here."

They found Cusard waiting up the street and climbed aboard the wagon. After a brief whispered explanation from Crack, Cusard whistled and said, "Next time I moan about being left behind, remind me of this."

Nicholas and Reynard settled in the wagon bed, Crack climbing back to join them as Cusard urged the sleepy horses into motion.

They were silent for a time, watching the darkened houses pass by. The night was winding down in this part of the city and the loudest sound was the clop of hooves on stone.

"What do we do now?" Crack asked.

That's the first time he's ever asked, Nicholas thought. *No matter what was happening*. It was too bad he didn't have an answer.

"That's simple enough," Reynard told Crack. "Tomorrow night you and I will go out, find Octave, and commit his remains to the river."

"That's the one thing we can't do," Nicholas said. He met Reynard's eyes. "Octave couldn't have done all that alone. There must be others. There's his coachman, for one." The coachman wasn't the one Nicholas was worried about. There was someone else in this, someone who wasn't interested in Octave's spirit circles.

Reynard returned his gaze steadily. "Are you sure we can afford to wait?"

Nicholas didn't look away. "No. But if there's even one other, he's got to be found. Octave knows too much about us. His colleagues must also."

"That wasn't the reason I was thinking of," Reynard said quietly.

"I know." Despite the devil-may-care persona Reynard had carefully constructed, his sense of morality was better suited to the officer and gentleman he had once been. His impulses were always in the right direction. Nicholas's impulses were usually all in the wrong direction and it was only the intellectual knowledge of right and wrong painstakingly instilled in him by Edouard that allowed him to understand most moral decisions. But something in that room had struck him to the heart. He would stop it, but he had to do it his own way.

Reynard said nothing for a time. The wagon boards creaked as Crack shifted uneasily, but the henchman didn't venture an opinion. Finally Reynard sighed. "He's clever, Octave or whoever helps him, to take so many and not be caught, not start some sort of panic. He could keep at it for years."

Nicholas was staring at the street moving past. It was necromancy, obviously. Octave and his followers were performing—committing—some sort of necromantic magic. There was a memory, just on the edge of recall, that would seem to explain much if he could just capture it. He said, "I think I've seen something like that room somewhere before."

Even Crack looked to him in astonishment. Reynard snorted. "Where? In a slaughterhouse?"

"Not in person," Nicholas explained with a preoccupied frown. "In a book, an illustration in a book. I used to read the most appalling things as a child, my mother. . . . My mother bought torn-up, broken books by the stack for me, at the old shops near the river, and she didn't always have the leisure to look at what they were." He shook his head. "That's all I can recall of it. I'll look in Edouard's library—he used to read appalling things too."

Reynard said grimly, "Whether he's committing plagiarism or he's thought it all up on his own, Doctor Octave's got to die."

6

Madeline wasn't able to sleep. It was for no rational
reason: Nicholas had done far more dangerous things
than pose as a servant at a house party. At least, she
thought he had. Doctor Octave was such an unknown
quantity.

Unable to reason away her sleeplessness, she sat up
on the chaise in the bedroom, wrapped in her dressing
gown, with a glass of watered wine and a book she was
unable to pay proper attention to.

*It's not as if Octave is the first sorcerer we've had to
deal with,* she thought for perhaps the third time, tapping
one well-kept fingernail on the page before her and staring into space. They had once burgled the town home
of a sorcerer called Lemere and found their way through
a bewildering maze of magical protections. But Arisilde
had been more active then and well able to cope with
any attempt at retaliation. *If Octave is a sorcerer.* Perhaps it was the unknown that disturbed her.

She wished she could tell if it was ordinary nerves or
some long buried sense trying to warn her. Nearly all
the women in her family had strong talents and incli-
nations for witchcraft. Madeline had given all that up
for the stage and in truth, she didn't miss it. Her real
talent was for acting and the roles she played in pursuit
of Nicholas's goals were just as thrilling as lead ingenue
at the Elegante.

She shook her head at her own folly. Life was safer

at the Elegante. Any fool could see Nicholas was obsessed. With destroying Montesq mainly, but also in a broader sense he was obsessed with deception itself. And obsessed with playing the part of Donatien to Vienne's criminal underworld, and dancing in and out of Inspector Ronsarde's grasp, and a dozen other things to varying degrees. And now with stalking Octave, for all she knew.

Lately the obsession had been gaining the upper hand. Madeline supposed that if she were of literary bent she would see Donatien as a separate, distinct personality that was fast consuming Nicholas. That, in fact, would make a good play. *Davne Ruis could play Nicholas*, she thought. *And I could play me. Or maybe his mother; that would be a good part, too.* But she knew it wasn't the case. Nicholas and Donatien were too obviously the same personality; at heart and everywhere else that counted they were the same man, with only cosmetic differences to fool the onlookers. They both wanted the same things.

But then sometimes she wasn't sure she knew Nicholas at all. She suspected Reynard might know him better. He had been helping Nicholas with his various plots for about six years or so and Madeline had only been involved for half that time.

Not long after Nicholas had first taken her into his confidence, Madeline had had a tête-a-tête with Reynard, over brandy on the veranda of the Cafe Exquisite. She had asked him, point blank, if he and Nicholas had ever slept together, wishing to get that question resolved before she embarked on any deeper relationship with him. Sensing her seriousness, Reynard had replied, immediately and without baiting, that they hadn't. "Not that I didn't inquire once if he was interested, not long after we first met." After a moment he admitted, "I had the feeling that if I had pushed the issue, he would have given in. If you can imagine Nic giving in on any point whatsoever, which I admit is rather difficult."

"But you don't push issues," Madeline had said, swirling the warmed brandy in her glass.

"No, I don't. He didn't want me, he wanted affection

and understanding. I didn't really want him, I just wanted to try to learn how his mind worked. Neither of us would have gotten what we wanted and we both already had more trouble than we could handle.''

''You can't find out who someone is by sleeping with them,'' Madeline had pointed out.

''Thank you for the words of wisdom, my dear,'' Reynard had said, dryly. ''Now where were you twenty years ago when the advice would have done me some good?''

Reynard had been of some help, but instinct told Madeline that both of them knew exactly as much as Nicholas wanted them to know and not one hint more.

Such speculations were pointless. Madeline shifted restlessly and tugged her dressing gown more firmly around her. There was a soft scratch on the door and as she put her book aside it opened and Sarasate peered in. ''Madame, there's a telegram.''

''Is there?'' She stood hastily, tightening the belt of her gown. She had forgotten her slippers and the stone-flagged floor was cold. ''That's odd.''

She took the folded square of paper and read it, frowning; Sarasate didn't quite hover. She said, ''Nicholas wants me to make sure the attic storeroom hasn't been disturbed.''

''The attic? The old master's things?'' Sarasate had been a manservant here when Edouard was alive.

''Yes, I'd better go up right away.''

''I'll get you a lamp, Madame. Would you like me to accompany you?''

''No, that won't be necessary.'' She took a moment to tie back her hair and find an old pair of shoes at the bottom of the armoire, while Sarasate brought her a hand lamp.

Madeline climbed the stairs up to the third floor and opened the door of the library. She caught a faint scent of pipe tobacco and hesitated. It wasn't the type that Nicholas or Reynard used, but she recognized it just the same.

She smiled to herself and said softly, "Hello, Edouard."

There was no answer but she hadn't really expected one. Edouard Viller wasn't haunting his old home in the sense that most people understood the term, he was simply there. The way the beamed and coffered ceilings that made the upper floor rooms both oppressive and cozy were there. The way the odd-sized spaces and the old inelegant furniture were there. Edouard's personality lay over Coldcourt like a fine damask cloth.

There was nothing to fear from this haunting. Madeline had never met Edouard when he was alive and she knew he had been executed for one of the most heinous crimes under Ile-Rien law, but the traces of him that were left had convinced her of his innocence without a review of the facts of the case.

She paused to light the lamp on the round table near the center of the room, revealing book-lined walls and two overstuffed chairs, a secretaire with letterscales, inkstand and blotter, a faded Parscian rug on the floor and cretonne curtains cloaking the windows. She crossed to the bookcase against the far wall and selected the correct volume, placing her palm flat on the cover. It was, appropriately enough, *The Book of Ingenious Devices*.

The section of the bookcase in front of her slid backward, then lifted up into the air, accompanied by much squeaking of gears and wheels. A cool draft, smelling of must, moved her hair and fluttered the skirts of her gown.

She set the book aside. This portal was one of Edouard's and Arisilde's earliest collaborations. Only the key, a spell imprinted on the cover of the book, was true magic. The mechanism that lifted the door was one of Edouard's mechanical contrivances.

The section of bookcase rose up into the high ceiling of the chamber beyond it, revealing a narrow stairway curving up into dimness. Madeline gathered her skirts and started to climb.

The stairs curved up and around, reaching a heavy wooden door. The key was in the lock. Long ago, Nicholas had taken the key from the drawer where it was kept and left it up here, explaining that if the house was ever searched, a key that fit no obvious lock was sure to be remarked, while if anyone managed to get past the concealed entrance to the stair, an ordinary door was not likely to stop them, locked or not. Madeline thought the Vienne Prefecture unlikely to be quite so astute, but she had long since given up arguing those points with Nicholas; as far as she was concerned, she was in charge of costume and makeup, he was in charge of paranoia.

She opened the door, which creaked a little, and stepped into the room beyond.

There was a little light already in the large chamber— moonlight, falling through three little dormer windows high in the opposite wall. The roof stretched up overhead, the beams beginning just above the windows and vanishing into darkness in the peak somewhere above. A platform about twelve feet in height cut the room in half: it was just below the windows, with a narrow stair at one end of the room giving access to it. There were trunks and boxes piled atop it, though most of the space it afforded was empty. It was there to disguise the real purpose of the attic; if you looked in through the dormer windows from the roof, you saw only a rather odd-sized box room. Edouard's experiments occupied the lower half of the chamber, under the platform.

Madeline made her way forward, sneezing at the dust. The area below the platform was like a cave; her lamp seemed hardly to penetrate it at all. Shelves lining the back wall held notebooks and bound manuscripts— years of Edouard Viller's research, saved from destruction at the hands of the Crown Court. Piled around were various bits of machinery, pipes, gears, wheels, several large leather bladder-like things that were obviously made to hold air, but for what purpose she couldn't imagine. There was a sort of metal cage lying on its side that loomed overhead like a whale's skeleton and seemed to be connected to half the other odd things around it; it reminded Madeline of the book where the shipwreck survivors landed on an island, which turned out to be the back of an immense sea beast.

She had been up here before in the daylight, but it wasn't any easier to tell what anything was then, either. It was as if a blacksmith's work room, a train yard, and a theater propmaker's shop had all been shaken together and the results carefully collected on the attic floor. But she knew Nicholas hadn't been concerned about any of these things. She pressed on, making her way toward the far wall.

In a cupboard at the very back of the space, she found her goal. Lined up neatly on one of the shelves were three spherical devices. They were small, each not much larger than a melon, and someone who knew nothing about either magic or navigation would have said they were tarnished armillary spheres. But instead of empty space each seemed to be filled with tiny gears and wheels, all linked together.

Madeline touched one and felt her fingertips tingle.

Though Edouard Viller had designed the spheres, each one needed a spark of real human sorcery, a spell of delicate complexity, to make it live and perform whatever its purpose was. The first one, the oldest one, had been brought to life by Wirhan Asilva, an old sorcerer at Lodun who had worked with Edouard while he was still perfecting his design. She touched Asilva's sphere; it was cold and there was no answering tingle of awareness. The spell had only lasted a few years, Nicholas told her. Asilva hadn't been very enthusiastic about Edouard's experiments and eventually he had refused to work with him anymore. But it had also been Asilva who had helped Nicholas save most of the important contents from Edouard's workrooms at Lodun, only a few steps ahead of the Crown officials sent to destroy it.

The other spheres had been built with Arisilde's help and he was the only one who knew anything at all about them.

She touched the third, partly out of thoroughness and partly because she liked that little thrill of power that seemed to course off the warm metal, and snatched her hand back in shock. The third sphere was vibrating. She reached for it again and a spark of blue light travelled along the spiral gears and winked out abruptly.

She lifted it off the shelf and, probably foolishly, tried to peer into it. *This is nothing for a lapsed and never-worth-much-in-the-first-place witch to be fooling with*, she told herself.

It didn't explode or blast her thoughts out of her head, but continued to shiver against her hands, like a frightened animal. She tried to see into the depths of it, to discover if any of the delicate works were damaged, but her lamp was no help.

Madeline tucked the sphere under her arm and carried it out of the confined space of the work area and up the narrow stair to the top half of the chamber. Moonlight flooded the platform, a clear colorless illumination almost strong enough to read print by. She ducked her head under the low-hung beams and crouched near the middle window, balancing the sphere on her knees. Again she looked deep into it.

She couldn't see any damage, or parts shifting around, but deep inside, still following some invisible path, was the blue spark.

Madeline felt a cold spot between her shoulderblades, as if a breeze had touched her in the dead still attic air. She lifted her head and looked out the window.

There was something crouched outside on the parapet, watching her. Tattered clothes, shroud-like in the wind, a skeletal head, teeth, clawlike hands grinding into the stone. She clutched the sphere to her chest and stood up in pure reflex, thumping her head on a ceiling beam.

The thing outside rared back, almost falling off its perch. The sphere shivered violently against her and the creature snarled and vanished over the wall.

Madeline was frozen, but only for an instant. She swore violently and leaned forward to see if it was still out there. She was careful not to touch the window, which was supposed to be warded. *It must still be warded*, she thought, *or that thing would have broken in and killed me*. She could only think it was one of the creatures Nicholas had seen in the Mondollot House cellars.

She looked down at the sphere she was still clutching to her. The shivering had stopped and it was only tingling gently, as it always did, the outermost manifestation of the power trapped inside. The creature might have fled the sphere. If it was sensitive to human magic the way the fay were, the sphere would smell of Arisilde, who had been at the height of his power when he had helped Edouard build it.

Worry it out later, she told herself, making her way to the stair. She had to collect her lamp, get back downstairs, check that the ward stones were still there, and make sure everyone in Coldcourt was still alive.

Nicholas had Cusard drop him off at the Philosopher's Cross. He wanted to talk to Arisilde now, even if he had to wake him, and he wanted Crack and Reynard to go on to Coldcourt, to make sure all was well there and to tell Madeline what they had discovered.

The Cross was still lively and wild, even this late, but far more safe than the streets of Riverside or the Gabardin, and many of the people promenading on the walks were of the *beau monde*. The cabarets and coffeehouses were still open, the streets well-lit and comfortably crowded, and there were peddlers and beggars gathered on every corner, while a truly astonishing number of prostitutes waited on the after-theater crowd. It would be relatively easy to find a hire cabriolet when he was done, if he could manage to get aboard before the driver got a good look at the current state of his clothes.

Even Arisilde's normally quiet tenement seemed teeming with life. Nicholas edged past the concierge, who was bargaining room rates with a lady of the night and her tophatted client. Climbing the stairs turned out to be a greater task than he had anticipated and he knocked on Arisilde's door greatly exhausted.

The door was thrown open with unexpected violence. Nicholas started back before he recognized Arisilde standing in the doorway. The sorcerer's eyes were red-rimmed and mad, his fair hair escaped from its braid and hanging in lank strings around his face. He looked like a member of the Unseelie Court from one of Bienuilis's more excessive paintings.

He stared at Nicholas without recognition, then said, "Ah, it's you." Glancing over his shoulder as if he feared pursuit from within the apartment, he leapt back down the little hallway into his rooms. "Quick, inside!"

Nicholas leaned his head against the dusty wall. "Oh, God." He was too tired for this. He thought of walking away, going back down to the street and finding a cab. But wearily he pushed away from the wall and followed Arisilde, pausing only to pull the door closed behind him.

The candles had guttered in the room with the skylights and the fire had been reduced to coal. The curtains had all been torn down from the windows, exposing the little apartment to the night sky. Most Vienne dwellers, especially in the poor neighborhoods, kept their windows shuttered at night for superstitious fear of nightflying fay, though none had been spotted near the city since the railroad lines had been laid. Obviously that was not something Arisilde worried about. *And even in his present condition*, Nicholas thought, *he is probably more than a match for any creature the fay could produce.* That was one of the tragedies of it. No one would ever know what Arisilde was or how powerful he could have been.

Arisilde was standing over the table, tearing through a pile of papers and books, scattering them onto the floor. Nicholas eased down into one of the torn armchairs near the hearth, wincing as his bruises made contact with the understuffed cushions.

Arisilde whipped around, ran a hand through his disordered hair and whispered, "I can't remember what I was going to tell you."

Nicholas sank back in the chair and closed his eyes. He could already tell that getting any sense out of his friend, about the possibility of someone stealing Edouard's work or the connection between Octave and the disappearances, was patently hopeless, at least for tonight. But the climb back down the steep stairs of the decaying tenement was more than he could stand to contemplate just now. He said, "I'll wait. Perhaps you'll think of it."

He didn't realize Arisilde had crossed the room until he felt the sorcerer's breath on his cheek. He opened his eyes to find Arisilde leaning over him, braced on the arms of the chair, his face scant inches away. A pitifully earnest expression in his violet eyes, the sorcerer said, "It was important."

Nicholas said, "I know." He hesitated. That Arisilde was in a worse state than usual had already occurred to him. That perhaps he should not have ventured into the garret under these circumstances hadn't crossed his mind—until now. Cautiously, he asked, "Where's your man Isham?"

Arisilde blinked. For a moment his expression was desperate, as if any concentration was painful. Then he smiled in weary relief and said, "At Coldcourt. I sent him to look for you."

"That makes sense." Nicholas told himself he was being a fool. When he had closed his eyes he had seen that room at Valent House again and it was making him imagine things; Arisilde couldn't bear to step on ants. *In his right mind*, a traitor voice whispered.

"Doesn't it?" Arisilde was suddenly elated. "That must be it, then!"

Nicholas pushed him back, so he could see his face more clearly, and asked, "Did you have more opium than you usually do, today?"

Arisilde said, "I didn't have any today," and tore away from him so abruptly Nicholas almost tumbled out of the chair. He stood, watching in bewilderment as Arisilde swept the rest of the books and papers off the table and began rubbing his hands over the unpolished surface, as if he was searching for something hidden there. Nicholas said, "None at all?"

"None." Arisilde shook his head. "I had to be careful. I had to be very, very careful. But I found it out, I did, the thing I wanted to find out.'' He slammed his hands against the table, with a force that should have broken his slender wrists. ''But now I can't remember what it was!''

Nicholas went to him, moving slowly so as not to startle, and tried to turn him away from the table, but Arisilde flung himself toward the opposite end of the room, upsetting a chair and careening off another table, sending a collection of little jars and plants crashing to the floor.

Nicholas took a deep breath. He had to get the sorcerer's attention, keep him from turning that energy on himself. ''Was it something to do with the things I brought you to look at, the ashes of the golem, maybe?''

Arisilde seemed to pause in thought, leaning on the far wall as if he had fetched up against it in a storm. The shadows were deep there and Nicholas could see nothing of his expression. ''No,'' the sorcerer said slowly. ''It wasn't anything here. I went out today. Oh, damn.'' He slid to the floor, helplessly. ''Next time I'll write a letter.''

Nicholas went to him, stumbling a little over the scattered debris in the half-light. He knelt in front of Arisilde, who had buried his face in his hands. ''Ari. . . .'' Nicholas cleared his throat. It was ridiculously difficult to speak. He wanted to say that if Arisilde had given up the drug for one day, couldn't he give it up for the next, and the next after that? But past attempts had taught him how useless any kind of remonstrance was; Arisilde would simply refuse to listen, or stop speaking to him at all.

The sorcerer lifted his head, took Nicholas's hand and ran a thumb along the lifeline, as if he was doing a palm-reading by touch, which he very well might be. He said, ''I watched them hang Edouard, do you remember?''

Let's not do this, not tonight, Nicholas thought, too weary to do anything more than close his eyes in resignation. He had come to realize that the main reason he was uncomfortable in Arisilde's company was not his disgust for what the opium did to his friend, but the fact that sometimes Arisilde said things like this. *Do you remember when Edouard took us to Duncanny, do you remember that day at the river in the spring, do you remember. . . .* When it was at its worst, it was like this: *do you remember the day at the trial when Afgin testified, do you remember when Edouard was hanged.* Nicholas didn't want to remember the good times or the bad. He wanted to think about revenge, about Montesq paying for what he had done. He couldn't afford to be distracted. But he let out his breath, looked at Arisilde again and said, "I remember."

"If I had stayed in Vienne with Edouard instead of going back to Lodun—"

"Ari, dammit, there was no reason for you to stay." Nicholas couldn't conceal his bitter anger. They had had this conversation before too. "No one knew what was about to happen. You can't blame yourself for that." Sorcerers could gain knowledge of the present and the past, but only if they knew where to look.

"I was the family witness because you couldn't bring yourself to it. . . ."

"That was a mistake." It also wasn't quite true, or perhaps Arisilde was being polite. They had kept Nicholas from trying to free Edouard or disrupting the execution by holding him down on a bed and forcibly dosing him with laudanum. When Nicholas had finally been conscious and coherent enough to realize the execution was over, he had broken every window, lamp and glass object in the house, so enraged he had no idea what he was doing. But the rage had burned away and what it had left in its place was no less hurtful, but far more useful.

"What?" The light from the hearth behind them gleamed off the whites of Arisilde's eyes but his voice sounded almost normal. "Do you think all this wreck and ruin came from that moment? Oh no, oh no, never think that. Watching a good friend hang is a terrible thing but it didn't do this. I did this." Arisilde leaned forward. His voice dropped to a whisper but it was as intense as if he shouted. "I wanted to kill them all. It's not what they did, you see, it's what they didn't do. I wanted to pull Lodun down stone by burning stone. I wanted to destroy every man, woman, and child in it, I wanted to burn them alive and watch them scream in Hell. And I could have done it. They trained me to do it. But. . . .'' Arisilde started to laugh. It was an agonizing sound. "But I never could bear to see anyone hurt. Isn't it ridiculous?''

"That's the difference between us, Ari. You wanted to do it; I would have done it." But the words disturbed him. Arisilde had said some odd things under the influence of opium but hearing him talk this way was almost shocking. Nicholas had never known why his friend had taken this path into ruin and despair. God knew he had seen it happen often enough before; in the teeming streets where he had spent his childhood, men and women fell into this same trap every day.

Arisilde rubbed his face until the skin seemed like to break and Nicholas caught his wrists and pulled his hands away, afraid that he was going to blind himself. The sorcerer peered up at him urgently. "You knew I thought Edouard was guilty. You knew because I told you and we talked about it, and then later after the execution I came to you and I said you had been right and I had been wrong, remember? And it was proved later, of course, Ronsarde proved it later, remember?''

"Of course I do. That was when. . . .'' *I decided not to kill Ronsarde.* Nicholas couldn't finish the thought aloud, not even to Ari who wouldn't recall this conversation by morning anyway.

"But I didn't tell you how I knew." Arisilde let the words trail off. Nicholas thought that was all he meant to say and tried to urge him to stand, but the sorcerer shook his head. His voice perceptibly stronger, he said, "I went to Ilamires Rohan. He was Master of Lodun, then, remember?''

"Of course I remember, Ari, he tried to defend Edouard.''

Arisilde stood up suddenly, dragging Nicholas with him. Ari was so slender, seeming so weak and languid most of the time, Nicholas had forgotten how strong he was. Ari's hands were buried in the front of his shirt, almost lifting him off his feet, and Nicholas didn't think he could free himself without hurting him. The sorcerer said, softly, terribly, "He didn't defend him well enough."

"What?"

"I went to see him in his study at Lodun. Oh, that beautiful room. I was afraid that my judgement was faulty because I had let Edouard fool me, and he said my judgement was not impaired. He said he knew Edouard was innocent. But he had let the trial go on, because a man of Edouard's knowledge was too dangerous to live."

"No." Nicholas felt oddly hollow. One more betrayal after all the others of that terrible time, what did it really matter? But as the words sank in, and Nicholas remembered the old man, Master of Lodun, sitting with them at the trial as if in sympathy and support, he was astonished to discover that it did still matter. It mattered a great deal.

Arisilde was saying, "Yes, the simple truth, after all the lies. I could have killed him."

"You should have told me," Nicholas whispered. "I would have."

"I know. That's why I didn't." Arisilde smiled, and Nicholas saw the other truth. Ari said, "But don't think he escaped unpunished. He loved me like a son, you know. So I destroyed something he loved."

Nicholas pulled away and Arisilde released him. The sorcerer was still wearing that mad, gentle smile. Nicholas walked back toward the hearth, not quite aware of what he was doing. The fire was nothing but glowing coals, winking out as he watched. Behind him, Arisilde said, "And Rohan became such a bitter old man, who lost his greatest student, his hand-picked successor. . . ." His voice broke. "That wasn't what I was going to tell you . . . I really have to remember that, it was very important."

Nicholas turned back as Arisilde slumped to the floor

again, but the sorcerer's madness seemed to have died with the fire. He let Nicholas guide him to the big tumbled bed in one of the little rooms off the hall. The most powerful sorcerer in the history of Lodun lay there quietly, saying nothing more, until the servant Isham returned and Nicholas left him to his care.

7

It was still dark when Nicholas had the hire cab let him off at the top of Coldcourt's drive. He could see every window in the sprawling stone house was lit and there were a couple of servants with lamps patrolling the roof between the towers. It didn't look like there was trouble now; the wide sweep of lawn was an empty landscape of shadows, broken only by the one lone towering oak and the drive. He started toward the house, almost lame from exhaustion, the gravel crunching under his boots. When he entered the circle of light from the lamps hung on either side of the front entrance, the doors swung open and Madeline hurried down the steps to meet him.

Her embrace, in his current state, almost knocked him off his feet. She said, "I was getting worried. The others thought you would be right behind them."

"It . . . took longer with Ari than I thought," he told her. "What's happened here?"

They entered the welcome warmth of the entrance hall and Madeline paused to secure the doors, saying, "There was something, I think it was the same sort of creature that you saw under Mondollot House, up on the roof. It was peering into Edouard's old attic. Nothing seemed disturbed and no one was hurt, so perhaps it was only scouting us out. I don't know what it wanted."

"I don't know anything anymore." Nicholas laughed bitterly. "I suppose Reynard told you what we found."

"Yes." Madeline's face was drawn and harsh in the

lamplight as she turned back toward him. "Could Arisilde tell you anything of use?"

Nicholas stopped at the foot of the stairs to look at her. Sometimes Madeline surprised even him. Any other woman would have had the decency to be shocked out of her wits, or to be made ill, or to invoke heavenly wrath on the perpetrators. He didn't know whether to attribute it to her general bloody-mindedness or the self-absorption and self-possession that usually characterized potentially brilliant actors. He ran his hands through his hair, trying to get his thoughts together. "I don't think Ari's going to be of much help."

"The opium?"

"I think it's finally got the better of him. He was telling me things. . . ." Nicholas shook his head. "I don't know. Either that or he's gone mad. Somehow Octave has had access to Edouard's work. That's how he's managing these spirit circles. He has a sphere, like the ones Edouard made with Ari and Asilva. Where that butchery in Valent House comes into it, I don't know. . . ."

Madeline linked arms with him and towed him up the stairs. "You're exhausted. Sleep until dawn, and then make plans."

"Damned optimist."

"Damned realist," she corrected with a weary smile.

Nicholas left Madeline to make the arrangements for a second, more thorough search of Valent House while he tried to sleep for what was left of the night. What he actually did was retire to his study on the second floor to lay out the notebooks and the scraps of paper their first search had brought to light.

The notebooks proved to be what he had originally thought, a student's copying from a probably forbidden text on necromancy. Reading through them, he couldn't see any evidence of the copyist inserting opinion. *He hasn't scribbled his name, present direction, and future plans for destroying the world in the margin either,* Nicholas thought sourly. *It's always helpful when they do that.* It might be illuminating to ascertain which text the notes had come from. Arisilde, of course, would probably recognize it at a glance. If Arisilde was sane and in any state vaguely approaching sobriety. But Arisilde had been out of touch with Lodun for years and would no longer know who kept such books in their private libraries, so perhaps there was not much point in it anyway. *But to find out whose student Octave was, and when. . . .* Perhaps he would ask Arisilde anyway.

The scraps of paper from the desk were more intriguing, though not much more helpful. The fragments of words were indecipherable, though Nicholas wanted to say that he recognized something about the handwriting. It wasn't Edouard's, which would have been too much to hope for. Though perhaps it didn't matter either. He knew Octave had somehow re-created Edouard's work. Perhaps the method was immaterial. *Yes, keep telling yourself that.*

Speaking of method. . . . Nicholas took down a heavy volume from the bookcase above the desk. It contained the memoirs of a very methodical man, the bureaucrat who had been responsible for cutting the new streets and plazas through the decaying slums of Vienne. It wasn't so much a memoir as it was a chronicle of work, describing in exacting detail the alterations that had been wrought on the ancient city. Nicholas had always found it extremely helpful since few reliable maps had ever been made of Vienne.

He flipped through the worn pages, looking for the section on Ducal Court Street. *And here it is. . . . Tearing down tenements, the old theater, what was left of the Bisran ambassador's home after the last time they burned it down . . . Ah. "I informed the Duke it would not be necessary to sacrifice Mondollot House"—I'm sure he was pleased—"but that its neighbor Ventarin House would have to be taken down."* The bureaucrat, a man not entirely without finer feelings, had regretted this, finding that Ventarin House was more pleasing to the eye and would have made a better ornament to his street than Mondollot. Ventarin, however, was in the wrong place and presently occupied only by servant caretakers, the family having moved to a country estate to finish dwindling into obscurity in peace. They had not opposed the destruction. *"They had no need of the old place, having not indulged in public life for many generations . . . One of their most illustrious ancestors was Gabard Alis Ventarin, a notable of some two centuries past . . . who held the position of Court Sorcerer under King Rogere."*

Nicholas closed the book and sat for a while, staring at nothing, tapping one finger on the polished wood of the desk. So the chamber that Octave's ghoul had broken into had once been part of the cellars under the home of a former court sorcerer. Had the old Duke of Mondollot known what was there? Had he perhaps opened that door, seen what it guarded, and ordered it sealed up again? That was undoubtedly what Octave had wanted to know when he had tried to convince the Duchess to let him contact the late Duke. *Something was there, and Octave's ghouls took it away. But it wasn't right. Either it wasn't what he wanted, or something was missing from it.* One of the best uses for necromancy was the discerning of secret things, whether past or present. There were other ways for sorcerers to divine the hidden, but none so easy as necromancy provided. It also taught methods of creating illusions that were solid to the touch, ways of affecting the minds and wills of people, animals, even spirits.

In the end Nicholas swept all the fragments together with the notebooks and carefully locked them away in one of the concealed drawers of his desk, and then trudged wearily to a bath and bed.

Nicholas managed to rest for only an hour, feeling the sun rise behind the heavy drapes over the window and listening to the mantel clock tick almost but not quite in time to his heartbeat. Madeline was sleeping deeply, her time in the crowded accommodations used by chorus performers having inured her to any amount of restless twitching on Nicholas's part. He kept having to fight the impulse to wake her, either to make love or to talk or

anything to keep his mind off Octave's theft of
Edouard's work. Finally he got out of bed, half furious
and half depressed, dressed and went down to the library.

It was a long room at the back of the house, the floor
to ceiling shelves overflowing with books. Books piled
on the warm upholstered armchairs and the rich Parscian
carpet, books stuffed into the two boulle cabinets and
the satinwood escritoire. *I'm going to need a bigger
house*, Nicholas thought, looking at it. His gaze stopped
at the tiny framed miniature on the desk. It was the only
remaining portrait of his mother, painted to be placed
inside a gold locket which had been sold when she had
brought him to Vienne. His father had commissioned the
piece not long after the wedding, when there had still
been money for such things, though no doubt his family
had made a great deal of trouble over the expense. They
had not begun to actively plot against her then, but they
would have argued over any money being spent on
something not directly related to their own comfort. It
was not a good likeness of her anyway, at least not according to Nicholas's memory. The portrait showed only
a young, fine-featured woman with dark curling hair, and
the artist had captured no nuance of expression or gesture that would have given the little image life. Of
course, his father had probably paid three times what the
painting had been worth and never knew he was being
cheated. Nicholas looked away, banishing the old memories.

He meant to make a thorough search of the historical
texts, both the dry scholarly and the lurid popular, for
that trace of memory that had bothered him so at Valent
House. The more he thought about it, or tried not to
think about it, the more vivid that shadow picture became. *It was a woodcut*, he thought. *And the page was
stained*. That didn't help. He didn't have any of his old
books from childhood. All those had gone when his
mother died, along with most of their possessions. The
books in this room had been Edouard's or had been
bought since Nicholas had come here years ago. But the

history section took up the entire west wall of the room and from his earlier delvings into it he had high hopes.

He searched, thoroughly engrossed, barely noticing when Sarasate brought in a tray with coffee and rolls. Between Cadarsa's *History of Ile-Rien in Eight Volumes* and an ancient copy of *Sorceries of Lodun*, he stumbled on *The Pirates of Chaire*, a children's storybook with illustrations. "What in God's name is this doing here. . . ." Nicholas muttered, flipping the much battered book open to the flyleaf. There was writing there and he stared at it a moment, taken aback.

It was in Edouard's hand and it read *Don't you dare get rid of this book.*

Nicholas smiled. Edouard Viller had known him better than anyone.

The only reason Nicholas was alive now was that some forgotten benefactor had told Edouard that the Prefecture were always picking up stray children in Riverside. When Edouard had decided he needed a son to fill the lonely days after his wife died, he had gone down to the cells at Almsgate to look for one.

Nicholas barely remembered his own father and the moldering, disgraced, debt-ridden ancestral estate where he had spent the first few years of his life. His mother had brought him to Vienne when he was six and taken back her maiden name of Valiarde, preferring the slums of the great city to coexistence with her husband's relations. She had made her living by piecework laundry and sewing and if she had ever had to supplement her income by the form of employment more common to destitute women in Vienne, she had never allowed him to find out about it. When he was ten she had died, of some congestive lung ailment that every year carried off hundreds of the poor who crowded into the broken-down buildings in Riverside and the other slums. Nicholas had already dabbled in thieving. After her death he had taken it up as a profession.

He had been lucky enough to encounter Cusard, and before that worthy's second stint in prison, Nicholas had learned from him the pickpocket's and cracksman's skills that would give him an edge over the other street boys. By twelve he had been leader of a local gang and had made them all wealthy and wildly successful by ambitious burglaries and by dealing with fences rather than rag and bone shops. This success brought the attention of the Prefecture. They had set a trap for him with the help of a disgruntled rival and Nicholas had ended his first illegal career in the filth of the Almsgate cells, beaten within an inch of his life and waiting to be hauled off to the real hell of the city prison.

He had been cursing the guards in fluent Aderassi, which his mother had taught him. There had been a fashion at the time for young gentlemen to learn the language so they could go to the court of Adera to complete their social education and she had never forgotten that his father's family had been noble, despite their poverty and well-deserved obscurity. Nicholas had discovered that he could call people the most terrible things in it and they would not understand him.

Edouard had come to the barred door and called, in the same language, "You have a very foul mouth. Can you read?"

"Yes," Nicholas had replied, annoyed.

"In what language, Aderassi or Rienish?"

"Both."

"Perfect," Edouard had said to the jailer. "I wouldn't want one I had to start from the beginning, you know. I'll take him."

And that had been that. Nicholas replaced the storybook on the shelf.

This time they entered Valent House through the front door. Nicholas was prepared to prove he was an estate agent for a firm on the other side of the river and that Cusard, Crack and Lamane were builders, here to give advice on possible renovations.

For all these elaborate preparations, the street was deserted and no one demanded to know their business, though the builders' wagon standing outside was probably explanation enough for the curious.

Earlier that morning, when the sun was almost high enough to officially qualify as dawn, Nicholas had gone into the guest bedroom to waken Reynard. Waiting impatiently until the cursing stopped, Nicholas had asked him to make the rounds of the cafes and clubs today to find out when Octave's next appointment for a spirit circle was, and to delicately ascertain if the good doctor had asked any of his other summoned spirits about lost family wealth. To Nicholas's unexpressed relief, Madeline had decided she could be of more help finding out about Madame Everset's late brother, and what had been aboard his ill-fated ship that Octave had been so interested in, than as one more searcher in Valent House.

Standing now in the dust and ruin of the house's foyer, Nicholas was sure he was right about Octave's original purpose in holding the circles. It only remained to discover how and why Octave had turned from thievery to necromancy.

Cusard had also brought Lyon Althise, who had trained as a medical doctor but been asked to leave the College of Physicians because of a fondness for drink. He was well known in Vienne's criminal underclass as being willing to use his medical skills for almost any purpose as long as he was well paid, but Nicholas doubted even he had ever seen anything like this. Althise and Nicholas made another examination of the bodies while the others searched the house under Crack's direction.

They came up for air after what seemed an interminable time and stood in the kitchen with the scullery door open for the cool breeze. Nicholas was wearing one of his Donatien disguises, the one that made him look about ten years older. Althise didn't know him as Nicholas Valiarde and he intended to keep it that way.

Althise, leaning on the cracked counter, shook his head. "I can't do much more than confirm what you've already discovered for yourself. Yes, he was alive when it happened, though not for long. Whoever did it used a very sharp knife, and it probably happened no more than a day before you found him. The remaining eye is cloudy and the skin is discoloring. The others have been here much longer, some days, some weeks.'' He looked up at Nicholas wearily. He was an older man, his hair graying and his face marked by perpetual weariness and defeat. ''I know I'm not being much help.'' Althise had been told what was basically the truth: that Donatien had been pursuing a man who had threatened him and stumbled on this house.

Nicholas shook his head. ''I've begun to realize I may not be able to do much with this. We can't keep sneaking in here to investigate—someone is sure to report us.'' Althise had tried his best but his best hadn't been good enough for the College of Physicians, either. *Doctor Cyran Halle may be Ronsarde's mouthpiece and a pompous bastard, but I wish I had him here now*, Nicholas thought reluctantly.

A startled gasp from Althise brought him out of his own thoughts and he jerked his head toward the open scullery door. There was a figure framed there, between the shadow of the room and the wan light from the ragged garden. It took Nicholas moments to realize it was Arisilde Damal.

''Ari, I didn't think you'd come,'' he said, startled.

Althise sagged back against the counter, relieved that the apparition was evidently expected, and muttered, ''And I thought my nerves were gone before I came here.''

''Yes, well, Madeline's message said it was urgent.'' Arisilde came into the kitchen slowly, as cautious as a cat treading on unfamiliar ground. His greatcoat had once been of very good material though now it was threadbare. He hadn't bothered with a hat and his fine hair was standing up in wisps all over his head. He nodded a distracted greeting to Althise, then looked down at Nicholas, his violet eyes confused. ''I'm not at my best today, I'm afraid. We don't know the people who live here, do we?''

''No, we don't. In fact—''

''That's good.'' Arisilde was relieved. Pale and battered and somehow otherworldly, he could have been mistaken for a particularly feather-headed member of the fay, but the size of his pupils was almost normal and his hands weren't trembling. "Because something terrible's happened here."

"Hey," Lamane called from the foyer. "We found something else in the cellar!"

Nicholas refused to allow himself to speculate as he followed the man down the cellar stairs and into the stinking chambers below. Arisilde trailed after him but Althise stayed behind in the kitchen. Nicholas was glad of it. He had told Arisilde not to mention names in front of strangers but it was simply better not to rely on his discretion. They turned down toward the opposite end of the hall, lit now with several oil lamps. As Cusard, Crack and Lamane made way for Nicholas, he felt a cool rush of dank air.

The passage had appeared to end in a bare wall. Now a section a few feet wide and about half a man's height stood out from it, revealing a dark opening. Nicholas knelt to look inside and saw a rough tunnel supported by moldy brick walls, leading down into pitch blackness. Crack knelt beside him and said, "Look."

He held the lantern out over the floor of the tunnel, a mix of dirt and brick chips, then pushed the slide down. There was a faint glow emanating from the floor and walls. "Perfect," Nicholas said softly. "How did you discover it?"

Crack put the slide up again. With Crack, it was always difficult to tell, but Nicholas thought he was excited at the discovery. "We knocked on the walls. Cusard made the lock work."

Nicholas stood up to look as Cusard showed him the small hole on the outer side of the false door. "It's an old trick," he explained. "Slide your finger in that hole, push up on the lever, and snick goes the bolt." He added grimly, "You can open it from the other side, too. Lets you in and out, this door does."

Arisilde had taken Nicholas's place at the tunnel entrance, crawling half into it. He sat back now, closely examining some substance on his fingers. "Nic, this is the same stuff that was on that coat you brought me, and those pieces of fabric from that drowned boy's clothes. It's a residue caused by a type of necromantic powder that hasn't been used in Ile-Rien for hundreds of years. Isn't that odd? I can't think who would have made it."

Nicholas stared at him and Arisilde's vague eyes grew worried. The sorcerer said, "That was you that brought me those things to look at, wasn't it?"

"Yes, of course, but—"

Arisilde sighed. "Thank God. I thought I was going mad."

"But I didn't think you'd looked at them at all. Why didn't you tell me last night?"

"You saw me last night?" the sorcerer demanded. "What was I doing?"

"You don't remember—You said you had something important to tell me. Was that it?"

Arisilde sat down on the filthy floor and tapped his cheek thoughtfully. "It might have been. Did I give you any hints?"

Nicholas ran a hand through his hair and took a deep breath. "What about the powder from the golem? Did you learn anything from that?"

"The powder from the what?"

Nicholas looked sourly at Cusard, who was regarding the ceiling with pursed lips, and Crack, who was staring down at the sorcerer with a puzzled expression, and gave in. "Never mind."

"Maybe I'll recall it, you can never tell." Arisilde was on his hands and knees now, crawling into the tunnel. "Let's see where this goes. I love secret tunnels, don't you?"

"My back's bad," Cusard said quickly.

Lamane immediately asserted that his back was bad, too. "I know, I know," Nicholas said impatiently. "I want to see it for myself, anyway."

Crack was already following Arisilde. Nicholas crawled after them.

"You don't need the lamp," Arisilde was saying,

partly to Crack and partly to himself. "Well, I used to know how to do this." Light flared in the tunnel suddenly, soft and white. "There we go," Arisilde said, pleased. The spell light seemed to emanate from all over his body.

Nicholas's fear was that the tunnel would prove to be only a repository for more bodies, but that didn't seem to be the case. Crack glanced back at him and muttered, "I should go first, in case we run into something."

"It's all right," Nicholas told him. "Arisilde is more capable than he appears." In fact, the sorcerer was acting more like himself than he had for a long time. Nicholas added, "But thank you for not claiming a bad back."

"I like this," Crack said simply. Then, as if realizing that statement needed more explanation, added, "Finding things out. I like it better than stealing."

So do I, Nicholas thought, but he wouldn't say it aloud.

"The tunnel gets wider here," Arisilde reported cheerfully. "I think we found the sewer." In another moment this supposition was confirmed by the sound of trickling water and the fetid smell of sewage.

The tunnel widened and opened into a ledge, a few feet above a stream of putrid water flowing through a round, brick-lined sewer. Nicholas got to his feet, one hand on the damp wall to steady himself. Arisilde swept his hands over his battered coat, gathering the spell light into a ball, then set it in midair where it hung suspended by nothing and illuminating the tunnel. "Here we are," Arisilde said. "Is this where you thought it would lead?"

"It's where the one in the Mondollot House cellars led," Nicholas told him, thinking of the hole in the wall of the wine vaults that the first ghoul had fled through. He heard a scrabbling and put it down to rats. "I think—"

It came up from below the ledge, too fast for him to move, to shout a warning. He could only fall back against the wall as the claws grasped for his neck and the maw gaped in the withered, hate-filled face. Crack shoved an arm between them, trying to seize it around the neck, and its teeth started to sink into his arm. This gave Nicholas the chance to grab its head, to push it away, but it was too strong. Then Arisilde was suddenly behind it, catching the thing from behind with a handful of its lank dead hair. The spell light flickered and suddenly the tremendous force shoving Nicholas against the wall was gone. He stumbled, caught Crack's arm and steadied him as the other man almost fell backward over the edge.

The creature lying at their feet bore little resemblance to the ghoul that had whipped up from beneath the ledge and nearly torn them apart. Nicholas stared down at it, amazed. This thing was barely a pile of rag and bone, held together by shreds of skin and tendon. He managed to clear his throat and release Crack's arm. "One of the ghouls," he explained.

Arisilde squatted next to it, careless of his balance on the ledge, and picked up one of the bones thoughtfully.

Crack was rubbing his forearm where the creature had planted its teeth. "Did it get you?" Nicholas asked, worried. Crack shook his head and showed his coat sleeve, unpunctured. "In another moment, Ari...." Nicholas found himself almost speechless, which didn't happen often.

"Yes?" Arisilde looked up inquiringly.

"Thank you."

The sorcerer waved it away. "Oh, no trouble at all, no trouble at all."

Nicholas looked around again. *They travel through the sewers, but we knew that already.* There didn't appear to be anything else here to see. Octave, connected with this house, with the ghouls, with necromancy.

"This isn't a ghoul, precisely," Arisilde said suddenly. "It's a lich. The necromancer obtains a long-dead corpse—very long dead, in this poor fellow's case—then animates it with a spirit that has been enchained to do the necromancer's bidding. Of course, the easiest way to obtain such a spirit is to kill an innocent victim in an act of ceremonial magic.''

''Like that man was killed in the cellar?'' Nicholas asked.

''No, that was something else, another way to raise power.'' Arisilde glanced around the tunnel expectantly. ''There's another aspect to the lich-making process. The remains that contained the enchained spirit still, um, hang about, you know. As revenants. Mindless, soul-dead creatures. I don't see any around here, though.'' Arisilde waggled his brows thoughtfully and frowned up at Nicholas. ''Necromancy is such a messy business, and someone's been very busy at it. Very, very busy.''

The woman who called herself Madame Talvera looked darkly at the passersby on the other side of the railing and said, ''Communication with the spirits isn't a game. For those of us who embrace it truly, it is a religion.''

Nicholas nodded encouragingly. Knowing he needed to question another practitioner of spiritualism about Octave, he had been working to arrange this meeting since the day before yesterday. He had found Madame Talvera by asking a couple of old acquaintances whom he knew dabbled in the pastime and also in confidence work. Neither of them had heard of Octave before he had appeared on the scene this year, but both had recommended Madame Talvera as a reliable source of information.

The cafe was on the Street of Flowers, just within the borders of the Philosopher's Cross. Madame Talvera hadn't wanted to go any further into that area, because she said she was afraid of witches. Nicholas was glad she didn't seem to know what Arisilde was; if she had realized that the vague young man sitting next to her and rendering cream pastries into their component parts before devouring them was a powerful Lodun-trained sorcerer, she might not have been as forthcoming.

He had been agreeably surprised that Arisilde had wanted to come with him. After crawling back out of the tunnel, he had had Cusard and the others close the door and leave Valent House. Before going, he had made Arisilde look at the oddly melted wall in the room with the vivisected body. All the sorcerer could tell him was that it had been done by a great release of power, definitely magical. When Nicholas had asked him what sort of magical power, Arisilde had replied, "Very bad power," and that was all he would say.

The other tables under the striped awning were occupied by tradespeople, but they were close enough to the vicinity of the Cross that no one cared too much about the state of their clothes, which had suffered greatly from the crawl through the tunnel. Nicholas had only had time to remove his Donatien disguise, which he didn't wear during the day in public if he could help it.

A wind stirred the trees in the strip of garden that ran down the center of the street and the strong scent of rain filled the air. Nicholas stirred his coffee and said, "Is it proper to use one's religion to earn money?"

"No, not at all. A gift is permissible, but it should be freely given and not more than the giver can easily part with." She made a sharp gesture. She was Aderassi, olive-skinned and hawk-featured, dark hair pulled back into a severe bun, serious dark eyes. She wore a black, plainly cut dress with a high collar and her hat had a small veil. "There are tricksters, who make tables rock with their toes, and imitate strange voices. You've heard of these things?" At his nod she shook her head grimly. "Such things are to be expected. There are men who make their living pretending to be priests, also."

She touched her glass thoughtfully. He had offered to buy her lunch, but all she would have was water. "It is not a thing of sorcery. The etheric plane is free to anyone who will strive to open their mind to it. The Great Teachers of spiritualism, the Sisters Polacera, have written of many techniques for schooling the senses to embrace it. Speaking to the dead is only a negligible part of what we do. Truly, taken altogether, it is a way of life."

It's a cult, Nicholas thought, *though a rather harmless*

one as cults go. He knew about the Polaceras and the other intellectuals who had started the spiritualism craze. "Do you know of a man purporting to be a spiritualist who calls himself Doctor Octave?"

"Oh, him. Everyone knows of him." She looked disgusted. "I see why you wish to know these things. He has taken money from you perhaps? From someone in your family?"

"He's been most troubling to me, yes."

"I first saw him six or seven years ago, when the Polacera Sisters still lived in Vienne. They live in the country now, outside of Chaire. Much more conducive to spiritual living, the country. And of course it's very nice there, near the sea. But anyway," Warming to her story, she leaned over the table intently. "He had been to circles held at other houses, by lesser devotees of the movement, but when he came to one of the Polaceras' circles at their old house in Sitare Court—" She shook her head. "Madame Amelia Polacera ordered him to go, saying his shadow in the ether was as dark as a well at twilight and she would give him none of her teaching. Many important people were there. Doctor Adalmas. Biendere, the writer. Lady Galaise. I'm sure it was most embarrassing for Octave, but—" She shrugged and admitted frankly, "I was glad she sent him away."

Madame Amelia Polacera may have something after all. Either that or she's simply a marvelous judge of character. Nicholas asked, "And you saw no more of him after that?"

"I heard he left the city and was studying privately with someone. It was not my concern, so I paid little attention. Then early this year, he returned and became very fashionable, holding circles for wealthy patrons. Many people are curious about spiritualism, but the true devotees will not hold circles for any but the pure and those who truly wish to learn. Octave does it as a party trick." Her lip curled. "The Madames Polacera will be greatly angered when they hear of it."

"Did Octave ever show any sign of knowing sorcery?"

She looked startled. "No, he was no sorcerer. Madame Polacera would have known, if he was."

Nicholas nodded. Perhaps she would at that. "There is just one more thing, Madame. If you wanted to contact a spirit, would you need something from the dead person's corpse? A lock of hair, perhaps?"

Madame Talvera frowned. "No, of course not. Hair, once it is cut, is dead. It would be of no more use than a cut flower. There is a technique that allows one to see visions of a person, living or dead, using something that they once wore close to their skin. Jewelry is best. Metal is very good at holding the impressions of the glow of ether that surrounds every living soul."

Arisilde was nodding agreement. "Hair, skin, bones are more useful in necromancy," he added.

Madame Talvera shuddered. "I have no knowledge of that and I wish none." She stood abruptly, collecting her little black-beaded reticule. "If that is all you wish to ask me. . . ."

Nicholas stood and thanked her, and watched as she made her way through the tables and out to the street. A light rain had started, which she seemed not to notice. "I hope I didn't frighten her off," Arisilde said, worried.

"You may have, but she'd already told us everything she knew of use." Nicholas left some coins for the waiter and they strolled out onto the promenade. "She's bound to be nervous of being associated with necromancy."

"I see."

Nicholas had held off on questioning the sorcerer about Edouard's work, knowing that if what Arisilde had told him last night was the truth, then the less he thought about Edouard the better. If Ilamires Rohan had known Edouard was innocent and still let him be executed, revenge was all well and good, but. . . . *But I'd rather have Arisilde*, Nicholas found himself thinking. "I know how Octave is contacting the dead," he said carefully.

"Oh, I must have missed that part. How?"

Nicholas felt some misgivings at further involving Arisilde in this. But he remembered how the sorcerer had destroyed the ghoul in the sewer, so casually, as if that display of power was not even worth comment. *I suppose he's in less danger from Octave than the rest of us are.* "He's using a device very like the ones Edouard made with you and Asilva. He must have had access to Edouard's notes to create it, but everything that survived the trial is at Coldcourt and hasn't been disturbed. That leaves you and Asilva. . . ."

Arisilde stopped abruptly, heedless of the sprinkle of rain and the people hurrying past, the wagons splashing in the street. He stared into space, concentrating so hard that Nicholas thought he was performing a spell. The sorcerer shook his head suddenly and gazed down at Nicholas seriously. "No, I don't think I told anyone about the spheres. I'm sure I'd remember if I had. And Edouard wouldn't have wanted me to, you see. No, I'm sure I'd remember that."

Nicholas smiled. "That's good to know, but I didn't really suppose you had."

Arisilde looked relieved. "Good. If you were sure it was me, of course I'd have to take your word for it."

They continued up the street, a torrent of water flung up from the wheels of a passing coach narrowly missing them. "I can't see Asilva telling anyone about them, either," Arisilde added. "He didn't really approve of Edouard's experiments with magic, you know. It didn't stop him from participating at first—he believed very strongly in knowledge for its own sake, which is not a dictate that everyone at Lodun follows."

Nicholas glanced up at him and saw Arisilde's face had taken on a hunted look. He said cautiously, "You mentioned something about that last night, in connection with Ilamires Rohan."

"Did I?" Arisilde's smile was quick and not completely convincing. "It doesn't do to take everything I say too seriously."

Nicholas decided not to pursue the point. *He's more coherent today than I've seen him in the past year—I don't want to send him back to oblivion with prying questions.* It was safer to stick to the present. "That room in the cellar, where the man was killed. Have you ever seen anything like it?''

''I should hope not.''

''I think I've seen a drawing, or a woodcut actually, in a book describing it. I'm wondering if it means that this was some sort of specific ritual of necromancy.'' Arisilde was frowning down at the wet pavement and didn't respond. Nicholas added, ''If we could identify what our opponent was trying to do, we would be a little further along.''

''I can't remember anything offhand—of course we both know what that's worth.'' Arisilde smiled a little wryly, then brightened. ''I'll look for it. That will be my job now, won't it?''

''If you like.'' Nicholas wasn't sure what Arisilde meant to look for, but you never could tell. ''We still need to know where Octave got his information and you know the most about Edouard's research. Was there anyone else who could have known enough to be of help to Octave?''

''That's the question, isn't it?'' Arisilde wandered into the path of two well-dressed ladies and Nicholas tipped his hat by way of apology and took his friend's elbow, guiding him out of the middle of the promenade and closer to the wall. ''It bears thinking about.'' His face growing serious, Arisilde said, ''I'm glad you're looking into this, Nicholas. We can't really have these goings-on, you know.''

Nicholas had arranged to meet Madeline at the indoor garden in the Conservatory of Arts. It was crowded as more people sought shelter from the rain that was trickling down the glass-paned walls and making music against the arched metal panels of the roof high overhead. Most of the little wrought iron tables scattered throughout the large, light chamber were full and it was hard to see past the hanging baskets of greenery and the potted fruit trees. He finally spotted her beneath an orange tree. She was dressed in burgundy velvet and a very extravagant hat and had simply managed to fade in with the fashionably dressed crowd.

"Did you discover anything about Madame Everset's late brother?" Nicholas asked as they took seats.

"Yes, but first tell me what you found out at that house." Madeline rested her elbows on the table and leaned forward anxiously.

Nicholas let out his breath in annoyance. She was always accusing him of not sharing his plans with her. "Madeline—"

Arisilde pointed at the remains of Madeline's iced fruit and said, "Are you going to finish that?"

She slid the china plate toward him and said to Nicholas, "Yes, yes, I know I'm a great burden. Now talk."

So as the light rain streamed down over the glass walls and the waiters hurried by, he told her about their morning at Valent House, the ghoul and the tunnel to the sewers, and what Madame Talvera had said of Octave's background.

"Another ghoul? How many of those creatures are we going to run into?"

"The dead brother, Madeline," Nicholas prompted. "What did you find out about him?"

"Oh, that. Yes, it was as you thought. The ship he was on went down with a very expensive cargo."

That confirmed his suspicions about what Octave's game was with the circles. *But using spiritualism to fleece the wealthy out of riches their dead relatives might have had some knowledge of is one thing; what we found in Valent House is quite another,* Nicholas thought.

"Oh," Madeline continued, "I ran into Reynard and he wanted me to tell you that he spoke to Madame Algretto and she said Octave has apparently taken rooms at the Hotel Galvaz. Everset never did confront him about the odd events at the end of the circle last night, but that's to be expected, I suppose."

"The Hotel Galvaz, hmm?" Nicholas looked thoughtful. That was only a few streets over.

They obtained the number of Octave's room by a trick that must have been invented at the dawn of creation shortly after the building of the first hotel: Madeline fluttered up to the porter's desk and asked for her friend Doctor Octave. The porter glanced at the rows of cubbies for keys in the wall behind him and said the good doctor was not in at present. Madeline borrowed a page of hotel stationery to write a brief note, folded it and handed it to the porter, who turned and slipped it into the cubby for the seventh room on the fifth floor. Madeline suddenly recalled that she would be seeing the doctor later at the home of another friend and asked for the note back.

As they climbed the broad stairs up from the grand foyer and the other public rooms, Arisilde used what was for him an easily performed illusion, obscuring their presence with a mild reflection of the available light that caused the eye to turn away without ever quite knowing from what it had turned. It could be broken by anyone whose suspicions were aroused enough to stare hard at them, but in the middle of the afternoon at the Hotel Galvaz, with people streaming back from late luncheons to prepare for evening entertainments, there was no one whose suspicions were aroused.

The fifth floor hall was presently occupied only by a basket of dried flowers on a spindly legged console table and the light was dim. Madeline hung back at the landing to watch the stairs and give warning if anyone approached. Nicholas knocked first on the door, waited until he was sure there was no answer, then took out his lockpicks. He glanced at Arisilde, who was studying the vine-covered wallpaper intently, and cleared his throat.

"Hmm?" Arisilde stared blankly at him, distracted. "Oh, that's right." He touched the door with the back of his hand and frowned for an instant. "No, nothing sorcerous. Carry on."

That didn't exactly engender confidence, Nicholas thought. He looked down the hall at Madeline, who was rubbing her temples as if her head hurt. She signalled that no one was approaching and, holding his breath, Nicholas inserted a pick into the lock. Nothing happened. Breathing a trifle easier, he started to work the lock. There couldn't be too much danger; after all, members of the hotel staff would be in and out several times a day. But a very clever sorcerer could have set a trap that was only tripped if the door was forced or opened without a key. Either Octave's sorcerer was not very clever or. . . . *There's nothing in the room worth the trouble to guard*, Nicholas thought grimly. After a few moments more he was able to ease the door open.

The small parlor just inside was shadowy, lit only by a little daylight creeping through the heavy drapes covering the window. There was a bedroom just beyond, also dark. Octave had been able to afford one of the better class of rooms: the furniture was finely made and well upholstered, and the carpets, hangings and wallpapers were of a style only recently in fashion. Arisilde slipped in after Nicholas and took a quick turn around the parlor, touching the ornaments on the mantel, bending over to poke cautiously at the coal scuttle. Nicholas watched him with a raised eyebrow, but Arisilde didn't voice any kind of warning, so he continued his own search.

He went through the drawers and shelves of the small drop-leaf desk first, finding nothing but unused stationery and writing implements. The blotting paper revealed only past notes to a tailor and to two aristocratic ladies who had written thanking Octave for holding circles in their homes. Neither was from Madame Everset. Nicholas removed the blotting paper for a sample of Octave's handwriting, knowing the good doctor would assume the floor maid had done it when she refreshed the writing supplies.

Reynard had said that Octave seemed to have the air of a professional confidence man and Nicholas felt that supposition was confirmed by an examination of the doctor's belongings. He went through the suits and coats hanging in the wardrobe, carefully searching the pockets, finding the clothes were a mix of items well cared for but in poor quality and items of excellent quality but not cared for overmuch. *When he is in funds, he becomes careless*, Nicholas noted. The state of Octave's personal effects confirmed several of Nicholas's theories about the man's personality.

None of which disguised the fact that there was nothing of importance here.

Nothing under the bed, between the mattresses, in the back of the wardrobe, behind the framed pictures, and no mysterious slits in the cushions or lumps under the carpet. Nicholas searched the sensible places first, then the less likely, finally progressing to the places only an idiot would hide anything. *No papers, no sphere*, he thought in disgust, resisting the sudden violent urge to kick a delicate table. There were no books to be found, not even a recent novel. *He took this room for show; his real headquarters is somewhere else.* Somewhere in the city there was another Valent House in the making. *And he's using one of Edouard's spheres.* For a moment rage made it difficult to think.

"Hah. Found it," Arisilde reported, leaning around the door. "Want to see?"

"Found what?" Nicholas stepped back into the parlor.

Arisilde was looking at the small framed mirror above the mantel. "It's a bit like that little job I did for you. The painting of *The Scribe*. This works on the same principle. I had the feeling there was something here, not something dangerous, just something...." He touched the mirror's gilt frame gently. "It's for speaking back and forth, I'm fairly certain, not spying. Hard to tell, though. It works like mine, with the spell all in the other end."

Nicholas studied the mirror, frowning. "You mean.... You told me the painting was a Great Spell."

Arisilde nodded vigorously. "Oh, it is."

"So the sorcerer who did this is capable of performing Great Spells?" Not Octave. If the spiritualist had been so powerful he would have had no need for a confidence game. Madame Talvera had said that Amelia Polacera had sent Octave away because his shadow in the ether was dark. Perhaps it hadn't been Octave's shadow she had seen.

Arisilde nodded again, preoccupied. "Yes, I suppose that's the case. He's asleep right now, I think, or perhaps in some sort of trance state. Whatever it is, I can't tell anything about him. If he wakes and looks in the mirror, I can get a better sense of him."

Feeling a prickle of unease crawl up his spine, Nicholas took hold of Arisilde's arm under the elbow and urged him gently to the door. Resisting the impulse to whisper, he said, "But if he wakes, he could see us, Ari."

Arisilde stared at him in puzzlement, reluctant to leave this interesting problem. "Oh, yes, of course." He started. "Oh, yes, that's right. We'd better go."

Nicholas took one last quick glance around the room, making sure nothing was disturbed. *Perhaps I shouldn't have brought Arisilde.* The other sorcerer might be able to sense his past presence here the same way Arisilde had sniffed out the spell in the mirror. *But if you hadn't brought Ari, you would never have known about the mirror and you might have lingered too long, or tried to confront Octave here.* And there was no telling what might have happened then.

Nicholas closed the door behind them and locked it, leaving the mirror to reflect only the dark, empty room.

8

This particular private dining chamber at Lusaude's
boasted a little bow-shaped balcony and over its brass
railing Nicholas had a good view of the famous grill
room below. The banquettes and chairs were of rich dark
wood and red drapes framed the engraved mirrors.
Women in extravagant gowns and men in evening dress
strolled on the marble floor, or sat at the tables between
stands of hothouse Parscian plants and Vienne bronzes,
their laughter and talk and the clatter of their plates echoing up to the figured ceiling. The air smelled of smoke,
perfume, salmon steak and truffle.

Nicholas took out his watch and checked the time,
again: the only nervous gesture he would allow himself
to make.

The private chamber was small and intimate, its walls
covered in red brocade and the mirror above the mantelpiece etched with names, dates, and mangled verses
by diamond rings. On the virgin white cloth of the table
stood an unopened absinthe bottle and a silver serving
set with the other paraphernalia necessary for drinking
it. Nicholas normally preferred wine but for this night
he favored the dangerous uncertainty of the wormwood
liqueur. For now he was drinking coffee, cut with seltzer
water.

He glanced up as the door opened. Reynard sauntered
in, crossing the room to lean heavily on the table.

"They've just arrived—they're getting out of the coaches now," he murmured.

His evening dress was a little disheveled and Nicholas could smell brandy on his breath but he knew Reynard was only pretending to be drunk. In the doorway behind him were several young men and women, laughing, leaning on each other tipsily. One of the young men was watching Reynard jealously. Nicholas pitched his voice too low for them to hear. "Very good. Will you be free to alert the others?"

"Yes." Reynard jerked his head to indicate his companions. "I'm about to shed the window dressing and head for the hotel." He took Nicholas's hand and dropped a lingering kiss on his fingers.

Nicholas lifted an eyebrow. "Reynard, really."

"It will make your reputation," Reynard explained. "I'm quite fashionable this week." He released him and turned to gesture airily to his audience. "Wrong room," he announced.

Nicholas smiled and sat back as Reynard left, pulling the door closed behind him. No one in the merry group would have the least bit of difficulty believing that Reynard had gone to an assignation when he disappeared from their company in the next half hour.

He lost his amusement as the main doors in the grill room opened to emit a new party from the foyer. Several men and women entered, among them Madame Dompeller. On the fringe of the group was Doctor Octave.

One of the things Reynard had discovered today was that Octave would be performing another circle tonight at the Dompeller town residence near the palace. It was not a house Reynard could gain entrance to, but he had also discovered that Madame Dompeller meant to finish the evening with a late supper at Lusaude's, the better to advertise the fact that she had just hosted a spiritual gathering.

Nicholas tugged the bellpull to summon the waiter and with a brief instruction handed him the folded square of notepaper he had prepared earlier.

Below, the Dompeller party was still greeting acquaintances and foiling the majordomo's attempt to lead them to their private dining room. Nicholas watched the waiter deliver the note to Octave.

The spiritualist read the note, refolded it and carefully tucked it away in a vest pocket. Then he excused himself to his puzzled hostess and moved quickly through the crowd, out of Nicholas's field of view.

In another moment, there was a knock at the door.

"Come," Nicholas said.

Octave stepped inside, quietly closing the door behind him. Nicholas gestured to the other brocaded armchair. "Do sit down."

Octave had received the note calmly enough but now his face was pallid and his eyes angry. He moved to the table and put his hand on the back of the empty chair. He had removed his gloves and his nails were dirty. He said, "I know who you are, now. You're Donatien. The Prefecture has searched for you since you stole the Romele Jewels five years ago."

"Ah, so you know. Your source of information is good. Too bad you can't afford to tell anyone." Nicholas put his cup and saucer aside and reached for the absinthe. "Would you care for a drink?" After last night, he had expected Octave to discover his other persona, sooner or later. The game was deep indeed and Octave wasn't the only player on the other side.

"And what is it that prevents me from speaking of what I know?" Octave was outwardly confident but sweat beaded on his pale forehead and the question was cautious.

He's wary now, too, Nicholas thought. *We've made explorations into each other's territory, and perhaps both of us have made discoveries that we had rather not.* "I've been to Valent House," Nicholas said simply. He opened the bottle and poured himself out a measure of the green liqueur. "You didn't say if you'd like a drink?"

There was a long silence. Nicholas didn't bother to look up. He busied himself with the absinthe, placing the perforated spoon containing chunks of hard sugar over the top of the glass, then adding a measure of water from the silver carafe to dissolve the sugar and make the intensely bitter stuff drinkable.

In one nervous motion Octave pulled the chair out and sat down. "Yes, thank you. I see we need to speak further."

"That's certainly one way of phrasing it." Nicholas poured out a measure for Octave, then took his own glass and leaned back in his chair. "I'll taste mine first, if that will make you more comfortable. Though I assure you that adding poison to absinthe is redundant."

Octave added sugar to his glass, his hand trembling just a little as he held the spoon and carafe. He said, "I realize now that I made a mistake in sending my messenger to you, the night of the ball. I thought you were attempting to meddle in my affairs."

"You're not a sorcerer yourself, are you? You didn't send that golem. Who did?"

"That's not your concern," Octave said, then he smiled, giving the impression of a man trying to settle a silly argument with a little cool reason. "I didn't realize your presence in Mondollot's cellars was due to the family jewels. I apologize, and we can consider the matter between us closed."

Nicholas's eyes narrowed. He tasted the liqueur. The bitter flavor was still intense, even watered down and sweetened. Drinking the stuff at strength or in quantity caused hallucinations and madness. He said, "It's too late for that, Doctor. I told you, I've seen Valent House. You seem to have left the place alive, which apparently isn't a feat that many people managed to accomplish."

"Then what do you want?" Octave leaned forward intently, his pose forgotten.

"I want him. The man who filled that house with corpses. His name, and his present location. I'll do the rest."

Octave looked away. For a moment, the expression in his protuberant eyes was hunted. "That may be more difficult than you think."

Nicholas didn't react. He had suspected that Octave

had a more powerful partner and now the good doctor had confirmed it. "But that's not all I want. I must also know how you obtained enough access to Doctor Edouard Viller's work to enable you to construct one of his devices." Mustn't place too much emphasis on that. He didn't want Octave to realize how angry he was over that theft of knowledge. *If he realizes that, he'll know I can't possibly mean to let him escape.* "I must know that, and I must know that you will stop using it to fleece people out of their dearly departed's lost treasures."

Octave eyed him resentfully. He took the folded square of notepaper out of his pocket and dropped it on the table. On it was written "*Marita Sun*, carrying gold coins for deposit with the Bank of Vienne from the Sultan of Tambarta." Octave said, "So this was not a bluff."

Nicholas lifted a brow, annoyed. "I don't bluff, Doctor." He picked up the note. "This ship sank last year. The fateful result of a complicated and rather dull transaction, involving an attempt to secure a loan from the Crown of Ile-Rien for the disadvantaged little nation of Tambarta. One lifeboat full of confused passengers and some debris survived. Only a crewman who went down with the ship could give an accurate enough description of her position to make salvage possible." He crumbled the note and met Octave's eyes. "You should have asked for longitude and latitude. The instructions he gave you were still too vague. It was too ambitious a project for you, Doctor. Better stick to Madame Bienardo's silver chests, stuck behind the old wine vault in the cellar, or the Viscount of Vencein's stock of gold plate buried in the garden by a mad grandfather—"

Octave struck the table with his fist, making the glasses jump and the silver spoons rattle on their tray. "So you know that much—"

"I know it all, Doctor." Nicholas allowed his disgust to show. "Edouard Viller found a way to meld machinery and magic, to create devices that would actually initiate spells on demand. His creations were so complex that no one has been able to duplicate them since he was framed for necromantic murder and hung. No one except you, that is.'' His lip curled. ''And you use them to ask the dead where they've buried the family silver, so you can come sneaking back and dig it up—''

Octave stood abruptly, knocking his chair back, breathing hard. His white face was shiny with sweat. ''What do you care? You're nothing but a common thief.''

''Oh, there's nothing common about me, Doctor.'' The words were out before Nicholas could stop them. He plunged on, knowing that to try to cover it would only draw more attention to his slip. ''What of the ghouls? Are they a byproduct of the process you use to communicate with the dead? And what of the man who needs to murder the way other men need this filth?'' He set the absinthe down on the table, hard enough for a little of the green liqueur to slosh out and stain the cloth. ''Is he a byproduct, too, or was he drawn to you by it? Can you get rid of him even if you want to?''

Octave drew back stiffly. ''If you want to live, you'll stay out of my affairs, Donatien.''

Nicholas rested his elbows on the table, smiling to himself. He waited until Octave's hand was on the door-knob before he said, ''Perhaps I don't want to live as badly as you do, Doctor. Think on that.''

Octave hesitated, then thrust open the door and stepped out.

Nicholas gave him a few moments head start, sitting at the table and tapping the arm of his chair impatiently, then stood and slipped out the door.

He took the back stairs, passing a couple of heavily veiled women on their way up to assignations, and went down the narrow hall, past doors into the kitchen that disgorged fragrant steam and harried staff. He paused in the alcove near the rear entrance, to collect his coat and deliver a generous payment to his attentive waiter, then stepped into the back alley. The lightest possible rain was falling out of the cloud-covered, nearly pitch dark sky, and with any luck the fog was already rising.

The dark cabriolet was waiting near the mouth of the

alley and one of the horses stamped impatiently as he approached. Crack was on the box with Devis and Nicholas knew part of their plan, at least, had already gone awry. He tore open the swing door and leaned inside. "Well?"

Madeline was within, wrapped up in a dark cloak. "Octave's coach is under a lamp, right next to the front entrance of Serduni's. There's such a crowd there that if we take the driver now we might as well do it on the stage at the Grand Opera during the third act of *Iragone*," she reported, sounding annoyed. "But I did get a good look at him."

Nicholas swore. *I knew that was going to be a problem on this street.* There was no help for it. "You'll do it at the hotel then, if he goes there," he said, and swung inside the cramped cab, pulling the little door closed. The windows had no glass, as was common on this type of conveyance, and it also made it far easier to see out in the dark streets.

"It will be easier there," Madeline admitted. She began to readjust her costume for the next part of the plan, removing the dowdy hat she wore and stuffing it into the bag at her feet. Her cloak fell open, revealing that she was already dressed in a man's dark suit. The cloak had completely concealed it and the large hat had allowed her to scout out the spiritualist's coach without anyone being the wiser. "Did you frighten Octave?" she asked, pulling a folded greatcoat out of her bag.

"He was already frightened." Nicholas scrunched over as far as he could to give her room and looked out the window, though the alley wall cut off any view of the front entrance of Lusaude's. Crack and Devis would be watching for a signal from the man posted across the street. "Where do you keep family jewelry?"

"In a strongbox in that little cupboard under the third floor stairs. Why?"

"Not you personally, Madeline, but in general."

"Oh. In a safe, of course."

"Upstairs."

"Of course. In my dressing room, I should think. At

least, that's where most of the ladies I know keep theirs.'' Madeline fell back on the seat, a little breathless from wrestling with the voluminous cloak and the heavy coat in the confined space.

Nicholas glanced back at her. In the darkened coach, it was difficult to see how well the disguise worked, but she had done this before and he knew how convincing she could be. "Octave inferred we were in Mondollot House's cellars to steal the Mondollot jewels."

"That's ridiculous. Can you see the Duchess's lady's maid trooping down to those dank cellars every time the woman wants to wear her emeralds to dinner? Why, she goes to formal court at least seven times a month and she has to wear the presentation pieces then or the Queen would be terribly offended. . . ." She tapped her lower lip, thoughtfully. "He didn't know about the gold she was hiding, did he?"

"No, I don't think so. He hadn't even tried to persuade the Duchess to let him contact the late Duke yet, so he didn't find out about any hidden wealth that way. He was searching for something he already knew was there."

"Did he find it, I wonder?"

"Someone found something. There was that empty room that had been broken into, with the plinth that had been recently occupied. It was originally part of the cellar of Ventarin House, whose only claim on history is that it was once the home of Gabard Ventarin, who was court sorcerer two hundred years ago, give or take a decade or two."

"So he was after something buried under the house of a long-dead sorcerer?" Madeline's voice was worried. "That sounds rather . . . dangerous."

"It does, indeed." Nicholas leaned out the window, unable to contain his impatience. There was still no sign of Octave. "If he calmly sits down to dinner with the Dompeller party—"

"We'll feel very foolish."

Crack leaned down toward the window then and whispered, "He's out front, waving at his man."

Nicholas sat back against the cushions. "At last. He must have stopped to make his excuses to Madame Dompeller. It means he's not exactly panic-stricken."

"Then I don't suppose he's going to run straight to his accomplices."

"No, but that was a forlorn hope, anyway. If he was that incautious, he wouldn't have abandoned Valent House last night when he realized someone was following him." He heard the harness jingle and the cabriolet jerked into motion, moving out of the alley into the crowded street. He had reasoned that if Octave didn't immediately panic and head for his accomplices' hiding place, he would return to his hotel, leave his coach and driver, and go on foot.

Devis was adept at this game and his team quicker and more responsive than the nags that usually drove hire carriages. He kept one or two other vehicles between the cab and Octave's coach while always keeping the quarry in sight.

Nicholas had no trouble recognizing the streets they were on tonight. "So it is to be the hotel." If his accusations had failed to panic the good doctor, what they were about to do would not.

Octave's coach reined in at the walk in front of the Hotel Galvaz's impressive gaslit facade. Devis followed his instructions, driving on by. Nicholas, shielding his face with a hand on his hat brim, caught sight of Octave hurrying between the dancing caryatids on either side of the entrance.

The cab turned the corner, drove past the hire stables the hotel used and took the next corner into an alley. There it rolled to a stop and Madeline fished a top hat out of the bag at her feet and said, "I'm on. Wish me luck."

Nicholas caught her hand, pulled her to him, and kissed her far more briefly than he wanted to. "Luck."

Madeline slipped out of the cab and hurried back down the alley, Crack jumping down from the box to follow her.

*   *   *

Madeline adjusted her cravat, tipped her hat back at a jaunty angle, and lengthened her stride as she walked to the head of the alley. Her hair was bound up tightly around her head, under a short wig and her hat. Subtle application of theatrical makeup coarsened her features and changed the line of her brows, and pouches in her cheeks thickened her face. Padding helped conceal her figure under the vest, coat, and trousers, and the bulky greatcoat capped the disguise. As long as she didn't remove her gloves, she would be fine.

It was important that the coachman be removed without any sort of attention being drawn to the act. Octave might have accomplices within the hotel and they didn't want to alert them. She walked past the open stable doors, lamplight and loud talk spilling out onto the muddy stones. Behind her, she knew Crack would be taking up a position at the head of the alley.

She rounded the corner, passing under the weathered arabesques and curlicues of the building's carved façade. A large group was exiting a line of carriages in the street. She mingled with them as she climbed the steps and entered the hotel.

She made her way across the brightly lit foyer and up the stairs to the Grand Salon. The room was decorated with the usual profusion of carved and gilded panelling, with large mirrors rising to the swagged cornice. An enormous arrangement of plants and flowers dominated the center and reached almost to the bottom dangles of the chandelier. There were a number of men in evening dress scattered about the room in conversational groups. None of them was Octave.

Madeline made her way to the back wall, which was open to a view of the rear foyer below and the grand staircase. She had to make sure Octave left before she proceeded with her part of the plan.

Leaning on the carved balustrade, she didn't spot Reynard until he stepped up beside her. "He's gone up to his rooms," Reynard murmured. "If this is to work, he should be down again in a moment."

"It'll work," Madeline said. "He'll want to tell his

friends that they've been found out.'' If Octave saw Reynard after the experience at the Eversets' circle, the doctor would surely become suspicious, but no one else in their organization was as well qualified to idle in the salons of an expensive hotel as Reynard was. Madeline, even in her respectable dark suit, was drawing some attention from a porter who was crossing the salon. It was because she hadn't given up her greatcoat to the cloakroom and so obviously wasn't a guest. She swore under her breath as the porter approached. This hotel had enough trouble with its reputation, it couldn't afford to allow in a possible pickpocket or sneakthief.

Reynard spotted the man approaching and put a hand on Madeline's shoulder, drawing her to him. The porter veered away.

''Thank you, I—'' She tensed. ''There he is.''

Octave was hurrying down the grand staircase, having changed his evening dress for a plainer suit and cloak.

Reynard didn't turn to look. He was pretending to straighten Madeline's cravat. ''We have all the entrances covered, but I suspect he'll go for the back. He doesn't strike me as being overly endowed with imagination.''

Madeline leaned one elbow on the balustrade, standing as if coyly enjoying Reynard's attentions, watching Octave until he disappeared below her level of view. A moment or two, and the spiritualist appeared in the marble-floored chamber below them, moving briskly toward the doors that led to the back street entrance. ''Right again,'' she said.

''I'll walk you out.''

There was a crowd around the front entrance now and they drew several curious looks. ''You must tell me who your tailor is,'' Reynard said to her, as if continuing a conversation, with just the right amount of amused condescension in his tone.

Madeline kept her expression innocently flattered and then they were out on the street.

Madeline stopped at the stable door and Reynard kept walking. Nicholas's cabriolet, with Devis at the reins, was already at the mouth of the alley. Madeline waited until Reynard had stepped inside and the cab turned up the street before she casually strolled into the stables. She made her way past the carriage stalls to the wooden stairs that led up to the second floor. The liveried hotel servants ignored her, assuming she was someone's coachman or servant.

The stairs opened onto a low-ceilinged chamber that seemed to serve as a common room for the men quartered here. It was crowded and the air was warm and damp and smelled strongly of horse from the stalls below. There was a dice game in progress on the straw-strewn floorboards and Madeline circled it, scanning the participants for Octave's coachman. She had gotten a good look at him in the street outside Lusaude's. He was a short, square-built man with coarse, heavy features and dead eyes.

He wasn't among the dice players. *Well, he didn't look the sociable sort.* No, there he was, standing against the far wall, alone. Madeline edged her way through the crowd, catching snatches of conversation in a variety of different accents, until she was near enough to her quarry for a few private words.

Much to Nicholas's consternation, she hadn't planned exactly how to lure the coachman into their clutches. She liked carefully planned schemes as much as he did, but with no prior knowledge of what the man might be doing, it was impossible to tell how best to proceed.

Besides, she did some of her finest acting under the pressure of desperation. "I have a message," she said, pitching her voice low and giving herself a faint Aderassi accent.

He eyed her, a sulky expression on his broad face. "From who?" he asked, suspicious.

Madeline realized she could say "From the doctor," but so could anyone else and she had no corroborating detail to give him. Nicholas had postulated the involvement of a powerful sorcerer, and Arisilde had confirmed it when he had found the enspelled mirror in Octave's hotel room. Taking a stab in the dark, she said, "The doctor's friend."

The man blinked and actually went white around the mouth. He pushed away from the wall and she led the way back across the room to the stairs.

She lengthened her stride as they reached the street, glancing back at him to motion him along, keeping her head down as if she feared pursuit. He quickened his steps to keep up with her.

She rounded the corner into the alley, passing a shadow hunched against the wall that she hoped was Crack. Blocking the alley was the back end of Cusard's ostler's wagon.

She turned, gesturing to it as if about to speak, saw the man's brows lower in suspicion. Then Crack moved, silent and quick, getting a forearm around the larger man's throat before he could cry out.

The coachman tried to throw his attacker off, then tried to slam him against the alley wall, but Crack held on grimly and the struggling was only making the stranglehold work faster. The only sound was wheezing grunts from the coachman and the scrape of their feet on the muddy stones.

Madeline kept an eye on the mouth of the alley, but no one passed by. Finally the coachman slumped limply to the ground and she hurried forward to help Crack haul him to the wagon.

Following a nervous man on foot wasn't as easy as following a nervous man in a coach and four. Nicholas had Devis keep the cabriolet hanging back as far as possible. He had chosen it specifically with this in mind, since it was an unobtrusive vehicle and tended to blend in to the city streets.

It didn't make waiting any easier.

"Really," Reynard said finally. "I'd rather you fidget than sit there like a bomb about to explode."

"Sorry," Nicholas said. The neighborhood they were entering was not quite what he had expected. The buildings were dark on either side of the wide street, the infrequent gas lamps wreathed in night mist, but this was a business district, heavily populated during the day. The traffic was light and they might have to get out and follow Octave on foot. "There's something wrong here."

"He didn't see me and even if he had spotted Madeline in that get-up, I don't see how he could have known who she was. I almost didn't recognize her and I knew what to expect."

"That mirror in Octave's room," Nicholas said. "If his sorcerer warned him through it. . . ."

"But how would he know? Is he following us?"

"Damned if I know." He shook his head. "I wish I could hand this over to someone else. This is too complicated, too urgent for me to deal with when all my attention and my resources should be devoted to the plot against Montesq."

"The sooner this is over with the better," Reynard agreed. "I'm a little confused as to how the Master Criminal of Ile-Rien ended up hot on the trail of a petty confidence man and his friend the murderer, and I was along from the first."

"Please don't call me a Master Criminal. It's overly dramatic. And inaccurate. And the bastard has one of Edouard's spheres, that's why I want him." *He's using Edouard's work to murder innocent people,* Nicholas thought. *I can't let that go on one moment more.* If Edouard was still alive he would have been leading the chase himself; he had never meant his work to be used to harm anyone.

Reynard was silent a moment, what little light there was from the street limning his strong profile. "I'm thinking of Valent House. Who could you possibly hand that over to? A sorcerer?"

Nicholas hesitated, though he wasn't sure why. "Inspector Ronsarde, of course. If he's good enough to almost catch us—"

"He's good enough to catch Octave and his friends. Of course. It's too bad you can't simply drop the whole matter on his lap, though I admit I would like to be in at the end."

It was too bad, but such a course was impossible.

Octave knew too much about them. If Ronsarde found Octave, he found Donatien/Nicholas Valiarde, and if he found Nicholas, he found everyone else. Nicholas tapped his fingers impatiently on the leather sill of the cab window. *I want this done and over with. I want to concentrate on Montesq. We're so close. . . .*

Reynard added, "Though I'm surprised to hear you say it."

Nicholas frowned at him. "Why?"

"You do have a tendency to become . . . unduly consumed with certain things, don't you? Are you sure you aren't putting off that plan against Montesq?"

"What do you mean?"

"When Montesq is hanged—a laudable goal in itself—that means you no longer have an excuse."

"I don't need an excuse." Nicholas kept looking out the window, watching the damp mostly empty street, making sure that was still Octave stepping out of the shadows under the next lamp. Reynard was one of the few people who would say such things to him, but Reynard wasn't afraid of anything. And if Nicholas became "unduly consumed" with things he felt Reynard erred in the other direction, by pretending not to care until it burned him away within. At least Nicholas wore his fire on the outside. "We all do what we have to do, don't we?"

Reynard was silent a moment, his face enigmatic in the shadows. He finally said, "I worry about you, that's all. All this can only go so far."

They reached a cross street that seemed completely deserted and Nicholas tapped on the ceiling, signalling for Devis to draw rein.

Nicholas waited until Octave turned the corner then swung the door open and stepped out. He motioned to Devis to stay back here, where there were still a few passing coaches and people to explain the cab's presence, and he and Reynard hurried down the dark street.

They saw Octave still moving away as they reached the corner and followed him cautiously, avoiding the infrequent pools of gaslight from the flickering street lamps. This street was completely deserted, the buildings lining each side as silent and dark as immense tombs in some giant's mortuary. Nicholas's walking stick was a sword cane and for tonight's work Reynard carried a revolver in the pocket of his greatcoat.

They stopped as Octave crossed the street and turned down an alley at the side of a tall, bleak building, a deserted manufactory that was solid and square, with dozens of unlovely chimneys thrusting up from the flat roof. Stone steps led up to a wooden double door, the street entrance, but Octave had gone down the alley. "It can't be," Nicholas muttered.

"I agree," Reynard whispered. "Too many people about during the day. Why, we're only two streets over from the Counting Row."

"The windows are boarded up," Nicholas said thoughtfully. "I don't think he saw us."

"Perhaps there's something behind it. We'd better move or we'll lose him."

I suppose, Nicholas thought. He smelled a trap. *Perhaps it would be best to spring it*. They crossed the silent street and Nicholas said, "He didn't see us, but still he knew he was being followed."

"Yes, dammit," Reynard said. "Someone could have warned him, but the only time he was out of our sight was when he went up to his hotel room. I suppose he could have been warned through that mirror thing you found, but how would they know about us?"

"If it was a sorcerer—a real sorcerer and not a damn fool like Octave—he'd know." And only a real sorcerer could have created that mirror. Nicholas had deliberately staged the meeting at Lusaude's to keep Octave from having any time to plan or prepare or think, but someone hadn't needed time.

They reached the side alley and went down it, ignoring the mud and trash their boots disturbed. The door was a small one, set into a slight recess in the stone wall. It was almost too dark to see it, the distant street lamps providing little illumination in these depths. Nicholas touched the door lightly, with the back of his hand, but felt nothing. He did the same to the metal handle, again without effect. *I wish Arisilde were here*, he thought, and slowly tried the handle.

He exerted just enough pressure to find that it turned. He stopped and stepped back. "It's not locked," he told Reynard. "Fancy that."

"Oh, dear. The good doctor does have a gift for the obvious."

"But he set this trap under instructions from someone else. It's that person I worry about." Nicholas rubbed his chin thoughtfully, then felt in the various pockets of his suit and greatcoat, mentally inventorying the various tools he had brought with him. Whoever had arranged this trap hadn't had much time; he knew it took hours, often days for the casting of the Great Spells, even if the sorcerer already knew the architecture he was trying to create. *And that would be a terrible amount of work simply to eliminate us. Especially when they have other resources at their command.*

He found what he was looking for, a small holiday candle, ideal for causing mass confusion in snatch robberies in crowded places. "Step back," he told Reynard. "And watch the door."

Nicholas took out a box of matches and lit the candle. It sparked in the dimness, lighting the alley around them, its white light casting stark shadows on the dark walls. Then he flung the door open and tossed it inside.

The candle sparked, sputtered and burst, emitting dozens of tiny flares that lit up a dingy foyer, floorboards thick with dust and spiderwebs depending from the mottled plasterboard. It also cast reflections into a dozen pairs of eyes, some crouched near the floor, some hanging from the ceiling or apparently perched halfway up the wall.

Nicholas heard Reynard swear under his breath. He heartily agreed that they had seen enough. He yanked the door closed, took out a short metal bar used for prying at reluctant locks and thrust it through the handle to wedge it against the wooden frame. It wouldn't last long, but they only needed a short head start.

As they reached the street Nicholas thought he heard the door burst open behind them and a frustrated snarl. That might have been his imagination. He knew the pairs of eyes, arrested by the brilliance of the sparking candle, had not.

The house was in an old carriage court called Lethe Square, off Erin Street across the river. It was only two stories and seemed on the verge of tumbling down. Surrounded by busy tenements with small shops crammed into the lower floors and right on the edge of a better district, it was an area where there were comings and goings at every hour of the night and the residents didn't pay much attention to new faces in the neighborhood.

The coach let Nicholas and Reynard off at the top of the alley, then headed for the stables at the end of the street. The infrequent gas lights turned the rising ground fog to yellow and cast odd shadows against the walls. There were other people in the street or passing through the alley to the courts beyond: tradesmen or day workers hurrying home, a few prostitutes and idlers, a group that was obviously down here to slum among the cabarets and brandy houses, despite their dress and attempts at aping the manners of the working class. *Why don't they go to Riverside if they're so interested in seeing how the lower orders live*, Nicholas thought, as he and Reynard hurried up the alley. *I'm sure our neighbors across the river would love their company*. . . . The answer of course was that this was a safe slum, filled with the working poor and those living in genteel poverty. Riverside was something else altogether.

They crossed the old carriage court, one side of which was occupied by a lively brandy house and the others by closed shops. Nicholas stopped at the stoop of the little house and knocked twice on the door.

After a moment it opened and Cusard stepped back to let them enter. "Any luck?" he asked.

"Yes and no," Nicholas answered, heading down the short hallway.

"Yes, we're still alive, and no, he didn't lead us anywhere useful," Reynard elaborated. "It was a trap."

Cusard swore under his breath as he locked the door behind him. "We've done a bit better. You won't believe what we been hearing from this poor bastard."

"I'd better believe it, for his sake." Nicholas opened the parlor door.

Inside was a small room, lit by one flickering lamp on a battered deal table. There was one window, shuttered and boarded over on the outside. Madeline was here, leaning against the dingy wall with her arms folded, still in male dress. She met his eyes and smiled grimly.

Lamane stood near the door and Crack, who was cleaning his fingernails with a knife, near the prisoner. Octave's driver sat in a straight-backed chair, blindfolded, his hands bound behind the chair back.

Reynard pulled the door closed and Nicholas nodded to Madeline. She said, "Tell us again. Who killed the people we found at Valent House?" Her voice was low and husky. Nicholas would not have recognized it as hers, or even as female, if he hadn't known her. Sometimes he forgot how good an actress she really was.

"The doctor's friend." The driver's voice was hoarse from fear. Nicholas recognized it as the voice of the man who had driven Octave's coach last night, who had climbed down from the vehicle to search for him along the muddy riverbank.

"Why did he kill them?"

"For his magic."

Nicholas frowned at Madeline, who shook her head minutely, telling him to wait. The driver continued, "He needs it. It's how he does his spells."

Nothing we didn't already know, Nicholas thought. Arisilde's explanations had been more cogent. "And who is this man?" Madeline asked.

"I told you, I don't know his name. I don't see him much. Before he showed up, it was just the doctor and us." Beyond the fear, the man sounded sulky, as if he resented the intrusion of the "doctor's friend." "Me and the two others, his servants, I told you about them. The doctor held the circles for money. We started in Duncanny and he used that gadget he has."

Nicholas pressed his lips together. The "gadget" must be Edouard's device. Madeline asked, "How did he get the gadget?"

"I don't know. He had it before I came into it. He paid us well. Then his friend showed up once we were in Vienne, and everything changed. He's a sorcerer and you have to do what he says. I didn't have nothing to do with killing anybody, that was all him, for his magic."

Magic which was necromancy of the very worst kind. Nicholas remembered the melting of the plaster and wood on the walls in that horrible room and Arisilde's opinion on it. He had been trying to decide what to do with the driver once the man had told them everything he knew of use. *He was in that house. He knew what was happening.* These facts made the decision considerably easier.

"But Octave himself isn't a sorcerer," Madeline was saying.

"No, he just had that gadget. But his friend is. He knows things too. He told the doctor Donatien was after him, and it was the doctor's fault, for mixing into things he didn't understand."

"Where are Octave and his friend now?"

"I don't know."

Crack reacted for the first time, snorting derisively. The driver flinched and protested desperately, "I don't. I told you. We split up after they said we had to leave Valent House. I been with the doctor. He knows, but he didn't tell me."

Nicholas glanced at Crack who shrugged noncommittally. *It's very likely the truth*, Nicholas decided. It sounded as if Octave's former compatriots were being increasingly cut out of the scheme.

"What did he want in the cellars of Mondollot House?"

"I don't know," the driver said miserably, certain this further protestation of ignorance wouldn't be believed either. "I know he didn't find it. He told the doctor it must have been moved, when the Duke rebuilt the house."

That was why Octave had tried to arrange the circle with the Duchess. Octave's sorcerer must have entered the house first, to break the wards and allow the ghouls to breach the cellar and search it. Somehow the creatures must have communicated to him that the search was unsuccessful, so Octave was sent to attempt to arrange the circle to speak to the old Duke of Mondollot. But something had been removed from the plinth in that room and not long before he and Crack had arrived. Did Octave's sorcerer friend have a rival for this prize, whatever it was? A rival who had also broken into Mondollot House that night? *No, we would have seen signs of him.*

A sudden noise startled him, a muffled report like a pistol shot in the next room. Nicholas was the only one who didn't reach spasmodically for a weapon in an inner coat pocket. Reynard was closest to the door and tore it open to reveal Cusard, standing unhurt in the center of the outer room, his own pistol drawn.

"Was that you?" Reynard demanded.

Confused, Cusard shook his head. "No, I think it was from outside."

Muffled cracks and bangs erupted from the direction of the street door. "Stay here and keep an eye on him," Nicholas told Madeline. She nodded and Crack handed her his extra pistol.

Reynard was already heading down the short hall to the outer door, Cusard behind him. There was another outside door in the disused pantry at the back of the house. Nicholas motioned for Lamane to cover it and stepped to the center of the parlor so he could see down the front hall. Crack moved up beside him. Vienne lived up to its unsettled past at frequent intervals, but gunfire in the streets was rare; this was more likely to be a trap arranged by Octave.

Reynard opened the spydoor and peered through it. Cusard, standing behind him, craned his neck to look over his shoulder. "Well?" Nicholas asked.

"A lot of people standing about and staring," Reynard muttered. He unbolted the door and stepped out, moving a few paces into the court.

Nicholas swallowed a curse at this incaution, but no shots rang out. He stepped into the archway. Through the open door at the end of the dim hall he could see a few figures milling in the center of the court. "Hey there, did you hear that too?" someone called.

"Yes," Reynard answered. "Did it come from the street?"

Suddenly the floor moved under Nicholas's feet and he grabbed the wall for support. Reynard and the others standing in the court staggered. Nicholas felt splinters sink into his hand as the wood and plaster cracked from the stress of the shifting foundation. It was the most disturbing sensation he had ever experienced, as if something deep inside the earth had suddenly turned liquid. He thought of stories naturalists had brought back from Parscia and further places, of the earth moving and cracking; he thought of the spell Arisilde had made to hide valuables in the warehouse. Then the sounds came again and this time he heard them clearly. Not muffled shots, they were cracks. The heavy stones that paved the court, snapping like twigs under some pressure from below. The sound was coming from behind him now, from under the house.

Madeline, Nicholas thought. He turned, plunging across the moving floor toward the parlor. He made it two paces before the floorboards in front of him seemed to explode. He shielded his arms as wood splinters and clods of dirt flew upward.

Sprawled only a few feet from the gaping hole in the floor, Nicholas felt cold air rush past. The single lamp winked out. The house was shaking, groaning as it shifted on the damaged foundation. Before he could try to stand, something massive shot up through the broken flooring and struck the ceiling.

Nicholas pushed himself away until his back struck the wall. All he could see of the thing was a dark shape against the light-colored walls, a deceptively large shadow in the dim light coming through the still-open door. He knew Crack had been standing near him, but he couldn't hear anyone else moving in the room.

The thing shifted and the wooden floor cracked in protest. *It's hunting for us*, Nicholas thought. Standing up in the small room would be suicidal. He edged along the wall, toward the archway that led into the entry way. If Crack was still here but unconscious, he would be near that narrow opening.

He didn't see the creature move but suddenly a more solid darkness loomed over him and Nicholas threw himself sideways, rolling away from it. He heard it slam into the boards just behind him, felt the tremor that travelled through what was left of the floor and upped his estimate of its size. He scrambled forward, knowing it would have him in the next instant. A door was suddenly flung open, throwing light across the wreck of the room. Nicholas fell against the side of the archway and looked back.

He caught only a glimpse of gray skin, knobby and rough like stone. It moved, turning away from him toward the light. A figure appeared in the door and fired three shots, loud as cannon blasts in the confined space, then the light went out again.

The thing flung itself against the door. *That was Madeline firing at it, she's still in that room.* Nicholas staggered, grabbed a broken chair. He had to distract it to give her time to escape.

Someone caught hold of the back of his collar and flung him away, back toward the outer door. He was outside, staggering on the pavement in front of the house, before he saw that it was Crack.

People were screaming, running. Nicholas tore himself free and looked through the door. He ducked back immediately. Dirt clods and shards of stone were flying out of the interior of the house, striking the steps and the court. Crack caught his arm and tried to drag him away. "She's still in there!" Nicholas shouted, twisting his arm to free himself.

They both must have remembered the boarded-up

window at the same moment and instead of fighting they were running for the corner of the little house, knocking into each other in their haste. Lighter on his feet, Nicholas reached it first and as he dug at the first board to rip it free he heard breaking glass from inside the room. *She's alive, she's breaking in the window from inside*, he thought, tearing down the board. Crack was helping, then Reynard was there, taller than both of them and able to get a better grip on the top boards, then Lamane caught up to them.

The last board came free and Madeline launched herself through the window and into Nicholas's arms, the last glass fragments tearing at her clothes. Over her shoulder as he pulled her free he saw the body of the driver, lying in the open doorway of the room. One of the walls was bowed inward and as the lamp flickered and went out Nicholas heard the crash of the ceiling coming down. Then they were all running down the alley toward the street.

Nicholas realized Cusard wasn't with them. He knew the old man had gotten out of the house. He had been right behind Reynard. He wondered if Cusard had panicked and left them; he would've thought Lamane would break before the old thief.

They came out of the alley into the street. The din from the carriage court was audible and people, a few tradesmen, a couple of puzzled prostitutes, were stopping and staring, though coach traffic was still moving. Others were standing in doorways or peering out windows. Nicholas saw Devis on the box of their cabriolet heading toward them, and behind the smaller vehicle Cusard driving his bulky wagon. More relieved than he liked to admit, Nicholas thought, *of course, he went to warn Devis we needed to make a quick escape.*

Nicholas pointed at the wagon and Lamane ran for it without further need of instruction. "What happened?" Reynard was asking Madeline.

"I cut the driver loose," she said. She had lost her hat and when she ran a hand through her disordered hair, forgetting for the moment her men's clothing, the dark curls tumbled down to her shoulders. "I wanted to give him a chance. It couldn't get in the door, but it started striking the wall and one of the beams hit him."

"Not here," Nicholas said, urgently. "Later."

The cabriolet drew even with them and they tumbled in.

9

"I never got a good look at it," Madeline confessed. "Did you?"

"No, it was too dark." They were a good distance from the ill-fated court, almost to the river. Reynard had told them how Crack had been thrown out the front door when the creature had first burst through the floor; the henchman had kept the others from running back down the passage, creeping slowly down it himself to retrieve Nicholas. *And probably saved all our lives*, Nicholas thought. If anyone had run into that room with a lamp, none of them would have had a chance. For someone who had been accused of killing several men in an unprovoked rage, Crack was awfully good at keeping his head in a crisis. It was too bad the judges at his trial hadn't bothered to discern that fact.

Once they had crossed the river, Nicholas tapped on the ceiling for Devis to stop. They drew rein in an unoccupied side street and he stepped out of the cabriolet to consult briefly with the coachman and to tell Cusard and Lamane to break off and return to the warehouse.

He climbed back into the little vehicle, noticing for the first time he had splinters in his hands from ripping at the board-covered window.

Madeline had heard his directions to Devis and now asked, "We're going to Arisilde?"

"Yes. We need to know how that thing found us." *We need help*, Nicholas thought. He settled back into the seat as the cab jolted forward. Cusard's wagon passed them, Lamane lifting one hand in a nervous salute as the cumbersome vehicle turned down a cross street. Nicholas had to assume everyone who had been in the house was now known to Octave's sorcerer; they had to keep moving until he could get Arisilde's protection for them.

"Is that worth it?" Reynard said. He had only met the sorcerer a few times in the past years and hadn't known Arisilde when he was at Lodun and at the height of his powers. "I mean, will it be of any use?"

"He was well enough today at Valent House when he destroyed one of Octave's ghouls. We'll just have to hope he hasn't succumbed since this afternoon," Nicholas said, but thought *fond hope.*

"You think that thing is going to try again?" Reynard asked, watching him.

"It's the safest assumption to make," Nicholas admitted.

Madeline glanced up from her contemplation of the dark street. "I think it's the only assumption to make."

No word of the disturbance across the river had reached the Street of Flowers and the Philosopher's Cross yet and all was as usual, colored lights lit over the market stalls and gay laughter and tinny music in the cool night air. Nicholas stepped down from the cab in the dark alley next to Arisilde's tenement and immediately felt something was out of place. He turned to help Madeline down and she gripped his arm, her dark eyes worried. "Something's wrong, can you feel it?" she asked.

He didn't want to answer her. He waited until Reynard had climbed out of the coach and then he started for the door.

The concierge was gone again. Nicholas took the rickety steps two and three at a time.

Arisilde's door was in the right place and he banged on it peremptorily. He glanced back as the others reached the landing.

He heard footsteps in the apartment, then the door

opened to reveal Isham, Arisilde's Parscian servant. For an instant Nicholas felt a rush of relief, then he saw the man's face.

Isham had always seemed ageless, like a wall-carving on one of the temples of his country, but now he looked old. The dark skin of his face seemed to sag, showing the network of wrinkles as fine gray lines and his eyes were wretched.

Nicholas said, "What's happened?"

Isham motioned for him to follow and turned back down the little hall. Nicholas pushed past him, stopped at the door to the bedchamber.

The low-ceilinged windowless room smelled of a bizarre variety of incenses, the tiny dresser and cabinet were crammed with books and papers, the carpet dusty and the wide bed disordered. Arisilde lay on that bed, a colorfully patterned coverlet drawn up to his chest. It was almost as Nicholas had left him last night, except that now Arisilde wasn't breathing.

Nicholas went to stand next to the bed. He touched Arisilde's hands, folded across the coverlet. The skin was still warm. This close he could see Arisilde was still breathing, but it was a slow, shallow respiration.

"I fear he will die soon," Isham said bitterly, in perfectly pronounced Rienish. Nicholas realized he had never heard the man speak before. "The drugs he took, they make the heart weak. I think it is only his great power that keeps him alive."

"When did it happen?" Madeline asked from the doorway.

Isham turned to her. "He seemed well this morning. He went out, I don't know where—"

"He was with me," Nicholas said. He was surprised at how normal his voice sounded. He touched Arisilde's face and then, moving like an automaton, he lifted the eyelids and felt for the pulse at the sorcerer's wrist. There had been times when he had wished Arisilde dead and thought it would be a welcome release from the torment the sorcerer put himself, and everyone close to him, through. But when he had stood in the doorway looking on what had seemed a lifeless body. . . . *Maybe it's not fear for Ari*, he thought, bitterly. *Maybe it's fear for yourself*. Arisilde was the last vestige of his old life. If he was gone, Nicholas Valiarde, sometime scholar and only son of Edouard Viller, was gone too, and nothing would be left but Donatien. "Have you sent for a physician?"

"I sent the person who watches the downstairs door for one, but he has not yet returned." Isham spread his hands, resigned. "It is late and he will have difficulty convincing anyone to come tonight. I would have gone myself, but I thought I would have even more difficulty."

As a Parscian immigrant, Isham would be lucky to get a decent physician's servants to even open the door to speak to him, especially at this time of night. And the concierge probably knew only the local quack healers. Even an honest hedgewitch would be better than that. Nicholas said, "Reynard. . . ."

"I'll go." Reynard was already moving toward the door. "There's a Doctor Brile who lives not far from here. He's not a sorcerer-healer but he's a member of the Royal Physicians College and he owes me a favor."

Nicholas looked down at Arisilde again as Reynard left. "Was it the drugs?" he asked roughly.

"I don't know." Isham shook his head. "When he came back today he seemed tired, but not sickly. He was pursuing his researches, so I went out. When I came back, I saw that he was in bed, with the lamps extinguished." Isham rubbed the bridge of his nose, wincing. "I didn't notice at first. I thought he was sleeping. Then I felt the spells, the wards and the little charms, start to fade and grow cold. Then I came in and lit the lamp, and saw."

Nicholas frowned. "You're a sorcerer too?" he asked the old man. "I didn't realize. . . ."

"Not a sorcerer. I am *interlerari*, for which there is no proper word in Rienish. I have some gift of power and I study the gift of those greater in power than I, so I may teach. I came here from Parscia to study with him." He looked up. "I sent a wire to you at Coldcourt but they told me it would not be delivered until later tonight. Did it reach you so soon?"

"No, we were already on our way," Nicholas answered, and thought, *How many years have you known Isham, and yet not known him at all?* Had he been that single-minded?

For a while there was nothing to do but wait. Not long after Reynard left the concierge returned empty-handed, unable to convince even one of the local quacks to come. "They know what he is," the man explained with a shrug. He had a thick Aderassi accent and a philosophical outlook. "I tell them he's a good wizard, only a little crazy and not in a bad way, but they're afraid."

Nicholas had tipped him more generously than he had originally intended for that and sent him to the nearest telegraph station with a coded message for Cusard at the warehouse. If Arisilde could no longer protect himself, Nicholas didn't want to leave him unguarded. His own presence here was dangerous enough.

Madeline and Isham had gone into the other room and Nicholas sat alone on the edge of Arisilde's bed until an unfamiliar footstep startled him. An older man in a dark greatcoat carrying a doctor's bag stood in the bedchamber's doorway, eyeing the poorly-lit room somewhat warily. Then his gaze fell on Arisilde and the wariness changed to a professional blankness. Stepping into the room, he said, "What does he take?"

"Opium, mostly, isn't it?" Reynard said, following the doctor in and glancing at Nicholas for confirmation.

Nicholas nodded. "And ether."

The doctor sighed in weary disgust and opened his bag.

Nicholas waited tensely through the examination, leaning on a bureau in a far corner of the room. Isham had moved quietly to assist the doctor and probably also to keep a cautious eye on what he did to Arisilde, but Nicholas could tell Brile seemed more than competent. Reynard came to stand next to him and Nicholas asked, low-voiced, "How did you get him to come here?"

"Threatened to tell his wife," Reynard answered casually.

Nicholas regarded him with a raised brow. "Well, no, not really," Reynard admitted. "He was attached to my regiment and caught a bullet when we were in retreat from Leis-thetla, and I stopped to throw him over the back of a donkey, or something, I can't recall, so he feels he owes me a favor. But the other makes a better story, don't you think?"

"Occasionally I forget that you're not as debauched as you'd like everyone to believe," Nicholas murmured.

Reynard pretended to seem disturbed. "Keep it to yourself, would you?"

Brile sat back, shaking his head. "It's not the opium. He doesn't have the signs of it. Oh, I can tell he's an addict and that it's destroyed his health, but it's not what's causing this, or at least it isn't directly responsible. This is some sort of seizure or catatonia." He looked up at them. "I'll need to send my driver to my surgery."

Reynard nodded. "Write down what you need and I'll take it to him."

More waiting, that meant. Nicholas walked out, into the main room, unable to hold still for another moment.

The curtains torn down during Arisilde's fit the other night had been replaced and a fire was burning, but the room still seemed cold and empty. Madeline was sitting in front of the hearth, near a writing desk overflowing with paper, books, pens and other trifles. She looked up as Nicholas came in. "Well?"

"He says it doesn't appear to be the drugs, at least."

Madeline frowned. "I'm not sure whether to be cheered by that or not. It doesn't leave us with any comfortable options. Could it have been Octave and his sorcerer, attacking him as they did us?"

Nicholas shook his head. "I don't think so. If Arisilde had fought a battle, we would have known it." The entire city would have known it. No, he could see what had happened all too clearly. Arisilde had had a disturbing episode last night, then today, when he had seemed so much better, he had used his power as casually as when he had been a student at Lodun. "He hasn't been in the best of health for years, and after everything else he's done to himself, I'm afraid his body has just . . . given out." Isham was probably right in that it was only Arisilde's power keeping him alive.

Reynard came into the parlor and a moment later Isham followed. Nicholas asked, "Well?"

Reynard shrugged. "Brile said he's not getting any worse, but he's not getting any better, either. There's no immediate danger and there's nothing else he can do tonight."

"Which means he doesn't know what to do."

"Exactly."

Nicholas looked away. *We need a sorcerer-healer*, he thought. *One that won't ask difficult questions. One that isn't afraid to tend a man who is probably far more powerful than he is and with a history of illness and instability.* It was a tall order. He said, "Isham, we have good reason to believe we're being pursued by another sorcerer. That's why we came, but we can't chance leading an enemy here with Arisilde in this state. I've set some men to watch the building and I want you to keep me informed of anything that occurs."

"I will do this," Isham assured him. "In what manner are you being pursued?"

Madeline had been turning over one of the books on the desk, her brows knitted in thought. "I think someone may have cast a Sending on one of us."

Nicholas frowned. "Why do you say that?"

"I know we weren't followed there, yet it found us so quickly. And there was just something about it. . . ." She glanced up and saw that he was regarding her skeptically, and glared. "It's only a feeling. I feel it to be so. I can't give you a hard and fast reason, all right?"

"Yes, but—"

"It is easily settled," Isham interrupted. "I can do a throwing of salt and ash to ascertain if this is the case."

As Isham lit two of the lamps above the mantelpiece, Reynard said, "I'm sure I don't really want to know this, but what is a Sending and why do you think it's after one of us?"

Madeline didn't respond immediately, so Nicholas answered, "A Sending is a spell to cause death. A sorcerer fixes it on a specific person, and then casts it. It exists until it destroys its target, or until another sorcerer destroys the Sending." He looked at Madeline. "I didn't know they could take on corporeal forms. I always thought they came as diseases, or apparent accidents. And I thought the victim had to accept some sort of token from the sorcerer before he could be made a target."

Madeline shook her head. "That's true now. But Sendings are old magic. Hundreds of years ago, they were far more . . . elemental."

"Very true," Isham agreed, lifting an embossed metal box down from one of the shelves. "Three hundred years ago the satrap of Ilikiat in my native land had a sorcerer cast a Sending against the God-King. It was not necessary to send a token to the God-King, and indeed it would have been impossible to get such a thing to him through the defenses of his own sorcerers. The Sending destroyed the west wing of the Palace of Winds, before the great Silimirin managed to turn it back on the one who cast it. But that was three hundred years ago and sorcerers are not what they were then, for which the Infinite in its wisdom is to be thanked."

"Why not?" Reynard asked.

Isham had opened the box, taking out various glass vials. He started to clear a space on the table and Nicholas and Reynard helped him lift down the piles of books. The old man explained, "Such profligate outpourings of power can only come from bargains with etheric beings. Fay, for example. And such things have been shown to be more deadly to the bargainer than to any of his enemies."

Isham swept the dust off the table with his hand and began to lay out a pattern of concentric circles, using ash from the fireplace and various powdered substances from the glass vials.

Quietly, not wanting to disturb the old man's concentration, Nicholas asked Madeline, "But what makes you suspect a Sending?"

She sighed. "If I knew, I'd tell you."

Isham finished the diagram and now took a water-smoothed pebble from the box and placed it gently in the center of the lines of ash. He motioned them to gather around the table. As Nicholas stepped forward he saw the pebble tremble. When he stood next to the table, the pebble rolled toward him, stopping at the edge.

Brows drawn together in concentration, Isham nudged the pebble back to the center of the diagram. "It seems it is a Sending, and it is focused on you." He picked the pebble up and rolled it between his fingers. "What form did it take when it appeared to you?"

"We couldn't really see it clearly." Nicholas described what had happened at the house, letting Madeline tell what she had seen after Crack had gotten him out. That the Sending was attuned to him he had no trouble believing. He had been expecting it since Madeline had brought up the possibility. That might even have been the purpose behind the trap at the manufactory. He had been the only one to touch the door; the Sending might have focused on that.

"It reacted to the bullets from your revolver?" Isham was asking Madeline.

"It drew back, yes. It's what kept it off me long enough for the others to get the boards off the window." She frowned, twisting a length of her hair. "You think it could be something of the fay?"

"It could be. The most powerful Sendings are made from a natural or etherical force. For example, the Sending cast against the God-King was said to be made from a whirlwind that had formed on the plain below Karsat. I would think to use something of the fay would be even more complicated than that, not that I have the slightest idea how to go about it."

"This man is a necromancer," Nicholas said.

Isham hesitated, lost in thought. He said, "It occurs to me that there must be the remains of many dead fay buried beneath Vienne.'' The old man spread his hands. ''I'm afraid I can't tell you any more than this. I am almost at the limit of my skill now.''

''We need the help of a powerful sorcerer,'' Madeline said. She moved to stand in front of the hearth, the fire-light casting highlights on her hair. ''Who else can we go to?''

''It has to be a sorcerer we can trust,'' Nicholas added. ''That's not as easily come by. . . . It will have to be Wirhan Asilva.'' Asilva had been a loyal friend to Edouard and maintained the connection with Nicholas after the trial, but he knew nothing of Nicholas's career as Donatien. He was also a very old man by now, but he was the only other living sorcerer whose abilities came anywhere close to being comparable with Aris-ilde's, and who Nicholas knew well enough to take a chance on. ''He still lives at Lodun. He might be able to help Arisilde as well, or at least direct us to someone who can.''

Isham had followed the conversation with a worried frown, and now said urgently, ''I don't know much of this Sending, but I do know this. You will be in the most danger during the hours of the night. And if this is a remnant of some fay monster, cold iron will still be a protection. The iron in the buildings, the water pipes, the underground railways offers some safety. Leaving the city could be most dangerous.''

Nicholas smiled. He wasn't beaten yet. ''Not if I leave the city on the train.''

Nicholas followed the others down the hall, but as he passed Arisilde's door, he found he had to take one last look. He stepped into the bedchamber.

The lamplight was flickering on the sorcerer's wispy hair, his pale features. It was hard to believe this wasn't death. Then Nicholas noticed the book lying on the patched velvet of the coverlet, not far from the sorcerer's left hand.

It might have been instinct that made him return to the bed and pick up the book, or some latent magical talent, but it was more likely only that he knew Arisilde so well.

The volume was very old and not well-cared for, the cover mottled with damp and the pages brown. The embossed letters of the title had worn away to illegibility and Nicholas opened it at random.

He was looking at a woodcut and for a moment he thought it depicted a modern medical dissecting room. Then he held it closer to the lamp and saw it was the scene from Valent House: an indistinct room, a man tied to a table, with his gut opened and his entrails exposed. But in this scene the victim was still terribly alive and the Vivisectionist was still present: a strange figure, stooping and leering like a character in an old morality play, dressed in a doublet and a high-collared lace ruff, a fashion out of date for at least a century or two. The caption read ''The Necromancer, Constant Macob, at work before his execution.'' The date given was a little less than two hundred years ago.

The page was stained, just as in his childhood memory. He turned to the frontispiece and there, in faded ink and childish scrawl, was written *Nicholas Valiarde.*

I'm looking for a book. . . .

How like Arisilde. He hadn't found another copy. He had found the very one Nicholas had owned as a boy.

Nicholas closed the book and carefully tucked it into his coat pocket, looking down at Arisilde once more. *No, you're not dead yet, are you? Hold on, if you can. I'll be back.*

Vienne's central train station was like a great cathedral of iron girders and glass. Even at this time of night it was comfortably busy, if not crowded. People in all sorts of dress from every part of Ile-Rien hurried back and forth across the vast central area. Nicholas heard the distinctive whistle and checked his pocket watch, then moved to one of the bay windows that overlooked the main platform. The *Night Royal* was rumbling in, a huge cloud of warm steam engulfing the track ahead of it. Grinding to a halt, it was a black monstrosity with bright-polished brass rails and only about twenty minutes late.

Madeline should be back any moment, Nicholas thought. He refused to allow himself to look at his pocket watch again. She was sending the wires that contained his instructions to the rest of the organization and he knew that right now she was safer alone than with him.

Before they had left the others, Crack had handed Nicholas his pistol and now it lay heavily in the pocket of his coat. The henchman had not been happy at being left behind, but Nicholas had refused to argue the point; he didn't mean to get everyone he knew killed. *Just Madeline?* he asked himself wryly. She had been grimly insistent about accompanying him.

He moved away from the window and strolled back to the center of the main area. Sleepy families were huddled on the benches against the wall, waiting for trains or for someone to meet them. There was a lounge for first class passengers on the gallery level and every so often, past the mingled voices and the dull roar of the trains he could hear the music from the string quartet that entertained there. Nicholas preferred the anonymity of the main waiting area, especially when something was trying to kill him.

His instructions had amounted to telling everyone to go to ground for the next few days. Reynard would watch Doctor Octave, but from a distance, and Cusard would do everything necessary to put off the plans for entering Count Montesq's Great House. Nicholas had sent a wire to Coldcourt, to warn Sarasate, and he only hoped Isham was right and that the Sending would concentrate on him and leave everyone else alone.

A delegation of lower-level Parscian nobility were disembarking from the *Night Royal*, their servants shouting, gesturing and requiring the assistance of almost every porter on duty for the large number of heavy trunks. That would slow things down a little more. The *Night Royal*'s next stop was Lodun and Nicholas intended to be on it.

It would be better for Madeline if she didn't return in time, he thought wryly. The Sending had only turned on her when he was out of its reach, though he had to admit, Lodun was probably the safest place for both of them. But if he left without her, she would only take the next train and be considerably put out with him when she arrived.

He saw a figure coming up the concourse then and recognized her walk. *No, it isn't her walk*, he realized a moment later. Madeline was walking as if she had a heavy dueling rapier slung at her hip; it was the way the character Robisais walked, from the play *Robisais and Athen*. It was one of Madeline's first major roles, that of a young girl who disguised herself as a soldier to cross the border and rescue her lover from a Bisran slave camp, during the Great Bisran War. He wasn't surprised he recognized the walk; he must've seen the damn play twenty times and Madeline had been the only worthwhile aspect of it. She must be very tired, to slip from her character of Young Man to Robisais. Of course, she could probably do Robisais in her sleep.

She climbed the steps and nodded to him briskly. She had borrowed a hat from Reynard and gathered her hair back up under the wig, so there was nothing to reveal her disguise. "Everyone is warned, now. I suppose that's the best we can do," she said. She glanced around the waiting area. "Nothing's happened here?"

"No," Nicholas said. At the last moment he remembered to link arms with her as he would with a man and not take her arm as he would a woman's. "We'll have a little time. Not much, but a little. Our sorcerous opponent shouldn't have drawn so much attention to himself. The Crown will take notice of this. After tonight, he'll have the court sorcerers, the Queen's Guard, and everyone else after him."

"And they will all be looking for us, too, if we're not careful," she pointed out.

"They can't trace ownership of that house, I've made sure of that. The driver's body can't be identified. We're safe enough." Nicholas felt the book in his pocket thump his leg as they strolled toward the platform and thought, *Safety is always relative, of course.*

Madeline's brows lifted skeptically but she made no comment.

The flurry of porters around the *Night Royal* had calmed, indicating the train was almost ready, and in another moment the bell above the booking area rang and the conductors began to call for boarding.

They took their place with the other passengers gathering in the damp cold air on the platform and through persistence and not being encumbered by baggage they soon managed to successfully board the train.

Nicholas found them an empty compartment and drew the curtain over the etched glass of the inner door to discourage company. Sinking down into the comfortably padded upholstery, the gaslit warmth, the familiar smell of combined dust, cigar smoke, coffee, and worn fabric, he realized he was exhausted as well.

Settling next to him, Madeline said, "I wonder if the dining car still has those cream tarts."

Nicholas glanced at her fondly. And this woman had the audacity to suggest that he was distanced from reality. He dug the book out of the pocket of his greatcoat and handed it to her. "Don't let this ruin your enjoyment of the trip."

He had left the page with the woodcut of Constant Macob folded down and she stared at it, then turned to the accompanying text.

Nicholas wiped the fogged window to look out at the gradually clearing chaos on the platform. He had read the section earlier, as he had waited for Madeline in the station. It briefly, and probably inaccurately, described Constant Macob's history as the sorcerer whose experiments with necromancy had turned it from a despised and barely tolerated branch of sorcery to a capital offense. *A capital offense, if you live until the trial,* Nicholas thought. In the past several sorcerers, most of them probably innocent, had been hung in the street by mobs before the accusations could even be investigated.

Madeline closed the book and laid it back in his lap.

"Doctor Octave's sorcerer friend is imitating this Constant Macob."

"Yes, or he believes he is Constant Macob. He is practicing the worst sort of necromancy, the spells that require pain or a human death to work, as Macob did. He is taking his victims from among the poorest class, apparently in the belief that the disappearances won't be noticed, as Macob did. And, like Macob, he can't tell the difference between beggars and the poor working class and occasionally takes a perfectly respectable dressmaker's assistant or some laborer's children and gets himself into the penny sheets." Nicholas turned away from the window. "Inspector Ronsarde must be very close to finding him."

"Yes, he was watching Doctor Octave at Gabrill House and he sent Doctor Halle to look at that drowned boy in the Morgue. He studies historical crimes, doesn't he? He must have looked at all the disappearances reported to the Prefecture, and recognized Macob's methods. That means—"

"He's only a step or two away from us. When he takes Octave—and if he realizes Octave is involved with the creature that destroyed the house in Lethe Square, he might very well take him tonight—Octave will tell them everything he knows about us."

"And we can't dispose of Octave while he has this pet necromancer defending him." Madeline tapped impatient fingers on the seat.

"After what we saw tonight, I know we can't take the chance. Not now. Not without help. This sorcerer could be using Octave and Edouard's device to contact Macob, or at least he thinks he's contacting Macob. But it would explain where all their knowledge of necromancy is coming from." He shook his head. "If I can get this Sending disposed of. . . ."

Madeline sat back in the seat, staring in a preoccupied way at nothing. Whistles and bells sounded outside on the platform and the compartment shook as the engine built up steam. "Why didn't you tell Reynard about this?"

"Because if the Sending follows us to Lodun and kills us, I didn't want him trying to avenge us."

"Then there won't be anyone to stop them," Madeline protested, brushing aside the idea of her own death.

"Yes, there will be. Ronsarde and Halle will stop them."

"For deadly enemies, you have a great deal of faith in Ronsarde and Halle."

"There are deadly enemies, and there are deadly enemies," Nicholas said. "Now let's go and see if the dining car still has cream tarts."

10

Lodun was a lovely town. Houses and cottages painted white, or ocher and blue, or a warm honey-color lined the ancient stone streets. Most had vines creeping up their walls and gardens or large courts with old cow-barns and dovecotes, relics of the time when they were farmsteads in open country, before the town had expanded to embrace them. Nicholas remembered it as even more beautiful in the spring, when the flowers in the window boxes and the wisteria were in bloom.

Asilva lived close to the rambling walls of the university, almost in the shadow of its heavy stone towers. The house was on a narrow side street, flanked by similar dwellings, each with a small stable on the ground floor. The entrance to the living area was reached by a short flight of steps leading up to an open veranda on the second floor. Asilva's veranda was cloaked by vines and crowded with potted plants, some still covered for protection from the last of the cold weather.

Nicholas hadn't liked the implication of the tightly shuttered windows and when he had climbed to the veranda, his knocking at the blue-painted door had brought no response. A neighbor had appeared on the recessed balcony of the next house, to explain that Asilva had left over a week ago and that they didn't expect the old man back for at least a month.

Cursing under his breath, Nicholas went back down to street level and through the little stone barn beneath the house and into the garden. He knew that as Asilva had grown older, the sorcerer had come to find Lodun more and more confining and had taken to travelling for several weeks at a time throughout the year. *I expected my luck to hold*, Nicholas thought, disgusted at his own presumption more than anything else.

Madeline was standing on a stone-flagged path, almost hip deep in winter-brown grasses, contemplating an assault on the back of the house.

"He's gone for an indeterminate period," Nicholas reported. It was early morning and the air was mild; it would be warm later. He pushed his hat back, looking over the garden. "We can't stay here long." With a sorcerer living on practically every street there was breathing space, though not much. And if the Sending came after him here and was destroyed by any of the number of sorcerers whose attention it would attract, the questions raised would be impossible to answer.

Madeline rubbed her eyes wearily. They had had coffee and pastries in the dining car on the train and very little sleep. The overgrown garden around them was mostly herbs, dry and bushy from the end of winter. Herb gardens were everywhere in Lodun, grown not only for the benefit of cooking pots but for their magical uses and for the dispensaries at the medical college. Nicholas was conscious of movement in the undergrowth, quicksilver sparkles of light. Asilva had always allowed flower fay to inhabit his garden, another example of his eccentricity. The colorful little creatures, as harmless as they were brainless, were drawn by the warmth of human magic, apparently heedless of the fact that the owner of this garden could destroy them with a gesture.

"There's no one else, I suppose," Madeline said thoughtfully. "Asilva was the last of Edouard's old colleagues."

"Yes." Nicholas looked toward the towers of the university. Seeking help there meant explanations, discovery. "I haven't been here in years. He's the only one who might have helped us and kept quiet about it."

Nicholas realized he was saying that he didn't know what to do next, an admission that would normally have to be forced out of him under torture, yet he could say it to her without a sensation of panic; it was odd.

A gossamer puff of blue-violet, with a tiny emaciated mock-human figure in its center, settled on Madeline's shoulder. He flicked it off and it tumbled in the air with an annoyed squeak.

"I might know of someone." Madeline became very interested in the dead weeds at her feet.

"Might know? Who?"

"An old . . . friend."

Nicholas gritted his teeth. Madeline's fellow artists in the theater mostly behaved as witlessly as the flower fay gamboling in the weeds around them now. Occasionally, when she was unsure of herself, Madeline imitated their behavior, apparently because it took up little of her attention, allowing her to devote her resources to finding a way out of whatever dilemma she was in. It drove Nicholas insane when she did it to him. He said, "Take your time. I do have all the time in the world, you know."

The look she gave him was dark, almost tormented. "I should let the dead past lay buried. It's a mistake to trouble still waters but—"

"That's from the second act of *Arantha*," he snapped, "and if you're going to behave in this nonsensical way and expect me not to notice you could at least do me the courtesy of not employing the dialogue from your favorite play."

"Oh, all right." Madeline cast her arms up in capitulation. "Her name is Madele, she lives a few miles out of town, and if anyone can help us, she can."

"You're certain?"

She let out her breath in annoyance. "No, I'm not certain. I thought a wild goose chase would occupy us until certain death tonight."

Nicholas contemplated the morning sky. "Madeline—"

"Yes, yes, I'm certain." She added more reasonably,

"We can get there by this afternoon if we hire a trap or a dogcart or something. We'd better get started."

"But. . . ." *You never told me you knew any sorcerers.* He was beginning to realize why she had been so determined to accompany him to Lodun. She had known of an alternative to Wirhan Asilva all along but she hadn't wanted to suggest it until she was certain all other possibilities were exhausted. He knew she knew something of magic, but supposed she had picked it up somewhere the way he had from simply living and studying at Lodun. He had the suspicion this was going to lead to a longer conversation than they could afford to have in Wirhan Asilva's fay-haunted garden with a Sending on their trail. He said, "Very well. Let's go."

Nicholas hired a pony trap from the stables on the street that led up to the university gates and they drove west away from the main part of the town.

The shop-lined streets gave way to laborers' cottages and summer residences with large garden plots, then finally to farmsteads and small orchards. This gave way in turn to fields of corn or flax, some standing fallow, all separated by earthen banks a few feet high planted with trees. The houses, whether they were tumbledown shacks or fine homes, all had runes set into the brickwork, painted on the walls, or cut into posts and shutters. A reminder that this was Lodun and it had seen stranger things than the Sending that currently hounded them.

It was close to noon and Nicholas was all too aware the hours of light left to them were limited. "Is it much further?" he asked.

"We're almost there," Madeline said.

It was the first words they had spoken to each other since leaving Asilva's garden.

Finally they reached a cart-track that led off the old stone road and Madeline indicated they should follow it. It led them past gently rolling hills and through a copse of sycamore and ash, then out into cultivated fields again. On a rise overlooking the track were the remains of a fortified manor house. As the wagon passed beneath the tumbled-down walls, Madeline said, "There's a story Madele told me, that an evil baron lived here and that she did something awful to him, tricked him into turning himself over to the Unseelie Court or something." She added, "It couldn't have been a baron, of course. What's left of the house is too small. And I think this land is part of the County of Ismarne, anyway."

Nicholas smiled at her. "Perhaps an evil gentleman farmer," he suggested. The breeze lifted a few strands of Madeline's hair that had escaped from under her hat and wig. "This could be very dangerous for your friend."

"I know."

"Do you think she would be able to do something for Arisilde, as well?"

"I hope so."

Could you be any less forthcoming? Nicholas wanted to ask, but he reminded himself that he was avoiding a quarrel.

There were a couple of farmsteads in the distance; Nicholas could see the smoke from their chimneys and hear the lowing of cows on the wind, but the area they were travelling through seemed deserted. Then the wagon track circled a hill and a house appeared as suddenly as if it had leapt out of the bushes.

It was of light-colored stone, two stories with a stable or cowbarn tucked in below and an old dovecote rising like a tower to one side. Vines, dried and brown from winter, climbed the steps and the arches of the stables, and the whole was shaded by an ancient oak tree, far larger than the house it sheltered, its lowest branches as large around as wine barrels and so heavy they had come to rest on the ground. The windows had carved casements and paned glass and the doors and shutters were well-made, though painted a dull brown. It was a substantial house; somehow Nicholas had been expecting a tiny cottage.

He drew rein in the dirt and graveled yard and Madeline jumped down from the box.

An old woman was standing in the doorway where a

set of stone steps led up to the second floor. Small and wiry, her gray hair knotted up in braids, her skin dulled by age, she was almost invisible against the weathered stone wall. She wore a smock and a dull-colored skirt: peasant clothes, oddly incongruous if she owned this prosperous house. No peasant, even in countryside as rich as this, would own such a large dwelling.

She put her hands on her hips and said, "So you've come to see me, hey, girl? You wouldn't if you didn't have to, I suppose. You reek of dark magic, I suppose you realize. If you'd stuck with your real calling you wouldn't need my help with whatever it is."

Madeline looked around, consulting an imaginary audience. "Has anyone got the time? What was that, one minute, two? How many instants have I been here before the same old song starts again? I suppose the rest of the family will be along to chime in on the chorus before the hour's out."

Nicholas sighed and rubbed the bridge of his nose, trying to discourage an incipient headache. *This is going well so far.*

The old woman sniffed. "You've brought a man with you."

"An astute observation." Madeline folded her arms. "I await further wisdom."

"And you've done something awful to your hair."

"It's a wig, Madele, a wig." She snatched it off and brandished it, scattering pins on the dusty ground.

"That's a relief. You could at least introduce me."

To the wig? Nicholas thought, stepping down from the wagon, then realized she meant him.

Madeline took a deep breath and said, "Madame Madele Avignon, may I present Nicholas Valiarde." She turned to Nicholas. "Madele is my grandmother."

For a moment, all he could do was stare at Madeline. As if sensing the trouble, the old woman coughed, and said, "I'll just step in and put some water on to boil, if you want to shout at me some more later."

She went back inside the house, leaving the door standing open. Madeline snorted. "She's listening to us,

of course. She has the manners of a precocious child.''
She smiled faintly, and added, ''But now you know
where I get it from.''

Nicholas didn't fall for this attempted distraction. He
said, ''Your grandmother is a sorceress?'' An old friend,
an old lover even, he had been prepared for.

''Well, yes, she is.'' She let out her breath, as if in
resignation.

Nicholas looked away, over the rolling fields. ''Why
don't you go and tell her about our little problem, and
I'll take care of the horse.''

Madeline looked a little uncertain, as if she had expected a different response. ''All right,'' she said finally,
and went toward the house.

Nicholas unharnessed the biddable horse and led it
into the little barn beneath the house. The mule and the
two goats penned there greeted his appearance with enthusiasm, as if they expected every human they encountered to be delivering food. Upstairs in the house, he
could hear metal cooking pots slamming around.

Arisilde had known, he supposed. The sorcerer had
made some comment about giving his regards to her
grandmother that had seemed to startle Madeline. It
would be very like Arisilde to have somehow realized
Madeline's antecedents years ago and during one of his
drug-hazes to forget that she obviously wanted it kept
secret.

Nicholas finished tending the horse and went out and
up the stairs. The front door was still standing open and
he stepped inside to a long room, the walls limewashed
a cerulean blue and the floor of patterned brick. A ladder
led up to what was probably a sleeping loft and another
door indicated at least one more room on this level. Madeline was nowhere to be seen.

Madele was standing at the large cooking hearth,
which held pots on hooks and a crane, trivet, and kettle.
There was a settle inside, in good peasant style, and a
cloth frill to help the chimney draw. She eyed him a
moment, then gestured for him to take a seat. ''Madeline
says there's a Sending after you. Of course she doesn't

know what she's saying." Her voice was raspy and harsh, as unlike Madeline's as possible. Any resemblance in feature was disguised by a profusion of wrinkles. "She could have been more help to you if she had followed her calling."

Nicholas took a seat on the bench at the deeply scarred table. Over the mantelpiece there was a clock with a garden scene framing the enamel dial and a framed photograph of a stiffly posed family group, looking uncomfortable in their best clothes. There were two young girls in the group, either of which might have been Madeline, but the broad flowered hats made identification impossible. There were a few chairs, an enormous wooden dresser stacked with china, a shallow trough sink, a potager embedded in the wall and a wooden drying safe hanging from the ceiling. Dried herbs and fragments of knitting littered the shelf below the window. There was absolutely nothing to indicate that Madele was a sorceress. No books, nothing to write with or on, and he was willing to bet the ceramic jars on the table contained only comfit and cooking oil. He asked, "What calling was that?"

Madele eyed him, almost warily, then as an apparent nonsequitur muttered, "She's certainly found herself an interesting one, hasn't she?" She gazed out the window at nothing and answered, "The family calling. Magic. Or power, or whatever pretentious name it has at Lodun. All the women in my family have always had talent and they've all pursued it, except one. Well, except my cousin twice removed, and she was mad."

Nicholas managed not to comment. He was wondering if there was anything else Madeline hadn't told him.

Madele shook her head. "Let's see about this so-called Sending." She sat down across from him and took his hand. Her skin felt almost as rough and hard as the wood of the table. "Well, it is a Sending. A very powerful one." Her eyes, which were a warm brown and clear for her age, seemed to look straight through him. "It came at you in the dark, from under the earth. It took no form you could recognize. It was drawn from something that had been dead for some time, buried under the street, but the iron in the soil kept it from decay. It shuns the sun and seemed to withdraw from iron, but that was only because it remembers the fear of the cold metal from when it was alive.''

Is she a sorceress or a fortune-telling hedgewitch? Nicholas felt more than a touch of impatience. Had Madeline gone completely mad? Not only was she going to get herself killed when the creature came after him, but this old woman as well. He asked, ''If the Sending follows us here tonight, can you turn it away?''

''Oh, I'm no Kade Carrion, I'm only a little hedgewitch, but I'll do,'' she answered cheerfully, as if she had read his thought. She pursed her lips and released his hand. ''There's no 'if' about it, you know. It will follow you here.'' Her gaze sharpened. ''It's a very old sort of spell, this. Strange to see it used now. Strange to see that there is someone who can use it at all.''

Nicholas hesitated, then took the book out of his pocket and opened it to the woodcut of the necromancer. ''I think the man who is behind it is deliberately imitating, or believes himself to be, this person, Constant Macob.''

Madele took the little book, fumbled for a pair of spectacles on a ribbon around her neck, and studied the illustration carefully, chewing her lip in thought. She ran her thumb over the page, as if testing the texture of the paper. ''Believes himself to be Macob? Are you sure?''

Nicholas felt a flash of irritation. ''No, I'm not sure of anything.''

''I meant, it's more likely that he actually is Constant Macob.''

''How can that be possible?'' Nicholas said impatiently. ''The man was drawn and quartered over two hundred years ago.''

''I know that, young man.'' Her gaze was serious. ''Anything's possible.''

Madeline came out of the other room. She had changed into an old skirt and smock of Madele's and had brushed her hair and washed her face. She and Madele eyed one another warily.

Madele stood. "I've a couple of things to attend to outside."

As the front door banged shut behind her, Madeline said, "I suppose you want to talk."

Nicholas steepled his fingers. "Perhaps your supposition is incorrect."

"Nicholas. . . ."

He had meant to be cold, but found himself saying, "Why didn't you tell me your family were all sorcerers?"

"Grandmama's been talking, I see. Why would my antecedents be your concern?" She looked up, caught his expression before he could conceal it, and said, "That's not what I meant." She gestured, exasperated, though at herself or him he couldn't tell. "I suppose I was afraid."

"Afraid of what?"

Madeline sighed and played with the fringe on her shawl. She said slowly, "I want to be an actress just a little less than I want to keep living. It takes all the time and concentration that I have. Studying this. . . ." She waved a hand at the little room. "Power, and all the varied ways of it, would take all the time and concentration that I have. I had to choose one. I did. Not many people understand that."

Nicholas folded his arms. *Be reasonable*, he told himself. They couldn't afford to fight now. And maybe it was none of his business; they weren't married. But he had told her everything. She was the only one who knew the whole story. "And you assumed I would be one of them?"

"Yes, I did." She met his eyes gravely. "I want to be an actress the way you want to destroy Count Montesq. I know what that kind of wanting is like. I could be much more of a help to you if I pursued magic instead of the leading role at the Elegante. Especially with Arisilde going to Hell in a handcart." She looked away. "I realized why I suspected it was a Sending. When it was trying to get into the room with me, there was a feel, a smell, something. . . . When I was a child Madele took me to Lodun once for the midwinter festival and while we were there some old enemy tried to kill her by slipping her an apple with a Sending of disease on it. She said it was a trick old as time and turned it aside, but she had me hold it first, so I would know how it felt, and know not to take anything that gave me that feeling. It was subtle, but it was there. It felt like wanting, like lust. It was frightening." She smiled briefly. "She didn't even bother to find out who Sent it to her. At least that's what she told me; for all I know he's buried under the house." She gestured helplessly. "I don't know. I've given up something that other people have begged, stolen, schemed for all through time. Maybe I'm mad."

"All my closest friends are mad." What that said about him, he didn't want to closely consider. Nicholas sighed and rested his head in his hands. "I wouldn't ask you to do something that you didn't like. Especially knowing it would do no good to ask."

"But if you had asked, I might have considered it." She smiled ruefully. "But that's not your failing, is it?"

Nicholas shook his head. He didn't want to discuss this anymore. It came too close to the bone. He said, "Do you think your grandmother can deal with this Sending? She's only a hedgewitch. There's no point in risking her life." He turned to look at her. "We still have time to get back to Lodun if we leave now."

Madeline's brows rose. She asked, "Did she say that? That she was only a hedgewitch?"

"Yes."

Madeline squeezed her eyes shut, briefly. "Her definition of hedgewitch is a little different from everyone else's." She looked up at him. "The name they called her was Malice Maleficia."

"Oh." The woman known by that name hadn't been seen for more than fifty years, but Nicholas had heard the stories of her exploits. Including the one about the evil baron, though he hadn't been a baron and he hadn't lived here. It had been the Bishop of Seaborn, who had tried to turn all the followers of the Old Faith out of the city and had reportedly ended up as a permanent fixture on the disappearing island of Illcay. "I see."

Madele banged in through the door, pausing to scrape the mud off her wooden clogs. "If you're staying for dinner, I'd better pluck a chicken."

They waited. Just before dusk fell, Nicholas helped Madele close the shutters.

He had forgotten what night was like in the countryside. It might be darker in the city, where gas streetlights were still sparse and crumbling buildings could blot out moon and starlight and leave the streets and alleys like little narrow ribbons of pitch, but it was never so silent as on an isolated farmstead. It might have been a great void outside, nothing stirring but the wind, an empty world where this little house was the only habitation of the living.

Madeline had fallen asleep on a chair and Nicholas covered her with a blanket from the bed in the other room.

Madele was knitting, her brow furrowed with the kind of concentration usually reserved for intricate mathematical calculation or perhaps surgery. Watching her, Nicholas smiled. She was acting, he realized suddenly. It shouldn't have taken him so long to see it, but this was really the first quiet moment he had had for real observation. She was play-acting the role of an old, somewhat daft peasant woman, for an audience of one. God knew Madeline did it often enough, concealing her true feelings, character, or temper behind a role tailor-made for whomever she wished to fool. He saw now where she had caught the habit. To draw Madele out a little, he said, "So this is where great witches go to rest?"

Madele smiled. She was missing some teeth, but it was a remarkably predatory smile all the same. "She told you?"

"Yes. It gave me confidence."

She sniffed. "Well, I'm old, it doesn't change that. I haven't done a great magic or trafficked with the fay in a very long time. Can't hardly find the fay anymore; they're waning. But I've a few twists and turns left." She finished the row on her knitting, and said, "You're a thief."

Coming from Malice Maleficia, this was not so heavy an accusation. He said, "Sometimes. Sometimes not."

"Madeline didn't tell me," Madele added. "I saw it on your face when you came in."

"Thank you," Nicholas said, with a polite smile, as if she had complimented him.

Madele shot him a suspicious look from under lowered brows, but forbore to comment.

Outside the wind had risen and Nicholas heard something heavy shift. He tensed, then realized it must be the huge oak that half-embraced the house. He started to say something, then saw Madele's head had lifted and her eyes were alert.

Madeline woke with a start and sat up, the blanket sliding to the floor. The sound came again, less like a heavy tree branch lifted by the wind and more like earth moving. Madeline whispered, "Is that it?"

Madele motioned at her to be quiet. She stood, setting aside her knitting, and moved to the front of the hearth. Her head was tilted to one side intense, as she listened with complete concentration to the night.

Nicholas got to his feet, glancing at the front door to make sure the lock was turned, for all the good that might do.

Madele frowned. "Can you hear it, girl? My ears aren't as good as they were."

"No." Madeline shook her head, her brows drawn together in frustration. "Nothing but the wind. You know I was never good at that."

Madele snorted in denial, but said only, "I need to know where it is."

Madeline went to the front window and Nicholas headed toward the back room. It was crowded with furniture, bureaus, chests, and an enormous cabinet bed. He blew out the candlelamp on the wall and opened the shutters on the single window, standing to one side of it in case something broke through. He could see nothing through the dusty panes but a moonlit stretch of empty ground and a clump of trees and brush swaying in the wind. He went back to the doorway.

Madeline had cautiously twitched back the curtain on the front window and was kneeling on the floor, peering out. "I can't see anything," she reported. "There might be something just behind the big oak, but the side of the house is blocking the view."

"I need to know," Madele gasped the words. Her face was pinched and drawn, as if she was in pain.

"I'll go out the back and look," Nicholas told Madeline. "See if you can find a length of rope; I'll need it to get back in."

Madeline started to speak, stopped, then cursed under her breath and got to her feet. Nicholas took that for agreement.

He opened the catch on the back window and raised it slowly, hoping the wind would cover any betraying noise and that the Sending's hearing wasn't keen. The outdoor air was dry and sharp, without any scent of the rain that the clouds and wind seemed to promise. He slid one leg over the sill, found footing on a wooden beam below, and slipped out to cling to the stone facing.

He dropped to the ground, landing on packed dirt. He couldn't hear anything but the wind roaring through the trees and the dry winter grass of the fields; it was like standing on the beach at Chaire when the tide was coming in.

Nicholas found the wooden half-door and eased it open, slipping into the barn beneath the house. The docile horse stamped and snorted in its stall, agitated, and the goats were rushing back and forth in their pen from fear. He went to the door that led to the front yard and edged it open.

The wind swept dirt over the packed earth and made the oak tree stir and groan with the weight of its branches. The surrounding fields were empty in the snatches of moonlight. Nicholas pushed the door open a little further, meaning to step out, when suddenly the mule in the barn behind him brayed.

He saw it then, just past the giant shadow of the oak, a piece of darkness that the moon didn't touch, the wind couldn't shift. He was astonished at the size of it. *The thing that came up through the floor of the house was only part of it*, he realized. The creature itself, whatever form it took, was taller than the tree that towered over Madele's house.

He edged the door closed for all the protection that might give the animals within and crossed back to the opposite door, giving the mule a pat on the neck as he passed.

Madeline had already dropped the rope from the window and tied it off to the bedframe and he scrambled up it easily. She was standing nearby in the warm room, her arms folded and her face tense, and Madele was waiting in the bedroom doorway. "It's just past the oak tree," Nicholas told her, locking the window catch. "I couldn't tell what it was, except that it's immense—"

The roof creaked suddenly and a little dust fell from the beams.

"Ahh," Madele said. "That'll be it, then," and turned back to the main room.

Nicholas and Madeline exchanged a look and followed her.

The house started to shake. Nicholas put one hand on the table to steady himself. He wondered if it would come through the floor again. That seemed most likely. Or perhaps through the roof. This house was more sturdily built than the one in Lethe Square; more dust fell from the trembling roof beams but the walls still held.

Madele was staring at the fireplace, kneading her hands and muttering to herself incomprehensibly. The iron pots and hooks hanging above the hearth rattled against the stone; the flames crackled as fine dust and hardened chunks of soot fell into them.

Something drew Nicholas's eyes upward. The stones of the chimney near the ceiling bulged out suddenly, as if whatever was within was about to explode across the room. Impossibly the bulge travelled downward toward the hearth, the stones appearing almost liquid as it passed.

It burst out of the mouth of the hearth in a cloud of soot and ash, a giant hand, skeletal, yellowed by decay, too large to have fit through the chimney, larger now than the hearth behind it.

Nicholas thought he shouted, though he couldn't understand the words himself. He heard Madeline cursing. Madele hadn't moved. She was easily within its reach, standing like a statue, staring intently at the thing.

It hung there and Nicholas saw it was formed as if human, five fingers, the right number of bones. Time seemed distorted; he wanted to reach Madele to take her shoulder and pull her away from it, but he couldn't move.

Then it withdrew, drawing back into the hearth, disappearing up the chimney hole that was far too small for it to fit through. The bulge travelled back up the stone chimney, vanishing as it climbed past the ceiling.

Nicholas realized his knees were shaking, that his grip on the table was the only thing keeping him upright. He thought he had imagined it, except the pots had been knocked to the floor and he had seen the thing's knuckles brush them aside when it emerged.

Madele's head dropped and she buried her face in her hands. Madeline pushed past him to catch her shoulders, but the old woman shook her off. Madele lifted her head and her eyes were bright and wicked. "Open the door," she said. "Tell me what you see."

Nicholas went to the door and tore it open. He saw nothing at first. The wind had risen alarmingly, making the house groan and tossing the branches of the oak tree. Then he realized that the tree was making far too much noise; a wind of the strength to stir those immense branches would have knocked the house flat. Thunder shook the stone under him and in the blazing white crack of the lightning, he saw the Sending.

It was white and huge, wrapped in the branches of

the oak tree, struggling to free itself. He saw the hand that had reached down the chimney stretching up above the tossing branches, its claw-like fingers curled in agony. In the lightning flash of illumination, a branch whipped up and wrapped around the straining skeletal arm and snatched it back down into the tree.

The light was gone, leaving the yard to darkness and the rush of the wind. Nicholas slammed the door and leaned against it.

Madele was picking up the scattered pots from the floor, clucking to herself. "Well?" Madeline asked.

"The tree appears to be eating it," Nicholas reported soberly. He was glad his voice didn't shake.

"You're lucky you came here," Madele said. She straightened and rubbed her back. "That tree was a Great Spell. I made it years and years ago, when I was young and I first came to live here. The Sending isn't fighting me as I am now, old and withered and dry. It's fighting me as I was then, at my prime." She lifted her head, listening to the wind against the stones, and maybe to something else. "And whoever Sent it is far more powerful than I am. Then or now."

The wind didn't die down for another hour and after that Madele said it was safe to go outside. There was no trace of the Sending, except a scatter of broken twigs and detritus beneath the heavy branches of the guardian oak.

11

"It's a lovely day not to be under a death sentence from a Sending," Madeline said, as they came out into the morning light from the dark interior of the stables. They had driven back to Lodun, starting before dawn to reach the town in good time, and had just turned the hired horse and trap back over to the owner. Madeline was in male dress again, Madele having nothing suitable for town that she could borrow. They were both dusty, tired, and somewhat the worse for wear.

Before they left Madele's house, Nicholas had told the sorceress about Arisilde and asked for her help. She had stood next to their pony trap while he harnessed the horse and had said, "Arisilde Damal, hmm? And he studied at Lodun? I don't think I've heard of him."

Nicholas thought that was probably just as well and didn't comment.

After a long moment of thought, she asked, "Is Ian Vardis still Court Sorcerer?"

"No, he died years ago. Rahene Fallier has the position."

"Ahh," she said. "Don't know him. That's good." There was another long pause and Nicholas devoted his attention to adjusting the harness. He wouldn't beg her, if that's what she was waiting for. Finally she asked, "Is it a spell, or just an illness?"

"We weren't sure."

Her brows lifted in surprise.

He hesitated, then said, "He's an opium addict."

Madele was now favoring him with one of Madeline's expressions of sardonic incredulity that seemed to question his sanity. It was worse coming from her, since her thick gray brows heightened the effect. Stung, Nicholas said, "If you feel it's beyond your admittedly failing skills—"

Madele rolled her eyes, annoyed. "He a thief too?"

"Yes," Nicholas snapped.

"Then I'll come," she had said, smiling and showing her missing teeth. "I like thieves."

Madele had promised to come to Vienne tomorrow which would give her time for making various arrangements for the upkeep of the house and animals with her neighbors. Nicholas hadn't been sure she would really come, if he could really count on her help, but after Madeline emerged from the house to have a half-hour argument with her over what train the old woman would take from Lodun, he felt she did, at least, mean to travel to Vienne.

Now, here in Lodun, he could only hope she would keep her promise. "Can you arrange the train tickets and check at the hotel to see if there's any word from Reynard or Isham?" Nicholas asked Madeline. He had left both with instructions to send a telegram in care of the railroad hotel if there were any new developments with Octave or with Arisilde's condition. "I need to pursue another line of investigation."

Madeline brushed road dust from her lapels. "Concerning how Octave became so intimately acquainted with Edouard's work?"

Nicholas's expression was enigmatic. "Yes, and how did you ever guess that?"

"Edouard performed most of his experiments here, didn't he?" She leaned back against the post and tipped back her hat thoughtfully, very much in character as a young man. The street was sparsely occupied, mainly by townspeople on errands or farmers' carts, with a few students in ragged scholar's gowns hurrying along the walk toward the university gates, probably just recovering from a night spent in the cabarets. "I assume you don't suspect Wirhan Asilva, since we were going to him for help?"

"No, not Asilva." Asilva had helped Nicholas remove the contents of Edouard's Lodun workroom after the old philosopher's arrest, something that could have landed Nicholas in prison and put Asilva, as a sorcerer and subject to charges of necromancy, under a death sentence. He had also fought for Edouard's release up until the last moment, even as he had protested that Edouard's spheres were dangerous and should never have been created. He didn't think Asilva would betray his old friend, even years after Edouard's death. "There's something Arisilde said that has made me wonder about Ilamires Rohan. And if we eliminate Arisilde and Asilva, he's the only other sorcerer familiar with the situation who is still alive now."

"That we know of." Madeline looked doubtful. "Rohan was Master of Lodun and Arisilde's teacher. He could be extremely dangerous, to say the least."

"That depends." Nicholas took Madeline's arm.

"On what?"

"On whether he merely gave the information to Octave or if he is Octave's mad sorcerer."

"If that's the case, it won't be safe to confront him. Are you sure—"

"I'm sure of one thing. That 'safe' is not a state of being any of us are going to experience again until this is over."

Nicholas spoke to several old acquaintances at the cafe near the northern university gates and discovered that his quarry was not only in town, but that he would be at home later this afternoon entertaining guests. That was ideal for what Nicholas had in mind and it also gave him time to look for more information on Constant Macob.

For that the best place was the Albaran Library, currently housed in one of the oldest structures in Lodun. Standing in the foyer of that venerable building, in the smell of aged paper and dust and time, Nicholas's student days seemed only a short while ago, as if the intervening years had meant nothing. He dismissed that thought with annoyance. The past was the past, as dead as Edouard. But on impulse, he found one of the attendants and asked for Doctor Uberque.

The attendant led him to a room in the outer wall of the bastion that had once been part of an inner defensive corridor. There were still trapdoors high in the walls and the ceiling, originally placed there so boiling oil could be poured down on anyone who broke through the outer doors. But now the corridor had been partitioned off into half a dozen high-ceilinged rooms and the walls were lined with shelves. The narrow windows that had been crossbow or musket slits were now filled with stained glass. Doctor Uberque stood in front of a large table covered with books and papers. He waved away the attendant before the man could introduce them and said, "Nicholas Valiarde. Did you come back to finish your degree?" He was a tall man with sparse white hair and a lined, good-humored face. He wore a black and purple master scholar's gown open over his suit, as if he had just come from a tutoring session.

"No, sir." Nicholas managed not to smile. Uberque was single-minded in the extreme and was as unlikely to be curious about Nicholas's need for this information as if he was any other student trying to write a monograph. "I'm in town on business, but I need information about a subject I thought you could supply."

"Yes?"

"Constant Macob."

Uberque's eyes went distant. Nicholas had seen the same effect with storytellers in the marketplaces of Parscian cities. They were usually illiterate, but held thousands of lines of poetic sagas in their memories. After a moment Uberque said, "One of the executed sorcerers from the reign of King Rogere. A disreputable character."

"The sorcerer or the King?" Nicholas asked, taking a seat at the table.

Uberque took the question seriously. "Either, though that is a different topic entirely. Do you want a reference on Macob?"

"Please."

Doctor Uberque stepped to the shelves and paced along them thoughtfully. "Everyone remembers Macob as a necromancer and nothing more. Before him, you know, necromancy was frowned on, but it was quite legal. It was mainly concerned with methods of divination, then. Seeing ancient kings on one's fingernail, and asking them for secret information." Uberque smiled. "Macob went on quite as any other sorcerer for a number of years. Then his wife and several of his children died in one of the plagues."

"It's certain they died naturally?" Nicholas asked, one brow lifting in doubt.

"Well, he was suspected later of causing their deaths, but I don't think he did. No, I don't believe so. Healing magic only goes so far and the apothecaries at the time were nearly useless. I think it was after his eldest daughter died that Macob . . . changed."

"He went insane?"

"It's hard to say. Judging from his actions, he must have done. But he didn't behave like a madman. He was more than clever, more than cunning. His work during this time period was nothing short of brilliant. He continually astounded the masters of Lodun, he was given honors by the King, and he carried on an utterly normal private life in his home in the city. And he killed people. He was caught, in the end, only by accident. The house next to his was sold and the new owners were adding a stables. A courtyard wall collapsed due to incompetence and it knocked down the wall of a wing of Macob's house. He was away at the time. When the builders hastened to repair the damage, they found the first of the bodies." Uberque shrugged and continued, "No one will ever know how many he killed. Gabard Ventarin read Macob's secret journals before he burned them and discovered that Macob had been advancing the frontiers of necromancy in quite a different direction than divination. He had learned how to draw power from not only death, but pain.'' Doctor Uberque paused, touching the spine of a book lightly. '' 'He called the dark fay allies and conspired with everything of decadence and filth. He brought death to the innocent and concealed the traces of his passing with chaos. . . .' That's from *The Histories of Aderi Cathare.* You don't want that, it doesn't have anything helpful. *The Executions of Rogere,* that's better. It's only fifty years old and there's half a dozen copies at least, so I can loan you one with a clear conscience.'' He frowned at the shelves. ''It's not here. No, it's not here. We'll go and have a look for it, shall we?''

The Executions of Rogere secured at last and Doctor Uberque thanked, Nicholas left the musty dimness of the old library and crossed the open gallery to one of the newer brick buildings that grew like mushrooms on the side of the older structures. The view between the pillars of the gallery was of the towers and courts of the medical college. The day was sunny and the breeze mild; another sign that winter was over for the year. Nicholas touched the pistol in his pocket. He doubted his next appointment would end so congenially.

Ilamires Rohan, former Master of Lodun University, still spent most of the year at his home on the university grounds. The house was four floors of tan-colored stone that took on a golden glow in the afternoon light, with small ornamental turrets along the roof line. It stood in the center of a large garden surrounded by a low stone wall. On leaving the Albaran Library Nicholas had passed through a students' hall and picked up a reasonably presentable scholar's gown from the pile at the bottom of a stairwell, discarded there by young students eager to escape tutoring sessions and enjoy the day. With that over his somewhat dusty suit, no one gave him a second look as he crossed the various college courts on the way to Rohan's house.

The gardeners were preparing the flower beds for spring, and none of them gave him a second look either when Nicholas walked in the back gate and through the kitchen garden to the scullery door. It was long enough after lunch that the kitchen and pantries were deserted except for a pair of maids scrubbing pots, who acknowledged his passing with hasty head-bobs and went back to their conversation.

Nicholas left the gown on the coat rack in the butler's sitting room and went through a baize servants' door that led out into the front hallway. The house was lovely from the inside as well. The hall was filled with mellow light from the dozen or so narrow windows above the main door and the cabinets and console tables lining the hall were of well-polished rosewood, the rugs of an expensive weave from the hill country. But Rohan had always had exquisite taste, even when he had been a dean living in a tiny cottage behind the Apothecaries Guild Hall. *His star did rise fast, didn't it*, Nicholas thought. And for all its apparent peace Lodun was a competitive world, especially for sorcerers. Nicholas investigated a few receiving rooms, finding them unoccupied, then heard voices and followed them into the large parlor at the end of the hall.

There was a group of men just coming in from the room beyond, talking amiably. They were all older, dressed either in Master Scholars' gowns or impeccable frock coats. One of the things Nicholas had discovered in his morning reconnaissance was that Rohan was giving a luncheon for several dignitaries from the town and the university this afternoon; he was glad to see his informant had not been mistaken.

"Master Rohan," Nicholas said lightly.

The old man turned, startled. His face, thin and ascetic, marked by harsh lines and pale from too much time in poorly lit rooms, changed when he recognized his new visitor. That change told Nicholas everything he wanted to know. Rohan said, "I didn't realize you were here."

The words had been almost blurted, as if from guilt at forgetting his presence, yet Rohan had to know the butler hadn't admitted Nicholas or he would have been informed of it. Stiffening with annoyance at the display of ill-mannered impudence and demanding to know why he hadn't come to the front door like a gentleman would have been more convincing. Nicholas smiled. "Which didn't you realize: that I was here in town, or that I was here among the living?"

Rohan's eyes narrowed, as if he suspected mockery but wasn't sure of the inference, but he said only, "You wanted to speak to me? I'm presently occupied." His voice was colder. In a few moments enough of his self-control would have returned to allow him to confidently dismiss the intruder.

Nicholas strolled to the table, hands in his pockets, and met Rohan's eyes deliberately. "I had something to ask you about Edouard's Lodun affairs. You were doing such a marvelous job of handling them for me when I was younger, I thought surely you could assist me now."

The old man's gaze shifted. With a barely perceptible hesitation, he turned to the others. "You'll excuse me, gentlemen. An obligation to an old friend. . . ."

The other men assured him that of course it was no trouble at all and Nicholas followed Rohan into his study without pause. He had been seen by the Master of Doire Hall, three deans of the medical college, and the Lord Mayor of Lodun, none of them Rohan's fellow sorcerers. If Rohan wanted to kill him he wouldn't be able to do it in his home this afternoon.

The study was spacious, the walls covered in green ribbed silk and lined with glass-fronted bookcases interrupted only by a lacquered map cabinet and several busts of classical figures on carved pedestals. There was a landscape by Sithare over the marble mantel, a strong sign that Rohan was not having any difficulty with his finances.

Rohan moved to the desk and sat down behind it, as if Nicholas were a student called in for a dressing down, not a very friendly gesture toward an old friend's son. He said, "I hope this won't take long. As you saw I am—"

"There's only one thing I still need to know; the rest is only curiosity," Nicholas interrupted. He let the old man wait a heartbeat. "The material you gave to Doctor Octave. Where did it come from? Did you take it from Edouard's laboratory?"

Rohan sighed. "I didn't steal it, if that's what you're implying." He leaned on the desk and rubbed the bridge of his nose. "Some of the notebooks were Edouard's, the rest were mine." He raised his head, wearily. "The sphere was mine. Edouard constructed it and I devised the spells."

Nicholas didn't allow his expression to change and kept his grip on the revolver in his pocket. This might be a trick. *Readily admit what you already know you can't conceal, and strike as soon as my guard is down.* He remembered the teasingly familiar handwriting on the scraps of paper they had found at Valent House; it must have been Rohan's. His voice deceptively mild, he said, "I didn't realize you had worked with Edouard. You said—"

"I said I didn't approve. I said what he did was nonsense." Rohan slammed a hand down on the desk, then took a deep breath, reaching for calm. "I was afraid. I made it a condition when I agreed to work with him that he tell no one of my involvement. Wirhan Asilva was an old man with no ambitions, even then. He could afford to be mixed up in such things. Arisilde. . . ." When he spoke the name Rohan's voice almost broke with bitterness. "Arisilde was a precocious boy. No one could touch him and he knew it. But I was Master of Lodun, and vulnerable."

This sounded too much like the truth. Nicholas said, "He kept his word to you. He told no one. You could have testified—"

"He was a natural philosopher who wanted to talk to his dead wife and they hanged him for necromancy. I was a sorcerer in a position of power. What do you think they would have done to me?" Rohan shook his head. "I know, I know. Asilva testified and it did no good. I convinced myself that Edouard might be guilty, that he might have killed that woman for his experiment, that he might have concealed the true nature. . . . And I was afraid. Then Edouard was dead, and then Ronsarde proved it was all a mistake, and there seemed no point in dredging it up again.'' He rubbed his face tiredly, then spread his gnarled hands out on the desk. "Octave wouldn't tell me what he wanted with the sphere. I suppose he went to you for the same purpose. I knew there were things missing from Edouard's rooms here when the Crown seized the contents and I knew you and Asilva must have taken them, but I didn't tell Octave that. That's not something that can be laid at my door. Did he threaten to expose you as well? Since Edouard was found innocent I don't think it would be a crime. . . .''

Rohan was speaking quickly, his hands nervously touching the things on the desk. Nicholas stopped listening. There was something tawdry and anticlimactic about it, to come here expecting evil and find only weakness. He asked, "What did Octave threaten you with?''

Rohan was silent a moment. "It wasn't the first time I had dabbled in necromancy.'' He looked up and added dryly, "I see you're not shocked. Most sorcerers of my generation have some experience with it, though few will admit it. Octave came to me here, two years ago. He knew. I don't know how. He knew about my work with it in the past, my work with Edouard, he knew everything. I gave him what he wanted, and he went away.'' Rohan winced. "I shouldn't have, I know that. Edouard meant it to be a method of communication with the etheric plane, but it never worked quite the way he wanted.'' Seeing Nicholas's expression he added, "I can't be more specific than that. Edouard built the thing; all I did was contribute the necessary spells. I know he wanted it to work for anyone, but it would only function for a person who had some talent for magic. It might be a small talent, just a bare awareness of it, but that was enough.''

But how did Octave know you had it? Nicholas had the feeling that if he could answer that question then all the half-glimpsed plots would unravel. "Is Octave a sorcerer then?"

Rohan shook his head. "He has a little talent, no skill. He isn't a sorcerer. But with the sphere. . . . I don't know. I can't tell you any more." He sat up a little straighter. "If that is all you have to ask, please go."

It might all be an act but that seemed unlikely. This was Rohan's sole involvement with the plot, as the victim of blackmail for past crimes and disloyalties. Nicholas took his hand out of the pocket with the pistol and went to the door. He paused on the threshold, glanced back, and said, "I'm sure Arisilde would send you his regards. If he could remember who you were," and quietly closed the door behind him.

Nicholas found Madeline waiting at a table outside the little cafe where they had arranged to meet. She stood as he came near, saying, "There was a wire waiting at the hotel from Reynard. He says there's been a development and we need to return immediately."

Nicholas spotted Reynard in the crowd on the platform of the Vienne station as he and Madeline stepped off the train. Since they had no baggage to collect they avoided the congestion and were able to make their way over to him and withdraw into one of the recessed waiting areas, left empty by the arrival of the Express. It was a little room lined with upholstered benches, smelling strongly of tobacco and the steam exhaust of trains.

"What's happened?" Nicholas demanded immediately.

Reynard was as carefully dressed as ever but he looked as if he hadn't slept. He said, "Ronsarde's been arrested."

"What?" Nicholas glanced at Madeline, saw her expression was incredulous, and knew he couldn't have misheard. "What the devil for?"

"The charge is officially burglary," Reynard said. From his skeptical expression it was evident what he thought the likelihood of that was. "Apparently he broke into a house in pursuit of evidence and was careless enough to get caught at it. But Cusard says there's a rumor in the streets that he was assisting a necromancer.''

The mental leap from housebreaking to necromancy was a long one, even for Vienne's hysterical rumormongers. Nicholas felt a curious sense of vertigo; perhaps he was more tired than he realized. ''How did that get started?''

Reynard shook his head. ''I should tell you from the beginning. The morning after you left for Lodun, the Prefecture found Valent House. Ronsarde was investigating the murders yesterday when he broke into this place he's accused of breaking into.'' Anticipating the question Nicholas was trying to interrupt with, he added, ''And no, I don't know the name of the house. It wasn't in the papers and Cusard couldn't find out from his sources in the Prefecture, either. Which makes it sound like a noble family, doesn't it?''

''An ignoble family, perhaps.'' Nicholas was thinking of Montesq. Octave's initial interest in Edouard Viller, his theft of the scholar's work, his knowledge of Coldcourt, even the way he had approached Ilamires Rohan. Like footprints on wet pavement they led back to Montesq. *Could he be at the root of it? Supporting Octave and his lunatic sorcerer? That would be so . . . convenient.* Convenient and in a way disappointing. He didn't want Montesq executed for a crime the man had actually committed. That would ruin the whole point of the thing.

''Wait,'' Madeline said, exasperated. ''I've missed something. How did the Prefecture get the idea that Ronsarde was behind the murders at Valent House?''

''They don't have that idea, of course,'' Reynard told her impatiently. ''He was done for burglary and whoever managed to pull that off must be damn high up in the ranks, that's all I can say.'' He gestured helplessly. ''But this rumor that he's involved with necromancers is everywhere. There was a small riot last night in front of Valent House. Took a troop of City Guards to keep them from burning the place down.''

"And half of Riverside with it, I imagine." Madeline's brow creased as she looked at Nicholas.

Nicholas dragged a hand through his hair. Several women and a porter laden with baggage passed the open doorway, but no one entered. He muttered, "Oh, he must be close. He must be right on top of them."

Reynard checked his pocket watch. "He's due to go before the magistrate in an hour. I thought it might help to hear what goes on there."

"Yes, we'd better go there at once." Nicholas turned to Madeline. "I want the other spheres removed from Coldcourt. Can you do that while we're at court?"

"Yes. You think Octave will try for them."

"No. But I may need them as bait and I don't want to risk going to Coldcourt again. I don't want their attention on it. Take the spheres to the warehouse and put them in Arisilde's safe. I wager even the real Constant Macob couldn't find them in there."

"I have the impression," Reynard began, his eyes grim, "that I'm underinformed. Who the hell is Constant Macob?"

"I'll explain on the way."

Madeline found a hire cabriolet to take her on her mission to Coldcourt and Nicholas and Reynard went to the coach. Devis was driving and Crack was waiting on the box. Crack's greeting was a restrained nod. Standing so as to block any curious onlooker's view, Nicholas handed Crack back his pistol and touched his hat brim to him.

"It's very odd," Reynard commented, once he had seen the book and had Nicholas's theory on their opponent explained to him, "to be rushing off to see Inspector Ronsarde arraigned before the magistrates. I always expected to be on the other side of the bench, as it were."

"Odd is a mild word for it," Nicholas said, his expression hard. Now that he had gotten over the initial shock, he was almost light-headed with rage at Octave and his lunatic sorcerer. They had stolen Edouard's work, they had tried to kill himself and Madeline, and now. . . . *And now Ronsarde*. He should be grateful to them for destroying the great Inspector Ronsarde, something that he had never been able to do. *Except I stopped trying to destroy him years ago*. He wasn't grateful, he was homicidal. It wasn't enough that they endanger his friends and servants, they had to attack his most valued enemy as well. "Where's Octave?"

"The night of our little upset in Lethe Square he moved out of the Hotel Galvaz and into the Dormier, using a false name. Some of Cusard's men are keeping an eye on him. Oh, and Lamane and I went back to that manufactory that Octave led us to. There was nothing there, just an old, empty building."

Nicholas grimaced in annoyance. Octave's behavior was inexplicable. He thought it would be greatly improved by a couple of hard blows to the spiritualist's head with a crowbar. "Octave should have left the city, at least until we were taken care of."

"Except that he has an appointment for a circle at Fontainon House. I don't think he wants to miss that."

"Fontainon House?" Nicholas didn't like the cold edge of prescience that simple statement gave him. Fontainon House was the home of the Queen's maternal cousin, an older woman of few ambitions beyond social achievement, but the house itself was within sight of the palace. It might even be caught in the edge of the palace wards. The idea of Octave holding a circle at Fontainon House didn't have the feel of another confidence game; it felt like a goal.

"Does that tell you something?" Reynard asked, watching Nicholas's expression.

"It makes a rather unpleasant suggestion. How did you hear about it?"

"I ran into Madame Algretto at Lusaude's. They've been invited. She wasn't keen on it after what happened at Gabrill House, but then she hasn't much choice in her engagements, from what I can tell," Reynard answered. He watched Nicholas sharply. "This worries you, doesn't it. Why?"

Nicholas shook his head. His suspicions were almost too nebulous to articulate. Octave had been working his way quickly up through Vienne's social scale. The Queen's cousin was practically at the top of that and there had been rumors for years about her odd pastimes. He said, "I never thought there was a plan. I thought Octave was out for what he could get and that this sorcerer was simply mad. But. . . ."

"But this makes you think differently."

"Yes." Nicholas drummed his fingers on the windowsill impatiently. "We need Arisilde. If I'd paid more attention the last time I spoke to him, perhaps—"

Reynard swore. "You can't live on ifs, Nic. If I had burned the damn letter from Bran instead of keeping it in a moment of sentimental excess, if I'd become suspicious when I realized it was missing instead of shrugging it off to carelessness, the little fool would still be alive. And if I kept living those mistakes over and over again, I'd be as far gone into opium and self-pity as your sorcerer friend."

Nicholas let out his breath and didn't answer for a moment, knowing very well he had said something similar to Arisilde the night of the sorcerer's last fit. For a time, when they had first met, he had wondered if Reynard had loved the young man who had killed himself over the blackmail letter. He had decided since that it was not very likely. But the young man had been a friend and Reynard had felt protective of him and responsible for his undoing. Nicholas thought most of Reynard's excesses concealed an overdeveloped sense of responsibility. *I wonder what my excesses conceal*, Nicholas thought. Better not to speculate on that. Dryly, he said, "Don't worry on that account. If I succumb to self-pity I'll probably do something far more immediate and spectacular than a simple addiction to opium." That sounded a deal more serious than he had meant it to, so he added, "But I'll have to get Madeline's permission first."

Reynard's mouth twisted, not in amusement, but he

accepted the attempt to lighten the mood. "I'm amazed that Madeline puts up with you."

"Madeline ... has her own life and concerns." Maybe this wasn't such an innocuous topic after all.

"Yes, fortuitously so, since it makes her remarkably tolerant of aspects of your personality that would require me to thump your head against the nearest wall."

"When you meet her grandmother, it will give you an inkling of how she acquired her thick skin."

As their coach drew near the city prison, Nicholas saw no evidence of the unrest Reynard had spoken of. The streets of Vienne seemed busy as always, as calm as they ever were. He was sure the damage caused by the Sending in Lethe Square had stirred up some trouble but Vienne had a long history and had seen far worse.

Then the coach passed the Ministry of Finance and entered the Courts Plaza.

The prison took up one side of the sweeping length of the open plaza. Its walls were of a mottled dark stone, several stories high, linking six enormous turreted towers. It had long ago been a fortification for the old city wall and the places where the numerous gates had been filled in with newer stone were still easily visible. There were actually several entirely separate structures that made up the prison within those high walls, with a courtyard in the center, but they had all been interconnected and the court roofed over decades ago. The last time Nicholas had been inside it was years ago, when he had first started to uncover some of Count Montesq's criminal dealings. He had discovered that a brutal murder that was the talk of Vienne had actually been committed by two men in Montesq's pay. The man who had been sent to prison for it had simply been in the wrong place at the wrong time and been framed by the actual perpetrators. Nicholas had had no evidence and little faith in Vienne's justice, so he had taken steps to obtain the innocent man's release. That was how he had first made Crack's acquaintance.

Engineering Crack's escape from the prison had been an unqualified success, especially since as far as the prison authorities knew, there had been no escape. Officially Crack was dead and buried in one of the paupers' fields in the city outskirts.

As their coach crossed the plaza, it passed the spot where an old gallows stood, a grim monument to Vienne's courts of justice. It hadn't been used for the past fifty years, since the Ministry had directed executions to take place inside the prison to prevent the gathering of huge unruly crowds. After Edouard's death, Nicholas had come every day to this plaza to look at that gallows, to touch it if he could do so unobtrusively, to confront it and all it stood for.

Ronsarde wouldn't be held in the prison itself, but in the offices of the Prefecture built out from the far side of the prison wall, extending halfway across the back of the plaza. The Prefecture's headquarters was a strange appendage to the grim prison and had many windows with carving around the gables and fancy ironwork. On the other side of the plaza was the Magistrates Courts and the Law Precincts. These structures were even more ornate, from the pillared portico over the entrance to the wickedly grinning gargoyles carved on the eaves and the depictions of Lady Justice wearing the regalia of the Crown of Ile-Rien above every entrance.

There was a massive fountain in the center of the plaza, with several statues of ancient sea gods spewing water from horns and tridents, and there were usually peddlers and penny sheet vendors to cater to the constant stream of foot traffic. Nicholas frowned. Today the plaza was far more crowded than usual and the milling figures lacked the purposeful air of tradespeople or clerks moving to and from work. They were a mob and they were in an unpleasant mood.

Nicholas signalled for Devis to stop and he and Reynard stepped down from the coach. They had to keep moving to avoid being jostled and shoved by the crowd as Nicholas made his way along the edge of the plaza, trying to get closer to the end of the Justiciary closest to the prison.

The usual peddlers and food vendors were out but

there was an angry group clustered around each one, debating loudly about necromancers and dark magic and taxes, and the failure of the Prefecture and the Crown to protect ordinary folk. There were a large number of beggars and idlers, but also clerks and shopworkers, women with market baskets over their arms and children in tow, house servants and workers from the manufactories just across the river. He heard mention several times of Valent House, and also of Lethe Square. He supposed their adventure there hadn't helped the panic any. And there was no quick way to spread the word that that particular manifestation had been dealt with, except among the criminal classes.

Nicholas stopped at the steps that led down from the central fountain's dais, unable to make his way closer to the buildings. He was nearer the Courts than the prison and could easily see through the windows of the bridge that connected them on the second floor. Reynard stepped up beside him, muttering, "I'd like to know what the devil stirred up all this so quickly."

Nicholas shook his head, unable to answer. He had read *The Executions of Rogere* on the train ride, but what he thought of now was the fragment of *The Histories of Aderi Cathare* that Doctor Uberque had quoted. *He concealed the traces of his passing with chaos. . . .*

Crack was standing only a few paces away, watching the crowd around them with concentrated suspicion. Nicholas motioned for him to step closer and said, "Send Devis to tell Cusard to come here with as many of his men as he can bring. Hurry."

Crack nodded sharply and started back toward the coach.

Reynard stroked his mustache thoughtfully. "Are we anticipating trouble, or starting it?" he asked, low-voiced.

"Both, I think," Nicholas said. He raised a brow as uniformed constables forced some bolder curiosity seekers off the steps of the Courts. "Definitely both."

*   *   *

They waited. Crack rejoined them after sending Devis for Cusard and through sheer persistence they made their way almost to the edge of the Courts' steps. Only one large foul-smelling individual objected to their presence: Nicholas gestured to Crack, who seized the man by the throat, yanked him down to eye level and made a low-voiced comment which caused the offender to mutter an apology and back rapidly away when he was released.

The time scheduled for Ronsarde's hearing passed and Nicholas could tell they weren't opening the court yet, even for people who might have a legitimate purpose there. He thought that a mistake; they should have started as soon as possible and allowed anyone who could squeeze in to have a seat in the gallery. Then there would be no reason for most of the spectators to remain and they would drift off back to their own concerns. Delaying the hearing only fed the atmosphere of strained excitement.

The sky was growing cloudy, but the morning breeze seemed to have died away completely. It was becoming warm and close in the plaza with so many bodies jammed into what was rapidly becoming a small area, which wasn't helping anyone's mood either. *He couldn't have chosen a better day for this*, Nicholas thought, *whoever "he" is. I'll have to remember to keep the weather conditions in mind should I ever need to start a riot.* He looked away from the Courts in time to see Cusard with Lamane at his heels making a path toward them. Reynard cursed suddenly and Nicholas snapped his gaze back.

At first he saw only a group of constables on the steps of the Prefecture. Then he swore under his breath. Ronsarde was standing in their midst. On the steps of the Prefecture, not on the overhead bridge, where felons could be conducted across to the Courts out of the reach of angry mobs.

"There he is!" someone shouted and the crowd pushed forward.

Nicholas plunged forward too, shouldering aside the men blocking him, using his elbow and his walking stick to jab ribs if they failed to give way. He and Reynard had seen Ronsarde many times before and had both recognized him easily. That the troublemakers who had pushed their way nearest to the buildings had also recognized him, when their only exposure to him should have been as a fuzzy pencil sketch in the penny sheets, was a confirmation of his worst fear. Whoever had arranged Ronsarde's arrest was still at work and had no intention of allowing the Inspector to ever reach the magistrate's bench.

The steps were awash in people fighting, pushing. He saw one of the constables shoved to the ground and the others were already buried under the press of bodies. Nicholas paused to get his bearings and a man dressed in a ragged working coat seized his collar and jerked him half off his feet. He slammed the knob of his walking stick into the man's stomach, then cracked him over the head with it as his opponent released him and doubled over. Someone bumped into him from behind; Nicholas ducked, then realized it was Reynard.

More constables were pouring out of the Prefecture to vanish into the chaos and struggling figures pressed close around them. Everyone seemed to be shouting, screaming. Suddenly there was breathing space; Nicholas looked back and saw Reynard had drawn the blade from his sword cane.

That proves half these people are hired agitators, Nicholas thought, *real Vienne anarchists wouldn't hesitate to throw themselves on a sword.* He had seen enough spontaneous riots in Riverside to know the difference. He managed to push his way up two more steps for a vantage point, Reynard close behind him. He couldn't see Ronsarde, but the nearest exit to the Plaza was choked with people fleeing the fighting—sightseers escaping before the Crown intervened with a horse troop.

Crack tore his way out of the crowd and fetched up against them. "Can you see him?" Nicholas asked him, having to shout to be heard over the din.

Crack shook his head. "Maybe they got him inside."

Maybe . . . No, this was staged too carefully. They wouldn't have allowed the constables to save him. . . . Nicholas swore in frustration. "We need to get closer."

"There!" Reynard shouted suddenly.

Nicholas turned. Reynard had been guarding their backs, facing out into the plaza. Searching the press of bodies behind them, he saw the purposeful knot of men with Ronsarde among them. The Inspector threw a punch and managed a few steps back toward the Prefecture, then someone struck him from behind and he disappeared into the crowd.

They were taking him toward the prison side of the plaza. Nicholas started after them. Reynard caught his arm. "What are we doing, dammit?"

Nicholas hesitated, but only briefly. He had a dozen reasons for this, but the one that currently made the most sense was that someone badly wanted Ronsarde dead, the same someone who wanted them dead, and knowing the reason could tell him a great deal. "Find Ronsarde and get him out of here."

"I was afraid of that," Reynard snarled and whipped his blade up, abruptly clearing a path for them.

They fought their way forward, the crowd giving way before Reynard's weapon and their persistence. Nicholas couldn't see Ronsarde anymore but kept his eyes on the man who had struck the Inspector: he was a big man wearing a hat with a round crown and he remained just barely in sight over the bobbing heads around them. They broke through into a clear space and Nicholas saw there were at least six others accompanying Ronsarde's captor and that the Inspector was being dragged between two of them. They were taking him. . . . *Toward the old prison gate? Why the hell . . . ?* Nicholas felt suddenly cold. *No, toward the old gallows.*

A firm shove sent him staggering forward a few steps; he sensed rather than saw the passage of something heavy and metal through the air behind him. He turned in time to see the tip of Reynard's sword cane protruding from the back of a man. The man's weapon, a makeshift club, fell to the pavement.

Nicholas pushed forward toward the gallows, hoping that Reynard and Crack could follow. The wooden trap had fallen in years ago, so if the Inspector's captors managed to hang him it would be slow strangulation rather than a quick snapping of the neck—that might buy Nicholas some time.

Another knot of rioters blocked his path. He plunged through them rather than taking the time to go around and found himself ducking as a wild-eyed man swung a broken broom handle at his head. The man staggered and took another swing at him and Nicholas realized he was drunk.

Nicholas dodged around the obstacle, came up from behind and seized him by the shoulders. The man obligingly kept swinging his club, apparently grateful for the temporary support. Nicholas steered his human battering ram in the right direction and the other combatants scattered out of his way.

Ronsarde's captors were taking the time to hang him because it was the sort of murder that would be attributed to a mob; if they had simply shot him someone might have been suspicious. *This wasn't Octave or his pet sorcerer*, Nicholas thought. *Whoever planned this knew Vienne too well.*

They broke through into another clear stretch of pavement. He aimed the man off to the side in case Reynard or Crack were making their way through behind them and gave him a push. The drunk staggered away in search of more targets and Nicholas ran.

Two of the men were hauling Ronsarde up the steps of the gallows. One of the others spotted Nicholas coming and blocked his path. Nicholas saw the man's expression change from a malicious grin to sudden alarm. He reached into a coat pocket and Nicholas saw the glint of light on metal. He swung his walking stick, cracking the man across the forearm and the revolver he had been about to draw went skittering across the pavement.

The sight of the revolver made Nicholas realize he was somewhat unprepared for this particular undertaking and he dove for the weapon. He hit the pavement and grasped the barrel just as someone caught hold of the back of his coat. There was a strangled cry and his attacker abruptly released him. He rolled over to see Reynard withdrawing his sword cane from the man's rib cage, Crack guarding his back. Another man was charging down the gallows steps toward them; as Nicholas struggled to his feet he shouted to catch Crack's attention, then tossed him the walking stick. Crack turned and slugged the newcomer in the stomach with the heavy wooden stick, hard enough to puncture his gut, then caught him by the collar as he staggered and slung him out of the way.

Two down, Nicholas thought, *five remaining*. He plunged up the steps to the platform which was creaking ominously under the weight of the men atop it. Three of them were wrestling with Ronsarde, who was still resisting despite a bloody face from repeated blows to the head. One was throwing the rope over the scaffold and the other was standing and looking on. *The ringleader, obviously*. Nicholas motioned for Reynard and Crack to stay back, then pointed the revolver at the leader and said, "Stop."

They all stared at him, temporarily frozen. Ronsarde was on his knees, blinking, barely seeming conscious. His captors all had the rough clothing and heavy builds of laborers, and from the visible facial scars and the coshes they all seemed equipped with, they did precious little in the way of honest work. The very sort of men who worked for Nicholas. He smiled. "Let's be reasonable. Release him, and you can leave."

The ringleader took the smile for weakness. He grinned contemptuously and said, "He won't shoot. Go on—"

Nicholas pulled the trigger. The bullet struck the man in the chest, sending him staggering back into one of the heavy piers that supported the gallows, where he slumped to the platform, leaving a dark stain on the old wood. Nicholas moved the gun slightly to point it at the man holding the rope, the next likely ringleader candidate. Still smiling, he said, "Let's begin again. Release him, and you can leave."

The men holding Ronsarde dropped him and backed away, without waiting for a consensus from the rest of the group. The Inspector swayed and almost collapsed, but managed to stay upright. The one with the rope put up his hands nervously. Nicholas gestured with the pistol toward the edge of the platform. "Very good. Now run away and don't come back."

The men scrambled to the edge of the gallows and leapt down. Nicholas put the pistol in his coat pocket and crossed to where Ronsarde had slumped against one of the piers. As he pulled him up Reynard stepped around to take the wounded man's other arm and said, "I hope you have some idea of what we're to do now?" His expression was skeptical. Crack, who was hovering warily a few steps away, looked too nervous of Ronsarde to question Nicholas's next course of action.

Surveying the chaos around them, Nicholas muttered, "Why Reynard, you sound dubious." He couldn't spot Cusard and Lamane among the crowd; they must have been lost in the confusion. The riot seemed to be gaining momentum. More constables had poured out into the plaza and their efforts to clear the area in front of the Courts were drawing an increasing number of previously neutral onlookers into the fray. Warders in dark brown uniform coats were streaming around the gallows to join the fighting; Nicholas looked back and saw a small iron door now stood open in the prison wall behind them. The sunlight had been completely blotted out by heavy gray clouds; if it suddenly started to pour down rain, the situation might improve, but otherwise it was sure to get worse.

They could hand Ronsarde back over to the Prefecture, under the guise of good citizens preventing a mob murder. The problem was that whoever had arranged for Ronsarde to be exposed to the crowd in the first place had worked from within; they could be turning the Inspector over to the very man who had tried to kill him. "We can't give him back to the constables," Nicholas decided. That was as close as he meant to come to admitting that he didn't know what to do next, even to Reynard. "Let's just get him out of here first."

"I couldn't agree more." This was so unexpected that Nicholas almost dropped Ronsarde. The Inspector's voice held only a little strain and his tone was as commonplace as if he were sitting in a drawing room, instead of leaning on his rescuers, his face bruised and blackened and dripping blood onto their shoes. He smiled at Nicholas, and added, "I too lack confidence in our good constables at the moment."

Nicholas tried to answer and found his throat locked. Reynard must have been able to read something in his blank expression, because he said, "That's settled, then. Our coach is probably stuck outside the plaza. If we can just get to it—"

A sudden wind struck them sharply: if Nicholas hadn't already been braced to support Ronsarde he would have stumbled backward. He gasped and choked on the foul taint in the air. The Inspector and Reynard were coughing too. Except for the worst pockets of fighting, the crowd seemed to pause. Stepping close to Nicholas, Crack muttered, "It smells like that room."

Not again, Nicholas thought. He said, "We have to get out of here." *Not the same Sending, it couldn't be.* It hadn't been able to come out in daylight and he had the evidence of his own eyes, besides Madele's word, that it was dead. This had to be something else.

He and Reynard got Ronsarde down the steps, then Crack grabbed Nicholas's arm, pointing at the opposite side of the plaza.

A mist was rolling over the pitched slate roof of the Courts. It was thin enough that even in the dying light the shapes of the gargoyles and the gables of the building could be seen through it, but there was something about its advance that was inexorable, as if it was destroying everything in its path. It rolled almost majestically down the front of the Magistrates Courts, like a wall of water off a cliff, to pool on the steps at the base. Then Nicholas saw movement behind it. Chips of stone were falling from the gables, striking the pavement below. *It's going to destroy the Courts*, Nicholas thought, unable to see the purpose of it. The quicker-witted individuals in the crowd were streaming toward the street exits of the plaza, though some pockets of fighters still seemed oblivious to what was occurring. Then something far larger than a stone chip landed on the pavement at the base of the building; the solid sound of flesh striking stone was audible even at this distance. Then it scrambled awkwardly to its feet and waddled out of the mist. It was large, gray, bent over like one of the orange apes from the jungles in the farthest parts of Parscia, but vestigial wings sprouted from its back. For an instant, Nicholas thought he was seeing a goblin, like some illustration in a book come to life. Then he realized it was one of the stone gargoyles from the building's gables, but it was stone no longer. In a heartbeat it was joined by two more, then a dozen, then another dozen.

It was too far across the plaza for them to reach the street exit, especially with Ronsarde as injured as he was. Nicholas looked around desperately, then focused on the prison wall behind them. The small door there was closed, but the guards had been running out that way only moments before. It might have been left un-locked. "Go that way." There was no other way to go. The prison had no other entrances on this side and the Prefecture was too far away to reach in time.

"It's obviously some sort of sorcerous attack, ani-mating the decorative stonework," Ronsarde said calmly, as Nicholas and Reynard half-carried him to-ward the door. "Who do you think it is directed to-ward?"

Reynard muttered, "I think I can guess." He glanced back over his shoulder. "They're coming this way—quickly."

"I didn't really want to know that." Nicholas mo-tioned Crack ahead toward the door. The henchman reached it and pulled on the handle, then whipped a jim-mie out of his pocket and jammed it into the lock.

Nicholas cursed under his breath and looked over his

shoulder. The mist and the clouds had blotted out almost all the light: it might have been twilight rather than afternoon. People were still running away up the streets, but the ungainly gray shapes in the mist were all moving this way. He gritted his teeth and resisted the impulse to tell Crack to hurry; the last thing he wanted to do at the moment was break the man's concentration.

Finally Crack stepped back, shoving the jimmie into his pocket and drawing his pistol. He fired at the lock and on the fifth shot the door gave way with a whine of strained metal. Crack threw his weight on the handle, swung it wide open, and Nicholas and Reynard dragged the Inspector inside. The door wedged against the stone pavement when Crack tried to close it and he fought with it silently. Nicholas leapt to help him and together they tugged it closed, shutting out the approaching mist. Something outside howled angrily just as the door slammed shut and Reynard shoved the heavy locking bar into place. Nicholas stepped back from the door, reflecting that if one of the prison warders had thought to bar it he and the others would be dead now. Reynard leaned against the door, looking annoyed more than anything else, and Crack wiped sweat from his forehead with his coat sleeve.

"This is a rather tense situation," Ronsarde said, conversationally. He was supporting himself on the wall, watching them thoughtfully. "What's our next course of action?"

12

Madeline walked the short distance from Coldcourt to the city gate and there got a ride on the public omnibus. She had learned from past experience that a public conveyance was always best when transporting valuable objects; even though it meant taking a more roundabout route to the warehouse, the omnibus was safer than a hire cab.

The spheres were in the carpetbag she was holding in her lap. Once at Coldcourt, she had taken time only to change from her dusty suit into a dress and jacket she thought of as Parlormaid's Day Out and stuff her hair under a dowdy and concealing hat. If she ran into any close acquaintances who recognized her as Madeline Denare, it would be easy enough to invent a story about some romantic escapade or wager. Most of her theater acquaintances were fools, and were sure to believe any lie as long as it sounded risqué enough. *You sound like Nicholas*, she told herself. *When did you become so cynical? Sometime after sorcerers started trying to kill me*, she answered. *Sometime after I met Nicholas*. She had also brought a muff pistol with her which was now tucked under her shirtwaist.

The omnibus was a long open-sided carriage with bench seats accommodating about twenty persons if they were willing to become over familiar with one another. It was about half full now, and Madeline had managed to secure a seat not far behind the driver's box. She was staring abstractly at the people passing on the street, thinking of their current problem, when she noticed the sky. *When did it turn so dark?* She fumbled for the watch pinned to her plain bodice. It was still early afternoon. *Those clouds came in quickly; it'll rain in a moment.*

There was something happening in the street up ahead, people were running, shouting. Madeline sat up straighter, trying to see, and finally resorted to standing up and leaning out to see around the box. Other carriages, slowed by the sudden increase in foot traffic, blocked the way and the omnibus driver reined in.

Madeline frowned, tightening her hold on her carpetbag. The other passengers shifted and complained and one impatient man in a top hat got off to continue on foot. The driver was shouting for the other carriages to get out of his way or tell him what the devil was wrong.

"There's riot in Prefecture plaza!" one of the other drivers shouted. "Go around!"

"Not riot, sorcery!" A bedraggled man, his coat torn and his face bloodied, staggered out of the confusion of coaches and addressed the passengers of the omnibus and the other halted conveyances as though he was preaching to a packed hall. "Sorcery, ruin! Demons overrun the halls of justice. We are doomed! Flee the demons in the Courts Plaza!"

The omnibus driver watched this performance in silence, then took a piece of fruit from the bag at his feet, stood and shied it at the speaker's head. Missiles from the other coaches and a few of Madeline's fellow passengers followed and the man ran away. The driver took his seat again, cursing, and began to try to turn the wagon. Madeline stepped off before this awkward operation could get underway and hurried across the crowded street to the promenade.

Demons weren't difficult to imagine after the Sending. *And the ghouls.* She supposed there were other people in Vienne who might currently be drawing that sort of sorcerous attention but that they would also be visiting the Courts Plaza this afternoon was a bit too much for coincidence. No, it had to be Octave's pet sorcerer.

Madeline hesitated for only a moment. The warehouse was a mile or two away and the plaza was barely two streets over.

She cut through alleys until she reached Pettlewand Street, which paralleled the plaza. She passed enough people fleeing the other way and heard enough confused reports of mayhem to confirm that there was riot, at least. She reached the avenue that would take her past the Prefecture building and the southern entrance of the plaza. It was ominously deserted, bare and colorless under the gray sky. She passed a darkened shop window and caught flashes of her own reflection out of the corner of her eye. She adjusted the strap of her carpetbag on her shoulder and kept walking. She could see the fanciful designs on the cornices of the Prefecture and the flight of steps flanked by two gas lamps in ornamental iron sconces. The sudden silence was so disconcerting it was almost a reassuring sight. Madeline told herself they were sure to know what had happened there, whether it was riot or sorcery, and if by some chance Nicholas and the others had been arrested. . . . Well, it was the best place to find that out, too.

Madeline stopped abruptly as shouts sounded from up ahead. A group of men, uniformed constables and what appeared to be a mixed bag of court clerks, shopkeepers, and street layabouts tumbled around the corner of the Prefecture. Madeline stepped back against the wall of a shop, flattening herself against the dirty bricks as one of the constables pointed a pistol at someone just out of her line of sight and fired. She winced as the loud report echoed off the stone. If the riot moved into this street the Prefecture was likely to become a fortress under siege; she couldn't afford to be trapped there. She edged back toward the nearest alley.

The constable fired again and his target lurched into view.

Madeline swore, loud enough that one of the men glanced her way. The thing moving toward them was like a cross between a goblin and an ape, with a rictus grin and vestigial wings, its skin gray and pitted as weathered stone. It lurched forward again, moving with unexpected speed, and the constable who had fired at it dodged back out of its reach. *Well, my dear, it's definitely sorcery*, Madeline thought grimly, fumbling for her muff pistol. Having the little pistol in her hand made her feel better but she suspected the sense of security was only illusory. *Something of a higher caliber would be more comforting*. Through the heavy material of the carpetbag she felt one of the spheres start to hum and tremble, as it had when the ghoul had approached the attic window at Coldcourt. She clutched the bag to her chest, willing it to be quiet. *Not now*. The creature, goblin, whatever it was was a bare twenty paces away and she didn't want to attract its attention. It darted at one of the unarmed men and she raised her pistol, though she couldn't tell if bullets had any effect or if the constables who were already firing at it were just poor marksmen.

Something grabbed her arm and yanked her into the alley. She knew instantly it wasn't human, even in the semi-darkness of the narrow, cave-like alleyway. The grip was cold, hard as rock, inescapable. Instinctively she tried to throw her weight away from it, a move that would have sent a human attacker staggering, but the thing only gripped her arm more tightly. Her pistol went off as her fingers contracted at the pain. The little gun only held two shots; she gasped and barely managed to bring the lever back so she could try to fire again. Her throat was closed from fear and shock; she couldn't even scream when the creature squeezed her arm again and sent her to her knees.

Her eyes watering, she looked up at a creature almost identical to the one that menaced the men in the street. The body was the same but this one had horns sprouting from its broad forehead. It lifted its free hand in a fist; one blow would crush her skull. Madeline forced her numb hand to move, twisting the pistol down despite the bone-crushing pain and triggering it. The sound deafened her and a shard of rock struck her cheek, making her think she had missed and fired into the alley wall, but the creature roared in pain. It released her arm and she collapsed.

Do something, run, fight, get up. Her right arm was numb to the shoulder and she managed only to roll away. She came up against something soft and lumpy that buzzed as if it contained a beehive. Her carpetbag. *The spheres.* She awkwardly ripped open the bag with her one good hand and snatched out the topmost sphere.

The creature was looming above her and she thrust the sphere up at it.

The world went briefly white, as if overwhelmed by light. Time seemed to hang suspended. She could hear a great roaring and something seemed to tell her that she was seeing sound and hearing color. Then she blinked and time washed back over the alley.

The creature was still standing over her but it was motionless, as if frozen into a block of ice. Cautiously she reached up and touched the rough surface of its chest. *Not ice, stone.* Madeline lowered the still humming sphere to her lap. Now that she had leisure to study the creature she could see it was a gargoyle. An ordinary roof gargoyle like the ones that guarded most of the private and public buildings in Vienne. She had an urge to push this one over and break it on the cobblestones. *Oh, for a hammer.* She started to stand and gritted her teeth at the pain in her right arm.

There was an explosion out in the street, followed by a peculiar thump, of something heavy striking the pavement. Madeline groped at the alley wall and managed to get to her feet, moving forward enough to peer cautiously out.

There were three gargoyles in the street now but one had been turned back to stone and lay in pieces across the walk. As she watched, another one suddenly halted in the act of seizing a constable and toppled over to shatter with a dull crash. In another moment she spotted the sorcerer.

The doors into the Prefecture building stood open and a spectacled young man in a frock coat was leaning on the stair railing, staring at the last remaining gargoyle and muttering to himself. As he said his spell, the still restive sphere Madeline was holding shook violently.

She didn't wait to see the creature destroyed, but turned back to gather the other two spheres and tuck them hastily into the carpetbag. She had to get them away. If she could sense the power in them with her small talent, the Prefecture's sorcerer was sure to. She slung the bag awkwardly over her shoulder, still nursing her right arm. That was all she needed, to spend hours in a cell while court sorcerers determined that the spheres had had nothing to do with the sorcery in the plaza, while Nicholas and the others were God knows where doing God knows what.

She stumbled out into the street only to be swept up in another wave of refugees, heading for the Prefecture. Madeline tried to push her way free, but someone jostled her bad arm and she couldn't suppress a cry at the pain.

"This lady is injured!" someone called out. Madeline glanced around in confusion and realized he meant her. She was suddenly boxed in by a young constable and an elderly man, both staring aghast at her. Her sleeve was torn, revealing the discolored flesh of her forearm.

"No, really, it's just bruised," she managed to protest. "I must get home—"

They weren't listening to her. "There's a doctor inside," the constable said, urging her toward the Prefecture steps. The older man was helpfully gesturing at the others, exhorting them to look at what one of the horrible creatures had done to the poor girl.

Madeline planted her feet and started to express her wish to be let alone in no uncertain terms, then realized she was barely two paces away from the young sorcerer. She couldn't afford to draw his attention. She bit back a curse and let herself be guided up the steps and into the Prefecture.

The Prefecture's foyer was large but packed with shouting, pushing people. Coming into it suddenly from the daylight, Madeline was nearly blind in the gaslit dimness. One of her erstwhile rescuers took a firm hold of her good arm and guided her through the confusion. One could scarcely bludgeon someone in the foyer of the Prefecture and get away with it, crisis or not, especially when he was just trying to be helpful. Madeline decided she would just have to let the doctor tend to her arm before making her escape.

A constable threw open the door to a room where the gaslight was turned up and high windows allowed in wan daylight. Madeline had barely a chance to focus on the group of men gathered around a table talking loudly before the constable said, "Doctor Halle, there's a lady injured here."

Oh, damn, Madeline thought weakly. Of course, Doctor Halle was in the Prefecture. Ronsarde had been about to go before the magistrates; where else would Halle be?

Doctor Halle swung around with an impatient glance that turned into a worried frown when he focused on her. He came forward to take her injured arm and Madeline found herself being ushered into a nearby chair.

One of the men standing around the table was Captain Defanse of the Prefecture. He was saying, "The attack is centered on the prison now, that's obvious." Defanse was a stout man with thinning dark hair. He was one of Ronsarde's chief supporters and had investigated Donatien's activities on numerous occasions but most of the time without knowing it was Donatien he was after. If he recognized Madeline, it would be from seeing her on the stage at the Elegante.

"But the Courts—" someone protested.

"That's where the creatures came from. They were moving toward the prison," Defanse corrected, shaking his head.

"The important question, gentlemen, is who arranged for the sorcery?" The speaker was a tall man with graying hair and handsome if harsh features. *Oh, hell*, Madeline thought, light-headed from repeated shocks. *That's Rahene Fallier, the Court Sorcerer.* She wasn't sure how it could get any worse. *The Queen will be in here in a moment, I'm sure.*

Madeline shoved her carpetbag under the chair and

put her feet on it. She was trembling from sheer nerves but Halle would interpret that as reasonable due to her injury. She had never been this close to him before and this was his best chance to recognize her as the woman he had seen in disguise on other occasions, but his attention was torn between her injured arm and the men arguing in the other part of the room. Madeline allowed herself a small sense of relief; with luck he would never look more than cursorily at her face. "Nothing broken. . . ." he muttered to himself, carefully palpating her forearm.

"No, just badly bruised," she whispered. She didn't want him to hear her voice. He was an avid theater-goer and she didn't want him to recognize her as Madeline Denare, either. "I do need to be getting home—"

"One of the constables saw Ronsarde and the men who saved him from the mob go toward the prison," one of the men at the table said. He was another Prefecture captain; she couldn't remember his name.

Halle glanced back at the speaker, his lips compressed as if in effort not to make an outburst.

Defanse gestured in exasperation. "You think they were in league with the Inspector? Impossible!"

"You think this is all coincidence? To happen just as Ronsarde was being taken into the Magistrates Court?"

"The man was attacked by rioters and almost killed, surely you can't believe this was somehow arranged as an escape attempt? I gave strict orders for the constables to escort the Inspector across the bridge, out of reach of the mob. I would ask them who countermanded those orders but all four men are dead."

"You suspect a conspiracy? Ridiculous!"

"Ronsarde would not use sorcery to cover his escape, not against his own constables," Fallier said suddenly. "Someone planned this without his knowledge."

"You're right, it's only bruised. You're lucky." Halle noticed Madeline's torn sleeve and looked up at the constable still waiting near the door. "Get this lady a coat so she can leave."

He was impatient to return to the argument and defend

his friend Ronsarde but he still had time to think about her modesty. "Thank you," Madeline whispered, keeping her voice pitched low.

Halle met her eyes and hesitated, but said only, "You're welcome, young woman," and got to his feet.

Madeline grabbed her carpetbag, accepted the young constable's uniform jacket to cover her torn dress, and made her escape.

Nicholas knew they had to move now, while the prison was still in a state of chaos.

The room they stood in was bare and empty, lit by a solitary gas jet high in one lime-washed wall, and obviously intended for no purpose other than as one more obstruction to the way outside. The floor was stone-flagged and there was one other door, a solid oak portal with heavy iron plates protecting the lock. Nicholas looked at it and felt a twist in his stomach. He didn't have the proper tools with him to drill through those plates, even if he had had the hours necessary to do it. *If that's locked, we're done for right here and now.* He stepped forward and seized the handle and felt almost light-headed from relief when it turned. He pulled it open, cautiously, and found himself in a corridor, narrow and low-ceilinged, lit by intermittent gas lamps and leading in one direction toward another heavy door and in the other roughly paralleling the outer wall.

"That's mildly encouraging," Reynard said in a low voice, stepping into the doorway after him. "That we're not trapped in here for the pleasure of whatever's after us, I mean. As to what we do now . . . ?"

Nicholas hesitated. Ronsarde's presence made the situation several times more problematic. "We could try the main gate, or throw ourselves on the mercy of the first official we meet, but. . . ." He glanced back at Ronsarde.

The Inspector smiled grimly. "But explanations would be difficult? At the moment I also prefer a more unobtrusive exit." He would not be able to move with much haste. He was bleeding from a cut on the head and one eye was already swelling and he limped with every step.

Very well, Nicholas thought. *Then we do it the hard way.* His eyes still on the Inspector, he asked, "Do you know this place at all?"

"No, only the public areas, unfortunately."

Crack was watching Nicholas worriedly. Of all of them, Crack had spent the most time here, but his experience had been limited to the cellblock. Nicholas preferred not to get any closer to that section of the prison than absolutely necessary. "Give me a moment," he said, half turning away and shutting his eyes in an effort to concentrate. "I've been here before under similar circumstances." Not here, exactly, but on the upper floors.

He had committed a map of the place to memory when he had arranged Crack's escape, but that had been years ago. *Of course, you were dressed as a guard then, and you had keys to the connecting passages, and Crack was pretending to be dead.* Doing it without keys, a suitable disguise, or an apparently plague-ridden corpse to fend off casual interest would be considerably more difficult. Sections of the map were coming back to him. He knew where they had to go; it was getting there that was going to be the problem. He said, "That open way looks easier, but it actually leads toward the warders' barracks and the stairs up to the governor's quarters and the other offices. Straight ahead toward that door will take us to a point where we can get down to the level below this one, which will be much easier to move through." It was made up of the old cellars and dungeons, connected by a criss-crossing warren of corridors and passages. That was where they needed to go, where there would be far less chance of detection. The lower levels were inaccessible from the cellblocks and not well guarded. "The only problem is that past that door is likely to be a guard point."

"How many guards?" Reynard asked.

"At least two." Nicholas eyed the door. Crack's pistol was empty, its bullets expended on opening the outer door. The weapon Nicholas had taken from Ronsarde's abductors had only five shots left. "Do you have your revolver?" he asked Reynard.

"No. I didn't think it necessary in the Magistrates Court," he answered, glancing speculatively around the bare room. "Crack, hand me your pistol."

"It's empty."

"They won't know that."

While they were settling that, Nicholas took his scarf and tied it around the lower half of his face. He didn't want to make it too easy for the guards to recognize him later. He waited until Reynard had done the same, then he went to the door. "Get ready to force your way in behind me."

It was sheathed in heavy iron; there would be no way to force it with the materials they had at hand. Nicholas approached it quietly and listened but could hear nothing through the layers of wood and metal. He drew a deep breath and pounded on it. "Open up, quick, it's right behind us!" he yelled, pitching his voice toward the edge of hysteria.

He heard something from the other side, someone shouting about what the devil was going on, and he continued pounding and yelling. Moments passed, enough time for the men within to make a decision, to realize this door led away from the cellblocks, not toward them, and that this couldn't be an escape attempt, and to fumble with their keys. The door jerked and started to swing inward. Nicholas set his shoulder and slammed his weight against it.

The man on the other side of the door staggered back and Nicholas caught his coat collar and shoved the pistol up under his chin, snarling, "Don't move."

This was directed at the second man in the room, caught just standing up from a desk. Reynard pushed through the door behind Nicholas, caught the other guard by the arm and slung him to the ground.

Nicholas stepped back so his man wouldn't be able to grab the pistol and said, "Turn around and lie face down on the floor."

"What—What do you—"

He was an older man, with thinning gray hair, gape-faced with astonishment. The one Reynard had flung down looked to be barely out of his teens. Nicholas found himself hoping he didn't have to shoot them. "Just do it," he snapped.

The two guards were unarmed, since unless there was some emergency, prison warders only carried clubs. When both men were lying face down on the floor, Nicholas motioned for Crack and the Inspector to move on through the room. He tore the keys off the first guard's belt and handed them up to Crack as the hench-man helped Ronsarde past.

"Their uniforms?" Reynard suggested.

"Yes, at least the coats," Nicholas said. "You take—" They both heard it at once, pounding footsteps echoing against the stone walls, coming from the corridor they had just passed through. "No time," Nicholas snapped. "Just keep moving."

Crack had unlocked the other door. Nicholas waited until the others were through and then backed toward it himself, saying, "Don't move, gentlemen, and no one will get hurt."

"You won't get away with this!" the older one said.

"Very likely you're right," Nicholas muttered. He stepped back through the door and gestured for Crack to pull it to and lock it. Without the keys, the two guards would have to wait for their fellows before they could open this door again. Not that that was likely to be more than a few moments. Nicholas looked around, trying to get his bearings.

They were in another small dim antechamber with two more doors and another corridor branching off. Nicholas hesitated, thinking hard, then took the keys from Crack and stepped to the first door. He unlocked it and yanked it open, revealing a narrow staircase twisting down into darkness. He gestured the others ahead, then turned back to unlock the other door, the one that should, if he re-membered correctly, lead to the long straight corridor to the lower cellblocks. He flung it open and turned back toward the stairs. Just let their pursuers believe they had taken that route, just long enough to let them lose themselves in the catacombs below. *They should have no trouble thinking us confused enough to go toward the cellblocks*, Nicholas thought, starting down the stairs and pulling the heavy door shut behind him. He shook it to make sure the lock had set again. *We're breaking into a prison, after all.*

He almost tumbled down the stairs in the dark, catching himself on the wall at the bottom under a barely burning gas sconce and almost falling into Reynard. They were in a narrow, low-ceilinged corridor of dark stone patched with old brick, passages leading off in three different directions. There were a few gas sconces visible, obviously new additions, with their pipes running on the outside of the walls. Crack was supporting Ronsarde. Nicholas motioned for them to be silent, though he doubted that would do any good if the guards decided to check down here.

The moments stretched. They heard a muted thump as someone tried the door above to make sure it was locked, then silence.

"It worked," Ronsarde said, quiet approval in his voice. "Simple but elegant."

Reynard looked at Nicholas. "Well, which way? Or do we flip a coin?"

Good question, Nicholas thought. He didn't know this level as well as the others. It had been a backup route for him in his original plan to engineer Crack's escape years ago, but he hadn't had to use it. "We'll try this way first."

The others followed, Reynard immediately behind him, with Ronsarde coming after, supporting himself with one hand on Crack's shoulder and the other on the slightly greasy stones of the wall. In the narrow corridor there was only room for one of them to help him at a time. That was going to tire Ronsarde more quickly and slow the rest of them down. *Worry about it later.* Keeping his voice low, Nicholas explained to Reynard, "What we have to make for is the southwest corner. That's the old chapel and mortuary and there's an outside door there for removal of the bodies. That's our only choice besides the entrance we came in and the main gate.''

''Rather appropriate, if you think about it,'' Reynard commented, and Nicholas couldn't find it in himself to disagree. The further away from the outer door, the more stale the air became. Stale, and with a foulness under it that made the back of Nicholas's neck prickle.

His voice strained from the pain of his injuries and from trying to keep up, Ronsarde said, ''If events turn any further against us, this may be our only opportunity to pool our resources. You saw the gentlemen who were pursuing me; I take it the sorcerer who animated the Courts' architecture is interested in you?''

''I suspect they may have been sent by the same person, whether they know it or not.'' Nicholas glanced back over his shoulder. ''Do you know who arranged your arrest?''

''Within the Prefecture, no. Halle is currently attempting to uncover that intelligence, but since he can no longer risk trusting our former allies, it will be difficult. As to who ordered my arrest, I can only suspect Count Rive Montesq.''

Nicholas stopped dead, for a moment all thought suspended, hearing that name. *Count Rive Montesq. . . .*

Reynard thumped him in the back then, saying, ''Escape first, revenge later.''

Nicholas started forward again. *Careful, careful.* He would have to reveal a little to get more information, but he didn't want Ronsarde to realize how deeply he was involved. The Inspector must have recognized him as Nicholas Valiarde, or he would soon enough. If he recognized him as Donatien. . . . *You would have to kill him.* As ironic as that would be, after risking his life as well as Reynard's and Crack's to rescue him. *There would be no choice.* Not when going to prison meant taking Madeline and the others with him. ''Do you know anything about the sorcerer who is involved in this?''

''I know that there is one, that he is practicing necromancy, and that he is completely insane,'' Ronsarde said. "I might have discovered much more if I hadn't been interrupted so precipitously by my arrest."

"It's very possible he—" *believes himself to be Constant Macob*, Nicholas started to say, but the scream echoing down the corridor from somewhere ahead cut off the words.

They halted in startled silence and Nicholas felt for the revolver in his pocket but the sound wasn't repeated. After a tense moment, Reynard said, "I know people must scream somewhat in the normal course of things in a place like this, but—"

"But not normally this far below the cellblock," Nicholas finished for him. "There shouldn't be anyone down here." Of course, Octave's mad sorcerer had gone to great lengths to get to them already, he wasn't going to let prison walls stop him.

There was another scream, startling out of the deep silence of the place, and Nicholas could tell it was much closer. "Back the other way," he said.

Madeline hurried down the street away from the Prefecture, but instead of turning toward the warehouse she took the other way, working her way closer to the plaza. When the official had mentioned the men who had run into the prison with Ronsarde she had had a distinctly sinking feeling in the pit of her stomach. There was no guarantee it was Nicholas and the others, but. . . . If he had sent someone for help, he would have sent to the warehouse only a few streets away and that meant Cusard and Lamane.

She scouted the streets and alleys bordering the plaza, passing confused, fleeing people. Finally she spotted Cusard's wagon on the roadside, the horses tied to the rails of a public water trough. She approached cautiously, but then she saw Cusard and Lamane, standing near the front of the wagon in agitated conversation.

They looked relieved at the sight of her and Madeline suspected that meant they were about to hand her a tricky problem. This thought was confirmed when Cusard greeted her with, "We're in trouble."

"Nicholas and the others?"

"In the prison."

Madeline swore a particularly vile oath, a luxury she usually didn't permit herself in front of people. Lamane even looked startled. She said to Cusard, "That's what I was afraid of. How?"

Cusard glanced toward a group of constables moving up the street, then gestured her toward the nearest alley. They moved a few paces down it, Madeline catching up her skirt out of habit to protect it against the filth-covered cobbles. The alley was open-ended and they could see a black wall across the street at its farther end. The prison wall.

"The Inspector was set-on as they brought him out of the Prefecture," Cusard said. "There was a huge crowd gathered, a mob. Himself smelled a trap and he sent Devis for us, only we didn't get there in time to do nothing but watch."

"What did you see?"

"Some bullyboys took the Inspector off the constables and were going to hang him at the old gallows. I lost sight of where Nic and the captain and Crack went until they popped up there. They took the Inspector off the bullyboys and chased them away, and I thought, now they'll want a quick escape, but then the sorcery started."

"Those stone things off the buildings, yes, I saw those. Then what?"

"Then they ran in the prison, with those living statues right behind them. Just like Lethe Square, it's us this sorcerer's after, all right."

"Miss."

Madeline flinched and turned, badly startled. Not five paces away was Doctor Cyran Halle. He must have stood just out of sight, around the corner of the alley.

"I heard your conversation," he said.

Lamane started to reach for something in his coat pocket and Cusard caught his arm. *No weapons, for God's sake*, Madeline thought. *We haven't done anything wrong, not that he's witnessed.* This was Ile-Rien, not Bisra, and thoughts and talk didn't count for as much. "What do you mean?" she choked out, trying to sound indignant.

"I followed you here from the Prefecture and I heard everything you said," Halle answered. His brow was furrowed with worry but his voice was calm. "I must . speak with you."

"You can't prove nothing," Cusard spoke almost automatically. "It's your word against all three of ours."

Halle held up his hands, palms out, and Madeline wondered if he was asking to be heard out or showing he was unarmed. He said, "I recognized you. You were the nurse, in the morgue that day."

"That means nothing," Madeline managed to say. Her throat was dry. Pretending to be offended was no use. The circumstances were too suspicious.

Halle took a step closer, halted when Lamane shifted nervously. "I heard you just now," he repeated. "Your friends are the men who saved Ronsarde, who ran into the prison to get away from the sorcery. You want to get them out without the Prefecture being involved. I want to help you."

"Why?"

"You were in that room just now, you heard them. Someone arranged for that mob to be present and ordered the constables to take Ronsarde out on the steps instead of across the bridge, so the hired thugs could get to him. If he's taken by the Prefecture, it will just give whomever it was another chance to kill him." Halle hesitated. "If you are who I think you are. . . ."

Madeline caught her breath. She felt as if someone had punched her in the stomach. Next to her, Cusard made an involuntary noise in his throat, but didn't react in any other way. She said, "Who do you think we are?"

"Ronsarde hypothesized your existence. He knew that this rogue sorcerer was encountering resistance from some person or group, and that there had to be something preventing that person or group from coming forward and reporting the sorcerer's activity. The incident

in Lethe Square seemed to confirm this." Halle paused
deliberately. "As to whatever it is that kept you from
coming forward when the sorcerer attacked you, I don't
know what it is and I venture to say that at this stage it
hardly matters."

Madeline exchanged a look with Cusard. They were
both too well-schooled at keeping appearances to show
relief, but he looked a little white around the mouth.
Madeline turned back to Halle. *He doesn't know about
Donatien—yet.* Ronsarde would recognize Nicholas as
the son of Edouard Viller, but that would be all. *I need
to come up with a story, something to explain what
we're doing and why. . . . He doesn't want to know now,
or thinks he doesn't, but he will soon. . . .*

"Please," Halle said urgently. "The streets are in
confusion, the Prefecture is helpless, we need to do this
now or we will lose our chance."

Madeline bit her lip. Her instincts said to trust him
but it was her instincts that she didn't trust right now.
It came from knowing your enemy too well. She had
heard all the stories Nicholas told, of Ronsarde and Halle
at Edouard's trial, she had read Halle's accounts of the
cases they had been involved in before that pivotal point,
the cases since. The times she had tricked them herself,
the disguises she had worn or designed for others specifically to fool them, the plots she had participated in
to circumvent them; she had become far too familiar
with them. *God help me, I almost think of them as colleagues.* She had been startled when they had encountered Halle at the city morgue, but now standing here
and speaking to him felt almost natural. *And you told
Nicholas he wasn't wary enough; this man could have
you sent to prison for the rest of your life.* She looked
toward the dark stone wall, just visible through the open
end of the alley passage. No, not that. She would put a
pistol to her head before that.

Halle was watching her desperately. He said, "The
only possible way in now is through the prison Infirmary. I've assisted the surgeons there before. There

are guards but I can get you past them without violence—"

"There's not been no violence, never, that wasn't self-defense," Cusard interrupted. "It was that sorcerer, whoever he is. Three, four times he tried to kill us with those ghouls and he killed all the people in that house—"

Madeline held up a hand to stop him. She said to Halle, "I'll need your word that nothing we say or do in the course of our association will be passed on to any official of the Prefecture."

"You have it," Halle answered readily. "But I'll need your word that no constables or civilians will be hurt or killed in what we're about to undertake."

She hesitated. "I can't promise that without reservation. If someone fires at me, I'll certainly shoot back, but I won't just kill someone for the sake of doing it, if that's what you mean."

Halle let out his breath. "That is satisfactory. I won't expect you to let yourself be shot for my scruples."

Madeline accepted that with a nod and turned to Cusard. "I'll need blasting powder. Go and fetch some for me."

Lamane looked as if he might faint. Cusard gaped at her. "Since when do you know how to set a charge?"

"You're going to show me how before we go."

Cusard closed his eyes, apparently in silent prayer. "Oh, no."

Halle said, doubtfully, "Blasting powder?"

"We can get in without violence, as you put it, but we won't get out, not with Ronsarde a wanted felon. We can't just steal a warder's uniform for him; too many of the constables have seen him, worked with him. We'll have to make our own way out."

"Young lady, you have a very . . . clear view of our situation." He took a deep breath and she realized this hadn't been easy for Halle either, that it was just as hard for him to trust her. *And he doesn't know as much about me as I know about him. He doesn't know I have a sense of honor, that I wouldn't break my word and shoot him as soon as I don't need him anymore.* He had been brave enough to approach her with Cusard and Lamane here; she knew they were cracksmen and housebreakers, not killers, but he didn't. He said, "We have no time to lose."

She nodded to Cusard. "You heard him. Hurry."

Cusard cursed, stamped his feet, and went.

"You won't regret this," Halle said, his eyes earnest.

Madeline nodded distractedly and began to pull the braid off her borrowed constable's jacket. *I regret it already*, she thought. *If this fails and I get us all arrested, I won't have to put a pistol to my head because Nicholas will kill me. And in all fairness I'll just have to let him.*

It was becoming more and more apparent that something was hunting them through the darkened corridors of the prison.

Nicholas cursed when he saw their path blocked by another door. So far they had run into four locked doors that the keys Nicholas had taken from the guard upstairs refused to open, but two Crack had been able to force with his jimmie. Two had been too heavily plated to open with that method and they had had to change their route. There were not supposed to be doors blocking these passages; they must have been added in the last few years, perhaps as a response to more escapes.

He gestured Crack toward the door and leaned back against the dirty stone to let him pass. Ronsarde braced himself against the wall, his breathing harsh. Nicholas exchanged a worried look with Reynard. If they kept to this pace much longer they might kill the Inspector. Somewhere up one of the corridors a crash of splintered wood echoed, then a thump and a human cry, abruptly choked off.

"God, it's got another one," Reynard muttered. "How many does that make?"

"Four," Nicholas answered. He was watching Crack work the door. This one looked like it might be forced, with luck at least. When they hadn't been captured in the cellblock area, prison warders or constables must have been sent down to this level to search for them. Fortunately, the creature the sorcerer had sent after them was indiscriminate in who it killed. "If it knew where we were going, it would have had us by now. It's just . . . hunting."

"Maybe it's time to start hunting it," Reynard said.

Nicholas met his eyes, frowning. "What do you mean?"

"I'll slip back the way we came and try to kill it," Reynard explained. He looked back down the corridor. "That's the only course of action that makes sense. From what we've heard it moves fast; there's little chance of all of us outrunning it, not with an injured man and having to stop to break open doors every few minutes."

"You don't know the prison," Nicholas pointed out. He had considered taking this option himself but he was reluctant to do it until he could think of a sure way to destroy the creature that was trailing them. The most likely method he had come up with so far involved the gas jets the passages were lit with, but he couldn't think of a way to accomplish it without self-immolation and he didn't think the situation warranted that yet. "If you survived the encounter with this creature, you wouldn't be able to follow us out." *If we ever find the way ourselves, which is very much in doubt at the moment.*

"I don't have to find my way out. The Inspector is the one who is the fugitive from the Prefecture. Alone, I'm just another damn fool who ran in here to escape the sorcery."

"You'll need the pistol," Nicholas tried again. It would be certain death to confront the thing alone and he estimated he had until Crack forced the door to talk Reynard out of it. "And right now I've got it."

Reynard eyed him deliberately and smiled. "I bet I could persuade you to give it to me."

Someone else might have thought Reynard was threatening violence; Nicholas knew better. What did the leaders of other criminal organizations do when one of their men threatened to embarrass them into handing over a weapon? He lifted an eyebrow. "Not in front of the Inspector, surely. And besides, what would Madeline think? She'd have to challenge you to a duel." This was not facetious; Madeline had fought a duel before, using pistols, with a fellow actress who had insulted her. Reynard had acted as her second.

Crack was hunching his shoulders, trying to divorce himself from the altercation. Ronsarde merely watched silently.

"True, and I would feel obligated to let her win," Reynard admitted, obviously torn. He knew Madeline's temper. "But still—"

The lock gave way with a creak and snap of old metal and Crack pushed it open and stood.

Nicholas quickly offered the most pertinent objection, "But we only have the one pistol, with only five bullets left, and if the creature gets past you, or you miss it in these corridors, we won't have a chance against it." This was what had stopped Nicholas from trying it himself and until he perfected his theory concerning the gas jets, it remained the main objection. He gestured toward the now open door. "I suggest we get moving before this discussion becomes academic."

"True." Reynard looked convinced, for now at least. "I hadn't considered that."

Nicholas hid his relief. "Perhaps we can find another horror for you to fight at a more convenient time," he said politely, as Reynard stepped toward the door.

"Oh, but I thought you had your heart set on us all dying together?"

Nicholas decided to let Reynard have that one and turned back to take the Inspector's arm and help him through. Ronsarde's expression had gone from quiet observation to quizzical amusement, which quickly shifted back to bland politeness when he caught Nicholas's eye. Nicholas was left with the rather nervous feeling that they had just revealed more about themselves than they should.

They made their way through the door, Crack shutting it and wedging it closed behind them.

Nicholas handed Crack the revolver without further comment from Reynard and Crack took the lead, with Nicholas assisting Ronsarde and Reynard behind them. About fifty paces down the dimly-lit corridor, Crack lifted a hand to stop them. Nicholas waited, until Crack glanced back and whispered, "Smell that?"

Nicholas frowned, trying to detect something in the stale air besides the normal stink of the prison. Then he had it. There was an animal odor, a foulness like the one that hung around rat-infested buildings, but far worse and growing stronger.

"It's gotten ahead of us," Reynard whispered.

"We're so turned around we may have gotten ahead of it," Nicholas answered. "Can you see anything moving up ahead?" He could see the open area where the corridor joined another passage, this one with a lower ceiling and fewer lights.

"No. Can't hear anything."

"The other victims probably couldn't hear anything, either," Ronsarde pointed out quietly.

Reynard and Nicholas exchanged a look. "He's fitting in well, don't you think?" Reynard commented, sparing a smile for the Inspector.

Nicholas decided he didn't have time to be annoyed. "Move forward—slowly," he said.

Crack reached the intersection first and held up a warning hand to halt them. They stopped, Reynard taking a firmer grip on his sword cane.

After a moment Crack motioned them forward.

On the floor of the wider area where the two passages met, a man in a prison warder's dark uniform lay in a crumpled bundle, face down, one arm twisted into an unnatural position, a spray of drying blood around him. A heavy steel door barred one end of the intersecting passage, the other led off to the left, the intermittent gaslights along its length revealing nothing but bare stone.

Nicholas could see the door was firmly shut and locked and he knew the creature hadn't come down the corridor they had just come up. He looked down the apparently empty passage. *It's there. It just doesn't know we're here. Yet.*

Nicholas motioned Crack to hand the revolver to Reynard, then pointed to the guard and mouthed the word "keys." Crack nodded.

Reynard took the pistol and stepped silently across the corridor where he could cover the open passage. He glanced worriedly at Nicholas, who knew what he was thinking. *We can be as quiet as we like, now*, Nicholas thought, *but it is going to hear that door open.*

Crack found the ring of keys on the warder's belt then stepped to the door. He fit the key into the lock and carefully turned it. The tumblers clicked loudly in the silence.

There was no sound from the open passage.

Nicholas quickly helped Ronsarde past the dead prison guard and through the door. As Reynard turned to follow them there was a rush of air and the nearest gas jets dimmed faintly. Nicholas let the Inspector go, his shouted warning instinctive and incoherent. It was enough for Reynard, who dove through the door, Crack slamming it shut almost on his heels.

Something heavy struck the thick metal with a thump that made the stones under their feet tremble. There was a pause, and then the handle jerked as it was pulled from the other side. "The keys?" Nicholas whispered, his throat dry.

Crack held up the bundle of keys and there was a collective exhalation of relief. *If those had been left in the lock. . . .* Nicholas thought. *Well, our troubles would have been over much sooner.*

"Good man," Reynard told Crack. "Now let's get out of here before it finds another way past that door."

Nicholas took the bundle of keys from Crack. They could move faster now at any rate, and take a more direct route to their goal, if they could avoid the guards. He just hoped they could move fast enough.

13

The entrance to the prison Infirmary was dangerously near the Prefecture, but Madeline hoped that the confusion that still reigned in the plaza on the other side of the building would keep anyone from noticing them. She and Halle were waiting on the opposite street corner, using the projecting bay window of a china shop to stay out of the prison guards' view. Even now, with people running everywhere, the guards might be alert for someone showing too much interest in their position outside the gate.

The Infirmary door was set back in the dark stone wall, not as large as the main gate but still imposing, and there seemed to be four uniformed warders armed with rifles on duty all the time. Madeline smoothed down the front of her borrowed constable's coat; she had removed the braid from it so it was only a plain dark jacket. With her gray dress and the jacket covering the tear in her sleeve, she should make a passable nurse. She knew there were also cellblocks for women convicts; once inside she might be able to assume a wardress's costume and gain more freedom to search, but it was useless to plan when she didn't know what she would encounter once they passed those doors. She noted with annoyance that her hands were shaking. She always got stage fright before her best performances.

Halle paced nearby, his agitation evident, but he hadn't attempted to engage her in conversation. She was glad of that. She saw Cusard approaching again and straightened expectantly, taking a deep calming breath. It was always worst right before the curtain went up.

Cusard stepped a little further down the alley, drawing a brown paper-wrapped parcel out of his coat. "Here it is." He handed it to Madeline carefully. "You remember all I told you?"

"Yes. A fourth of a cap for a wooden door, a whole one for a steel door, at least four for an outer wall of stone and plaster, and a coffin full for a supporting wall, because that's what I'll need if I use it on one." She looked at Halle. "Can we put this in your bag, Doctor?"

Halle nodded, his face preoccupied. "Probably wise. If they searched you—"

"It would be disastrous." She waited for Halle to open the bag and lift out the top tray of instruments so she could place the small package carefully within.

Cusard eyed Halle thoughtfully, then said to Madeline, "And I brought you this, just in case." He handed her a six shot revolver and a small tin box of extra bullets.

Madeline checked it automatically to make sure it was properly loaded, then started to put it in the bag. Cusard coughed sharply.

Madeline knew what that meant but shook her head firmly. "I can't carry a pistol into the prison in my pocket. They know Doctor Halle, they know he investigates for the Prefecture. If they find it in his bag the most they will do is take it away."

Halle was looking toward the prison. "I fear my reputation won't be of much use to anyone after this." He glanced back at her. "But I'll worry about that later."

Madeline hesitated. There was something else she couldn't risk carrying into the prison in her pocket. She had given the two quiescent spheres in her carpetbag to Cusard to take back to the warehouse safehole. The active one, that she knew had been created with Arisilde's help, was wrapped in her handkerchief and currently weighing down her coat pocket. Both logic and instinct had said to hold on to it. *Witches' instinct*, Madeline thought. Not always worth listening to when you weren't one. Logic, and something she thought of as artist's instinct, told her to trust Halle.

She drew the sphere out of her pocket, carefully, feeling it thrum lightly against her fingers, and lowered it into the bag.

"What's that?" Halle asked, frowning.

Cusard looked puzzled as well. Knowing him, he had put the whole carpetbag in the safe without opening it. *Knowing Nicholas, Cusard was probably afraid Count Montesq's head was in it*, Madeline thought. She explained, "This is a magical device that may help us if we run into any more of those walking statues, or any other sorcery."

"Ah." Halle sounded relieved. "How do you use it?"

Good question, Madeline thought wryly. "I don't know. It works by itself."

Halle's expression was doubtful and Cusard rolled his eyes in eloquent comment; Madeline ignored both of them. She said, "May I carry your bag, Doctor? The guards know you, but I need a prop." That was true in more ways than one. She hadn't realized before what a calming effect donning makeup and proper costume had had on her.

Halle closed the bag and handed it to her.

As they hurried across the street toward the prison, Madeline wondered if she had gone mad and what Nicholas would say. *Nicholas damn well better not say a word*, she thought suddenly, remembering he had been the one to go into the damn place first, with Inspector Ronsarde of all people, and cause all this. Then they were in the shadow of the wall and under the arch that protected the entrance, the pavement damp underfoot and the stone radiating cold, and it was time to stop thinking entirely.

The man who stepped forward to stop them was a constable, not a prison warder. "There was a report of men injured here," Doctor Halle said quickly, before the man could speak. He managed to sound both out of breath and anxious, though undoubtedly the anxiety was real. Madeline thought his approach was ideal; guards from the prison had been involved in the riot and were sure to have been injured. No one could know if they had all been attended to yet or not.

The constable looked confused and mulish but one of the prison warders came forward, saying, "I thought they was all took to the surgeons. They said—"

"No, there are more still inside," Halle interrupted. "I spoke to Captain Defanse not an hour ago."

The prison warder swore and gestured emphatically at the heavy iron door. There was a grill in the center of it where another sentry could peer through; it swung open with a creak and then Halle was hurrying inside and Madeline was following him.

They passed through at least three grim chambers each guarded by heavy doors, iron gates, blank-eyed men, existing only to prevent those inside from getting out. Madeline tried not to think about the getting out part. *Find Nicholas and the others first, then worry about the rest.*

The next ironbound door opened into a tiny gray-walled court, little more than a shaft to let in light and air, then another door opened for them and she knew from the thick odor of carbolic that they were passing into the prison Infirmary.

It was a high, stone-walled chamber, with a vaulted ceiling overhead, with still visible oval patches of newer stone high on the walls where windows had been filled in long ago. The further end was walled off by wooden partitions but the beds in the two long rows nearest them seemed to be mostly occupied by constables or warders. There were guards at the door they had just come through and a few women in dresses of the dull brown of the prison warder uniform: wardresses probably hastily pressed into service to tend the injured.

From the shape and size of the place it had probably once been an old chapel. Madeline saw another door at the opposite end that would lead further into the prison interior. Then she spotted a man who must be the Infirmarian, a stoop-shouldered young man with a frazzled appearance and spectacles, dressed in an old suit with a stained apron over it. Halle saw him too but apparently not quite quickly enough, because he made to dodge behind a curtained partition and stopped when the Infirmarian called, "Doctor Halle! I didn't realize you were here."

Halle glanced at her and stepped forward to shake hands as the younger doctor hurried toward him, saying, "We've had quite a day, as you can see."

"Yes," Halle said, "I've been called in to speak to the governor about something. I'm not sure if he'll still be able to keep our appointment in this emergency, but I thought I'd better—"

"Of course, but while you're here, could you look at this one case, just for a moment. . . ."

Halle's lips thinned in frustration but he allowed himself to be led away. Madeline kept her eye on him, making sure the Infirmarian was only leading him down the row of beds a little ways, though she supposed it was too early to suspect traps. Halle's explanation had been offered smoothly enough, though a little too readily; fortunately the other doctor seemed too busy for suspicion. And who would suspect Doctor Cyran Halle of as mad a plan as this?

She should use the time to gather information and try to discover if Ronsarde had been recaptured and if there had been anyone with him. One of the prison wardresses was standing nearby, washing her hands in a metal sink against the wall. Madeline started toward her.

"Madame!" someone said. Madeline was too well-trained from stagework to jump guiltily or allow herself any other reaction. She ignored the preemptory summons and kept walking. Out of the corner of her eye she could see a man approaching her. *This is trouble*, she thought. He was older, stern-faced, dressed in a dark, very correct suit. Not another doctor. With the way her luck was running it was probably the prison governor himself.

He came straight toward her and she had to stop and acknowledge him with a nervous little duck of the head, the gesture a woman in her position would be expected to make. The nervous part wasn't hard to manage. "Who are you?" he demanded.

"Doctor Halle's nurse, sir." That should quiet him and send him off. Doctor Halle was a frequent visitor here.

Instead the man turned, spotted Halle with the other doctor and stared at him, his eyes darkening with suspicion. Madeline felt a coldness grow in the pit of her stomach.

Halle glanced up and saw him. He was too far away for Madeline to read his expression accurately, but she didn't think he looked happy. He excused himself to the Infirmarian and came toward them.

"Doctor Halle," the man said as he approached. "What are you doing here?"

Halle's expression was grim. He hesitated, then said, "Could we speak privately, Sir Redian?"

All Madeline felt was disgust at her luck. She didn't need to be told this was some high official of the prison, someone who wouldn't believe their hastily concocted lies. Redian eyed Halle a moment, then said, "Come this way."

Halle started after him but Madeline stayed where she was, trying to fade into the furniture. But Redian snapped, "Your nurse also, please."

Madeline swore under her breath. *Of course, I was always more accustomed to stealing scenes than to disappearing into the chorus.* Halle glanced back at her, his features betraying nothing, and she had no choice but to follow.

They were led away past a row of cubicles screened off by canvas partitions to a small office that must belong to the Infirmarian. It was cramped, the desk and shelves overflowing with papers, books, and medical glassware; not nearly grand enough for someone with a "Sir" in front of his name. Redian closed the door behind them and said, "Well?"

That single uncompromising word didn't give Halle much to work with and Madeline couldn't contribute without ruining her role. She stood with downcast eyes, her hands beginning to sweat on the handle of Doctor Halle's medical bag. The walls that blocked this office off from the rest of the Infirmary were thin and would conceal no loud noises. She wondered if she would have time to get the pistol out of the bag if Redian called for help, and exactly what good that might do her. The little room had no windows to leap out of. No, if Halle couldn't talk his way out of this, and it seemed unlikely, their only chance would be to take Redian hostage. *And that's no chance at all*, she thought.

Halle said, "I'm not sure what the cause is for this suspicion."

It was evasive but it made Redian talk. Glaring, he said, "The reason for suspicion is that your colleague Ronsarde escaped from the constables under what I lightly call extremely suspicious circumstances. The last reliable report we have is that he entered this institution. Now I find you here."

"That's ridiculous," Halle said, incredulous and annoyed. "Ronsarde was abducted, almost killed, you can't accuse him—"

"I was on the steps when the riot started," Redian retorted. "I know what I saw."

Halle had managed to distract him into a side issue but he was still only playing for time. "I don't care what you saw." Halle turned, took the medical bag from Madeline and opened it as if looking for something, then set it down in the chair she was standing next to, all the while saying angrily, "And if you knew anything at all you would realize the charges against him were complete fabrications."

Brilliant, Madeline thought and started to breathe again. He had placed the pistol easily within reach, almost directly under her hand. It wasn't quite as good as working with Nicholas but close, very close. Halle turned back to face Redian, shifting enough to the side that he blocked the man's view of both the bag and Madeline's right arm. That might give her the edge she

needed; if she didn't manage to surprise Redian, he
would have time to call for help.

"That is hardly the point," Redian was saying. "If
Ronsarde had a hand in this riot—" He stopped, grimaced and added, "And that is hardly the point either. I
want to know why you've come here, Halle. Do you
have anything to do with the armed men who forced
their way through one of the guard rooms after Ronsarde
escaped?"

"I can't believe you are accusing me—"

"Oh, we haven't caught them yet, but we will. Now
give me an answer or I'll have you turned over to the
Prefecture on suspicion of collusion in an escape."

Madeline dropped her handkerchief and bent down to
reach for it, reaching instead into the bag and finding
the grip of the pistol. The door burst open and Halle
started and turned. Madeline had a heartbeat to make the
decision and stayed where she was, half bent over, her
hand inside the bag. She looked at the door and saw a
young man in constable's uniform standing there, and
almost drew the gun, but he wasn't looking at her.

The constable was breathing hard, his eyes wide. He
said to Redian, "Sir! We found five dead men in the
lower level."

"What?"

"They're torn apart—it's sorcery, like what was outside."

Forgetting Halle, Redian strode to the door, following
the constable. Halle looked at Madeline, his face a study
in mixed relief and consternation. "Follow him?" he
asked softly.

"Yes," she whispered and pulled the pistol out of the
bag and slipped it into the pocket of her jacket.

Nicholas approached the archway carefully. Gas
hadn't been laid on in the last few corridors and it was
as dark as pitch. Their source of light was a stub of
candle Crack had had in his pocket, lit from one of the
last sconces. It was now dripping hot wax onto Nicholas's glove as he slid carefully along the damp wall. The

curve of it and the way it was constructed suggested the prison sewer outlet was just on the other side. He hoped they wouldn't have ghouls to contend with as well, though he didn't see any way in from the sewer tunnel.

Nicholas reached the darker shadow across the wall that was the low opening of the archway. A current of air came from it, also damp, but just as stale and flat as the atmosphere in all the passages. It was not an encouraging sign.

Improvements in the walls, gas laid on, new doors, Nicholas thought. Let them not have had time to block in the catacombs that led up from the old fortress's crypt to the new prison's mortuary. Let fate grant him that one small favor.

No ghouls or other inhuman products of an insane sorcerer's craft leapt out at him and he slipped inside the archway. He lifted the candle.

The jumbled contents of the low-ceilinged chamber were in the disarray he remembered. Old bones, splintered wood from coffins, broken fragments of fine stone that had once sealed grave vaults, all heaped on the stone-flagged floor and covered with dust and filth. Except that a path had been hewn through it, pushing the jumbled mounds to the walls, and at the far end the passage that should have led upward was sealed with nearly new brick.

Nicholas was too tired to curse Fate at the moment. He would have to remember to do it later. They must have had escapes, somehow. He couldn't take credit for that. When he had broken Crack out a few years ago he had left a reasonable substitute in the form of a recent corpse from the city morgue in his place; Crack was marked down in the prison records as dead. This debacle was the result of untidy persons who broke out on their own and left trails any fool could follow.

He ducked back out the archway and returned down the passage to where the others waited. "It's blocked. There's only one alternative."

"Steal guard uniforms and try to bluff our way out,"

Reynard said. His sour expression revealed how likely he thought the chances of success were.

Nicholas knew success was not only unlikely, but with Inspector Ronsarde along, wounded and sure to be recognized by any constable they might pass, it was damned impossible. At this point he was even desperate enough to risk the sewer, but they had no way to get to it. "I'm open to suggestions," he said dryly.

Leaning heavily against the wall, Ronsarde said promptly, "I have one."

"If it's the one you've had the last three times I asked, I don't want to hear it again," Nicholas said. He was aware his patience was wearing thin, making him more likely to make mistakes, but there was little he could do about it now.

Ronsarde only grew more determined. "You said yourself, if I am not with you it would be relatively easy to explain your presence. You could walk out of here with a blessing from the prison officials—"

"And leave you to bleed to death?" Nicholas interrupted. *What kind of man do you take me for?* He wanted to ask, and managed to hold it back just in time. Damn fool question to ask Ronsarde, when he didn't know himself.

"It is out of the question," Reynard said, but he said it in his cavalry captain's voice, very unlike the indolent tone of the bored sybarite that he usually affected. "Because it would be giving in to the bastard, whoever he is, who has gotten us into this with his damned sorcery. And that's what he wants us to do, so that is what must be avoided at all cost. That's elementary, for God's sake."

"This sorcerer wants you dead," Nicholas elaborated. He was grateful that Reynard was still supporting him; raised mostly in the slums among the criminal classes, among which he counted his paternal relatives, he wasn't accustomed to that kind of loyalty. "He went to an untold amount of trouble to arrange it. You must be close to discovering him. If you're taken by the authorities he'll move against you again, probably even more swiftly and probably taking quite a few other innocent bystanders down along with you.''

Ronsarde, who wasn't used to being argued with so effectively, said heatedly, ''You forget the most likely hypothesis is that the man is simply barking mad and has seized on me the same way he evidently has seized on you gentlemen, and he'll pursue us to the end no matter how close or how far we may be from discovering his identity or whereabouts.''

Nicholas and Reynard both started to answer but Crack, having reached the end of his patience, snapped, ''You're doing it again. You're standing still and arguing.''

Nicholas took a deep breath. ''You're right; let's keep moving.'' He turned and started back down the corridor.

Crack shouldered Ronsarde's arm despite the Inspector's mutinous glare and followed. Reynard caught up to Nicholas in a couple of long strides and asked, ''Where are we going?''

''If I knew—'' Nicholas began, speaking through gritted teeth.

Obviously feeling he had to make up for his earlier show of nobility, Reynard said, ''Sorry, sorry. Just trying to think ahead again; I can't seem to shake the habit.''

Nicholas said, ''Try.''

Madeline and Halle followed Redian out into the Infirmary again. There was a stretcher sitting on one of the long wooden tables holding the body of a man. Madeline caught a glimpse of flesh torn away to the bone and grabbed Doctor Halle's arm. This was partly in relief that the body was that of a constable and not Nicholas, Reynard or Crack, and partly to keep Halle from rushing up to it with the other doctors.

Redian stared down at the body of the constable, his expression sickened. He said, ''Has there been any sign of Ronsarde, or the men with him?''

''No, sir, nothing.'' The young constable looked ill. There were bloodstains on the sleeve of his uniform.

"We thought they were in the other wing so the search was concentrated there, and we only sent a few men down to the cellars."

Madeline drew Halle back from the frightened group around the stretcher and said, "Whatever did this is searching for Nicholas and the others."

He nodded. "There are a great many passages down in the lower levels. I don't know why they would have gone there unless they were forced to it . . . Wait, there was an escape using an old tunnel up from the crypt to the prison mortuary, so the tunnel was walled up. Could your friends have been making for it, thinking it was still in existence?"

Madeline bit her lip, considering. "When was it walled up?"

"Only last year."

"Yes, they could have thought it was still there."

Halle glanced back at Redian and began to move toward the corridor at the back of the Infirmary, drawing her with him. "Then I suggest we try to find them before anyone or anything else does."

"My thoughts exactly," Madeline murmured.

Nicholas traced their path back, finding a narrow stairway leading upward. They approached it with great caution since it was the only way up in this wing and the searchers might be watching it. But the intersection of corridors near the stairwell was just as empty as the other tunnels.

Leaving the others at the bottom, Nicholas went up to the first landing until he could lean around the wall and see what lay at the top. The head of the stairs was barred with a metal door with an iron grill in the top portion of it. He could tell the room beyond it was lit, that was all. After a moment of thought, he decided to risk it and crept upward toward the top of the stairs, glad that they were scarred stone instead of wood and there was no chance of creaking.

He edged cautiously up to the door and looked through the grill. Another guard room, with two warders and a constable deep in worried conversation. One of the warders had a rifle. *That can't be on our account, can it?* Nicholas thought. *We haven't even killed anyone yet.* No, it had to be for whatever was hunting them through this maze. They must know about the creature by now, surely. If the authorities killed the thing, at least it would be one less obstacle in their path, Nicholas decided, as he crept carefully back down the stairs. Of course it would also make it easier for the constables to hunt them. . . .

At the bottom of the stairwell the others were waiting anxiously. "Well?" Reynard asked.

"Two warders and a constable, well-armed." Nicholas described the door and the guard room briefly, then took a deep breath. This was not a good plan but it was all he could think of and they didn't have the time to sit about waiting for him to turn brilliant. "Crack will pretend to be a warder, and fumble with the keys to open the door." Crack nodded, not bothering to question this. His coat was dark brown, close in color to the coats the warders wore and in the dim light of the stairwell, it would be temporarily convincing. "You'll have a wounded man in tow to add an air of urgency."

"I shall be the wounded man, I think," Ronsarde said. He pointed to his right eye, which was nearly swollen shut and surrounded by a large purpling bruise. "This is rather convincing."

"It'll do." It was too bad they couldn't manage some more blood but. . . . Nicholas reminded himself not to get wrapped up in detail. "And once the door is opened, Reynard and I will push through and take them by surprise." *And then we shall all be shot and killed.* He looked at Reynard, expecting him to say something along those lines.

Reynard merely smiled and said, "It sounds perfect to me."

Just then they heard raised voices from the upper reaches of the stairwell, echoing down from the guard room through the grill in the door. A low mumble of male tones, then a woman's voice, the words muffled but clearly urgent. Frowning, Nicholas took an unconscious step up. It couldn't be. "That sounds like—"

"Madeline," Reynard finished, looking worriedly at Nicholas. "She wouldn't, surely she wouldn't."

Crack swore and clapped a hand to his forehead, the greatest emotional outburst Nicholas thought he had ever seen from his henchman. And it was all the confirmation he needed. He climbed the stairs to the first landing, listening hard.

From here he could pick out occasional words but nothing to make sense of this. He heard another man's voice with a more educated accent, saying something about medical attention. Ronsarde boosted himself up the last few steps and grabbed Reynard's arm for support. "That's Halle," he whispered, his tone incredulous. "What the—"

"Doctor Halle?" Nicholas asked, managing to keep his voice low, though what he wanted to do was rage.

"Yes, certainly."

Dammit, dammit. Nicholas gestured for the others to stay back and crept up to the door again. He flattened himself back against the wall and managed a quick glance through the grill. Madeline was in her dowdy nurse persona and carrying a doctor's bag, but the light in her eyes was dangerous and entirely her own. *She's distracted and slipping out of character—I'll have to speak to her about that,* he thought. *And a few other things.* He recognized the man with her as Doctor Halle and his mouth set in a grim line. *The nerve of the woman.*

All three of the guards were facing away now, arguing with Halle. And Nicholas's irritation with Madeline's precipitous behavior didn't change the fact that they would never have a better chance to get past this door. He stepped back down to the others and said softly, "Yes, it's them. Now let's go, just as we planned."

They scrambled quietly to get into position, Crack and Ronsarde moving to the step just below the landing, Nicholas and Reynard behind them and ducking down so they wouldn't be seen. At Nicholas's signal, Crack banged on the door suddenly, shouting, "Open up, it's right behind us!" With Ronsarde moaning in pain, he stuck one of the keys in the lock and jiggled it, as if in his panic he couldn't make it turn.

There was shouting from the other side of the door, then the lock clicked and one of the guards jerked it open. Ronsarde pitched forward to collapse at the man's feet, immobilizing him and keeping the door from being slammed shut. Crack lurched forward, apparently stumbling over his wounded companion, then he knocked the startled guard flat. Nicholas and Reynard pushed forward before the other two men could react, Reynard catching the rifle barrel just as it was lowering to cover them and slamming the wielder back against the wall. Nicholas looked frantically for the third man and saw Madeline had him by the collar with a pistol shoved under his ear.

Nicholas stepped back, letting Reynard tell their prisoners to lay down on the dirty floor. When Crack removed the constable from Madeline's grasp, Nicholas said, "Well, this is a surprise."

"We found you," Madeline said, sounding quite pleased with herself.

Nicholas stared at her, not sure if he couldn't answer because he was seething with rage or because he was merely exhausted. He glanced at Doctor Halle, who was trying to examine Ronsarde's injuries despite the Inspector's attempts to fend him off. "It's moderately helpful. Now there are six of us stuck in here."

Madeline's brows lowered dangerously. She opened the medical bag, burrowed in it, and produced a small paper-wrapped packet. "Did you think we would come in here with no notion of how to get out again?"

Reynard was tying up one of the warders with the man's own belt. He glanced up and laughed shortly. "We did."

Nicholas glared at Reynard, then said, "What's that?"

"Blasting powder. Cusard's special mix."

Nicholas gasped in relief. "Brilliant!" He snatched the packet from her.

"You're welcome," Madeline said with acerbity.

Then Nicholas saw what else was in the bag. "You brought one of the spheres? I told you to take them to—"

"I was," Madeline interrupted. "I thought it would be useful against all this sorcery—"

"Useful? How?"

Madeline lowered her voice to a hiss. "It's been doing things."

"Things?"

"Magical things. You saw those stone gargoyles that were chasing people all over the plaza?" At his nod she explained, "It turned one back to stone."

He took her arm and drew her out the door and down a few steps, out of earshot of the guards. He kept one hand on his pistol, mindful that they weren't alone in these corridors. "Just like that? You didn't do anything to it?"

"Just like that." Madeline gestured in exasperation. "Nicholas, this device is as far beyond me as the role of Elenge would be for my dresser. I don't know what it did, but it did it, of its own will, with no help from me."

"But it's never done anything before," Nicholas protested. He was unaccustomed to feeling foolish and he didn't like it much. He took the sphere out of the bag and examined it as best he could in the bad light. It looked no different than it ever had, a device of nested gears and wheels that apparently had no purpose, something that might be a child's toy.

"It was sitting on a shelf at Coldcourt. Maybe it never felt the need to do anything before."

That was true. Nicholas gave it back to her and ran a hand through his hair, trying to think how to handle this development. *Edouard, Edouard, couldn't you have stuck with natural philosophy?* "We don't have time to deal with it now, we've got to get out of here."

"How?" Reynard asked, coming down the stairs to them. He had the constable's rifle and Nicholas was relieved that they were a little better armed now. "Are you thinking of blasting open that blocked passage up to the mortuary? The whole place will know where we are and they'll be waiting for us at the other end.''

"I know, that's why we're going out through the sewer. Once in it, we can take any direction, leave it at almost any street. They won't have any hope of anticipating our direction.''

"Yes, perfect.'' Ronsarde seconded the motion. For one of the foremost representatives of law and order in the country, he seemed to be entering into lawbreaking with real enthusiasm.

"We're going to leave those men tied up?'' Halle said, as they followed Nicholas down the stairs. "With that thing roaming these corridors?''

"We left it trapped on the other side of an iron door, it will have to find a way past that first,'' Nicholas said. "Besides, it won't go up to the ground floor while we're still down here—it wants us. Crack, pull that door to and lock it.''

Nicholas led them back to the wall that adjoined the sewer. It was near the point where the corridor dead-ended into the catacombs, which meant they would be trapped down here if anything came in after them. *I hope that is actually the sewer behind this*, he thought, sitting on his heels to carefully unwrap the package and lay out the contents on the stone flags. If it wasn't, he was going to cause an awful commotion for nothing. He noted Reynard and Crack were taking the weapons to guard the open end of the corridor. That would buy them a few moments if they were discovered, but much depended on Nicholas getting this right the first time.

The blasting powder itself was contained within a small glass vial, carefully stoppered with a cork. Most of the package contained the accoutrements for it, including a long coiled fuse and small chisel to set the charge within a wall. Madeline knelt beside him, saying quietly, "Cusard tried to tell me how to do it myself if I had to, but I'm just as glad I don't.''

"Watch carefully, in case you ever have to again.'' Nicholas squinted up at the wall in the bad light, trying to judge the best point to set the charge. He had chosen a spot between two heavy support pillars, hoping they would hold up the ceiling if he made a mistake. He only wanted to make a small hole, just large enough for a human body to pass through easily.

"If you need assistance, do say so," Ronsarde said.

Nicholas glanced back and saw that Halle had retrieved his medical bag from Madeline and was redoing their makeshift bandage of Ronsarde's head injury. That was good; if they were going into the sewer, the less odor of blood about them the better. The sewers had been their enemy's territory up until now; for that reason Nicholas hoped what they were doing would be unexpected.

Madeline watched as he chiseled out a hole in the damp pitted surface of the wall. "Are you going to shout at me later for allying myself with Halle?" She sounded more abstractly curious than apprehensive at the prospect.

Nicholas glanced back at the Inspector and the doctor again. They were just out of earshot and deep in their own conversation. He said, "I suppose I could, for all the good it would do, since you would simply stand there and nod, going over the soliloquy from *Camielle* in your head. Of course, I'd be a hypocritical bastard, since all this came about because in a moment of weakness I decided to rescue Inspector Ronsarde." Nicholas finished the hole, then reached for the glass vial. "Stop breathing for the next few moments, please."

Madeline held her breath while he measured out a small quantity of the powder onto a piece of the packing paper and carefully slid it down into the spot prepared for it in the wall. When he nodded that it was all right, she said, "A moment of weakness?"

Nicholas picked up the fuse. "Yes. We'll see how weak if I end up having to break all of us out of here again, this time from the cellblocks after our trials."

Madeline's expression was serious. "Do you think he'll do that? Turn us in?"

Nicholas let out his breath. It had been a long day for hard questions. "If you were him, you wouldn't. If I was him, I might, in the right mood. I don't know.''

Madeline drew breath to speak, then made a startled exclamation instead. She lifted the sphere from her lap, looking into it. ''Something's coming.''

Nicholas stared down at the sphere, frowning, then at the empty corridor stretching away in the half-light. ''How do you know?''

''It's humming, it does that when it senses power. Touch it.''

Nicholas hesitated, then reached down and touched the metal of the sphere with a fingertip. It was oddly warm and Madeline was right, it was resonating slightly. ''We have a problem,'' Nicholas said, pitching his voice louder to get the others' attention.

Crack said suddenly, ''Wait, do you smell that? It's here again.''

''Yes,'' Reynard said, shifting his hold on the rifle. ''That's it.''

In another moment Nicholas knew what they meant. A foul odor was drifting down the corridor, the same miasma that had hung over the area where they had found the mutilated warder. He turned back to the wall, attaching the fuse, making himself work carefully; there would be no time to try again.

Madeline stood, still looking into the sphere, and moved up with Crack and Reynard. Reynard glanced at her and said, ''My dear, really—''

''Hush, I know what I'm doing,'' Madeline said, then added, ''I haven't the faintest idea of what I'm doing, but this thing seems to.''

Ronsarde struggled to his feet with Halle's help, saying, ''That is one of Edouard Viller's famous, or infamous, magical spheres. I hadn't thought to ever see one in use.''

''I rather hope we don't have to see it now,'' Halle said. ''Is there anything we can do to help?''

''I'm almost finished.'' Nicholas unrolled the fuse then quickly packed up the remains of the materials, though he hoped they wouldn't need them again. Halle came to help him and to put the package back into his medical bag. As Nicholas stood to tell the others he was ready, he heard it.

A scratching, like heavy nails against rock, accompanied by a sibilant hiss, echoed down the corridor. Madeline and Reynard glanced at each other and Crack stood like a stone, pistol held ready, waiting for whatever was out there to charge.

It can't be very big, Nicholas thought, *not and fit through these doors*. It couldn't be as powerful as the last Sending either, or they would all surely be dead by now. Maybe that had hurt their sorcerous opponent, to loose that great store of magical power and have it snuffed out by the Great Spell that protected Madele's house. Whatever it was, they couldn't see it yet, but that didn't mean it wasn't near. It had managed to kill at least several armed men so far. He unrolled the fuse, backing toward where the others were waiting, laying the cord out along the floor. This gave them about twenty feet of clearance. He wasn't sure that would be enough, but moving any further up the corridor was out of the question. Nicholas said, "I'm ready to set off the charge. When it goes off, the creature may come at us."

Leaning against the wall, Ronsarde said, "We've no choice."

"I'm aware of that," Nicholas said, managing to keep his voice mild and reaching for the candle.

Madeline shouted suddenly and Nicholas looked up to see the corridor ahead of them go dark, as if a wave of shadow was rolling down it. He lit the fuse and shouted, "Get down!"

The blast was a shock, louder than Nicholas had expected. He fell against the wall, ducking his head as his back was peppered with fragments of rock. He looked up to find himself blinded by dust and smoke and said, "Everyone all right?"

There were answering calls and some violent coughing.

Nicholas groped along the floor until he found the candle, blown out by the force of the explosion, then got to his feet. He shook his head, which did absolutely nothing for the ringing in his ears, and stumbled back toward the wall. Between the dust hanging in the heavy air and the darkness it was impossible to see and he had to feel along the wall for the opening. He tripped on a chunk of blasted stone and almost fell through the hole. It was at waist height, larger than he had expected; the stone hadn't been as thick as it had looked. *Lucky I didn't bring the ceiling down on top of us.* "Here!" he shouted.

As he got the candle lit again, the others managed to find him. They were all covered with brick dust, their faces smudged with smoke, and he supposed he looked as bad as they did.

Madeline was holding someone's handkerchief over her face, the sphere tucked securely under her arm. "It's not humming as loudly now," she reported. "The explosion must have frightened that thing."

"For the moment, at least," Nicholas agreed. The dust was settling, aided by the damp air from the sewer. He lifted the candle. Through the gaping rent in the wall he could see a wide tunnel with an arched roof, lined with uneven stone blocks. There were ledges along both sides and a stream of dark water running between. A stench rose off that water, striking him like a blow in the stomach. Ducking his head, he stepped through the hole.

Crack scrambled through after him, saying tersely, "Ghouls."

Nicholas tested his footing on the slimy stone. "I haven't seen any."

"Didn't see any last time, either."

There was a minor altercation occurring in the corridor, as Halle and Ronsarde tried to make Madeline go next and she protested, "No, I have the sphere, I should go last to cover our escape."

"Gentlemen, it is useless to argue with her," Nicholas told them grimly. He helped Ronsarde step through, then moved back to give Halle room on the ledge.

Reynard solved the Madeline problem by wrapping an arm around her waist and lifting her bodily through the gap, then stepping through after her. "If you'd seen what it did in the alley," she was saying, "you'd realize what I mean. It reacts to the presence of magic—Good God, what a stink."

"Half the prison knows where we are now," Reynard reminded them. "Which way?"

"Here," Nicholas said, moving forward to pick a path along the ledge. The sewer was running roughly eastward, toward the river. He hoped they didn't have to go that far. They had only a short time before the constables followed the sound of the blast and swarmed down here after them. Two streets over would be as far as they could safely go. Fortunately it would be growing dark outside and with every other odd thing that had happened in this part of the city today, people climbing out of the sewer would not be that much to remark on.

"The sphere is humming again," Madeline said, breathless at the stink and the effort of walking on the slick stone in her long skirts. "That creature didn't stay frightened for long."

Wonderful, Nicholas thought. *Perhaps it will stop and eat more constables.* He didn't think that was likely; there was no question it was after them.

They kept moving, muffled curses marking occasional stumbles. The sewer was a long tunnel, vanishing into darkness a few feet in front of their candle, dissolving into it behind them as they moved along. Vienne had literally miles of sewers, some new and easily traversed by the sewermen in sluice carts or boats, others old and so choked by refuse as to be almost impassable even by water. They were lucky that this was one of the newly built tunnels.

The filthy air was making it hard to breathe, but Nicholas noted the odor of rats was growing stronger, though the sewer seemed strangely empty of the rodents. The ledge grew narrow in places and Nicholas caught Madeline's arm both to steady her and to reassure himself. Most of her attention was on the sphere.

The sphere's humming was getting louder; Nicholas could hear it now himself. Madeline was holding it nervously; she had taken off her gloves and her bare hands left traces of moisture on the stained metal surface. The rank, animal odor was more intense, combining with the effluvia of filth from the water below and making it difficult to draw a full breath. It was how intelligent the thing was that really mattered and how afraid it was of the sphere, Nicholas realized.

"How much further?" Madeline said. Her voice was thick.

"Just far enough," Nicholas told her. "It would be a shame after all this to come up within sight of the Prefecture or the prison gates."

Madeline laughed, a short gasp that turned into a choking cough. *And if we manage to escape everything else that's after us, the stench may still kill us*, Nicholas thought.

"Nic," Reynard said suddenly. "There's something behind us."

"Keep moving," Nicholas said. Looking back, he caught a glimpse of a shadow shifting in the blackness, something that might be a trick of the light and his imagination. He knew it was all too real.

They managed perhaps another fifty yards down the sewer, before Nicholas said, "We've come far enough." He had been counting paces and even given a generous margin of error, they should be at least two streets east of the prison by now. "Look for an outlet."

"Thank God," Reynard muttered from behind him. "I thought we were going all the way to the river."

"There's a ladder up here," Halle said. Nicholas peered into the dimness ahead, then suddenly caught sight of it himself.

Nicholas handed Halle the candle and stepped up beneath the ladder, which led upward to a round metal cover in the curved roof. It was a street access for the sewermen. "Reynard, would you make certain we're in the right place?"

"The wrong place being the prison courtyard or the steps in front of the Magistrates Court, I presume." Reynard handed the rifle to Nicholas, then caught the lowest

rung of the ladder and swung up it. Nicholas faced back
the way they had come, the gunstock sweat-slick in his
hands. He heard the heavy metal cover slide over, grating on stone, then muted daylight suddenly washed
down through the tunnel. Nicholas thought he saw a
form scramble back to the edge of shadow. He had the
sudden conviction that it had changed, that it had taken
a shape more suited to this fetid underground river.
"Hurry," he suggested from between gritted teeth.

"It's Graci Street," Reynard said from above. "Come
on!"

Halle came forward, half-supporting Ronsarde, and
Nicholas realized the Inspector was in far worse case
than he had been before. In the wan daylight his face
was gray and he was gasping for breath. *He's old*, Nicholas thought suddenly. *He wasn't a young man when
Edouard died, but I didn't realize how old. . . .* Halle
climbed far enough to hand his medical bag up to Reynard, then reached down to pull Ronsarde up the ladder,
apparently on strength of will alone. It was going to be
slow. Nicholas told Crack, "Help them."

Crack hesitated and Nicholas gave him a push. "Go,
dammit, help them."

Crack pocketed his pistol and gave Ronsarde a boost
from behind, climbing up after him.

Nicholas looked back down the sewer. The darkness
was pressing close, a palpable barrier. He swallowed in
a dry throat. The next few moments would make all the
difference.

Crack was through the opening now and looking anxiously down at them.

Staring into the sphere, Madeline said tensely, "Go
on."

Nicholas caught her arm. "Madeline, I'm not going
to argue with you—"

The darkness surged forward, blotting out the fading
daylight from the opening overhead just as a burst of
white light flared with the strength of a bomb blast. Madeline cried out and they both fell back against the slick
wall.

It took long moments for Nicholas's vision to adjust to the dimness again, to be able to see anything beyond the spots of brilliance swimming in front of his eyes. The light from the opening overhead showed him nothing but empty ledges, the water below, the brick-lined tunnel leading off into the dark. But he could see further than he had before and there was nothing moving in those shadows but the flow of the stream. The others were shouting down from above, demanding to know what had happened.

Madeline pushed herself away from the wall and made a futile effort to brush at the stains on her dress. The sphere she was still holding carefully in the crook of her arm was silent. "I told you so," she said, pre-occupied. "Edouard built it for this, after all." She caught the rung of the ladder and swung up easily, one-handed.

I'm beginning to believe he did, Nicholas thought, and slung the rifle over his shoulder to climb after her.

14

It was full dark by the time they reached the warehouse
but Nicholas only meant to stop there temporarily. The
small offices there were fairly comfortless and he wanted
to avoid Coldcourt and every other place that Octave
might have some knowledge of. So after greetings and
exclamations of relief from Cusard and Lamane, he bundled everyone into Cusard's wagon and directed him to
a safehouse they had had some occasion to use in the
past, an apartment on the third floor of a small
limestone-faced tenement near the Boulevard Panzan.
There was no concierge to ask awkward questions and
few other tenants.

The wagon pulled into the carriage alley between the
buildings and Nicholas climbed down to unlock the side
door. The small lobby was dusty and undisturbed, but
he sent Crack up to make sure the stairs were clear anyway.

Madeline swung down from the wagonboard and
climbed the stoop to stand next to him. Her hair was in
wild disarray and she looked exhausted. She said, "Ronsarde doesn't look well. We're lucky Halle is here."

"I suppose." Leaning against the ornamental iron
railing around the stoop, Nicholas rubbed the bridge of
his nose. His head was still pounding from the explosion
and standing still for a moment had made him realize
how very badly he needed a bath and a change of clothing. And to fall down on a bed for a week. To fall down

on a bed for a week with Madeline would have been even better. "This day is not going quite as I had originally planned."

"Quite." Madeline's expression was wry.

"Thank you for saving our lives."

Her mouth twisted. "You're welcome, I suppose."

Before Nicholas could question that comment, Crack appeared in the darkened hall and gestured for them to come up.

Nicholas went first to unlock the door and briefly check the apartment. It was a modest town residence with a salon and parlor, dining room, bedchamber and dressing room, maid's room and kitchen. The air was stale and dusty and the windows were covered with thick draperies and shades, the furniture concealed under dust covers. He went through the small kitchen to check the back door, which gave on to an outer wooden stair that led down into a narrow alley next to the building's court; that and the small trapdoor in the pantry that allowed access to the roof were the chief reasons he had originally selected the place. After reassuring himself that all the outer doors and windows were securely locked and showed no signs of tampering, he returned to the front door and called softly for the others to come up.

He stepped back as Reynard and Doctor Halle helped Inspector Ronsarde inside. "Take him to the salon," Nicholas said, opening one of the doors off the small bare foyer. "There's a couch and the lamps are better."

Nicholas went down the hall and back to the kitchen, to lean against one of the cold stone counters and try to get his thoughts in order. He heard Crack rummaging in the pantry for the coal store, Madeline's voice giving instructions, the others tramping about.

Finally Madeline came in, eyed him a moment, then leaned against the china closet and said, "Well?"

Nicholas took in her appearance thoughtfully. "You look like a charwoman. I don't suppose there are any roles at the Elegante next season which require that?"

"Thank you," Madeline said, inclining her head graciously. "I shall certainly keep it in mind." Her expression turned serious. "I gave my word to Halle, you know."

"Is that what this is about?" Nicholas couldn't quite manage to laugh. "They are the least of our worries."

Madeline hesitated. "This sorcerer. . . ."

"Is determined to kill all of us, true, but that's not what I was thinking of. Donatien is dead, Madeline. It's over."

At the mention of the name, Madeline glanced reflexively at the closed door. "But they don't know—"

"I suspect Ronsarde does know. Whether he will act on that knowledge or not, I have no idea. After we saved his life, I think not. And he still needs our help."

She was silent a moment. "So it's over."

"Yes."

She looked away, as if she couldn't quite believe it. "Is that such a bad thing?"

Nicholas's jaw hardened. "It also means the plan for Montesq is over."

Madeline stared at him, startled. "I'd forgotten it. With everything . . . I can't believe I forgot about it." She shook her head, disturbed. "But we can't just let that go. Perhaps—"

It was Nicholas's turn to look away. That it all still meant something to Madeline was a relief but he wouldn't show it. "We can't continue with the plan. Ronsarde would know and that would destroy the whole point of it."

Madeline paced the cold tile floor, coming up with several objections which she started to voice and then reconsidered. Finally she stopped, hands on hips, and said, "So that's it. We're letting Montesq get away with it?"

Not necessarily, Nicholas thought. He would have to kill Montesq himself. It lacked the elegance of allowing the state to execute the Count for a crime he hadn't committed, but it would be accomplishing the same end, even if Nicholas himself didn't survive it. He said, "For all practical purposes."

Madeline did him the courtesy of looking worried instead of skeptical. She said, "Donatien would kill Ronsarde."

Nicholas pushed away from the counter. "You're the one who gets lost in your roles, my dear. Besides, Donatien isn't in charge anymore, I am."

"That's supposed to reassure me?"

Nicholas had no answer for that so he pretended not to hear her and went down the hall to stand in the open doorway of the salon. The lamps had been lit and Crack had gotten a fire started in the hearth, dissipating the cold dampness and making the room almost livable.

The dust covers had been pulled away from the broad divan and Doctor Halle was trying to tend to Ronsarde, who was fending him off with acerbic comments about physicians who thought their services indispensable; Halle deflected the sarcasm with the air of long practice and continued treating the Inspector's injuries. Reynard was leaning against the mantel, watching them. Nicholas waited until Halle had finished and was repacking the contents of his medical bag, then caught Reynard's eye. "I'd like a word alone with the Inspector, please."

"Of course," Reynard said easily, gesturing for Doctor Halle to precede him out. Halle went but his face was guarded; Reynard was worried too, though only someone who knew him well would have been able to discern it. Nicholas smiled bleakly to himself. So Reynard was uneasy about what attitude Nicholas would take to their new allies as well.

The only person who didn't appear uneasy was Ronsarde himself, who was smiling expectantly at him as Nicholas closed the door behind Reynard and Halle. Ronsarde was still pale and had a swollen eye and a darkening bruise on his jaw, but with the wound in his forehead stitched and the dried blood cleaned away, he looked considerably better. He said, "You were saying?"

Nicholas hesitated, but couldn't for the life of him think what Ronsarde meant. "Excuse me?"

"About the sorcerer who is so intimately involved in this affair. We are still pooling our resources?"

Ronsarde was continuing the conversation begun when they had first taken refuge in the prison, as if all the intervening struggles hadn't taken place, or had meant nothing. Well, perhaps they hadn't. Nicholas said, "I was saying that it is very possible he believes himself to be Constant Macob. But you already knew that."

Ronsarde shook his head. "Young man—"

Nicholas fought a flash of annoyance and lost. "You know my name, sir, don't pretend otherwise." This was no time for masquerades.

"Valiarde, then." But the Inspector said nothing for a moment, only watched Nicholas thoughtfully. "I had heard you meant to become a physician," he said finally.

"Events conspired against me." Nicholas moved to the window, lifting the musty damask curtain just enough to give him a view of the street. "I recognized you that night at Gabrill House, though I don't think you recognized me."

"No, I did not," Ronsarde admitted. "I thought your voice familiar, but it had been too long since we last spoke."

"Since the trial, you mean." *Ten years, eight months, fourteen days.* Nicholas performed the calculation automatically. "You must have recognized the sphere."

"Yes, that I knew only too well. I would have come to you eventually, if you had not come to me, so to speak." Ronsarde hesitated, then said, "Count Rive Montesq has had such a run of poor luck since that time, hasn't he?"

Nicholas dropped the curtain and turned slowly to face the older man, leaning back to sit on the windowsill and folding his arms. Ronsarde's expression was merely curious, that was all. Nicholas smiled and said, "Has he really?"

"Oh, yes. He has had several large losses of funds and property in the last few years. Not enough to bankrupt him, of course, but enough to seriously inconvenience. And then there have been the losses among his staff. One of his chief financiers, a solicitor, and two personal servants, all vanished without a trace."

"How terrible," Nicholas commented. He was glad at least that Ronsarde didn't know everything; Montesq had suffered more losses than that. "But then perhaps it's simply a visitation by Fate."

"Perhaps." Ronsarde shrugged, then winced as if the motion pained him. "If I didn't know that the solicitor was a blackmailer of the worse stripe, who had ruined a number of individuals and provoked the suicide of at least one victim, that the financier was his ally in that enterprise, and that the two servants had second careers as thugs and extortionists, I might have been moved to do something about it. But somehow I never quite found the time."

And am I expected to thank you for that? Nicholas thought. He looked away. This cat and mouse game was not particularly to his liking, even though they both seemed to be taking the role of the cat. "Why were you watching Doctor Octave that night?"

Ronsarde accepted the change in subject gracefully. "Several weeks ago a lady came to me for my assistance in a matter concerning Doctor Octave. Her mother was paying him to hold circles for her and produce various deceased relatives on command. As you might expect, the family was quite wealthy. I began to investigate the good doctor, but could prove nothing definite. He was very careful." Ronsarde stared into the middle distance, a rueful anger in his expression. "I realize now he was warned against me by this sorcerer whose necromantic activities he evidently supports. Sorcery gives the criminal an unfair advantage."

"There are ways to even the balance," Nicholas said, his voice dry.

Ronsarde's quick smile flickered and the good humor returned to his eyes. "I imagine you are quite familiar with them. But to continue, I managed to help the lady convince her mother to leave the dead in peace, but I still pursued Octave. I discovered that Lady Everset would be hosting a circle and that in all probability it would be held in her garden. This was the first opportunity I had had to observe a circle at close range, when

Octave had no knowledge that I would be present.''

"That's why I was there, too," Nicholas said, without thinking, and then grimaced and reminded himself not to say too much. All these years of caution and concealment and here he was talking to Ronsarde as if he were as close a colleague as Madeline or Reynard. Being hunted by mad sorcerers and ghouls had obviously unhinged him. "You didn't realize he was connected with the disappearances."

It was Ronsarde's turn to look uncomfortable. He tugged the blanket more closely around him with a short angry jerk. "No, I did not," he said. "Halle had examined the three bodies that had been recovered at various times from the river and he drew my attention to the lichen. It is a variety that flourishes in the presence of magic. That, and the style of the injuries made before death caused me to believe someone was imprisoning these individuals and killing them in the course of necromantic magics. I noted the similarities to the murders of Constant Macob, committed two centuries ago."

Nicholas frowned in annoyance. He hadn't noted it, not until the scene in the cellar of Valent House, when it had become obvious. *The Executions of Rogere*, the book Doctor Uberque had lent him, had been even more illuminating. One of the methods Macob had used to lure his victims was to poison them with an herbal mixture that caused symptoms anywhere from mild confusion all the way to unreasoning terror. How he had gotten his victims to ingest it was a mystery to the writer of the account, though Nicholas wondered if the stuff might be so potent it could be absorbed through the skin. It explained the confusion and odd behavior of Jeal Meule, as described by the penny sheet *The Review of the Day*, and why her neighbors had been unable to convince her to go home before her second disappearance. She must have escaped her captor at some point but the poison had clouded her mind and kept her helpless, until he had been able to collect her again. Nicholas asked Ronsarde, "Why did it suggest Macob so readily?"

"Macob's crimes and his trial were well documented

for the time and give much vital information regarding the mind of a man bent on mutilation and mass murder. I'd read the history of it before, but I found it especially useful three years ago in the case of the Viscount of March-Bannot, who was—''

''Cutting people's heads off and throwing them in the river. Yes, I vaguely recall it.''

''Octave and his associates made the mistake of disposing of one body under the bridge at Alter Point and not into the river itself. The presence of the lichen marked it as part of the same case and not one of the many other unfortunates who are found dead every day in Vienne. Mud adhering to the pants legs indicated the edge of Riverside where it bordered on the Gabardin.''

''Yes, I found Valent House as well.''

''Before I did.'' Ronsarde smiled faintly. ''Octave was frequently seen near the place, by a person who is at times my informant, who recognized the good doctor after he had been described to him.'' His expression turned pensive. ''After the circle at Gabrill House I knew someone else had Octave under observation. When I discovered Valent House two days ago it also became apparent that someone else had discovered it first. The signs that my quarry had left in haste and that his lair had been thoroughly searched were unmistakable. I wasn't certain if I had a second opponent, but I knew that Octave did.''

Nicholas didn't comment. It had been so very close. Ronsarde had been one step behind him, at the most. He said, ''Surely you weren't arrested for breaking into Valent House.''

''Oh, no,'' Ronsarde said, gesturing dismissively. ''I was arrested for breaking into Mondollot House.''

Yes, exactly. Nicholas kept his elation in check; there were still too many questions unanswered. ''You wanted to look at a small sealed room in one of the subcellars. If you got that far, you found it empty, but there were signs it had not been unoccupied for long.''

''Yes.'' Ronsarde was watching him as intently as if Nicholas were a suspect he was questioning. ''In actuality the chamber belongs to Ventarin House, destroyed years ago when Ducal Court Street was cut through. I realized Octave had an interest in the Ventarins during the first circle I watched. The family whose deceased relatives he was currently interfering with had been a distant connection of the Ventarins, virtually the only people left in the city of any relation to them whatsoever. Octave questioned their dead on the old Ventarin Great House's location and its cellars. I believed at the time that he was only after hidden family plate or other trinkets. It wasn't until I made the connection with Macob that the facts took on a more sinister tone.''

"Yes, two centuries ago Gabard Ventarin was King Rogere's Court Sorcerer and presided at Constant Macob's execution,'' Nicholas said. ''Do you know what was there, in the large box that was removed from the chamber?''

"I have no idea,'' Ronsarde admitted. He shook his head after a moment. ''We could draw the conclusion that this sorcerer, who seems to believe himself a reincarnation of the Necromancer Macob, had some reason to believe there were relics of his idol stored in the chamber and wished to retrieve them.''

"We could draw that conclusion,'' Nicholas said reluctantly, ''but we might also wonder why relics of a famous criminal were buried deep inside a sealed room beneath a powerful sorcerer's home, and not on display somewhere.''

"It isn't encouraging,'' Ronsarde agreed. ''Whatever it was, Ventarin seems to have felt that it needed to be concealed and guarded. And we must assume our sorcerer opponent has had it since. . . .''

"Four days ago,'' Nicholas supplied.

Ronsarde gazed curiously at him. ''How did you discover the chamber?''

"It was how I and my associates became embroiled in all this,'' Nicholas said, evasively. ''Through an entirely coincidental . . . occurrence.'' He was not going to tell Ronsarde he and Octave had both decided to rob Mondollot House on the same night. ''Octave believed

I had been to the room before him and removed something. Oddly enough, I hadn't. The room was empty when I entered it. Octave wanted to question the late Duke of Mondollot, I assume to ascertain if he discovered the room before his death and removed some part of the contents, but the Duchess refused to cooperate with him." Nicholas hesitated. "Why did you break into Mondollot House? Wouldn't the Duchess have given you access if you had asked?" *After she hid anything linking her to Bisran trading concerns, of course.*

"Possibly. After discovering Valent House I realized how very dangerous my opponents were and also, how very influential their friends." Ronsarde's expression was grimly amused. "It was intimated to me by my superiors, and I use the term lightly, that I just de-emphasize my investigation. To avoid panic, you see."

"Ah," Nicholas breathed. *De-emphasize an investigation of multiple abductions and murders, to avoid panic. Yes, that sounds like the Vienne Prefecture.* "Which brings us to Count Rive Montesq."

"Yes, he has been shown to have a pernicious influence on Lord Albier, who is currently acting head of the Prefecture." Ronsarde's gaze sharpened. "I am not surprised you knew that."

Careful, Nicholas reminded himself. *Very, very careful.* "My interest in Montesq is entirely academic," he said lightly.

"Of course. But all this aside, we must find this sorcerer, and to find him, we must question Octave." Ronsarde let out his breath in annoyance. "Unfortunately, when I was arrested, I lost track of his whereabouts."

Nicholas smiled. "Fortunately, I haven't."

Nicholas pushed open the kitchen door to find the others all gathered there, most of them standing and staring at the floor as if they were attending a particularly dreary wake. "Are you all just standing about in here?" he demanded. "What's wrong with you?"

"Everything all right?" Reynard asked, with an uncharacteristic air of caution.

"Of course." Nicholas ran a hand through his hair impatiently. "Madeline, we need to consult you on makeup and clothing for disguises, and Crack, you'll need to fetch Devis, and Reynard—"

"We?" Halle interrupted, his expression cautious.

"Yes, we. What are you all staring at?" Before anyone could formulate an answer, Ronsarde pushed open the door behind Nicholas. He was leaning heavily on the wall, an expression of grim determination on his features. "I see no reason why I cannot accompany you," the Inspector said, almost peevishly.

"Disguised as what?" Nicholas asked him. "A cripple selling matches?"

"That would be ideal."

"Until you have to run away!"

"I could sit in the coach," Ronsarde persisted.

"What would be the point of that?" Nicholas asked, exasperated. It was like dealing with a less sensible version of Madeline.

"He's right," Halle said, coming forward to take Ronsarde's arm and urge him back down the hall toward the salon. "You need rest if you're to be of any help. You can't go running about the city. . . ."

Their voices continued, raised in argument, and Nicholas rubbed his hands together, his mind already on the task ahead. "I need to make a list. We're going to need Cusard for this, too." As he left the kitchen he heard Reynard's ironic comment, "Oh, good, now there's two of them."

After setting some of the wheels in motion and sending Crack for Cusard, Nicholas found the others gathered in the salon, looking at the sphere which was set atop a pillow on a small table. It looked like nothing more than an odd sort of curio or ornament. Nicholas leaned in the doorway and folded his arms.

"How does it work?" Halle asked, touching the metal with cautious curiosity.

Madeline looked over at Nicholas, who shifted a little uncomfortably, and said, "We don't know."

"You don't know?" Ronsarde echoed.

"Edouard left no instructions," Nicholas explained reluctantly. "None of the intact spheres ever reacted to anything at all, until this one transformed one of the gargoyles back into stone when it attacked Madeline. It was pure chance she had it with her at all. There are two others, but one appears to be dead and the other didn't react to the gargoyles."

"You did nothing to cause this one to act?" Ronsarde asked, with a hard stare at Madeline. "You felt nothing?"

"I did nothing," Madeline replied, faintly exasperated. "I felt quite a number of things—fear, anger, the desire to shriek with hysteria. I've felt those emotions before and never had magic spontaneously erupt." She shook her head impatiently. "I have a small talent for witchery which I've never tried seriously to cultivate, but I've helped my grandmother with spells and I know what working one feels like. That thing acted all on its own account."

"Madeline's grandmother is a witch of some repute," Nicholas said, smiling slightly at the understatement. "She's agreed to attempt to help us with our difficulties and will be arriving soon from Lodun." *We hope*, he added to himself.

"Is there no sorcerer currently in town whose opinion we could seek?" Ronsarde persisted. He added wryly, "There are some attached to the Prefecture but I can no longer command their assistance. In fact they would be more likely to turn me in to the nearest constable at once."

Halle grunted agreement and Nicholas speculated that Ronsarde had made his opinions on sorcery known in no uncertain terms to the practitioners who worked for the Prefecture. "There is a sorcerer whose advice I would like to have. He was the one who helped Edouard construct this sphere," Nicholas admitted. "But he's badly ill, in a sort of paralysis."

"Arisilde Damal?" Ronsarde asked, brows lifting.

Nicholas nodded warily. He had forgotten how much

Ronsarde had learned about Edouard's work during the Crown investigation and the trial.

"It was the opinion of many that he had left the country," Ronsarde said thoughtfully. "I was asked several times by persons at Lodun to locate him, but was always unsuccessful."

"That isn't surprising. If Arisilde didn't want to be found, it would be impossible to locate him even if you were standing in the same room."

"An unfortunate tendency of sorcerers," Ronsarde agreed. "He is ill?"

"Yes." Nicholas hesitated. "We thought at first it might have been caused by our opponent—it occurred at a rather inopportune moment."

Reynard snorted at the choice of words.

"But it's more likely the result of poor health and an opium addiction," Nicholas finished.

Halle cleared his throat. "Has he been attended? I could examine him. . . ."

Nicholas shook his head. "He's being seen by a Doctor Brile, who has already brought in other physicians to consult with. I don't think there's anything anyone can do."

There was a moment of silence, then Halle said quietly, "I know Doctor Brile. He's a very accomplished physician and your friend is in good hands."

Nicholas realized he had everyone's attention and that he must have betrayed more than he meant to. He said, "But the point is there is no other sorcerer I will risk taking the sphere to." He looked down at the apparently innocuous device. "It's too unpredictable."

Fontainon House itself was unbreachable, at least without Arisilde's help, and there was simply no possibility of any of their group receiving last-minute invitations. Taking Octave at his hotel would have been the best solution, but they had little time to make arrangements and after a brief scouting mission Madeline reported that the prospects were not ideal. Octave seemed to realize his danger. He spent all his time either locked in his room or in one of the lounges surrounded by dozens of people.

The next best opportunity would have been late at night after the circle, when Octave was relaxed with his success and the other participants would be on the way home and the worse for the large quantities of wine and brandy consumed before and after the festivities. But for some reason he was not quite willing to articulate, even to himself, Nicholas felt it better not to allow Octave to perform the circle at all.

Madeline had questioned this in her usual fashion, during the long afternoon when Nicholas had been trying to work out details and make contact with the more far-flung elements of his organization. "Why should you care what happens to the woman, just because she's a relative of the Queen? I thought you said once that Ile-Rien could go hang."

"It can still go hang for all I care," Nicholas had replied with some acerbity. "It might be just another one of Octave's confidence schemes, but if it isn't, I don't want to give this fool who thinks he's Macob another victory."

Madeline had sighed and given up her game of trying to make him admit fond feelings for his home country. "If he was a fool, we wouldn't be in this mess, would we?"

"No," Nicholas had admitted. "No, we wouldn't."

At the first opportunity he and Madeline had put together disguises out of the things she had purchased for tonight and, with Crack along for protection, gone to Arisilde's garret in the Philosopher's Cross. Nicholas had taken the sphere with him, out of a hope he didn't dare voice to anyone else. But he knew it was a foolish hope when Madeline sat on the edge of Arisilde's bed with it and the sphere did nothing but hum and tremble, the way it did in the presence of any magic.

"It's no good," Madeline had said, when he followed her to the door. "It must be a natural illness, as the doctor thought, and not a spell."

"It was worth a try," Nicholas said. "You and Crack

go on and take the sphere back. I'll be along shortly.''

She had hesitated, but in the end she had gone without questions.

Nicholas went back to the bedchamber and took a chair near Isham, who was patiently guarding his friend. Arisilde looked the same as he had that first night, his face drawn and pinched, his skin pale as wax. "We've got some help for you. She should be arriving tomorrow," Nicholas told Isham, and explained about Madele.

"She will be much welcomed," Isham said. He was seated in a straight-backed chair at Arisilde's bedside and looked worn and tired. "The physicians say they can do nothing." Isham watched the sorcerer's still face for a time, then said, "I used to try to stop him, sometimes. I talked and talked, which did no good, and then I tried to hide his poisons, which was foolish. If I destroyed them he simply got more."

"Hiding things from Arisilde is rather problematic," Nicholas agreed. Isham was skirting the edge of something that had occupied his own thoughts. "I should have tried harder myself. He might have listened to me." Admitting even that much was an effort. Nicholas had never liked to give in or acknowledge defeat. Maybe if he hadn't been so afraid of failure he would have tried harder.

Isham shook his head. "We can only work with what we have."

On impulse Nicholas asked, "What did you make of the sphere?"

"I've never seen its like before." Isham had examined the device tentatively before Madeline had taken it away, but made no comment on it. "It's something Arisilde has made?"

"He helped make it. It's capable of working magic; Madeline used it once or twice but she isn't sure how. It seems to work if and when it likes."

"Rather like Arisilde," Isham observed.

"Rather like," Nicholas agreed, smiling.

Later, back at the apartment, they had held another council of war. They agreed that the only time to take

Octave would be when he was on the way to Fontainon House. This was complicated by Reynard's discovery that the royal cousin meant to send her own coach for the spiritualist.

"You realize of course that we're all going to be executed as anarchists," Reynard had pointed out.

"It may be a royal coach, but there's not going to be anyone royal in it, and it won't be guarded as if there were."

"So we'll only appear to be anarchists to the untrained eye."

Nicholas rubbed his forehead. "Reynard. . . ."

"If we succeed in capturing Octave, then what?" This was from Doctor Halle.

"Then we ask him where his sorcerer is." Nicholas leaned back against the escritoire and folded his arms, anticipating the next objection.

"And if he doesn't want to tell us?" Halle said.

Nicholas smiled. "Then we explain to him that it would be better if he did."

"I won't participate in that," Halle said flatly. "And I won't condone it."

"You saw Valent House," Nicholas said. "We know Octave condoned that. For all we know he participated."

"And I won't lower myself to that level."

You can't talk to these people, Nicholas thought. "I doubt we'll have to go quite as low as that," he said, lifting a brow. "Octave doesn't seem the stoic type to me."

Later, Nicholas had been walking down the passage outside the salon, when he heard Doctor Halle's voice from within and the words made him pause. "Are you certain you know what you're doing?"

Ronsarde's voice, preoccupied, replied, "You will have to be more specific, old man."

"I'm talking about Valiarde." Halle sounded impatient.

Ronsarde chuckled. "He's an ally, Cyran, and a good one. You and I are getting somewhat old for all this—"

"That's beside the point." Halle took a deep breath, then said quietly, "Have you looked into that young man's eyes?"

There was a moment's silence. Then in a far more serious tone, Ronsarde said, "Yes, I have. And I'm greatly afraid that I'm one of the men who helped place that cold opacity there. He wasn't like that before his foster father died."

"So you will, at least, be cautious."

"I'm always cautious."

"Now that's a damned lie. You would like to think yourself cautious but I can assure you—"

The conversation devolved into commonplaces and after a moment, Nicholas walked on. None of it meant anything, of course. Neither one of them knew him at all. But it took an effort of will to avoid the mirror at the end of the passage.

The mist was thick, pooling heavily around the nearest street lamp like the creature of the fay called the boneless, which had once haunted the less well-travelled country roads. Arisilde and some of the sorcerers who had spoken of their craft at Lodun favored the presence of mist for the working of illusions; Nicholas couldn't help but wonder if it aided the working of more dangerous magics as well.

He paced along the stone walk at the edge of the muddy street, rubbing his arms for warmth. The neighborhood was blessedly quiet. Directly behind Nicholas was a block of upper-class apartments with a row of arabesqued lintels under the second floor windows and an ornamental ironwork fence along the street level. The main entrance was on the cross street, and the inhabitants would mostly be out dining or at the theater at this time. Across from it was the massive, forbiddingly dark façade of an older Great House, closed for the season except for caretakers. On the upper corner was the side entrance of a quiet and highly respectable hotel.

There was little traffic except for the occasional passerby and the cabriolet parked near the walk. It was an older vehicle, purchased this afternoon for this purpose, and Devis was on the box, making occasional clucking noises at the two rented horses. Nicholas was dressed as a cabman too, in a slightly shabby greatcoat and fingerless gloves, and a round cap tipped back on his head. Together they must have made a convincing impression, since several people had tried to hire them, only to be told they had already been hired for someone inside the apartments.

For all the apparent quiet of the neighborhood, Fontainon House was only a few hundred yards down the street. Nicholas could see the gas lamps illuminating its carriage entrance, and sometimes hear the voices of an arriving party. Everyone had had something to say about his choice of site for the ambush, but there had been no other place on the possible routes between here and Octave's hotel that was fairly quiet and that Nicholas was sure the coach would have to pass.

They would just have to be quick and not only for fear of the constables and the detachment of the Royal Guard attached to Fontainon House. They were only safe from the sorcerer while he believed Nicholas and Ronsarde to be dead. *After this, he's going to know we're definitely not dead*, Nicholas thought grimly. *Out of our minds and flailing about like idiots maybe, but not dead.*

One of the horses lifted her head and snorted and an instant later Nicholas heard the clop of hooves from an approaching vehicle. He and Devis exchanged a look and Devis straightened up and adjusted his reins nervously.

Nicholas stepped into the street to meet the cabriolet as it materialized out of the mist. It was his own vehicle, the one Devis usually drove, with Crack and Reynard on the box. Nicholas caught the bridle of one of the horses, stroking the anxious animal's neck as it recognized him and began to aggressively snuffle at his pockets for treats. "They're not far behind us," Reynard said in a low voice as he leaned down. "Two coachmen, one groom on the back, no outriders. And the coach doesn't have the royal seal, only the Fontainon family crest."

"So we're not technically anarchists yet," Nicholas said, in mock innocence.

"Not technically," Reynard agreed, smiling sourly. "But we have hopes."

Crack allowed himself a mild grimace at the levity. Then Nicholas stepped back. A couple had emerged from the side entrance of the hotel on the corner and were strolling down the street in their direction. It was Madeline and Doctor Halle, and their appearance meant they had just seen the Fontainon coach turn onto the cross street that was visible from the windows of the hotel's cafe. Nicholas said, "Get ready."

Reynard swung down from the box, pretending to be doing something with the harness, and Nicholas moved with apparent idleness to the front of Devis's cab so he could give him the signal.

In another moment Nicholas heard the approach of a larger, heavier vehicle than a cabriolet, then he saw its shape approaching them out of the mist. The coach drew nearer and he could see the liveried driver and footman on the box. Nicholas turned away, leaning casually against the side of the cab, and fished in his pocket for the round firework packet that was standing in for an anarchist's bomb. He struck a match and lit the fuse, then as the noise of the approaching coach grew louder, turned and tossed it into the center of the street.

It went off with a loud pop that echoed back from the buildings around them. Smoke poured out of it as the horses screamed and reared and the Fontainon coach jolted to a halt. "A bomb!" Nicholas yelled, running across the street.

Devis allowed his frantic team to rear and then turned them, letting them sling the cab half across the street in front of the coach and blocking its escape. Halted near the smoke, the frightened horses continued to rear and buck, looking as if they meant to tear the cab apart and further terrifying the coach's team. Reynard had leapt down off the cabriolet and was now running around, yelling like a panic-stricken maniac. On the far promenade, Madeline shrieked and fainted convincingly into

Doctor Halle's arms. Crack stood up on the box, nearly tumbled off as his team tried to join the confused horses in the center of the street, then pointed down the alley next to the apartment block and shouted, "I saw him! He threw the bomb and went that way!"

When they had discussed the plan earlier today, Inspector Ronsarde had been especially fond of that touch.

Nicholas dodged through the growing wall of smoke and almost ran directly into the footman who had been riding on the back of the coach. The man's forehead was bleeding, as if he had fallen when the vehicle had jolted to a halt. Nicholas grabbed him and yelled frantically, "It was a bomb, go get help!" and sent him staggering away.

Nicholas reached the coach just as the door swung open and Octave fell out. Nicholas grabbed him by the front of his coat and threw him back against the vehicle. "Surprised?" he asked.

"What do you want?" Octave stammered. A flare from the sputtering firework showed Nicholas the other man's face: he was sickly pale in the white light, his staring eyes red-rimmed and his flesh sagging. Nicholas was bitterly glad the last few days had obviously not been kind to Doctor Octave, either.

"You know what I want—your sorcerer. Where is he?" They needed to get Octave into Devis's cab and away, but Nicholas could hear Reynard arguing with someone on the other side of the coach, saying something about an entire crew of anarchists running off down the alley. He considered trying to drag Octave to the cab alone, but if the spiritualist resisted at all and was seen, their plan would fall apart.

"I'll tell you. I'll tell you if you'll protect me—You don't know what he is—"

Nicholas shook him. "Where is he? Tell me, Doctor, it's your only chance."

"The palace . . . the palace on the river. He's been there—" Octave's voice rose to a sudden shriek. "There!"

Nicholas had only an instant to realize it wasn't a

trick. Something gripped his shoulder and he was flung to the ground. He rolled over on the muddy stone, the breath knocked out of him, and saw a figure standing over Doctor Octave.

In the poor light and the haze from the firework, he first thought it was a man. He could see the skirts of a greatcoat, a shape that might be a hat, but then he realized how it was towering over Octave, shaking him as if he was a child, and he knew that it wasn't human.

Nicholas fumbled for the revolver in his coat pocket. He had brought it reluctantly, not liking the thought of one of the coach drivers or footmen accidentally shot, but not meaning this night's work to fail, either. He drew the gun, aimed at the creature's head and fired.

It turned toward him, still keeping a grip on the struggling Octave's coat, and snarled. Nicholas scrambled backward, took aim and fired again, though he knew the first shot hadn't missed. *The Unseelie Court would be easier to fight*, he thought in exasperation. At least the fay were highly susceptible to gunfire; the creatures of human sorcery and necromancy obviously were not.

It dropped Octave then and started toward Nicholas, moving slowly, its steps deliberate. Nicholas struggled to his feet and backed away. The concealing smoke was still swirling around them and the coach was blocking the yellow light of the street lamp; he wanted to see what this thing was. Octave lay like a lump on the street, moving only feebly, and Nicholas cursed under his breath. Sacrificing himself so that Doctor Octave could escape a probably righteous and well-deserved fate hadn't been in his plans either, but he couldn't let the man be killed until he knew where the sorcerer was hiding.

The tall figure stalked him, stepping out of the shadow of the coach. Its face was that of an old man, with craggy, uneven features, but as the light shifted it became a death's head, the skin stretched over it to parchment thinness. Nicholas kept moving back, luring it further from Octave, who had managed to struggle to his knees and was trying to crawl away.

Octave must have made some noise, or perhaps it read something in Nicholas's expression, because it turned suddenly and bounded back toward the injured spiritualist. "No, dammit, no," Nicholas shouted, starting forward.

It reached Octave in one leap and swung at him with an almost careless backhanded blow. Nicholas saw Octave fall back to the street, spasm once, then go limp. He stopped, cursing, then realized the thing was turning toward him again.

Nicholas moved away, raising the pistol, though it hadn't done him much good before. He saw Reynard coming around the coach and waved him back. Reynard halted, surprised, then got a glimpse of the creature as it moved into the light again. He stepped back, reaching into his coat for his own revolver.

There was a shout and a loud clatter from up the street. Nicholas couldn't risk a quick glance behind him but whatever was coming the creature saw it and stopped where it was with a thwarted growl. Then it stepped back into the shadows.

Nicholas blinked, resisting the impulse to rub his eyes. The shape of the creature was growing darker, harder to see, fading into the pool of shadow on the street until it was gone.

Nicholas stared at the darkness where it had been, then looked for what had alarmed the thing.

A horse troop was coming toward them from down the street, at least twenty men. Nicholas swore under his breath. A mounted troop meant only one thing: Royal Guards. He whistled a signal that meant "cut and run" and the frantic activity around the coach grew more frantic as the cabriolet suddenly drove off. Nicholas stayed where he was. He was in the middle of the street, in the full light of the gas lamp. If he ran, the horsemen would chase him. The others were almost invisible in the shadows and the troop wouldn't be able to clear the wreckage of the coach quickly enough to chase Crack's vehicle.

Nicholas clicked on the revolver's safety, then dropped it into the street. As he turned back toward the coach, he casually kicked it into the gutter.

The smoke eddied in the still damp air as the firework sparked one last time and went out. Devis had vanished from the rented cab, leaving it and the confused horses to block the street. Madeline and Doctor Halle were nowhere to be seen, having had orders to retreat back to the hotel on the corner as soon as the confusion was well underway. He couldn't see Reynard either and hoped he had had time to swing aboard the cabriolet before it left. One of the Fontainon footmen was sitting on the curb, still stunned from falling from the box. The coachman had managed to calm his horses finally and now staggered around the side, stopping when he saw Octave.

He bent over the spiritualist anxiously, gripping his shoulder. Nicholas stopped beside him and saw the man needn't have bothered; Octave's head was twisted at an unnatural angle, the neck cleanly broken. He resisted an urge to kick the unresponsive body. "He's dead," the coachman said, suddenly realizing it. He looked up at Nicholas, confused. He had a shallow cut in his forehead that was bleeding into tangled gray hair. "Did you see what happened?"

Nicholas shook his head in bewilderment and in his best Riverside accent replied, "They said there was a bomb, but all I saw was that sparkler. Are you sure he's dead?" He sat on his heels beside Octave's body, flipping his coat open as if looking for a wound and unobtrusively searching the pockets. He was beginning to understand Octave's behavior. He had been afraid of being cornered by Nicholas, afraid of being caught by the Prefecture, but he had become even more terrified of his sorcerous ally.

"He looks dead," the coachman muttered, looking away and clutching his head. "I would've sworn it was a bomb."

Octave didn't have the sphere on him. *Damned fool*, Nicholas thought. *How was he going to perform a circle without it?* Unless this was the last circle and Octave had stayed for it only because he needed the money to flee. Lady Bianci wasn't a member of the *demi monde*, she was true aristocracy, and would have paid the spiritualist for trying even if he hadn't been able to produce any messages from the dead.

Then the horsetroop was surrounding them. Nicholas stood and stepped back against the coach to avoid being run down. From their badges and braid they were Royal Guard, probably dispatched from the nearby Prince's Gate to help defend Fontainon House. The lieutenant reined in just in time to keep from trampling the injured coachman and demanded, "What happened here?"

"We were attacked and this gentleman killed! What does it look like?" the coachman shouted, standing up suddenly. Before the lieutenant could reply, the older man swayed, clutching his head, and started to collapse. Nicholas stepped forward hastily to catch him and ease him to the ground, thinking he couldn't have arranged a better distraction himself.

There was more shouting and confusion, the two footmen were located, and the major-domo of Fontainon House and the corporal in charge of that Guard detachment appeared to add to the conflict. The coachman was revived enough to give his version of events, which disagreed with the footmen's version, to which Nicholas helpfully added conflicting detail, glad that the blustering Guard lieutenant hadn't the sense to split them up and question them separately. This resulted in the conclusion that there had been six anarchists, who had thrown a firework instead of a real bomb, and had probably meant to cause a Public Incident of some sort. Nicholas wasn't sure how they were defining Public Incident but reluctantly decided it was better not to call attention to himself by asking.

"But how was this man killed?" the lieutenant demanded, staring worriedly down at Octave. They had sent one of the Guards to bring Lady Bianci's personal physician from Fontainon House, but everyone knew it for an empty gesture. "His neck looks broken. Did he fall from the coach?"

Nicholas shifted uneasily and scratched his head in

bewilderment along with everyone else. Then the Fontainon major-domo suggested, "The coach door is open. Perhaps he tried to step out and when the horses reared he was thrown down?"

"Yes, that could very well be what happened," the lieutenant said, stroking his mustache thoughtfully. There were nods of agreement among the Fontainon servants. Octave's death might conceivably have been blamed on them and this was a convenient out. "Yes, that must be it," the lieutenant concluded and there were relieved sighs all around. He looked up then, frowning. "But who was shooting?"

Nicholas rubbed the bridge of his nose, annoyed. *That should have been your first question, you idiot.* "Must have been the anarchists, to scare the horses," he muttered, low under his breath.

One of the footmen heard him and took up the theme. "They was shooting, sir, to scare the horses!"

"Yes, that was it," the coachman seconded, and there were more nods of agreement and surreptitious relieved sighs. Nicholas smiled to himself. With all this obfuscation, by morning no one would remember what he had seen or who had claimed to see what, and that was just as well.

There was a clatter behind the wrecked coach as another party arrived from Fontainon House, led by a man in evening dress carrying a doctor's bag, who must be the lady's personal physician. He fought his way past the horses of the milling Guard troop and demanded, "Whose vehicle is this blocking the street? It will have to be moved so we can bring in a stretcher for the injured."

While the corporal and the major-domo were explaining that haste was no longer necessary on the injured man's behalf, Nicholas touched his cap to the lieutenant and said, "All right to move my cab, sir?"

The lieutenant nodded and waved him away distractedly. Nicholas went immediately to the cab, freeing the reins from where someone had tied them to the lamp post, murmuring some soothing words to the still restive horses. It hadn't been necessary to claim the cab as his; everyone had simply assumed that the person who looked like a cab man belonged to the only empty vehicle.

Nicholas had grabbed the rail and was stepping up to swing into the box, when someone just behind him said, "Stop."

Nicholas hesitated for a heartbeat, then made a conscious decision to obey. He was close to escape and didn't intend to ruin it by panicking for no reason. He looked back and saw a tall gray-haired man in formal evening dress. *Someone from Fontainon House*, Nicholas thought first, then he recognized him. It was Rahene Fallier, the Court Sorcerer. Nicholas's mouth went dry. He said, "Sir?"

Fallier took a step closer. He said, "There was sorcery here tonight. Did you witness it?"

Interfering bastard, Nicholas thought. It was too late to change his story; the Guard lieutenant wasn't that much of a fool. "No, sir, I didn't see nothing of the kind."

The corporal from Fontainon House was coming over. He was an older man than the lieutenant, with more intelligent eyes. He said, "Sir, did you want to question this man?" To Nicholas he called, "You there, step down."

They were drawing the attention of the mounted Guards still half searching the area for nonexistent anarchists. Nicholas protested, "They told me to move the cab," but he stepped back down to the scuffed paving stones. Fallier might not be as suspicious as he seemed.

Fallier took another step toward him, standing only a bare pace away, so that Nicholas had to look up at him. He was frowning, concentrating. *Working a spell?* Nicholas wondered, keeping his face blank. He remembered powerful sorcerers could sense the past presence of magic. The Sending Octave's sorcerer had unleashed on him might leave some residue. Or Fallier might detect traces of Arisilde's powerful spells from the sphere Nicholas had held earlier today.

Then Fallier said, "The resemblance is striking. And you are younger than you look, of course."

Nicholas let himself appear puzzled. *He knows who I am*, the thought burned as cold as ice thrust through the heart. He had never met Fallier in his own persona, never seen him at closer range than across the crowded pit at the opera. *"The resemblance is striking."* Fallier knew what he was, as well.

Fallier half-turned to the Guard corporal. "We must detain this man—"

Nicholas moved, not toward the waiting circle of horsemen but back toward the cab, turning and diving under its wheels in the oldest street trick there was. He rolled under the vehicle, narrowly avoiding a crushed skull as one of the horses started and the wheels rocked back, ducked out from under it and bolted away.

There were shouts behind him, the clatter of hooves, as he ran for the corner. Two turns away these broad well-lit streets gave way to the crowded byways and overhung tenements of the old city, where there were alleys so narrow the horses couldn't follow him. But first he had to get there.

He heard someone riding up on him from the right and dodged sideways so the mounted trooper plunged past him before he could stop. The man wrenched his horse around sharply and the animal reared. Nicholas ducked away from the flailing hooves and ran for the corner again.

Suddenly there was a solid wall not ten feet away, rising out of the lingering mist. Nicholas slid to a stop, baffled, then cursed his own stupidity as he realized what it must be. He flung himself forward but a riding crop cracked across his shoulders, sending him sprawling headlong over the raised curve of the promenade.

Before he could scramble up hands grabbed the back of his coat and dragged him to his feet. He was flung up against a wall—a real one, this time, not Fallier's illusory creation that was already fading gently away into the damp night air—and his arms were pinned behind him, as someone roughly searched his pockets.

He heard the Guard lieutenant saying, "Where do you want him taken? The nearest Prefecture is—"

Yes, the Prefecture, Nicholas thought, a sudden spark of hope blossoming. Being imprisoned as an anarchist was a better fate than some things that could happen and Fallier might not want to drag up ancient scandals. And he knew there wasn't a prison in Ile-Rien that could hold him for long. *Fallier might not know as much as he thinks he does. . . .*

"Not the Prefecture, the palace," the Court Sorcerer's voice said.

Well, that's that. Nicholas laughed, and the two Guards pinning him twitched as if startled. He said, "But really, the palace? Isn't that rather melodramatic?"

Someone must have gestured because he was jerked away from the cold stone and turned to face Fallier and the lieutenant. The Court Sorcerer didn't even have the grace to look triumphant. His expression was merely cool. The lieutenant looked a little wary, probably at Nicholas's sudden change of accent and voice. Then Fallier said, "It hasn't been a very well-fated destination for members of your family. I can only hope history repeats itself."

Nicholas smiled in acknowledgement. "The least you could do is tell me how you knew."

"No," Fallier said. "That is not the least I can do," and gestured to the Guards to take him away.

15

Madeline took the stairs up to the apartment two at a time. She reached the door and fumbled with the key, cursing herself when she saw how badly her hands were shaking. Finally the lock turned and she flung the door open.

Lamane was standing in the doorway to the salon, staring blankly at her. "Did Nicholas come back here?" she demanded.

He shook his head. "No, no one's come. What's happened?" Inspector Ronsarde appeared in the doorway past him, a blanket draped over his shoulders.

Madeline shut the door behind her. "No telegrams, messages?"

"No, there's been nothing." Lamane looked a little unnerved. Madeline didn't imagine her expression was terribly reassuring at the moment. She leaned back against the heavy wooden door. This had been her last hope. If Nicholas had been unable to meet them for reasons of his own he would have come here or sent a message. She rubbed her temples, trying to massage away the ache of tension.

Ronsarde let out his breath in exasperation and came forward to take her arm and draw her inside the salon. The fire was burning brightly and a card game was laid out on one of the little tables. Ronsarde led her firmly to one of the well-upholstered couches, saying, "Sit down, calm yourself, and tell me what has happened."

Madeline sat down, glaring at him. "Don't treat me like one of those stupid women who come to the Prefecture because they think their neighbors are shocking them with electric current—"

"Then don't become hysterical," he said sharply. "What has gone wrong?"

She looked away. It wasn't his fault and the last thing they needed to do now was argue. "I think Nicholas was caught."

Ronsarde's face hardened. "By whom?"

Madeline drew breath to speak and then hesitated, remembering who and what he was. *No, we're in this too deeply to hold back now*, she thought, exasperated at herself. *And Halle knows already*. But she trusted Halle more than she did Ronsarde. She said, "A detachment of the Royal Guard rode up as the others were leaving. Nicholas was trapped in the middle of the street and couldn't slip away." She quickly told him everything Reynard had witnessed during the carriage wreck concerning Octave's death and the intrusion of the sorcerer again. "The others are still searching for Nicholas, trying to discover if he was taken to the Prefecture or the palace. . . ." Madeline was the only one who knew what that might mean, that there was a reason other than the crimes he had committed as Donatien that the palace might be interested in Nicholas.

Ronsarde threw the blanket off and paced. Lamane had found a walking cane for him somewhere and his limp didn't seem to slow him down much, as if some of the old energy Halle had described in his articles was returning to him. He said, "This sorcerer's ability to anticipate our movements is distressing."

"He can't have put another Sending on us," Madeline protested, gesturing around her at the apartment. "We would all be dead."

"Oh yes, if he had been able to fix his power on one of us, we would never have gotten through the sewer alive and we certainly wouldn't have been able to take shelter here unmolested for so long. No, it was Doctor Octave he was following, watching somehow, knowing our next step would be to accost him." Ronsarde stopped in front of the hearth, staring into it, eyes narrowed. "He unites the ferocity of a madman with the cognitive ability of the sane; this is not a pleasant combination."

"What about Nicholas?" Madeline said, running a hand through her hair wearily. She wasn't accustomed to feeling helpless and it wasn't a sensation she found agreeable in the least.

"If he has been taken to the palace, I can help," Ronsarde said. His mouth twisted wryly. "I should say, I can try to help. Appealing to them directly was an avenue I meant to take once we had obtained more solid evidence for our theories. It's always risky to approach royalty, especially after one's just escaped from prison—you never know the attitude they are going to assume. But even without official assistance I can still secure entry to the place, at least for the present."

Madeline exchanged a look with Lamane, who shrugged, baffled. She thought Ronsarde was babbling and with everything else that had gone wrong, it didn't much surprise her at all.

The outer door rattled again and they all tensed, Lamane reaching for the pistol in his coat, but it was Crack who stepped through the salon door. He went immediately to Madeline, standing in front of her and breathing hard. He said, "It's the palace."

She swallowed in a suddenly dry throat. She hadn't believed it, not really, not until now. "How do you know?"

"The Captain found somebody who seen the troop go back in through Prince's Gate. He was with 'em."

"Then we are committed." Ronsarde nodded to himself. "We will pursue the best course we can and hope we are not making a possibly fatal mistake." He looked around the room thoughtfully, as if marshalling nonexistent troops, ignoring the way the others were staring at him. "I will need your help to obtain materials for a disguise, young lady. . . ."

* * *

Nicholas had never been to the palace before, not even in the areas on the north side which were open to the public during Bank Holidays. He had not thought it particularly politic, or sensible, to attend, even though there was said to be a museum display of items from the Bisran Wars in the old Summer Residence that he would have quite liked to see.

He did not think it was particularly politic, or sensible, to be entering the palace now, but then the choice wasn't his.

The plaza in front of Prince's Gate was lit by gas lamps and there were so many torches in the towers that the whole edifice looked as if it was on fire. The light washed the ancient stone blocks of the walls and the great iron-sheathed doors with a dull orange-red glow. There was a line of crested carriages waiting to enter the palace grounds for some occasion, with the usual crowd of idlers there to watch.

Nicholas was on horseback, one of the troopers leading his mount, the sound of the hooves muted by paving stones softened and polished by time. The Guards at the gate halted the carriages as the troop passed under the great arch of the Queen Ravenna Memorial. A few necks craned as the occupants tried to see who the troop was escorting, but Nicholas had been placed near the center and he thought no one could get a good view. They had bound his hands with a set of manacles held together by a lock that he would have found laughable under less serious circumstances. He had two pieces of wire sewn into the cuff of his shirtsleeve that would open it with little trouble. It was Fallier he was worried about.

The Court Sorcerer was riding ahead in his coach, a fashionable vehicle with the royal crest on its doors. The gate Guard saluted as it went by. Nicholas was watching the back of it even as they passed through Prince's Gate, more aware of it than the menace inherent in the battlemented walls and the armed men surrounding him.

Try as he might, he couldn't cast Rahene Fallier as Octave's mad sorcerer. He didn't know much about Fallier personally, but everything he knew about his political career suggested a more subtle man than the sorcerer who had transformed the Courts Plaza into a battle-ground.

As they drew away from the gate the torchlight faded and the shadows grew thick. The troop drew rein in a dark cobblestoned court whose uneven surface spoke of many years use. Gaslight and other such modern inno-vations evidently had not come to this part of the palace; there were only oil lamps and the scattered illumination from the windows above to light the court. It was sur-rounded, turned into a deep well almost, by old stone and timbered buildings of elegant design, by massive stone edifices with fantastically carved pediments and new structures of brick, which seemed stark and ugly against the older work. Nicholas realized with a shock that they had passed within the wards, must have passed them at some point outside the gate. *And I didn't even turn to stone*, he thought.

He saw that Fallier's coach continued on, vanishing under a deep archway. This was one of the oldest sec-tions of the whole walled complex, built to be a fortress and the center of Vienne's defenses. The newer section lay behind the ancient King's Bastion and was more open, designed more for comfort and entertainment, and less for defense. The old buildings crumbling around him were also the most powerful ethereal point in the city, perhaps in all of Ile-Rien, better warded and more powerfully protected than even Lodun.

Dismounting from the restive cavalry horse, Nicholas pretended to clumsiness, stumbling and letting one of the troopers catch his arm to steady him. Recovering, he looked around at the circle of armed men, all larger than he was. With a rueful expression he said, "Am I that dangerous? Why not draw up an artillery battery?"

One of the troopers chuckled. Walking ahead, the lieutenant glared back at them and snapped his riding crop.

Nicholas smiled to himself, looking down to conceal the expression. He wanted them to think him harmless and he might be succeeding. He had bruises from falling in the street and his shoulder was sore from having his arm wrenched around behind him, but it was nothing that should keep him from taking any opportunity that presented itself.

That was assuming an opportunity presented itself. *Oh, no*, Nicholas thought, as the troopers hauled him across the court, *I'm becoming an optimist. I've obviously been with Madeline too long*. That thought reminded him of how worried she and the others would be. Well, as far as sorcerous attacks went, there wasn't a safer place in Ile-Rien. It was all the other dangers he had to worry about.

They took him toward one of the older buildings, a stone and timber structure with three or four stories. As they approached it, Nicholas noted the heavy beams and frame around the door and the apparent lack of windows in the lower floor; it was a guard barracks then, a very old one. He was hustled inside and through a high, timbered hall, empty except for a few Guardsmen talking idly. They glanced at Nicholas curiously as the group passed but didn't offer any comments. Nicholas marked potential exits and hazards as his captors led him up a flight of wooden stairs at the end of the hall, then down a short corridor.

They stopped before a door and one of the Guards fumbled with keys. They had shed most of the troop by now, either down in the court or coming up through the main hall of the barracks, but there were still five of them and that was about four too many.

The door opened finally and he was led into a small room, windowless, walled with dingy plaster with a plain wooden chair and table the only furnishings. One of them took the manacles off, which was a consideration he hadn't expected, but then this wasn't the Prefecture. He said, "Wait. I haven't been told why I'm being held here."

One trooper hesitated but then shrugged and said, "I haven't, either," as he stepped out.

The troopers were standing right outside, though they hadn't closed the door. There were quiet voices in the corridor, then Rahene Fallier walked into the room.

Nicholas took a couple of steps back, putting the table between them, suddenly overcome by the gut-level conviction that Fallier was Octave's sorcerer compatriot, no matter what logic said. He told himself it was ridiculous. Fallier didn't look mad and surely no one could be mad enough to commit those acts without showing it somehow, in his eyes or in his demeanor. Nicholas said, "Now that we are, I assume, unobserved, will you tell me how you recognized me?"

Fallier stood near the table, removing his evening gloves. His expression enigmatic, he said, "You are as dark as your infamous ancestor was fair. But I've seen the Greanco portrait of Denzil Alsene, which is very like seeing the living person, and there is a resemblance."

Simply from that? Nicholas frowned. *Could it be true?* It would be impossible to believe, except for the fact that Greanco had had the second sight and his portraits had tended to capture the soul of their subjects, and that Fallier was a powerful sorcerer, with perhaps more insight into those semi-magical works of art than most. *And of course there was a portrait*, he thought sourly. Denzil Alsene had been a King's Favorite a century ago before he had hatched his plot to take the throne, and Greanco had been the most celebrated portrait painter of the age. "You could be mistaken."

"But I am not." Fallier's gaze was calm.

Nicholas was aware his palms were sweating through his torn gloves and he couldn't tell if he was successfully keeping his expression under control. He said, "I can't think why it's of interest to you. I have every right to be in this city."

"That is true to a certain extent," Fallier said. His face gave nothing away, not his motives, his intentions, and certainly no hint of how he felt about this encounter. There was nothing for Nicholas to grasp on to. The sorcerer continued, "I'll admit to some curiosity as to why you are in Vienne."

Fallier didn't sound very curious. Nicholas said, "I live here." The cold eyes didn't change and Nicholas found himself adding, "I'm only a scion of a disgraced family; I don't see why that piques your interest." The family was still technically of the nobility of Ile-Rien, though the charter of the duchy of Alsene had been revoked when Denzil Alsene had plotted to take the throne from the then King Roland. Nicholas's ancestry should be a historical curiosity, nothing more. Surely he wasn't the only person in Vienne at the moment who was descended from a famous traitor.

Of course you're not, Nicholas thought in self-disgust. *Now tell him you've had nothing to do with the Alsenes since your mother fled their moldering estate more than twenty-five years ago, that you use her maiden name of Valiarde, that you have a legitimate business as an importer. Then tell him why you're disguised as a cabman in the middle of an apparently anarchist attack on Lady Bianci's coach.* And Denzil's treachery hadn't simply been against his king. He had plunged the city into turmoil, caused countless deaths, exposed the people to attacks by the dark fay of the Unseelie Court, murdered enemies and allies alike. He was the most hated traitor in Ile-Rien's long history. His actions and subsequent death had turned the former duchy of Alsene into an enclave of hated outcasts, not that they didn't deserve that status on their own merit.

Fallier said, "That may well be true, but somehow I doubt it." A little sarcasm slipped through the stony façade. "I have previous engagements, so I'll leave you to think of a better excuse for your presence in the street tonight." The sorcerer stepped back, pulling the door closed behind him, the lock tumblers clicking into place with what Nicholas hoped was only symbolic finality.

He waited a moment, giving Fallier time to get down the corridor. *You idiot, you've done for yourself now.* He had trouble enough in the present without dragging the past into it. And the damnable part of all this was that he hadn't meant any harm whatsoever to the Queen's stupid bitch of a cousin, he had only wanted Octave.

He knelt next to the door to carefully examine the lock. It was old and not terribly secure. He touched it

lightly with the back of his hand, but there was no reaction. Fallier hadn't bothered to put any magical ward-
ing on it. He extracted the wires from his cuff, carefully
inserted one into the lock—an instant later he was rolling on the floor clutching his hand to his chest and biting
his lip to keep from crying out.

The pain faded rapidly and Nicholas lay on his back,
breathing hard, carefully working his fingers to make
sure the joints and muscles still worked. "You bastard,"
he said aloud. So Fallier had bothered to ward the lock.

After a moment, Nicholas sat up and looked around
the room. There was a yellowed map of the city environs
pinned to one wall, an empty bookshelf in the corner.
This wasn't a cell, it was only an old, unused chamber.
So why hadn't he been taken somewhere more secure?

All his knowledge of the palace came from what was
available in the popular press and a few half-
remembered tales passed down from his father's family,
which were all at least a century out of date and probably lies to begin with. But he knew there were better
areas for holding prisoners than this, probably in the
King's Bastion. Why hadn't Fallier had him taken there?

Fallier was taking no chances. He didn't want anyone
else to know Nicholas was here.

Nicholas edged back to the door and through painful
trial and error managed to ascertain that the ward didn't
extend beyond the metal of the lock. He pressed his ear
to the wooden door, listening for noise from the corridor.
He was willing to bet there was at least one guard outside, probably two. After a moment he heard a voice,
transformed into an unintelligible mumble by the thick-
ness of the wood, and another answering mumble.

He sat back. *Damn it.* Given time, he thought he could
get past the ward on the lock. Pain wasn't as effective
a deterrent as some other methods, such as the spell that
caused you to be distracted by movement glimpsed from
the corners of your eyes whenever you focused on the
warded object. He could train himself to become accustomed to the pain long enough to work the lock, and the
ward might not react to a splinter of wood as quickly as

it did to a metal lockpick. But he couldn't get past the guards.

Nicholas stood and began to pace.

Looking at Ronsarde, Madeline had to shake her head in admiration. The Inspector was as adept at disguise as she and Nicholas.

It was cold and very dark and the air had the feel of the deep night well past midnight, when only those people and spirits up to no good were about. *Which includes us*, Madeline thought grimly. They stood one street over from the palace, in the open court of a closed porter's yard, using Cusard's wagon to shield them from casual view. Down the street Madeline could see the plaza in front of the Prince's Gate, the circle of gas lamps illuminating one side of the massive arch of the Queen Ravenna Memorial and the classical fountain at its base. The plaza had been busier earlier in the night, carriages carrying guests through the gates, peddlers hawking to the small crowd of sightseers, but it was mostly deserted now except for a coach or two passing by. Madeline knew that if this sorcerer who thought himself Constant Macob somehow found them now, they wouldn't have a chance of escape. *He was following Octave*, she reminded herself. *And Octave is dead.*

It had taken an hour or more to get them to this point. Ronsarde had a special pass that allowed him to enter the palace at any time of the day or night, for the purpose of consulting with the Captains of the Queen's Guard and the Royal Guard, and since it named the bearer only as a "senior officer of the Prefecture" he could still use it to get in without alerting anyone to his identity. It had been left in the desk in his study in his apartment on Avenue Fount, which was sure to be under observation by the constables. Cusard had had to burgle the apartment to get it, going in through the attic to avoid capture himself. And it had taken Ronsarde some time to assume his disguise.

He had used hairpieces to alter the shapes of his beard and mustache and applied an unobtrusive scar just above the left eye that still served to focus the observer's attention. In clothes that fit the role and with the bruises and cuts from the fighting outside the prison covered with makeup, he looked an entirely different person.

He stood carefully now, folding the pass and tucking it away in his coat pocket. Everyone had had to admire that document, which was only a sheet of good quality stationery finely written with the Queen's own hand. "A damn shame there's not time to get old Besim to make a copy for us," Cusard had commented sotto-voce to Madeline. "Never know when it would come in handy."
The original is coming in damn handy now, Madeline thought. To Ronsarde she said, "You did agree now. You're going to go in, get Nicholas, and get out, and no appealing to anyone official for help, correct?" *I sound daft*, she thought. *This is the palace, for God's sake.* She reminded herself they had broken out of Vienne prison earlier today, but then Nicholas had done that before, if not under quite so spectacular circumstances.

"I shall do as I think best," Ronsarde agreed complacently. "An appeal to Captain Giarde of the Queen's Guard would be a last resort, of course."

Cusard groaned, and Reynard and Madeline exchanged a look. Crack stood like a stone, but his jaw muscles tensed. Even Doctor Halle rubbed his face and sighed. Reynard said, tightly, "I thought we had agreed—"

Ronsarde held up a hand. "I will do nothing that endangers our mission—"

"Our mission?" Cusard commented to Crack. "What about us?"

"—but I will not fail to take any opportunity that presents itself." Ronsarde's gaze went to Madeline. The ebony cane he carried was no prop, he needed it to walk, but the prospect of action seemed to have cured him of any other injury. He said, "I will find him, my dear. I swear it to you."

Madeline closed her eyes briefly, wishing she was religious enough to appeal to something supernatural, either of the old gods or the new, without feeling like a hypocrite. She and Reynard had argued over this while Ronsarde was assuming his disguise, but Madeline could think of no other way to proceed, and when pressed, neither could Reynard. She said, "Just remember that if this ends with all of us spending the rest of our lives in prison, he won't thank you for it."

Impatiently, Halle said, "Just get on with it, old man, you're driving everyone to distraction."

Ronsarde gave him an aggrieved look and adjusted the tilt of his hat. "Please, I'm concentrating." He nodded cordially to them all and walked out into the square.

There was nothing else to try, Madeline reminded herself. She didn't like the way Ronsarde was leaning so heavily on the cane, but he might be doing it intentionally, to alter his customary step and mannerisms, which was the essential part of any effective disguise.

"He won't make it," Reynard said, voicing it for all of them. Madeline had never seen him so worried and it wasn't helping her nerves any, either.

But Doctor Halle said calmly, "Oh yes, he will. He helped them work out all their guard procedures several years ago and he knows the palace intimately. If anyone can break it, he can."

Reynard pressed his lips together and didn't appear convinced. He motioned for Madeline to step back from the others and when they had drawn a short distance away, he said, "I'm acquainted with Captain Giarde. He was in the First Cavalry before he was appointed to court and we were both stationed in the Bahkri."

"Well?" Madeline prompted.

"Well, he's a bastard, but he's a very discerning bastard. If Ronsarde encounters him, he will be extremely difficult to fool." Reynard eyed her a moment, his expression a little sardonic. "Is there something I haven't been told, Madeline?"

"Yes." Madeline rubbed her face wearily. She was tired of secrets. She was tired, period. "But it's not something you're going to care much about, if you understand me."

"But it's something others would care about?" Reynard persisted.

"Yes." She hesitated, then let out her breath in resignation. "Nicholas is related to a noble family who happen to be rather famous traitors to the Crown."

"That can't be all, surely? I'm related to a noble family of rather famous drunkards and it never hurt my standing at court. When I had one, that is."

"They weren't your run-of-the-mill traitors. Nicholas is related to the Alsenes, as in Denzil Alsene."

"Oh. That traitor. The traitor, I should say." Reynard's brows drew together as he turned over the implications. "Is there still an interdict about Alsenes leaving the old duchy? He's not committing a crime simply by being in the city, is he?"

"No, that was apparently revoked almost fifty years ago. But . . . it doesn't look good."

"No. No, I suppose it doesn't." Reynard looked down the dark street after Ronsarde. "Damn."

Nicholas had waited a long, tense hour, during which the guards had never left their posts outside the door and he had become increasingly frustrated. Then he heard steps out in the hall and the lock turning. He moved warily to the back of the room, but the man who entered wasn't Fallier. It was the guard lieutenant who had helped capture him.

The man closed the door deliberately behind him. Smiling, he took a seat in the chair at the battered table, saying, "I hope you find your quarters comfortable?"

"Comfortable enough," Nicholas replied. He folded his arms and eyed his visitor thoughtfully. He was a large man, strongly built, armed with a dress sword and a serviceable pistol. He obviously thought himself secure enough from an unarmed, slightly built man. "I only wish I knew why I've been brought here."

The lieutenant said, "Perhaps I could tell you, if you were to tell me who you are and why Rahene Fallier is so interested in you."

Ah, then you don't know either, Nicholas thought. He

looked at the man's sly, curious face and a plan sprang to mind, complete in practically every detail. He took a deep breath, looking away as if about to reveal some uncomfortable truth, and said, "I'm his bastard son."

The lieutenant stared, then tried to hide his astonishment and appear off-hand. "Not surprising."

Save me from amateur schemers, Nicholas thought dryly. If everything he understood from his checkered family history was true, then this man didn't stand a chance among the practiced plotters at work in the royal court. He said, "My mother is. . . ." The Queen was too young, in fact she was several years younger than himself, so that wouldn't do at all. *Ah, perfect.* ". . . . the Countess Winrie."

The lieutenant swore under his breath. The Countess Winrie had been a prostitute famous for the most outrageous practices before she had persuaded the aging but still hale Count to marry her. He had died a year or so after the marriage, leaving the wealthy Countess the unofficial leader of the *demi monde* and a perpetual thorn in the side of good society. "But. . . ." The lieutenant was frowning in concentration.

"You see what this would do to his reputation," Nicholas prompted. He began to pace again, slowly, getting his quarry used to the sight of him moving about. "If it were to become known. . . ."

"Ah." The lieutenant nodded sagely, finally picking up on the innuendo. "You've been threatening to come forward and he has been buying your silence."

Nicholas paused and glanced back at the man, managing a trapped expression, and swallowed as if in a dry throat. He wondered what Madeline would make of this performance. *She would probably say something sarcastic about the quality of my audience*, he thought. "I have no idea what he intends to do to me," he hinted hopefully.

The lieutenant assumed an expression of smug knowledge, which Nicholas felt safe in presuming meant he didn't have the slightest notion either. The man tipped his chair back, propping his booted feet up on the table, and said callously, "Keep you out of the way permanently, I suppose."

Nicholas felt a flash of anger on behalf of this persona he had just constructed, this powerless young bastard at the mercy of his sorcerer father, and reminded himself not to get too involved in the role. He said, "My father has paid me a great deal of money over the past years and the Countess, who feels some fondness toward me, is still quite wealthy. Anyone who helped me regain my freedom would be well rewarded."

The lieutenant's eyes shifted. He said, "I would need some guarantees. You can't expect me to trust you."

Nicholas read his expression easily. The man only wanted information to give him a possible advantage over Fallier; he wasn't quite foolish enough to oppose the Court Sorcerer directly. "Of course not," Nicholas agreed readily. "Perhaps if I show you this, you will realize my sincerity." He approached the table, reaching into his pocket.

The lieutenant watched him, trying to look arch but failing to cover his obvious greed. His eyes dropped to the hand Nicholas was withdrawing from the pocket of his old coat and Nicholas kicked the chair leg. Overbalanced, the lieutenant fell backward.

Nicholas stepped in and punched him, knocking the man's head back against the wall. The thumps hadn't gone unnoticed by the guards and he heard keys working frantically in the lock. He snatched the pistol from the dazed lieutenant's holster and leapt over the tangled heap of body and chair on the floor, putting his back to the wall just as the door flew open.

He pointed the gun at the lieutenant and both guards stumbled to a halt. "Any closer and I'll shoot him, gentlemen. And please don't call out," Nicholas said evenly.

The lieutenant gasped and made a garbled noise, trying to push himself up, and Nicholas kicked the supporting hand out from under him. He motioned with the gun. "Move away from the door, please."

The two men glanced at each other, then obeyed. As

they moved out of the way, Nicholas stepped quickly to the door and backed out into the corridor. Two heavy bodies struck the door as soon as it swung to, pounding on it and shouting, but Nicholas was already turning the key in the lock. Experimentally he took a couple of steps away, then smiled. The noise the captives were making was inaudible more than two steps away from the door; that would buy him some time at least. Nicholas pocketed the key and strode down the corridor away from the main staircase, turning the corner into the cross corridor. This was a barracks and there wouldn't be an unguarded servants' door; he would have to go out the way he had come in. Running now, he passed more closed doors, an open arch into an old practice room filled with wooden fencing dummies, more passages branching toward the back of the building. Around another corner he found a second staircase, smaller and less ornate than the one in the main hall. He hurried down it, keeping his steps quiet.

The stairwell led down into an anteroom, with an archway opening onto the main area. Nicholas paused at the edge of the arch, back against the wall, leaning around to get a view of the hall. The number of men there had greatly increased. Most were in Royal Guard uniforms but a few were in civilian dress. Nicholas cursed under his breath. *Of course, that was why the lieutenant had time to question me.* The guard was changing, with men going off-duty and their replacements coming on. The confusion might make it easier— if Fallier was trying to keep his capture quiet, most of the men coming on duty might not have been informed there was a prisoner in the barracks. What he needed to do now was steal a uniform coat and. . . . Nicholas's attention was suddenly caught by a man in civilian dress standing with his back to him, apparently studying the flags of old decommissioned guard troops displayed along the gallery, and engaged in animated conversation with a Royal Guard lieutenant. For a moment he thought he had recognized him. *But it couldn't be*, Nicholas told himself. *Not here.*

The man turned and Nicholas stared suspiciously at his face, his clothes. *It could very well be*, he thought grimly. The man was limping, he was the right height, the right build, about the right age, despite possible cosmetic alterations to his hair and features and—*and he is using an ebony cane with a carved ivory handle exactly like the one Reynard brought back from Parscia*. Nicholas resisted the urge to knock his head against the wall. *Damn them.*

There was a shout from the gallery and one of the guards Nicholas had left locked in his temporary prison careened down the stairs and ran across the hall, heading for the outside doors. The off-duty guards watched him go, some calling out questions. *He's going for Fallier*, Nicholas thought. *He must have ordered them to keep my capture secret.*

As the men in the hall went about their business, Nicholas snatched off his cap and ducked out into the milling crowd, keeping his head down, and managed to fetch up against the old man with the cane. "Were you looking for me, sir?" he asked, in a Riverside accent.

Inspector Ronsarde actually had the audacity to smile. "There you are, my good fellow." He turned to the Guard lieutenant standing at his elbow. This lieutenant was older than the man who had helped with Nicholas's capture and his gaze was sharper. "I sent my driver here to see if he could locate Sir Diandre. No luck then?"

This last was addressed to Nicholas, who shook his head and said, "No sir, no one here's heard tell of him." He kept his head ducked and fervently hoped Ronsarde had chosen the name of a man who was on leave or otherwise inaccessible.

"Ah, well, then. We'll keep at it. Simply must find him. . . ."

"Have you tried the Gallery Wing, sir? There is a ball tonight and he may be attending," the lieutenant said. He was choosing his words carefully and his expression was a little guarded. He did not appear an easy man to deceive. Ronsarde must have concocted quite a story to get this far.

"That's a thought. Yes, if he isn't here. . . . I shall try there immediately then, thank you very much." There was a flicker of suspicion in the man's eyes. Then Ronsarde paused and with a self-possession that Nicholas would have admired had he been less angry, said, "Could you accompany me or does duty call?"

The suspicion vanished and the lieutenant consulted his pocket watch. "No, I'm afraid I must stay here. I can assign someone to guide you if—"

"Oh, no, don't bother, I can find my way on my own. I was here for the Queen's Birthday, you know. Thank you again for your assistance. . . ."

The expostulations and good-byes seemed to go on forever. Nicholas felt sweat running down his back. But finally Ronsarde exchanged one last handshake with his new friend and they made their way down the length of the hall. Nicholas stayed behind the Inspector, who kept to a steady pace despite his limp and the need to hurry. They were almost to the arch of the stone-walled foyer when a Guard corporal stepped forward to accost Ronsarde. "Sir, are you—"

Ronsarde flourished a folded paper. "Here to see Captain Giarde, young man."

At the sight of the seal on the document and the name of the Queen's Guard Captain, the corporal backed away, saluting for good measure.

Nicholas didn't breathe, didn't dare lift his head until they were out of the main doors and down the steps. Once they were in the cold wind-swept court and out of range of the lamps, Nicholas grabbed Ronsarde's arm and dragged him to a sheltered corner. "What are you doing here?" he demanded.

"Looking for you, my boy. Really, what did you think? I would've been here sooner, but it took me some time to find where they had taken you. Discovering it was the old barracks was somewhat anticlimactic; I had anticipated having to free you from the holding cells under the Gate Tower."

"I'm so sorry you were disappointed," Nicholas said, through gritted teeth. "I risk everything to get you out of that damn prison and you come here?"

"Of course." Ronsarde glanced around the court. There were groups of people crossing between the shadowy hulks of the buildings around them, laughing and talking, some bearing lanterns. They didn't look like search parties but in the dark it was hard to tell. The Inspector asked, "Do you know where you are?"

"Not particularly."

"You were held in the old Queen's Guard barracks, or what's left of it. It was expanded when the Royal Guard was chartered."

"Ordinarily I have a deep appreciation for historical curiosities but at the present moment—"

"And that," Ronsarde continued, pointedly, "is the Albon Tower, which was enlarged to join the Old Palace, destroying much of the security provided by the old siege walls and bastions, but allowing us to make our way through the lower floors to the new section of the palace grounds, where there is a ball being given for the Lord Mayor in the Gallery Wing. Most of the guests will have left by now but St. Anne's Gate should still be relatively busy, and they will not be searching for you there."

"Then let's go."

The tower only lay across the court but Nicholas felt exposed and vulnerable as they made their way toward it. There was one guard on the door, standing under a lamp suspended from the mouth of a stone gargoyle. Ronsarde displayed his pass again and they were waved on.

Once inside they found themselves in a large drafty hall, the curved ceiling supported by heavy square pillars. The place had an almost unused air and there were only a few lamps to light the way through. Ronsarde hesitated, getting his bearings, then said, "This way," and strode forward.

They were almost to the center of the large room when the doors behind them crashed open. Nicholas spun, drawing the pistol. There were Guards pouring into the hall behind them. Ronsarde grabbed his arm and said, ''No, it's too late.''

Light flared behind Nicholas and he glanced over his shoulder to see more Guards with lamps moving to block the only other way out.

16

"Stop where you are, please."

Nicholas stopped. From a doorway a man was pointing a pistol at them. He was a little older than Nicholas, dark-haired, bearded, wearing evening dress. Nicholas thought at first it was one of the off-duty Guards, but then he saw the men behind him were in cavalry uniforms. No, not cavalry uniforms; the sashes were different. *Queen's Guard*, Nicholas thought, recognizing the style suddenly.

"Put the weapon on the floor."

Nicholas hesitated, but only for a heartbeat. The man's eyes told him that he would shoot without compunction. Keeping his movements slow and deliberate, he lowered the pistol to the floor.

"Very good," the man said. He stepped further into the room, the gun never wavering from its aim. Nicholas watched him grimly. The Queen's Guard had traditionally been the personal bodyguard of the Queens of Ile-Rien and since the current Queen ruled in her own right this made them the first armed troop in the palace and more politically powerful than the Royal Guard. If this man was their Captain he would not be as easy to escape as the hapless lieutenants they had outwitted.

Ronsarde said, "Captain Giarde, how very good to see you."

The man stopped, stared hard at the Inspector, then

glanced uncertainly at Nicholas. "I don't think I know—"

Ronsarde straightened up and deliberately began removing the extra hairpieces from his beard, mustaches and eyebrows. "Flattering of you not to recognize me," he said in his normal voice. "I threw this together in something of a hurry."

"Ronsarde?" Giarde's lips thinned in annoyance. "Good God, man, how dare you come here like this?" He looked again at Nicholas. "That's not Doctor Halle, is it?"

"No, this is my protege, Nicholas Valiarde."

Nicholas stared at Ronsarde in fury, barely managing the self-control not to voice an outraged denial. *Protege?*

"How did you find us, if you don't mind my asking?" Ronsarde continued easily. "You know I am always seeking to improve my technique."

"I've been following Fallier's movements, actually, and was curious to see who it was he brought here in such secret." Giarde's gaze went to Nicholas speculatively. "Your protege?"

"Our situation has become . . . complicated," Ronsarde admitted.

Giarde motioned them to back away, then moved forward to collect Nicholas's stolen pistol. As if aware this would not be over quickly, he leaned against the nearest pillar and said, "You know you're being hunted all across the city by your own men, of course, even if the charges do sound ridiculous. Why did you escape when you must have realized the Queen would intervene as soon as the Magistrates Court ruled? And what the hell are you doing here now?"

"I did not intend to escape from the Magistrates Court," Ronsarde said, as if it should be obvious to anyone. "I was seized, by men hired to insure my silence, and was about to be murdered when I was rescued by some friends and associates. We then spent the next several hours fleeing for our lives. That is the short version."

Giarde did not appear pleased. "I hope the long one is more illuminating."

Ronsarde cleared his throat. "Then, as we continued our investigations, Valiarde here was detained without cause and I came to retrieve him."

"Wait." Giarde held up a hand. He motioned one of the Guards over, spoke a moment, and sent the man away.

Nicholas stared at Ronsarde in mixed disgust and disbelief. "That's to be our story, is it? I was doing better as the illegitimate son of the Court Sorcerer," he said, keeping his voice low.

"Don't be alarmed," Ronsarde said, maddeningly. "The situation is well in hand."

Nicholas wished he had taken his chances with the pistol.

Giarde turned his attention back to them. He said, "It's odd that you claim this man is working for you, because my sources informed me the prisoner brought in by the Royal Guard Gate troop was involved in an anarchist attack on Lady Bianci's coach. He looked at Nicholas. "Is that why Fallier had you brought here?"

Nicholas would have wagered anything that Giarde already knew why Fallier had brought him here, or at least that he had guessed most of the truth. "I was a witness to the attack. The driver and the footmen can verify that," he said. "I was not arrested by the troop." Nicholas hesitated, reluctant to say it aloud, but there was no help for it. And the sooner Giarde was distracted from the coach incident the better. Nicholas said, "I'm an indirect descendent of Denzil Alsene. Fallier was extremely interested in me."

Disgusted, Ronsarde said, "Was that all?" but the Captain's face was impassive. Giarde said, "You told him who you were."

Nicholas smiled. "No. Fallier told me."

Giarde was silent a moment more, considering. "How exactly did this come about?"

"I haven't been to Alsene since I was a child," Nicholas said. "I don't use the name and I have no desire to. I was about to leave the scene of the coach accident so I could report to the Inspector.'' He couldn't help throwing a dark look at Ronsarde but the Inspector didn't seem to notice the sarcasm. ''Fallier said he recognized me from the Greanco portrait of Denzil Alsene. I have no idea if he was telling the truth or not.'' He suspected it was true but there was no harm in muddying the water a little. ''He had me brought here quite against my will.''

''I see.''

''All this aside,'' Ronsarde interrupted testily, ''the city is being menaced by a mad sorcerer and if I—'' He paused and corrected himself graciously, ''If we are to do anything about it, I must have a pardon and some assistance, thank you.''

''What are you talking about?'' Giarde demanded.

Ronsarde waved his arms in frustration, causing the watching Guards to stir nervously. ''The person who caused the disturbance in the Courts Plaza, the deaths in Vienne Prison and Valent House. He is most certainly a sorcerer, he is most assuredly mad, and I would have apprehended him by now without all this deliberate interference.''

''You know who he is?''

Ronsarde glanced at Nicholas. ''Not yet, but we have our suspicions. I need a pardon, Captain. The situation is urgent.''

Giarde's expression was difficult to read. He put his pistol into his coat pocket and said, ''It's very late.''

''She will be awake.''

He can't mean who I think he means, Nicholas thought, shifting uneasily. This experience was surreal enough already.

Giarde hesitated. ''You're not exaggerating this?''

Ronsarde's expression was grim. ''I only wish I was.''

''All right.'' Giarde tossed the pistol Nicholas had stolen to one of the Guards. ''Follow me.''

Ronsarde nodded as if pleased. Nicholas took a deep breath to calm his pounding heart.

Giarde led them through dark halls, further into the tower. With the lamps of the Guardsmen sending shadows chasing up old stone walls that bore marks of fire and at least one round impact that looked as if it could have come from a cannonball, they might have been passing back through time. Nicholas would not have been terribly surprised if they were leading him to one of the dungeons below these ancient floors. He thought about bolting down one of the cross corridors they passed but knew that would be useless; he didn't know the place and would probably be rounded up within minutes.

It was known there were areas in the lower levels of the palace still sealed off from when the Unseelie Court had occupied it for that short time over a hundred years ago. Corridors, storerooms, stairwells, huge echoing cellars, blocked off by falling walls and collapsed roofs, that had been left as they were with no effort expended to reclaim them from the earth.

But the double doors they eventually came to opened into an old if not ancient stairway, lit prosaically by gaslights. The gas pipes were mounted on the walls, since the plaster and wood panelling must be only a thin veneer over solid stone. Nicholas knew they had left the tower; this must be the King's Bastion.

They went up the stairs and through a few echoing halls with abrupt turns and occasional dead ends, until Nicholas realized he was thoroughly lost. He could tell they were approaching the more well-used portions of the palace when the floor underfoot turned from polished wood to white marble.

They passed several of the semi-public areas, seeing no one but a few quiet servants, then entered a reception room. Giarde said, "Wait here," and continued on, leaving the other Queen's Guards with them.

Nicholas folded his arms, resisting the urge to pace. The room was small, chill, with a marble floor and mantels and a set of delicate giltwood chairs that looked as if they would burst apart if sat on. He knew he looked an odd figure here, dressed all in tattered black and with an expression of dark outrage. It was perhaps an appropriate appearance for the first Alsene to visit the palace of Ile-Rien in so many years.

Leaning on his cane, Ronsarde said conversationally, "I discovered your rather colorful antecedents when I was first investigating your foster father. I thought it of no consequence, however."

Nicholas looked at him, eyes narrowed. "You're not endearing yourself to me, you know."

Giarde reappeared and motioned them to follow. As they did, Nicholas noticed the Queen's Guards remained behind. He glanced sideways at Ronsarde but couldn't tell if the Inspector seemed relieved or not. They went down another hall and then through an open doorway into a vast chamber.

There was an arched arcade running all along the upper half and a floor covered with parquet and very old Parscian carpets. An enormous chimneypiece of black and white marble would have dominated the room, except for the gold-framed mirrors, the elaborate floral designs of the figured ceiling, and the faded glory of the two-hundred-year-old tapestries. The furniture was all marquetry or vermeille, all in colors of old gold or amber, until the room seem to glow with it. Ronsarde nudged Nicholas with an elbow and pointed up. Three large gold lanterns of intricate design hung from the ceiling. "From the barge of the Grand Cardinal of Bisra, looted during the battle of Akis in the last Bisran War," he whispered. "The touch of the conquering barbarian among the splendors of civilization."

"I heard that."

There was a woman sitting in an armchair near the massive hearth. She was small and her face was very young, a girl's face almost, except it was too thin to be entirely childish. Her hair was red and worn piled up under a very old-fashioned lace cap, and her dark dress looked plain and almost dowdy, until the lamplight caught it and revealed it as a deep indigo velvet. She was laying out cards in a game of solitaire on the little table in front of her and she hadn't looked up at her visitors.

She said, "You were arrested." A quick, almost furtive glance revealed she was speaking to Ronsarde. Her voice was light and unexpectedly girlish for someone with such a serious mien.

"I was, my lady," the Inspector said calmly.

Nicholas felt the back of his neck prickle. Traditionally in Ile-Rien, officers of the royal court and personal servants addressed royalty as "my lady" or "my lord" instead of the more formal and cumbersome "your majesty." That Ronsarde had been granted that indulgence showed he was closer to the Crown's confidence than Nicholas had previously suspected.

"Can't have that," the Queen muttered, as if to herself. She turned over a card and ran her thumb along the edge, lost in thought. "I know who you are," she said. Another quick glance showed she was speaking to Nicholas now. "It was distressing that Rahene Fallier brought you here without informing me."

"Distressing, but not entirely unexpected," Giarde added.

The Queen shot Giarde a dark look. She made an abrupt gesture, as if embarrassed by this admission. "Politics, you understand."

"I avoid politics, your majesty," Nicholas said.

She looked up at him then, for the first time, eyes narrowed as if she suspected mockery. She probably was mocked, to her face or to her back, by the more sophisticated ladies of the court and by those of her advisors who didn't appreciate serving a woman who appeared barely out of childhood. If he remembered rightly she wasn't older than twenty-four. Apparently satisfied that he had spoken in all seriousness, she said, "Wise of you," and looked back down at her game. She placed the card carefully in the array on the table. "There is a resemblance. I think it's the eyes." She turned over another card and studied it. "And I suppose your mother must have been the first new blood in that family for several generations."

She was speaking of his resemblance to the long-dead Denzil. Nicholas damned Greanco's skill. "Circumstance has made them insular," he hesitated infinitesimally, "your majesty."

"It was a pretty damn deliberate circumstance," the Queen corrected, her voice dry. She glanced at him furtively. "When I was a child I met your aunt Celile once, at a garden party the Valmontes gave at Gardien-on-Bannot." She shuddered, not theatrically, but apparently in real horror at the memory. "Horrible woman."

"You should try having to face her over dinner." The words were out before Nicholas could stop them.

The Queen hesitated, her hand on a card. Her smile was so brief it might have been imaginary. She looked at him directly then, her large eyes utterly serious, and said, "I've seen the house, from a distance. It was horrible, too. What was it like there?"

Nicholas drew a breath but was temporarily unable to speak. He knew he needed to answer her but he hadn't expected this. If he had ever imagined this meeting, he would never in his wildest dreams have constructed it in this fashion. He thought of the decaying, faded glories of the Alsene Great House, the land meant to support it long gone, either sold off to pay debts or taken by the Crown as more punishment for Denzil's long-ago attempt to seize the throne. Roland Fontainon's throne, who was this woman's great-great-grandfather. He said, "Mercifully, I don't remember much of it." There were details, long buried beneath the surface, that insisted on springing to mind. He added only, "My father died and my mother fled with me to Vienne."

She blinked, her expression unchanging. "Are we related?"

"It's a distant connection." He suspected she knew it very well; the purpose of the question had been to ascertain if he knew it.

She sat back in her chair. "By the charters of Old Vienne and Riverside, and the Council of Margrave and the Barons of Viern, there is a proposed line of descent that gives you a claim on the throne." One eyebrow quirked, but her face was serious. "I might have to marry you."

The shock wasn't mild but Nicholas realized immediately that he was being tested, in ways both subtle and blunt. *It explained what Fallier wanted of me*, he thought, feeling a sinking sensation in the pit of his stomach. Perhaps that was why the family seldom left the estate. His father had only left long enough to court his mother. And there were those who had never left the slowly rotting house, who had spent their whole lives living for the past. He was probably the first Alsene to come to Vienne in generations. He said, "The Council of Margrave and the Barons of Viern was invalidated by the later action of the Ministry, in their first convening in Vienne."

"That's true." The Queen slumped back in her chair suddenly, frowning. "I'd forgotten."

Thank you, Doctor Uberque, for a thorough grounding in the history of court law, Nicholas thought, though he didn't believe for a moment the Queen had forgotten that obscure fact. It was like watching Madeline play a role, only underneath it all Madeline was basically harmless and the Queen was anything but. *The woman uses candor like a loaded pistol.* He still thought her courtiers probably mocked her, but if they did it within her hearing, they probably didn't do it twice. In his peripheral vision he saw Giarde wincing and rubbing the bridge of his nose.

She sat up straight again and Nicholas suspected he was about to be dealt another roundhouse blow. She said, "But you're still the heir to the Alsene properties."

"Like being the heir to Hell, only less glamorous," Nicholas said, keeping his voice light. But this was almost a relief. He had never expected nor wanted to inherit anything from the Alsenes and indeed he doubted they had anything worth wanting. He bowed, ironically. "I renounce my claim, your majesty."

"Really? Because when you say it to me, you know, it's official." The Queen pointed this out somewhat diffidently, as if embarrassed by it.

He hadn't known. He hadn't lived at Alsene long enough to be taught all the vagaries of the landed noble's relationship with the Crown. Nicholas said, "I want no part of the family of Alsene. I am not the heir." There was a curious sense of freedom in saying it.

She glanced at Giarde and said, "We'll write that into the court proceedings, remind me, please."

Giarde sighed audibly and the Queen glared at him again. Nicholas would have given a great deal to know what their relationship was. Queens of Ile-Rien had always taken lovers among their personal guard; it was practically a tradition.

A large ginger cat suddenly leapt up onto the table and with great deliberation, settled itself down on top of the card game. The Queen froze, card in hand, and stared at it with a grim set to her mouth. The cat returned her gaze with a challenging air and settled itself more comfortably. The Queen sighed, evidently conceding the point, and set the card aside. She leaned back in her chair and folded her hands, looking thoughtfully down at the carpet. "We were going on to that other matter. . . ."

Giarde evidently took that as a signal to continue. He cleared his throat and glanced at Ronsarde. "I've sent for Lord Albier. He's in charge of the investigation of the incident today. I thought he might benefit from this discussion."

Ronsarde and Nicholas exchanged a look. Lord Albier was the head of the Prefecture and no one had said yet whether they were under arrest or not.

"And I've asked Fallier to attend," Giarde continued. He smiled. "His reaction should be illuminating."

The Queen glanced up at him, her mouth twisting ironically. Her expression as she looked at her Guard Captain was much the same as when she had looked at her cat, holding both affection and resigned annoyance.

A butler caught Giarde's attention from the doorway and the Captain motioned him forward. As the servant conferred with the Queen and Giarde, Nicholas said, low-voiced, to Ronsarde, "Well, are we for prison or not?"

"I'm not sure," Ronsarde admitted. "It's always so hard to tell what the dear child is thinking. Giarde has some influence on her but not as much as appearances suggest." He shrugged philosophically. "You've escaped from the Vienne prison twice now, haven't you? Don't most sorcerous formulae suggest the third time should be lucky?"

Nicholas rubbed his forehead, to conceal his expression from the others. "Oh, if I'm to be sent to prison I'd prefer it to be for bashing in the head of a Prefecture Inspector and leaving his body in a midden." He was beginning to feel a deep sense of sympathy for Doctor Halle.

Ronsarde chuckled.

The butler retreated and Giarde glanced at them and explained, "Fallier and Albier are here."

The Queen shifted uneasily.

"This should be interesting," Ronsarde muttered.

Nicholas folded his arms. Interesting was a good word for it.

It was Fallier who entered first, Lord Albier following him. Nicholas knew the sorcerer was almost instantly aware of his presence even though he gave no sign of it.

Fallier paused, meeting the Queen's gaze without challenge but without apology, either. She said nothing, merely looked at him with a light in her eyes that might have been contempt. It was the imperturbable Court Sorcerer who was the first to look away. Turning to Giarde, he said, "I was told this was a matter of some urgency, Captain?" His voice was cool.

"Inspector Ronsarde has some intelligence concerning the sorcerous attack on the Courts," Giarde said. He looked thoughtfully at the sorcerer. "That is all."

Fallier's eyes narrowed slightly and he looked from Giarde to the Queen. Nicholas saw that her hand, resting on the delicate chair arm, the jeweled rings incongruous next to bitten nails, was trembling. *She is seething,* he thought. He suspected this wasn't the first time Fallier had attempted politics, as the Queen had called it.

In the meantime, Lord Albier was staring at Ronsarde, caught between astonishment and anger. He was a large, florid man, very much the type of the military officer. The state of his clothes suggested he had dressed hastily. "Captain, I demand an explanation. Inspector Ronsarde is a wanted man. What the—"

"The Inspector has reasons for his rather odd behavior," Giarde interjected, before Albier could commit the indignity of swearing in front of his sovereign.

Ronsarde smiled at Albier. "Have you been searching for me very hard, sir? If so, I suggest it's time for another review of the detective force, because I assure you I was not that difficult to find."

Albier reddened. He looked at Giarde and said harshly, "I should have been informed—"

"You're being informed now," Giarde interrupted, apparently tiring of Albier's discomfiture. "Have you made any progress on discovering who turned the Courts Plaza into a sorcerous spectacle yesterday?"

Albier retained his control with an effort. "We had nothing to investigate. The sorcerers we called in could find no trace of the identity of the person who caused the disruption." Albier was all but ignoring the Queen, which Nicholas thought was poor judgement indeed.

Giarde nodded to Ronsarde. "I believe the Inspector can shed some light on it. He and his . . . associate have been investigating the matter."

For the first time Fallier's gaze came to rest on Nicholas. He allowed himself one small smile at the sorcerer's expense and Fallier turned his attention to Ronsarde, without reacting. *He is a dangerous man*, Nicholas thought. He was making another enemy tonight, that much was obvious.

Ronsarde cleared his throat and began to describe the events of the past few days, beginning with his investigation of Octave.

Listening to him, Nicholas was pointedly reminded of

the current difficulties of his situation. Even his delight at Fallier's discomfort was dampened.

He had told Madeline that Donatien was dead, but perhaps he hadn't quite believed it himself until now.

The Inspector's quiet voice as he told their story was working on Nicholas's nerves like salt on raw flesh. *It has to be this way*, he told himself. To get this sorcerer, he would have to have help. He was running out of resources and time and more importantly, they had him dead to rights. There was no other choice.

When he looked back he realized the Queen's eyes were on him, that she had read his reaction as plainly as if he had spoken aloud. Her gaze flicked away as if she was ashamed to be caught watching him.

Ronsarde told them all they had discovered so far, his deductions and Nicholas's, their individual and shared discoveries, making it sound as though Nicholas had been working under Ronsarde's auspices from the very beginning. He left out anything that might hint at less than legal activities on Nicholas's part. The Inspector was making it sound as if he had known Nicholas all his life and that was, in a way, true, just not in the way Ronsarde was implying. *You should be grateful*, he thought, instead of standing here simmering with resentment. Sebastion Ronsarde, Inspector of the Prefecture, sworn to the Crown, was standing here lying like a market whore to save him. And he was telling those lies to the Queen, who was sitting there blinking solemnly and probably all too aware she wasn't hearing more than half the real story, but trusting Ronsarde anyway.

As the Inspector finished, Giarde and the Queen were looking at Albier. He coughed and said, "I had heard some part of this before—"

"And believed none of it—" Ronsarde interrupted.

"You had no proof," Albier said heatedly, "only outrageous speculations!"

"I assume the destruction and death yesterday is proof enough?" Ronsarde's voice was icy, for one moment revealing the bitterness he must have felt at his warnings going unheeded.

"Of course." Albier gestured to Giarde. "But even the great Inspector can give us no clue as to this person's whereabouts."

This was too much for Nicholas's abraded nerves. He interrupted, "There is, in fact, one clue."

That got everyone's attention, including Ronsarde, who stared at him, frowning. Nicholas said, "Doctor Octave, before he was killed by his associate, said that the sorcerer was hiding in a 'palace on the river.' "

"There are a number of deserted or unused Great Houses along the river or on the islands," Albier muttered.

"And they will be searched," Giarde said. He looked at the Court Sorcerer, who said, "I will put my apprentices at the disposal of Lord Albier."

The Queen said suddenly, "You're dismissed."

Albier looked startled, almost offended, and actually looked at Giarde for confirmation, but Fallier bowed and turned at once to go, crossing the parquet floor to the doors.

It must have finally dawned on Albier that there were undercurrents of which he was unaware. He bowed to the Queen and to Giarde said, "I'll make you aware of any progress." With another dark glance at Ronsarde, he followed Fallier out.

As the doors closed behind them Ronsarde shook his head. "I don't like to say it, but in light of what brought us here I find I do not entirely trust Fallier."

Giarde glanced at the Queen and seemed to receive some quiet and almost imperceptible signal. He said, "Fallier may be Court Sorcerer, but he is not her majesty's only advisor in things sorcerous. The person who holds that position is a very old woman who lives in a corner of the main kitchen in the North Bastion. To consult with her it's necessary to go to the kitchen in question and crouch on a coal scuttle, but she is always correct, and her advice is untainted by political pressures of any kind. I'll put this before her and see what she thinks.'' He added, ''She sent me a note a short time ago to tell me that within the past few hours there have been no less than three etherial assaults on the palace, all repelled by the wards.''

''That . . . isn't unexpected,'' Nicholas said. *He's still after us*, he thought. *Killing Octave didn't satisfy him.* Perhaps the man was mad. There was an odd sense of disappointment in that. He really would have preferred a sane opponent. But how could the man be a sorcerer in Ile-Rien and not know the palace at Vienne was the most heavily protected place, both physically and etherically, in this part of the world? The wards that guarded it were woven into the very stones of the oldest parts of the palace, they had been created and maintained by the most powerful sorcerers in Ile-Rien's history, and some of them were so old they were almost self-aware. How could the man think he could strike at them past that magical barrier? Except. . . . ''Fontainon House.''

Nicholas looked up to realize everyone was staring at him. Ronsarde nodded and said, ''Yes, the reason Octave stayed to perform his circle.''

Giarde swore. ''Fontainon House is inside the wards.''

The Queen was frowning. She looked at Nicholas, brows lowered, and he explained, ''During a circle Octave would apparently materialize ghosts. It's possible he meant to open a circle in Fontainon House, within the wards, and open a way for something else to materialize.''

''He leaves bodies strewn like discarded trash,'' the Queen said, suddenly. She stroked the now somnolent cat with a quick, nervous touch. ''I take it we assume he is a madman?''

''The indications are there, my lady,'' Ronsarde said.

She subsided again, staring bitterly at the carpet.

''Well?'' Giarde asked her. There was a stillness to his expression that brought Nicholas back from all thoughts of their sorcerous opponent. *He is asking her if we—I—should be released.* Ronsarde had done nothing except try to stay alive; Nicholas was the one who presented a problem.

The Queen's eyes lifted, met Nicholas's gaze shyly. *Shy doesn't mean weak*, Nicholas thought. It would be entertaining to live long enough for Fallier to realize that. She said, "You're certain?"

That one baffled him. "Your majesty?"

"About the inheritance? About giving it up?"

It was such an ingenuous question, yet he didn't doubt her seriousness. "I'm certain, your majesty. I was certain a long time ago." He found himself adding, "Of course, a true Alsene would say anything to get out of this, would swear allegiance to the devil even."

She sighed and looked at nothing in particular. Then she stood, gathering her cat in one large ginger armful. She stepped close to Nicholas before he could react, put her hand on his shoulder and said, gravely, "Your aunt Celile still writes to me. If you fail, I shall give her your address."

Then she was making her way to the door, the cat's tail snapping with irritation at its interrupted nap, while the men in the room hastily bowed.

As the doors closed behind her, Nicholas felt something unclench around his heart and distinctly heard Ronsarde draw a relieved breath. Giarde shook his head, as if in continued amazement at his sovereign's thought processes. With an air of resignation he asked Ronsarde, "Is there any other assistance you require?"

"Albier was correct on one point," the Inspector said. "We have to find this sorcerer first. We can do nothing until we know where he is."

"The Prefecture will search the abandoned structures along the river with the help of Fallier and his apprentices. Lord Albier will believe he is directing the investigation, but he'll take my advice, and I'll take yours."

"A pardon, so I can continue my investigations without impediment, would also be helpful," Ronsarde pointed out.

Giarde folded his arms. "Our influence with the Prefecture is not all inclusive. It will take some time to persuade the Lord Chief Commissioner that your rampage through the lower levels of the prison was done in the Crown's name." He added, "But I'm sure something can be arranged."

Ronsarde's bow was a trifle ironic. "In the meantime, I would prefer to stay with my associates and contact the Prefecture through you or Lord Albier."

"That would probably be wise."

Giarde led them out, pausing in the reception room to say, "Take care, Ronsarde. You have powerful enemies."

"Yes, that had begun to dawn on me," Ronsarde confessed.

Giarde sighed and glanced briefly heavenward. "I'm serious. If you leave the palace, I can't protect you."

"If I don't leave the palace, I can't catch him," Ronsarde said, patiently. "And that would be too dangerous for all of us."

Giarde watched him narrowly, then nodded. "We can get you outside the palace walls without drawing unwanted attention. There's a passage under St. Anne's Gate that leads to the underground station on the Street of Flowers. My men will take you that far." He glanced at Nicholas, his eyes hooded, then said, "I think you are keeping dangerous company, Inspector."

"Oh come now," Ronsarde said, smiling indulgently. "That's a terrible thing to say about old Halle."

Giarde glared at him in exasperation. "I'm the only thing that's standing between you and a few nights in the Prefecture cells, so I'd think you could at least pretend to show me a little diffidence."

"I'm sorry." Ronsarde managed a contrite expression that fooled no one. "I will try to do better."

"Get out, before I change my mind."

Following their escort of Queen's Guards down the opulent halls, Nicholas waited until they were a safe distance from Giarde and the royal environs, then said, accusingly, "You're enjoying this."

Ronsarde glanced at him, arching a brow. "And you aren't?"

There was no answer for that. Seething, Nicholas made no reply.

After a moment of silence, the Inspector said, "Don't be fooled by her majesty's rather unusual manner. Her habits of thought are devastatingly precise."

"Whatever gave you the idea I was fooled," Nicholas said, coldly. "It was everything I could do not to accept her offer of marriage at once. I think we would have taken Bisra and half of Parscia within the year."

"A frightening thought." Ronsarde watched him alertly for a moment, then as they reached the head of the staircase, stopped Nicholas with a hand on his sleeve.

Their escort halted on the steps below, looking back up at them impatiently. Low-voiced, Ronsarde said, "We'll find this madman. We'll find him because he doesn't know when to stop. He lacks the professional criminal's instinctive knowledge of when to cut and run." The expression in Ronsarde's eyes turned rueful. "That's why I never caught you. You knew when to stop."

Nicholas swallowed in a dry throat. He wanted to be away from here and pursuing the hunt so urgently it was almost a physical need. He wasn't sure he knew when to stop, not anymore. "He wants something," he said, starting down the stairs again. "Even if he's mad, he wants something and we have to know what it is."

17

The stench rising up from the dark swirling water in the stone pit was truly hellish; the handkerchief Nicholas had wrapped around his mouth and nose did little to mask it. He managed to draw enough of a breath to ask, "But have you noticed anything unusual in the refuse lately?"

The oldest sewerman frowned and paused to lean on his broad paddle, which he was using to direct the flow of sluice water down the channel of the main sewer into the collector pit. "Some days it's hard to say what is usual," he said, which was a more philosophical answer than Nicholas was hoping for. The man's much younger assistant, wielding a paddle on the other side of the channel, only nodded in perfect agreement.

Nicholas nodded too, keeping his expression sympathetic. This was only partly because he needed the sewermen's cooperation to get the information he wanted. After only a few minutes down here it was easy to see that you either became philosophical about your lot in life or you went quickly mad.

It had been three long days since his interview at the palace and the Prefecture's search along the river had turned up nothing so far, at least according to the frequent bulletins from Giarde. Nicholas was uncomfortable with having his connection to the Alsenes known, even though Halle had been too polite to bring the subject up and Crack, of course, had ventured no opinion at all and Cusard only worried that it would draw attention to them. Reynard had affected to think it amusing, and commented, "Now I know why you tried to hand the Duke of Mere-Bannot that bomb at the Queen's Birthday celebration two years ago."

"I was drunk, Reynard, that's why," Nicholas had reminded him tiredly. "And besides, Denzil Alsene wasn't an anarchist. He was a dedicated monarchist, he just thought it should have been him on the throne and not the legally crowned Fontainon who was currently occupying it. That he had to destroy the country to accomplish that goal was immaterial."

Notices in the penny sheets had cautioned people about the sorcerer's method of obtaining victims and there had been some panic in Riverside and many false reports, all of which diverted constables from the search. Oddly, there had been no more verifiable disappearances in the past few days. Nicholas found that more ominous than reassuring.

He had kept up his own observations of the Prefecture's efforts, spying on them from various vantage points with Crack's help and employing Cusard and Lamane's network of street children and petty thieves to follow their progress. He brought the information back to Ronsarde, who pored over it, muttering to himself, and sent terse orders to Lord Albier through Captain Giarde. Nicholas felt this procedure was highly unsatisfactory; if directing a methodical search was all that was needed, Albier and his cronies were as good at organizing that as anyone else in authority. What was needed was Ronsarde's reductive abilities, his genius for ferreting out apparently unrelated clues and finding the relationship between them. He needed to be on the scene, where the constables could report their findings directly to him. It infuriated Nicholas that the Prefecture was probably even now overlooking important information, simply because they didn't know what they were looking at. He knew the Inspector felt this as deeply as he did.

They had discovered yesterday through a friend of

Reynard's that the warrant issued for Doctor Halle's arrest had been formally rescinded. This had occasioned an almost violent argument, since Halle had wanted to join the search himself, hoping his experience with Ronsarde's methods would allow him to bring items of possible significance to the Inspector's attention that the constables and their officers might overlook. Nicholas had forbidden it on the grounds that their opponents knew Halle was a direct link to Ronsarde; if the doctor tried to take a visible role in the investigation, they would move against him as violently as they had moved against the Inspector. It was no accident that the Prefecture's principal investigator and the city's foremost medical expert in violent death had both been effectively stymied. Nicholas knew that there was at least one person behind all this who knew what he was about.

The argument had raged on until Madeline had stepped in to explain Nicholas's point of view, even though he had already explained it several times himself. Halle had grudgingly given in then and Nicholas had stormed out of the apartment to spend an hour kicking gutters in the Philosopher's Cross and had ended up sitting at Arisilde's bedside again, hoping for improvement. Part of his anger came from his suspicion that there were things Ronsarde wasn't telling him.

It was all being taken out of his hands but they couldn't stop him from pursuing his own line of inquiry.

Which was why he was currently some distance below the street, squatting on a walkway above the stagnant waters of a sewage collector, talking to sewermen and ratcatchers. The lamplight flickered off the oily stone curving above them, though this part of the sewer was well-tended and relatively clean. There were pipes overhead, splitting to cross the domed roof of the collector, some carrying potable water which had been brought in from outside Vienne by aqueducts ever since the city officials had given up the charmingly naive belief that the river water was drinkable if pumped from the deepest current. "This would be within the past five days, say," Nicholas persisted. This was the fifth work group he had spoken to and he had learned he didn't want to offer suggestions for the items that might have been found, since the sewermen were often of the type of witness who tended to say what you wanted to hear, simply to be polite.

The oldest sewerman straightened, one hand on his obviously aching back, and hailed the two men aboard the small boat that was plying the waters of the collector. "Hey, is there any talk of odd things found in the pits?"

An adroit push from a paddle brought the boat within easy speaking range. There was some chin-scratching and due consideration from the two men in the boat, then one said, "We don't ever find much in the way of coin or valuables. That's a myth people tell, like the one about the big lizards."

"I found a silverpiece last year," the youngest one commented helpfully.

"Perhaps I don't mean something unusual," Nicholas said, trying to think of a good way to explain. "Perhaps I mean an unusual amount of something you often find. Like a large concentration of sand, or bits of ironmongery, or—"

"Bones?" one of the boatmen suggested.

"Or bones," Nicholas agreed, concealing his reaction. "Was that the case?"

"Aye, the word was the Monde Street syphon came up full of bones two days ago. The Prefect figured a wall had broke through in one of the catacombs somewhere and that's where they come from."

"No," the oldest sewerman disagreed. "If that was it, the water level in Monde would drop and our collectors all down fifth precinct would go dry. There hasn't been enough rain to fill a catacomb."

The discussion abruptly turned highly technical, as water levels, drainage, rainfall, sluices, collectors, and connecting passages were all brought in as evidence for and against the catacomb hypothesis. Nicholas listened carefully. There were catacombs under Vienne and old covered-over rock quarries, and other places where a wily sorcerer could hide. It was a more likely place than an abandoned river palace, no matter what Octave had said.

The sewermen's lively discussion moved on to other topics and Nicholas interrupted long enough to bid them good-bye before he moved on to the next group. The sewers called for more research and he had many more questions to ask.

Madeline let herself into the apartment off the Boulevard Panzan, tired and cursing her luck. She had been following the progress of the Prefecture's search with the others but the frustration of being unable to participate actively was wearing on her. She would have preferred to be off with Reynard, who was pursuing Count Montesq's possible connection to their mad sorcerer, or Nicholas, who had been damnably uncommunicative about his pursuits.

Doctor Halle was in the salon, standing in front of the fire, apparently as preoccupied and discouraged as she was. He glanced at her as she flung herself down on the sofa and commented, "This inactivity rather grates on one, doesn't it?"

Madeline laughed ruefully. "I'm glad someone else feels it." She removed her hat, a plain gray affair to match her plain gray walking dress, an assemble guaranteed not to draw attention on the street and which did nothing to lift her flagging spirits.

Halle leaned on the mantel and cleaned out his pipe. "Ordinarily when the Prefecture has no use for me I see patients at the charity hospitals."

Madeline nodded in agreement. "I feel fortunate that I didn't take a role this season; I wouldn't have been able to do a farce justice with my mind on this."

His brows lifted. "So you are that Madeline Denare."

"Come now, you knew that."

"I did, but I wasn't sure I should mention it." He hesitated.

"I'm sure you have questions," Madeline said, carefully.

Halle smiled gently and shook his head. "Only impertinent ones. Why Reynard Morane persists in presenting himself to society as a debauched and dissipated wretch when he's as sound as a young horse. How a wandering scion of the infamous Alsenes made the acquaintance of so many congenial thieves.'' He looked at her gravely. ''And what you are doing here.''

He would ask a hard one, she thought. She shook her head. ''I'm not entirely sure of that myself,'' she admitted.

Halle didn't show surprise. He regarded her gravely. ''How long have you known Valiarde?''

''Since my first real ingenue role, as Eugenie in *The Scarlet Veil*. I got into a bit of trouble and Nicholas helped get me out.'' She saw the expression that Halle hadn't quite concealed in time and laughed. ''No, not that sort of trouble. I had gotten the attention of a rather terrible person called Lord Stevarin. Did you ever hear of him?''

''Vaguely.'' Halle frowned thoughtfully. ''He took his own life at his country home, didn't he?''

It had been so long Madeline had almost forgotten that part of the story. She nodded and said, ''Yes, I believe he did.'' She would have to judiciously edit the rest of her account. ''He was a great theater-goer, but not quite in the way other people are. He would go to look at the actresses, and when he took a fancy to one he would have her abducted, keep her at his town home for a few days—until he was tired of her, I suppose—then dump her out near the river somewhere, usually covered with bruises and too terrified to accuse him of anything. After all, they were only actresses, and he was a lord.''

''Good God,'' Halle said softly. After a moment he looked at her sharply. ''Then one day he chose you.''

''Yes. He had drugged champagne sent to my dressing room, and then sent his men to haul me off like I was a bag of laundry. Then—''

''You needn't tell me anymore if you don't wish—'' Halle interrupted hastily.

''No, he never got a chance.'' She smiled. ''I woke

in a bedchamber in his town home, he told me his intentions rather baldly, and I... brained him with a vase.'' She wondered what had possessed her to tell this story. *You should have made something up.* But she didn't like to lie to Halle and wasn't doing such a good job of it with a story that was mostly the truth. ''I was climbing out the window into the inner court when I met Nicholas climbing up. He had seen me in *The Scarlet Veil* too, and also had the idea of making my acquaintance but in a more conventional fashion. He saw Lord Stevarin's men taking away what he thought was a suspicious bundle, discovered I wasn't in my room and that my dresser had no notion where I'd gone, leapt to a conclusion no one else in his right mind would have leapt to, and followed them. So I got away.''

Halle looked at her a long moment, his gaze penetrating. ''And Lord Stevarin killed himself in remorse?'' he asked finally, as if he meant to believe her answer, whatever it was.

''No.'' Madeline hesitated, then shook her head. It suddenly seemed pointless to conceal it, what with everything else Halle knew. She said, ''That wasn't quite true. It wasn't a vase. He had a gun, you see, and I took it away from him and shot him with it. I wasn't afraid. As soon as I realized what he was, I knew I'd kill him.'' That was simple truth, though it sounded more like bragging. Madeline knew herself well enough to realize it had more to do with a disbelief in her own mortality than courage. *That could catch up to you at any moment,* she told herself. *And you call Nicholas reckless.*

Doctor Halle shook his head. ''A young woman, abducted and threatened? Not a court in Ile-Rien would see it as anything but self-defense.''

''Perhaps.'' Madeline shrugged. ''I never had much to do with courts and Nicholas had good reason not to trust them, after what happened to Edouard. Stevarin had sent his servants away so he wouldn't be interrupted and so it was very simple to take his coach and transport his body to his country home and make it look like suicide.

Nicholas knew how to make it appear as if Stevarin had held the gun, and put powder burns on his hand and around the wound, and all these other things I wouldn't have thought of if he hadn't mentioned them. I found it truly fascinating.''

Halle watched her a moment, a worried crease between his brows. ''Valiarde doesn't . . . use this against you, does he?''

''No, Nicholas only blackmails people he doesn't like.'' She bit her lip. She really wanted to make Halle understand, but she wasn't sure it was possible. She was only an actress; she didn't make up those eloquent speeches she gave on stage. ''It's not like that. Nicholas isn't just a clever criminal. If Edouard hadn't been killed, he would be a physician or a scholar or a dilettante or. . . . But if Edouard hadn't taken him in when he did . . . he would be a good deal worse.''

''Yet you trust him?''

''I do.''

Halle fiddled with his pipe a moment, then his eyes lifted to meet hers seriously. ''Should Ronsarde and I trust him?''

Madeline smiled. ''You ask me?''

''You strike me very much as a young woman who goes her own way.''

''Nicholas is a dangerous man,'' Madeline said honestly. ''But he's never betrayed anyone who kept faith with him.''

There was the sound of the outer door rattling as someone opened it with a key. Halle cleared his throat almost nervously and Madeline stood, fussing with her hideous hat and unaccountably embarrassed, her face reddening as if the conversation with the doctor had been of a far more intimate nature.

She forgot her embarrassment when Inspector Ronsarde appeared in the doorway, trailed by an expressionless Crack. Ronsarde was waving a telegram and his eyes gleamed with triumph. ''At long last, a development,'' he said. ''Summon the others at once!''

* * *

Nicholas walked back to the Philosopher's Cross, threading his way through street vendors and the mid-morning market crowd, until he reached Arisilde's tenement. He slipped past the concierge, who was arguing with a delivery boy, and started up the stairs.

Nicholas always approached Arisilde's garret cautiously, though it had remained under observation by Cusard's men and no one they didn't know had attempted to enter. Madeline had also visited here with Crack, though they were all careful to take different routes when they left to prevent anyone following them back to the Boulevard Panzan apartment. Nothing had happened here since Arisilde's illness and Nicholas was almost grudgingly willing to admit that it might be safe.

The door was whipped open before he could knock. Madele stood there, glaring at him. "What, you again?" she demanded. "Don't you trust me?"

"Since you ask," Nicholas said, stepping past her, "not particularly." Madele was dressed in what she considered "town clothes," a shapeless black dress and a hat with somewhat wilted fabric flowers jammed on her head. He stopped in the hallway to take off his coat and boots, not wanting to take the sewer stink that clung to them into Arisilde's room. Madele stood and stared at him, her arms folded, her brows lowered in suspicion. "What have you done with Isham?" he asked her.

"He's out at the shops," Madele said, defensively. "I've got to live."

If Nicholas had only the evidence of his eyes to go by, he would have said Madele had done nothing since Madeline had met her at the train station except sleep and devour whatever food was brought into the apartment. But Isham had told him that Madele spent every night seated on the floor of the parlor in front of the fire, working with the herbs and other supplies he found for her during the day. She had made a healing stone by the second night but so far it had done no good for Arisilde. It had, however, cured various fevers, lung ailments, piles, and other illnesses throughout the tenement, including a case of advanced venereal disease on the first floor, simply by its presence in the building, so Isham had no doubt of Madele's power. Madele had also rearranged the furnishings in the apartment with special attention to the potted plants, mirrors, and glass bric-a-brac. She had pretended to Isham that she was doing it out of sheer eccentricity, but he had recognized it as a very old method of channeling etherial substance and suspected she was trying to use whatever of Arisilde's power remained in the apartment to help sustain him. Madele had used none of Arisilde's extensive collection of magical texts and after some subtle observation Isham had concluded that she was illiterate. Nicholas had suspected it before and wasn't surprised to hear it confirmed. He said, "You realize you're 'living' enough for three or four old women, don't you?" and continued on to Arisilde's bedroom. Madele followed him, grumbling.

Nicholas stopped just inside the door to turn up the gas in the wall sconce. Medicine bottles and other medical paraphernalia littered the dresser near the bed, along with an incense burner and some bunches of herbs. "Did the physician come today?"

"Yes," Madele admitted, reluctantly. "Didn't do a damn thing. How much are we paying him?"

" 'We'? " Nicholas sat on the bed. Arisilde's face was white, his eyes sunken in their deep sockets. Isham had kept the sorcerer clean, forced enough water and broth down his throat to keep him alive, followed the physician's instructions, but there had been no change. Madele had ventured no opinion as to whether the sorcerer's condition had been caused by a spell or just the inevitable consequences of his much-abused health, but according to Isham she was exploring both possibilities.

One of the necromantic techniques for creating illness was to write an inscription in blood on a piece of linen or skin and bury it near the house of the victim. Isham had searched the neighborhood for anything of that kind with the help of a few hedgewitches of his acquaintance, but found nothing. Madele had looked again with the same result. *Can't you wake for a challenge, Arisilde? Wouldn't you appreciate the novelty of defeating a mad sorcerer in battle?* Nicholas thought. He said, "More than 'we' are paying 'you.' Are you asking for further compensation?" Madele had country sensibilities and her idea of compensation would probably be a new hat, which she certainly seemed to be badly in need of.

Madele sniffed and said nothing. Nicholas glanced at her and thought he read defeat in her expression. He looked away. Madele didn't have a Lodun degree but he suspected she was as knowledgeable as any sorcerer-healer they could find there. And she had been able to do nothing.

The day she had arrived in town Madeline had brought her to the Panzan apartment and they had shown her the sphere. She had held it in her work-roughened hands for a long time, turning it over, watching the wheels within wheels inside it move. Then she had looked up at them with a baffled expression and said, "What in hell is this?"

Madele might have forgotten more sorcery and herbal medicine than most practitioners knew at their best but the principles of natural philosophy that Edouard had used to construct the sphere were a closed book to her. She could sense the power within it but she had no notion of how to reach it.

There was a rattle from the hall as someone tried the outer door of the apartment. Madele darted out of the bedroom and Nicholas stood, reaching for the pistol in his inside jacket pocket. A moment later he heard Isham's voice and relaxed.

Isham came down the hall, handing off a string bag of bread and onions to Madele, saying, "Take this to the pantry, please, you horrible old woman. Is . . . Ah, you are here." Isham fished a folded telegram out of his sleeve and gave it to Nicholas. "The concierge had this, it arrived only a few moments ago. It is addressed to me but it is surely for you."

Nicholas tore it open quickly. *Important news—come at once. SR.* "Yes," he said, feeling his first flash of hope in three days. "It's for me."

*   *   *

They came to the place from the river aboard a small steam launch owned by a friend of Cusard's. Nicholas stood in the bow, ignoring the spray of foul river water. The light was failing but he could see the turrets and chimneys of the house they were approaching outlined against the reddening sky. It was a monolithic bulk, mostly featureless in the shadow, but swinging lamps lit the garden terraces above the river and the watergate.

Nicholas jammed his hands further into his pockets and braced his feet as a gust of wind tore at him. The air was cold and the water like black glass. The setting sun left the Great Houses lining this side of the embankment in darkness and lit the columns and classical pediments of the buildings on the far side with a pure golden glow. The Prefecture had found the house this morning and it had taken most of the day to convince Lord Albier that Ronsarde and Halle should be permitted to inspect the scene. The battle had been conducted entirely by telegram, with frequent missives fired off to Captain Giarde at the palace for support. In the end Albier had given in with poor grace and Ronsarde and Halle were formally invited to give advice. Nicholas had not been invited but he was here anyway. Madele had not been invited either but she was the only trustworthy source of sorcerous advice they had at present, so she was now huddled in the cabin of the boat, vocal in her displeasure at being forced to cross running water. Madeline had invited herself and was in her "young man" disguise to help forestall questions from Albier and the other representatives of the Prefecture. Crack had not been invited but he was here to guard their backs.

The chugging engine of the launch abruptly cut off. Nicholas turned back to the cabin and saw the captain standing, staring worriedly at the watergate the boat was still drifting toward. Nicholas glanced at it and saw that they had drawn near enough for the lamps to reveal the official markings on the launch already tied there and the uniforms of the men waiting at the gate.

"Constables," the captain said, and spat succinctly over the side. He was an old man, featureless under several layers of ragged coats and scarves, looking more like a dustman than a smuggler. Doctor Halle and Ronsarde exchanged a look, then Halle took a step toward the man.

"It's all right," Nicholas told the captain. "They're expecting us."

The captain grunted thoughtfully, then disappeared back into the cabin. A moment later the engine came to life again.

Ronsarde stepped up beside Nicholas, his eyes on the house ahead. He said, "Albier has been here all day."

The boat drew up to the watergate with a practiced ease, bumped gently against the pilings as Crack stepped over to the tiny stone dock to catch the lines. One of the constables hurried to help him tie it off and a young man in a dark coat and top hat stepped forward to greet Ronsarde. "Inspector, I'm glad you can assist us in this . . . matter." The lamps hanging on the pillars of the gate were shaped into elaborate wrought iron lilies; by their light the young man's bland, handsome face looked ill. He said, "Lord Albier—"

"Lord Albier wishes me in Hell," Ronsarde said briskly. He gripped Nicholas's shoulder to steady himself as he stepped off the boat. Halle was immediately beside him, handing him his cane. "So I doubt he was pleased to hear my assistance would be inflicted upon him. I only hope he and his minions haven't destroyed too many vital traces."

"Ah . . . Yes, well." The man's eyes widened at the number of people piling off the boat. Nicholas had followed Halle and Madeline was helping her grandmother. "These are . . . ?"

Ronsarde gestured sharply. "My associates." He started for the stone steps leading up to the house and the young man hurried after him.

"That's Viarn, Lord Albier's secretary," Doctor Halle explained to Nicholas as they followed.

The stairs climbed a terraced garden, cloaked in twilight and shadow, a constable's lamp illuminating small manicured hedges and stone flower urns. They passed the garden walls screening the entrance of the house from the river and found themselves on a broad court with benches and graceful statuary, lit by gas sconces framing the doorway. Nicholas looked up at the large windows on the second floor where lamps from inside the house revealed a conservatory filled with palms and hothouse flowers. Nicholas tried to think how many gardeners would have been employed to care for those tropical plants and for the gardens on the embankment. During the winter, and with the family at their country seat, surely only two or three.

The doors stood open as they probably never would had the house's real owners still been in command. A uniformed constable stood guard there. Ronsarde stepped into the foyer beyond, stopping abruptly as he realized there were muddy bootprints on the tiles. Then he saw the muddy boots of the constable at the door, swore violently and strode into the house. Doctor Halle grimaced and hurried after him.

"This is Chaldome House," Madeline spoke in a low husky voice, part of her "young man" disguise.

In the man's suit, greatcoat and hat she wore and with her face subtly made up she looked the role, but he hoped she would be able to maintain it once they saw what was sure to lay within. Stiffly, Nicholas said, "Are you sure you want to be here?"

Madeline looked at him, her dark eyes enigmatic, and followed Halle into the house.

Nicholas felt a tug at his coat sleeve and glanced down. Madele stood there, bundled up in several coats and shawls. She said, "Damp air is bad for my joints."

He offered her his arm. She took it, muttering to herself, and he helped her up the steps into the house.

The second floor of the entrance hall was open to the conservatory and air from the open doorway rustled in the heavy fronds and stirred the leaves, made the flames in the glass sconces flicker, brought the faint scent of the river into the house. Nicholas realized he had unconsciously braced himself for the heavy odor that had clung to Valent House. *But he wasn't here as long*, he thought. *There hasn't been time.*

He heard Ronsarde's voice and followed it through the open double doors at the end of the hall.

The sound led him to a ballroom, high-ceilinged, with a row of marble columns dividing it from another conservatory, this one a glass-walled oval extending out from the side of the house. The torcheres along the walls and the chandeliers were meant to hold candles, so the room was lit only by the kerosene lamps of the constables. Most of it was in shadow but Nicholas could tell the walls were covered with paintings of tropical islands, with plants, birds, exotic animals picked out in fine detail. Nicholas remembered that the current Lord Chaldome was a naturalist of some renown, a member of the Philosophers' Academy.

Uniformed men were searching, pulling the dustcovers off the furniture in the salons that gave onto the ballroom, even unrolling the rugs which were stacked along the far wall. There were eight tarp-covered forms stretched out on the floor in a line. Lord Albier stood near them, with his secretary and another man in a frock coat and top hat, arguing with restrained, bitter violence with Inspector Ronsarde. Halle was looking around at the shapes on the floor, shaking his head, Madeline standing near him.

Nicholas swore under his breath. "They moved the bodies. They destroyed the scene." He had dragged poor Madele and her bad joints here for nothing. He supposed it would do no good to explain to Albier that if they hadn't seen the murder room in Valent House as it was, they would never have realized it was necromancy, or known about the tie to Constant Macob.

Madele slipped her arm free of Nicholas's and moved away, studying the large chamber thoughtfully.

Madeline turned away from Halle and Ronsarde and Nicholas went forward to meet her. "We may have come here for nothing," she said, low-voiced. "Albier is a complete fool."

"Is he?" Nicholas said. Albier was now pointing at

them and gesturing to Ronsarde, obviously objecting to their presence. "Or did someone tell him to do this."

"That's the question." Madeline glanced around. "Where is grandmother?"

Nicholas turned, looking around the room. Madele was nowhere to be seen. He let out his breath in annoyance. "We'll find her when she wants to be found. Try to see as much as you can before we're thrown out." Before boarding the steam launch, Nicholas had told Madeline their primary goal was to search for the sphere Octave had made. He hadn't mentioned this to Ronsarde and Halle.

Madeline nodded and moved away. An agitated party of people were being conducted into the room through the doors in the far wall. Several men in business dress, one older woman who might be a housekeeper or upper servant. She saw the still forms lined up under the sheets and cried out in shock. Albier saw the newcomers, gave Ronsarde one last parting glare, then hurried across the room toward them.

Halle moved immediately toward the bodies and the other doctors who were conferring near them, taking advantage of Albier's distraction. Nicholas approached Ronsarde. "Well?"

The Inspector was leaning on his cane, an expression of thwarted fury on his face. His eyes still on the occupied Albier, he said, "The family is still in the country, but there was a small staff to maintain the house in their absence, including a housekeeper, maids, a footman, and two gardeners to keep up the grounds and conservatories. This morning a dairyman tried to make his usual delivery at the kitchen door. He was well-acquainted with the house and when he realized it appeared to be locked and empty, he brought it to the attention of the local constable. That the servants were all found here, dead, is all I have been able to ascertain, and from the state of the place that is all I will ever be able to ascertain."

"Did he discover when any of them were last seen alive?"

"The dairyman made a delivery three days ago and found them all quite alive and healthy. There are constables speaking with the other merchants in the area and the servants in the houses to either side, hoping to obtain confirmation of that."

Nicholas stared around in irritation. "They were killed here?" The ballroom floor was marked only by the dirt and mud from Prefecture boots.

Ronsarde slanted a look at him. "So Albier says."

"Then where's the blood?" His recent research told him that there were some of Constant Macob's necromantic magics that could be performed by strangling or suffocating the victim, but that wasn't enough for the powerful spells their sorcerer seemed to favor.

"A good question." Ronsarde looked at him, his eyes serious. "Albier claims that there is no need for haste or further investigation. He says he has the solution."

"Solution?" Nicholas looked around the ballroom again, baffled. "He's bluffing, trying to get rid of you."

"I fear that he is not." Ronsarde moved away, leaning heavily on his cane.

Worried, Nicholas watched him go. The new arrivals were being led over to the bodies, obviously to view them to establish their identity. Nicholas started to fade out of the way, but noticed, in the far corner of the ballroom, an unobtrusive set of panel doors, made obtrusive by the presence of two constables guarding them. This piqued his curiosity greatly, but he saw no way to discover what was there until Albier saw fit to reveal it. He left the ballroom through one of the attached salons.

He walked through the empty rooms, occasionally encountering constables who took him for one of the doctors or an aide to one of the Inspectors present. The only sound was quiet talk from the ballroom, punctuated by the loud sobs of the older woman as she identified the bodies.

Albier is either a fool or a liar, Nicholas thought. If the sorcerer had been here at all, he hadn't been here long. The house was clean, freshly swept, ready for the occupancy of its masters at any moment. Most of the furniture was still neatly covered, paintings still on the walls, silver dining services neatly arranged in unbroken glass cabinets. Nothing had been looted, nothing disturbed.

The house wasn't very old. The design was too modern, with too many public rooms and windows on the first floor. The owners would probably wish they had bought one of the older, more fortress-like Great Houses instead of building for comfort. Still, there had to be a sorcerer hired to ward it against theft. Nicholas made his way down to the kitchens to check the pantries and found Madeline coming up from the cellars. "Did you go down there alone?" he demanded.

She gave him a withering look as she fastened the door latch again. "No, Nicholas, Lord Albier escorted me personally. The constables have already been through it and there's nothing down there. I was looking at the cisterns."

Nicholas pinched the bridge of his nose, regained his calm, and asked, "Were they topped off?"

"Yes." She waved a hand toward the main kitchen. "The fires were banked and then let to burn out and there were beds disturbed in the servants' quarters. They must have been attacked at night."

He nodded. "And the intruders didn't use any water while they were here. To drink, or to clean up the blood."

Madeline gestured in exasperation. "I don't see how those people could have been killed here."

"They weren't."

"Well that clears everything up," Madeline said, annoyed.

Nicholas ignored the sarcasm and took the servants' passage back to the public rooms. It opened into one of the reception areas off the ballroom. Nicholas looked around at a room as clean and undisturbed as all the others, with jade figures ornamenting the mantelpiece, and swore aloud. He would have taken an oath on anything that no intruders had stayed long in this house.

Just long enough to abduct the servants, then to bring the bodies back.

The voices from the ballroom grew loud and agitated, then Doctor Halle appeared, supporting the older woman who had been called in to help identify the corpses. She was gasping for breath and even in the dim light Nicholas could see her face was going blue. He tore a cover off the nearest couch while Madeline shoved the ornamental tables out of the way. Halle lowered the woman to the couch as another doctor bustled in, digging in his medical bag.

Nicholas and Madeline backed away to give the physicians room and Madeline whispered, "Why did they make her look at them now? Surely they don't always do it that way, not when the death was violent."

"No, the relatives aren't brought in until the victims are at the morgue and have been washed and prepared by the undertaker. For some reason the Prefecture is in an unseemly hurry for identification." From the look of it, Halle would be busy here for a time. Nicholas went back into the ballroom, Madeline trailing him.

Ronsarde had cornered Albier again. As Nicholas drew near he heard him say, "I've been patient throughout this farce, Albier, now tell me what it is you think you have. Unless," Ronsarde added, smiling, "you are afraid it won't stand up to my scrutiny."

Albier returned the smile with the same lack of cordiality. "Very well. I was not trying to delay you, Ronsarde, only making sure of my facts. This way."

Albier led the way to the doors Nicholas had noted earlier, the ones barred by the constables. Albier nodded to the secretary Viarn, who hurried over, drawing a key out of his pocket.

Viarn unlocked the sliding panels, then pushed them open. The room within was dark, illuminated only by narrow windows high in the outside wall. Another gesture from Albier and one of the solemn constables brought a lamp.

Obviously as impatient with the theatrics as Nicholas,

Ronsarde took the lamp away from the constable and held it high, lighting the room.

Nicholas caught sight of another body on the floor, this one left in situ as the others had not been. He pushed forward, elbowing Viarn out of the way.

The body was that of a man, young, with a lanky build and dirty blond hair, sprawled on the parquet floor amid markings of ash and black dust or soot. What many of the marks had represented was permanently obscured by blood, most of it pooled around the man's body. His throat had been cut and the lamplight glinted off a knife still clutched in one discolored hand.

"There is your sorcerer," Albier said.

Nicholas looked at Ronsarde, whose expression of stunned incredulity said everything, then back at Lord Albier, who was complacently straightening his gloves. Since Ronsarde was apparently still speechless with rage, Nicholas cleared his throat and asked, "He killed everyone in the house, cleaned up after it, then cut his own throat, I suppose?"

Albier lifted his brows at this presumption, then noticed that everyone within earshot, constables, inspectors, their assistants, the doctors, was staring, waiting for the answer. He said sharply, "He was a sorcerer, called Merith Kahen, trained at Lodun and hired by Lord Chaldome to ward this house and the family estates in the provinces against theft and intrusions. I have been informed the remaining symbols on the floor of that room indicate the practice of necromancy. The conclusions are obvious."

"Are they?" Ronsarde's voice was admirably cool, the edge of sarcasm as sharp as a blade.

Albier's mouth tightened. "He was practicing necromancy at the house in the Gabardin and he became frightened when you discovered the place. He tried to eliminate you with the attack on the Courts Plaza. In the meantime, one of the unfortunate servants here also discovered some evidence of Kahen's activities, and perhaps confronted him. In his madness Kahen killed everyone in the house then—"

"Conveniently killed himself in remorse," Nicholas finished. "How very . . . tidy of him."

For a moment Albier's eyes were dangerous, then he turned away with a muttered curse.

Nicholas smiled tightly to himself. Viarn and the constables posted nearby were all pretending not to have noticed the altercation. Ronsarde had been too caught up in his study of the dead man to notice and now he handed Nicholas the lamp without looking at him and leaned down, studying the floor intently. Picking his spot with care, he took one step forward, then one more, so he could kneel awkwardly beside the body. Nicholas took his place in the doorway, holding the lamp so Ronsarde could see. He leaned in as far as he could, to examine the walls of the room. There was none of the melting that he had observed in the cellar chamber in Valent House where the necromancy had taken place. He would have been greatly surprised if there had been.

Ronsarde had carefully lifted the dead hand that was still clasped around the knife. Now he lowered it gently, and said, "Unfortunate young man."

"Did he cut his own throat?" Nicholas asked. "Not that it matters."

"He did. Not that it matters." In a tone of bitter disgust, Ronsarde added, "Magic."

Nicholas looked around the dark little room again. Albier wasn't a fool; if they could find any evidence that this scene was as stage-managed as a play at the Elegante, Albier would believe it, if reluctantly. But there would be no evidence. The young sorcerer had been enspelled to kill himself. From the traces of black dust on his hands, he had also been enspelled to draw the circle. *But was that simple expediency, or attention to detail?* Nicholas wondered. There was even a bucket of soot standing in the corner. *When they search his rooms, if they haven't already, will they find texts and notes on necromancy?* Their opponent was learning.

Ronsarde had come to the same conclusion. He said, "There is nothing of use here." He planted his cane and used it to lever himself to his feet, turning back toward the door. Nicholas stepped out of his way and handed the lantern off to the nearest constable.

There was an outcry from across the ballroom and the old woman that Halle and the other doctor had been tending came running toward them. Her face was red and streaked with tears, and she was gasping, "He wouldn't do it, he wouldn't do a thing like this, I swear it! You've got to believe—"

Ronsarde stepped forward and caught her hand, turning her away before she could get another look into the room. Nicholas quickly slid the doors closed and the secretary Viarn hastened to lock them.

"He didn't . . . he didn't . . ." the woman was still trying to say.

"I believe you," Ronsarde said to the hysterical woman, his voice firm. "Go to your home, mourn him and the others, and know that the accusations against him are vile lies, and in time he will be proved blameless."

The woman stared at him, as if she couldn't quite comprehend what he was saying, but her breathing calmed and her eyes were less wild. When the other doctor came to lead her away, she went without protest, only craning her neck to look back at the closed doors.

Halle had followed the woman in and now stepped close to Ronsarde and said in a low voice, "She was the housekeeper here and the boy, the young sorcerer, was her son. When they discovered he had the talent for magic Lord Chaldome paid for his education and sent him to Lodun. He was being paid well for his services here, enough so that his mother had no need to work. It sounds as if he had absolutely no motive to feel anger toward the family or the servants."

Nicholas cleared his throat and said, "His father . . . ?"

"I thought of that," Halle said impatiently. "His father was a barman at a local wineshop, who died only a few years ago. The possibility that he was a bastard of Lord Chaldome—"

"Is not worth considering," Ronsarde finished. He

looked around the ballroom again, his expression dark. "I greatly fear that this . . . charade has been designed to throw off pursuit long enough for our culprit to move to another city and begin his work again."

Nicholas said nothing. He wasn't so sure that was the case. To throw off pursuit, yes, but not to cover an escape. He saw Lord Albier coming back toward them and murmured, "Watch out, gentlemen."

Lord Albier advanced on Ronsarde, saying, "Calming the woman's hysterics with platitudes does her no good. Facing the facts—"

"I gave her the facts," Ronsarde said coldly. "You are the one who is deluding yourself. If you would be the only one to suffer from it, I would be happy to let you have your delusion. But the killing will continue, if not here, then somewhere else."

Nicholas moved away, leaving Ronsarde and Halle to argue with Albier. Madeline, he realized, had also disappeared, probably to pursue the search through the rest of the house. He felt fairly confident that she would find nothing.

Doing his best to stay unobtrusive, Nicholas made his own brief examination of the bodies of the unfortunate servants. The wounds on two of them were like those on the corpses found at Valent House, with the tattered, hideously stained clothing torn aside to reveal disembowelments, eyes gouged, rope marks on wrists and ankles. *He chose one man and one woman*, Nicholas noted. *Impartial bastard.* The others had been simply slaughtered, their throats cut. Only one large man, who by his coat and mud-stained trousers might have been one of the gardeners, had been killed by repeated blows to the head which had finally crushed his skull. The man must have fought or tried to escape. *So he used two for necromancy, and the others had to be killed because. . . .* Because they might have been able to swear to Merith Kahen's occupation with some harmless pursuit during the time when he was supposed to be killing people in the Gabardin or planning magical attacks on the Courts Plaza.

Nicholas dropped the sheet on the last corpse. He didn't know why he was doing this; he wasn't discovering anything Halle wouldn't be able to tell him.

"What are you doing?"

Nicholas turned on his heel, but the words weren't to him. Rahene Fallier stood over Madele who was kneeling on the floor and lifting a sheet to peer at one of the bodies. Nicholas stood slowly, his back stiffening. He hadn't known Fallier was here but he supposed it was inevitable. Despite his fall from grace in the palace, Fallier would still be working with the Prefecture. Nicholas started to move toward them.

Madele looked up at Fallier, her bright eyes wary, then she smiled, or at least showed her teeth. She said, "Think again."

Fallier stared down at her for a long moment then, though Madele had done nothing, or nothing obvious, he took a deliberate step back. Dressed in an impeccable dark suit and towering over the ragged old woman, he looked totally in command and it seemed an uneven contest. But Madele was the kind of woman who would fight like a feral animal when cornered and that wasn't taking her power into account. The sorcerer adjusted his gloves, his expression revealing nothing, and said, "Who are you?"

Madele said, "I came with Sebastion," and grinned at him.

Nicholas had no time to wonder when Madele had had the chance to get on a first name basis with Inspector Ronsarde. Fallier growled, "That hardly answers my question."

She said, "It didn't that, did it? Go on, now."

Fallier watched her a moment longer, his lips thinning with annoyance, then he gave her an edged smile and tipped his hat to her.

Nicholas approached cautiously as Fallier moved away. He sat on his heels next to her and said, "I was racing to your rescue but since you seem perfectly capable of rescuing yourself I thought I'd let discretion rule valor."

Madele turned from her rapt contemplation of Fallier's departing form to regard Nicholas with a raised brow. "If you were thirty years older or I was a hundred years younger—"

"I would run screaming," Nicholas assured her. "What have you found?"

Madele chuckled but she looked down at the sheeted body again and her face turned serious. She lifted the arm of the corpse. Nicholas noted it was a woman's arm and that it was discolored and the stiffness had passed off, showing that it was at least a day or more since the death, but Halle would have already made note of all that. Madele gently lifted one of the fingers and Nicholas frowned. The corpse wore a ring, a plain dull metal band. "I don't understand."

Instead of the sarcastic response he half-expected, Madele gently worked the ring up the finger, so he could see that the skin beneath it was blackened, burned. "What caused that?" Nicholas asked, frowning.

"A magic," she said. "Unfinished, and harmless." She tucked the arm back under the sheet, smoothing the cloth over it and giving it an absentminded pat, as if she was tucking in a child. "It makes me wonder if it was a second go."

"Can you be a trifle more obscure? I think I almost understood what you said that last time."

She shook her head impatiently. "He was making a magic, with the ring and this poor dead thing, but he didn't let it finish. Just a thought I had—I do have them occasionally. I need to ruminate on it a bit and take a look somewhere." She held out a hand and Nicholas helped her up.

Madele wandered away, her course apparently aimless. With Fallier here Nicholas thought he might as well make himself scarce, at least for a time, and he headed for the way out of the ballroom.

Nicholas saw the secretary Viarn hovering near the outer doorway, an expression of tired resignation on his face. He greeted him with a nod and Nicholas took the opportunity to ask, "Lord Albier said the dead sorcerer was trained at Lodun. Who did he study with?"

"I believe it was Ilamires Rohan." The secretary shook his head. "After all the opportunities Lord Chaldome gave him, it's hard to believe the young man would betray him so. But madness knows no reason."

"No," Nicholas agreed. "No, it doesn't, does it?" He walked on.

Out on the stone court the wind was in the right direction and the night air was fresh. The lamps flickered and the constables patrolled the grounds, endlessly searching. Nicholas jammed his hands in his pockets and paced to the end of the court where he could see the river. Octave had said, "The palace . . . the palace on the river. He's been there—" *He's been there and gone,* Nicholas thought. *Is that what he meant to say?* Octave had known about this house. From the state of the bodies, they could have been killed that very night. If the spiritualist had lived for one more breath, one more heartbeat, would they have known about this place in time to save the occupants? He wasn't sure why that should be such a bitter thought; this was none of his business.

No, that wasn't true. What would Edouard have thought if he had known his work had been used in aid of all this killing?

And that wasn't true, either. *Edouard's dead,* Nicholas thought. *Might as well admit that as well, if honesty is everything. None of this can hurt him.*

I want this sorcerer because I want him, there's no altruism about it. He has challenged me, he has interfered with me, and I'll see him in Hell if I have to escort him there personally.

Crack ghosted up and took a post at his elbow and Nicholas put those thoughts aside for the moment. He said, sourly, "Lord Albier's solved our little mystery—to his satisfaction."

Crack grunted noncommittally.

"You know what that means, of course."

Crack muttered, "We're on our own again, that's what."

* * *

Madele burst through the door of Arisilde's apartment, shedding scarves and shawls. She found Isham seated in an armchair in front of the parlor hearth, a book in his lap.

She dropped her last shawl, still damp from the river spray, and said, "He was making a corpse ring!"

Isham stared. "What?"

"This sorcerer. He's killed another lot of folk, and on one's hand I found the making of a corpse ring."

Madele's excitement was making her country accent thicken and Isham frowned in incomprehension, but he caught the last two words. "Corpse ring?" It was one of the oldest tricks of necromancy, a ring enspelled and left on the hand of a corpse for three days. When it was removed and placed on the hand of a living person, it would simulate death, or a state close to it. Isham shut his book and slammed it down on the table. "I already told you that that was the first thing I looked for! There were no strange tokens, nothing that was not his—"

Madele shook her head impatiently. "Looked with your eyes, or looked with your hands?"

Isham hesitated, then said something vile in Parscian and struggled to his feet.

Madele followed him to Arisilde's bedchamber, saying, "You said you went out and when you came back he seemed to sleep. Well, he must have gone to sleep, with a bit of his drug to help him along. And while he lay so it must have come in, whatever it was, and put it on him without waking him. . . ."

Still cursing his own stupidity in Parscian, Isham tore back the patched coverlet and grabbed for Arisilde's hands. He felt carefully around the base of each finger, moving upward slowly, deliberately turning his face away so he would have only the evidence of touch to go by. An illusion strong enough to hide a ring on the finger of a man who had been examined by physicians, who had been searched many times for any evidence of magical attack, could still be powerful enough to confuse the senses even when the searcher was certain it was there. He found nothing and shook his head in frustration.

Madele snatched the coverlet off the bed entirely and took Arisilde's right foot in one hand, feeling carefully along the toes. Isham watched, but the brief spark of hope was dying as she found nothing and moved on to the left foot.

Madele frowned, then her face went still suddenly, as her fingers reached the smallest toe.

Something else had occurred to Isham and he said urgently, "Madele—"

She was already slipping the ring off Arisilde's toe. Once it lay in her palm the illusion dissolved and she could see it as well as feel it, a small iron band, grimly stained. She met Isham's anxious gaze, and grinned. "Isn't it always the last place you look?"

18

It was late at night by the time Nicholas returned to the apartment off the Boulevard Panzan. The others had gone there directly from the docks while he had escorted Madele back to the Philosopher's Cross. The old woman had been preoccupied about something but he hadn't been able to pry it out of her. He had resolved to go over to Arisilde's in the morning to see if she was more willing to talk then.

The river spray and the damp had gotten into his clothes and he climbed the stairs up to the apartment wearily, cold to the bone.

It was a despondent group that greeted him in the salon. "I don't understand why Albier is persisting with this," Halle was saying, pacing agitatedly in front of the fire. Crack leaned against the wall near the doorway, Cusard was a dour figure huddled in a chair as far away from Ronsarde and Halle as possible, and Madeline was draped across one of the couches with her hat pulled over her face.

Ronsarde was in the chair near the window, smoking his pipe, with a serpent-like intensity in his gaze. He said, "The facts of the case are becoming known. Dozens of deaths in Riverside and the Gabardin and sorcerous attacks in the city make the Prefecture look ineffectual. He wants to produce a culprit, or at least pretend to produce one, to deflect criticism while the search for the real criminal goes on." He lifted one edge of the window curtain to look out at the dark street below. "It is nothing that has not been done before."

Nicholas paused in the doorway, feeling a twist in his gut. "We know," he said lightly, crossing into the room.

"Was Madele all right?" Madeline asked, sitting up on the couch and tossing her hat aside.

"Yes, only preoccupied."

She was trying to dig something out of her pocket and eventually produced a folded letter. "Sarasate sent a messenger with this. It came to Coldcourt this morning."

Nicholas took it from her and glanced at the address, then smiled. "Doctor Uberque." He sat down on the couch and tore the letter open immediately.

"Is that another sorcerer?" Cusard asked suspiciously.

"No, he's a doctor of history, at Lodun. I consulted him on Constant Macob and he was going to keep looking into the subject for me." He spread the closely written pages on his knees. Ronsarde's interest had been piqued at the name of the ancient necromancer and he came to stand at Nicholas's elbow.

The information Nicholas wanted had apparently led Doctor Uberque on a merry chase through the libraries of Lodun. But the historian seemed to combine an enthusiasm for the hunt with a detective instinct to rival Ronsarde's and an encompassing knowledge of his subject. "He's discovered what was in the chamber buried beneath Ventarin House," Nicholas reported after a moment. "That's the room we found broken into from the Duchess of Mondollot's cellars," he explained for Cusard and Crack's benefit.

Cusard glanced uneasily at Ronsarde, who was frowning down intently at the letter.

Madeline drew breath to expostulate at the delay and Nicholas continued, "It was Constant Macob's body."

"His body?" Ronsarde's expression was almost affronted.

"His bones, more probably, after this amount of time," Halle commented reasonably. "Did your informant discover the reason the corpse was concealed?''

"He believes Gabard Ventarin had the body sealed in the chamber as a precaution. He relates it to the custom present at the time for burying murderers at crossroads in case their predilection for bloodshed stemmed from an arcane source.'' Nicholas folded the letter and tapped it against his chin. Ronsarde captured the document and opened it to read for himself.

"I suppose that explains it,'' Madeline said, though she seemed troubled. "Octave needed a relic, a lock of hair or an old possession, of the dead people he wanted to speak to. His sorcerer wanted a relic of Macob so he could speak to him. After all this time Macob's bones must have been the best thing for it.''

"After all this time,'' Ronsarde echoed. "Doctor Uberque explains that he obtained this information from a letter penned by Gabard Ventarin, who was then holding the post of Court Sorcerer. The letter was sent to the sorcerer who was at that time Master of Lodun and whose papers and books are stored in the university's oldest archives. A difficult task, even for a historian familiar with the Lodun libraries.'' He frowned. "How did Octave and our sorcerer know of the corpse's location?''

That question had occurred to Nicholas as well. But he remembered how Arisilde had found the book he had described to him and felt wary of constructing any theory that contradicted that incontrovertible fact. "Sorcerers,'' he pointed out, "can find things that have been lost for years with little difficulty. Without more information, the only conclusion we can draw is that we are facing a very powerful sorcerer. Something we already knew,'' he added dryly.

Ronsarde did not look satisfied.

Nicholas hesitated. Now would be a good time to bring up the subject of the sewers and what he suspected an investigation of them would reveal, and he had planned to do so. But Ronsarde's comment on the Prefecture's methods had awakened old, and not-so-old, suspicions. He said only, "I'm going out again,'' and stood.

Crack stopped him in the hallway. "Me with you?" he asked.

Nicholas shook his head. "No, I want you to stay here. Watch the others."

Whether Crack had received a subtle message from that, Nicholas didn't know. He scarcely knew whether he meant it to convey one or not. But Crack made no protest, only nodded, and stepped back into the salon.

Nicholas went through the darkened bedchamber and into the dressing room, a small chamber with a table and a few chairs, a good mirror and some inadequate lamps. It currently looked like it was being used by at least half the cast of an amateur theatrical.

Madeline had followed him back to the dressing room, as he had hoped she would. But before he could say anything she kicked the door shut behind her and said, "You're being somewhat uncommunicative."

Her tone, honed to an edge of expression from years of training, stung more than her words. Nicholas's patience wasn't inexhaustible to begin with and his temper was short from long hours of work and continual frustrations. He snapped, "I haven't anything to communicate."

"You mean nothing definite," Madeline corrected, folding her arms.

Nicholas turned away and dug through the chaos of clothing and disguises spilling out of the wardrobe and onto the floor, cursing under his breath. *It's my apartment and this was all my idea. You would think I could find my goddamned trousers.* "All right, nothing definite to communicate."

"You won't discuss it with me because you're afraid I'll tell Ronsarde and you don't want your thunder stolen."

"That makes me sound like a complete fool." He found the remnants of his cabman outfit, which had the merit of being dry, at least, and began to strip.

Madeline didn't disagree with that statement. She eyed him narrowly, then said, "Halle asked me today if he and Ronsarde could trust you."

"Halle asked you that?" Nicholas paused with his shirt half off.

"Yes."

"Ungrateful bastard."

"You're jealous," she said.

"On your account, I assume?" As soon as he said it he knew it was a mistake, but it was too late to snatch the words back. *Idiot*, he snarled at himself.

But Madeline only gestured in annoyance. "No, I'm not that much of a fool. On Ronsarde's account. Halle's worked with him all these years, been involved in the investigations of all these fascinating crimes, been his confidant and his partner. That's what you would have wanted."

"That's ridiculous," he snapped, slinging things out of the way as he searched for his boots in the bottom of the closet. He wasn't sure which charge was more demeaning: the accusation of professional jealousy or her obvious belief that that was the only kind of jealousy he could possibly fall prey to.

"Is it? That's why you won't tell anyone what you've been doing. You want to impress everyone."

Nicholas finished dressing in suppressed fury. Finally he slung his battered black coat over his shoulders and pulled on the torn fingerless gloves. He grabbed his hat from the dressing table and went to pull back the curtains and shove the window open. He turned back and saw, from Madeline's expression, that she might regret what she had said, but it was far too late for that. He said, "I don't know what's worse, your inaccuracy or your patronizing attitude," and stepped out the window onto the ledge.

The decorative stonework let him boost himself up onto the roof where he could make his way down the outside stairs into the back courtyard.

It was too early for the appointment Nicholas had to keep, so he found himself in the theater district just off the Saints Procession Boulevard. He passed the façades of the Tragedian, the Elegante, and the Arcadella, with their well-proportioned columns and statues of the Graces and the patron saints of drama and the arts. The promenades were crowded with well-dressed patrons and the vendors and flower-sellers overflowed out into the street, impeding traffic. The carriage circle of the opera was almost choked with coaches with noble crests emblazoned on their doors and the ornamental lamps around the fountains in the center crowned the confusion with a blaze of light and moving water.

Nicholas kept moving, skirting the busy promenades and the constables who patrolled them, ducking into the street where he had to dodge between the lumbering coaches and the faster-moving cabriolets and curricles. The crowding became even worse when he came into sight of the less expensive theaters and the music halls, an area that flirted dangerously with the edges of the Gabardin and Riverside. He paused outside the High Follies, a theater that specialized in grandiose epics with shipwrecks on fayre islands, exploding steamers in stormy seas, and volcanic explosions. As a boy he would have given, or stolen, anything for the coins to attend a show here. As an adult with freedom and money in his pocket he would have thought the tawdry magic of the place would have palled, but it was amazing how tempting the doorway, framed by an enormous pair of gold-painted palm trees hung with giant snakes, still was. He reminded himself that the shows went for hours and he didn't have that much time to waste. *You can take the boy out of Riverside*, Nicholas thought ruefully, *but it's always in his blood.* Which showed you what fools the people were who believed heredity and bloodlines meant everything. His blood was of the pure aristocracy of Ile-Rien which the Alsenes were still members of, even if their disgrace kept them from participating in it. This would have been a comforting thought if he hadn't had the suspicion that his infamous ancestor, Denzil Alsene, would have got along rather well in any place of violence and cutthroat competition.

Nicholas walked on until the theaters became little hole-in-the-wall affairs and the music halls, as well as the prostitutes, became progressively smaller and dingier, and he was in Riverside proper.

There he found entertainment of a somewhat more active nature. He talked or traded insults with a wide variety of people, some of whom were old acquaintances, most of whom knew him by different names. He watched the robbery of a brandy house and ducked into an alley as the constables and the shouting owner ran past. He walked and thought and ended up sitting on what was left of the grand staircase of a ruined Great House with a street urchin, sharing a handful of hot chestnuts when he heard the nearest clocktower ring the hour.

His goal was only a few streets up, back toward the boulevard, but the area was very different. The streetlights illuminated few passersby and most of the tall brownstone buildings were offices, closed for the night and dark. There was only one building with lit windows, a much more elaborate affair with columns and a polished stone façade. It was the office that housed the Prefect of Public Works.

Nicholas went round the back, threading his way through the alleys, until he found himself in the quiet carriage court behind it. He knocked on the door there and in a few moments the man who answered passed him a tightly folded bundle of documents and Nicholas handed him an envelope of currency notes.

He went further up toward the Boulevard then, finding an open café whose lamps threw enough light onto a nearby bench and he sat there to study his prize. He stayed there long enough that the waiter decided he was an eccentric and began to include him in his circuit, so Nicholas was able to order coffee without having to disturb the arrangement of the documents.

He had been there some time when a voice behind him said, "You're not easy to find."

Nicholas glanced up. Madeline stood leaning on the back of the bench, dressed as a young man, wearing a ridiculously emphatic blue and gold waistcoat and with her hat tilted at a rakish angle. He said, dryly, "That assumes I want to be found."

Madeline sat on the bench next to him. "Oh, I think you wanted to be found, just a little. You did leave a trail through Riverside, though I did have quite a time until I picked up on it." She frowned at the papers in his lap. "What's that?"

"Sewer maps from the Public Works office. I bribed a clerk to steal copies for me. Ronsarde could have got them just by asking, of course, but then it would be in the penny sheets by tomorrow. The clerks there are eminently bribable." The dregs of the argument still lay between them but at this time of night it seemed pointless to pursue and Nicholas was disinclined to continue it.

"Hmm." Madeline looked like she badly wanted to ask what the maps were for, but managed, maddeningly, to restrain herself. She said, "Well, I actually had a reason for following you."

"Oh, good. I'd hate to be deluded into the thought that you were mildly fond of me."

Madeline's mouth twisted wryly. "A second reason. Reynard sent a telegram to the apartment; he wants you to meet him tonight. He has something important to tell you, I gather, unless there's something you haven't been telling me?"

"Madeline, you can't be jealous of Reynard; it's passé," Nicholas said, but he was already folding up the maps.

The first glow of dawn was lightening the sky to the east by the time they reached the Cafe Baudy. It was in the Deval Forest, a pleasure garden with wandering paths, streams, and picturesque waterfalls and grottos, always crowded in the warmer months. The cafe was built on two large firmly-anchored barges in a small lake and reached by footbridges. In the summer the water would have been cluttered with boaters and bathers, the rounded islands thick with flowers, but now it was still and dark, the banks shadowed by willows and poplars.

Only the cafe was bright, colored lanterns lighting the balcony and the raucous diners crowding it, music drifting over the still black water. Nicholas noted the resemblance to a scene out of one of Vanteil's Visions of Fayre oils.

Nicholas and Madeline made their way over one of the narrow bridges to the terrace of the cafe. Reynard had chosen the spot well; their unconventional dress, which would have kept them out of any of the better hotels and restaurants, was here not even acknowledged. As the waiter led them among the tables Nicholas saw that Madeline was by no means the only woman dressed as a man, or vice versa, in the crowd.

Reynard was seated at a table with its white linen littered with wine glasses and crumbs and the remains of a light meal. By the number of glasses Nicholas suspected he had had to fend off numerous friends and acquaintances while waiting for them. This impression was confirmed when he greeted them with "Where the hell have you been?"

"We were detained," Nicholas explained unhelpfully and Madeline assumed an expression of innocence. While the waiter fussed with fresh glasses and poured more wine, she poked at the remnants of the food, finding enough pâté to spread on one of the leftover rounds of toast. As soon as the man was gone, Reynard said, "You were right. It was Montesq got Ronsarde arrested."

Nicholas leaned forward. "Money?"

"How else? I suspected he had Lord Diero in his pocket—"

"Diero, not Albier?" Madeline interrupted, pâté-smeared bread forgotten in her hand.

"Not Albier," Reynard confirmed. "My sources of information—and I'll admit, most of them are prostitutes, either professionals or amateurs—all believe Diero to be heavily in debt to Montesq. Last week Diero was visited by Batherat, that solicitor you heard about last year—"

"Yes, the new one." Nicholas had been witness to a

meeting between Montesq and Batherat via Arisilde's portrait at Coldcourt.

"And the next day, Diero gave a very private order to have Ronsarde's movements checked."

"How did you discover that?" Madeline demanded. "You have a source in the upper levels of the Prefecture?"

"One of Diero's subordinates is a friend of a friend. It's surprising how many people come to the same places for their entertainment. This rather vital piece of information was confided to me over a late supper at the Loggia, as though it meant nothing, and of course to the person who told me it did mean nothing. But if you know the rest. . . ." He gestured eloquently.

"So Montesq is in league with our sorcerer," Madeline said. "But how did that happen? We watched him so closely. How—"

Nicholas's thoughts were going along the same path, but Reynard cleared his throat and said, "No, I don't think he is in league with our madman. I think he was after Ronsarde for an entirely different reason."

"What reason?" Nicholas had never forgotten that Ronsarde had advanced some suspicions of Montesq. He had wanted to follow up that tantalizing hint but had been afraid of exposing more about his own activities than Ronsarde could comfortably ignore. And there hadn't been time.

"Ronsarde apparently never dropped the case concerning Edouard Viller." Reynard advanced the topic cautiously, but Nicholas gestured at him to continue. As a victim of scandal himself, Reynard wasn't one to talk of rope in the house of the hanged, either literally or figuratively, and wouldn't mention it unless it was important. Reynard said, "This same person, Diero's subordinate, told me that Ronsarde had finally asked formal permission of Diero to reopen the court documents and interview witnesses officially, in front of a magistrate. Your name, Nic, was on the list of persons to be questioned in court."

The waiter arrived to pour more wine, appearing just

in time to hear Madeline utter an oath that disturbed a normally impenetrable demeanor to the point that the man actually cocked an eyebrow in reaction. They waited until he had moved on, then Reynard continued, "And that of course means nothing unless you know that Montesq arranged the evidence against Edouard Viller."

Nicholas smoothed the tablecloth, to keep his hands from knotting into fists. "Ronsarde said nothing about it."

"He wouldn't." Madeline was strangling her napkin in repressed excitement. Her voice shook with it. "He never knew who arranged his arrest. Halle tried to find out but he couldn't discover anything. Ronsarde doesn't know Diero is connected to Montesq. If he had he would have gone over his head, to Albier or Captain Giarde or the Queen herself, he could easily do it."

"That's not all," Reynard said impatiently. "Montesq didn't only move against Ronsarde. Batherat met with someone else last week as well, in a cabaret. The man evidently believes the lower class prostitutes that inhabit the place can't see or hear and won't recognize men they must see every night at the theaters, getting out of crested carriages. He met with Fallier, Nicholas, Rahene Fallier."

"Ah." Nicholas leaned back in his chair, and the too-warm, noisy room seemed to fade. "Of course he did."

"I don't know what he has on Fallier," Reynard added. "Montesq has been in the business of blackmail so long, it could be anything. Debts, youthful indiscretions—"

"Necromancy, past or present," Madeline added.

"Exactly."

"Your informant didn't know what Batherat and Fallier discussed," Nicholas said, thoughtfully.

"No," Reynard admitted. "But I think it must have been you."

"Yes." Nicholas nodded. "It would explain Fallier's sudden interest in me."

"What do you mean?" Madeline demanded.

"Fallier may or may not have recognized my resemblance to Denzil Alsene from a Greanco portrait. In fact, I think he must have; he did know me when we came face to face in the street. But he already knew who I was and not from past researches to uncover possible usurpers to the Crown. He knew because Montesq had Batherat tell him." Montesq could have sought information on the Valiarde family easily enough. Nicholas's mother's family denied her existence now but there would be old servants or far-flung relations who would readily admit that Sylvaine Valiarde had lived, married a disgraced Alsene, left her husband's family after his death and dropped out of sight in Vienne.

Madeline nodded. "Montesq knows you hate him, knows you believe he destroyed Edouard. Maybe he even knows you've been sticking your nose in his illegitimate dealings."

"But he doesn't know much, or he would have moved against you before now," Reynard added. "He wanted to get Ronsarde out of the way so he had these charges trumped up, then stirred up a riot so he'd have done with him permanently. He also wanted to discredit you, so he told Fallier about your past history."

"But I'd left Coldcourt and Fallier couldn't find me until he was called to the contretemps outside Fontainon House." Nicholas's eyes narrowed as he followed that line of logic. "And our sorcerer knew Montesq's movements and took advantage of his machinations for his own purposes." And why had Montesq acted against Ronsarde and himself now, after all this time? *Obviously he's afraid Ronsarde has new information. Or that I have new information.*

"So he is in league with Montesq?" Madeline said, with the air of being determined to settle at least one point.

"No." Nicholas was thinking of the enspelled mirror Arisilde had found in Octave's hotel room. "Our mad sorcerer has too many ways of finding things out. He is a necromancer, after all. But I would like to know how he knew where to look." He let out his breath. He hadn't wanted to discuss this with anyone, except perhaps Arisilde, who was too distanced from reality himself to find any theory far-fetched, no matter how outrageous it sounded. "I'm almost afraid that the reason he did know all this—"

A sudden shout from the doorway drew their attention. A raggedly dressed boy was at the entrance, gesturing urgently to a skeptical maitre'd. Nicholas recognized one of Cusard's messengers and nodded to Reynard, who signalled their waiter over and said, "I believe the boy has a message for me; have them let him in, will you?"

In another moment the boy stood panting at their table, much to the consternation and amusement of the other diners. "Captain Morane!" The boy held out a smudged square of folded notepaper. "This's for you."

Reynard handed the note to Nicholas and dismissed the boy with some coins and a couple of pastries from the table. Nicholas scanned Cusard's hasty and almost illegible handwriting quickly, swore, and got to his feet. "There's trouble. We have to get there immediately."

The cab let them off in the Philosopher's Cross, one street over from Arisilde's building. Without knowing what had happened, Nicholas wanted to be able to approach the place cautiously and on foot; Cusard's note had said only that there had been a "disaster" and that they must come to Arisilde's apartment at once.

The early morning light was gray and heavy, the air cold and damp. Nicholas was first down the alley and first to come within sight of the tenement.

He halted on the dirty paving stones of the promenade without quite knowing he had. Cusard had not exaggerated.

There was a hole in the upper stories of the old building, just where Arisilde's apartment was. It was a ragged, gaping cavity as if from a bomb blast and had torn a section out of the mansard roof. But there was no mark of fire and no smoke hung in the damp air, though broken stone and shingles littered the pavement.

Behind him he heard Reynard curse, then Madeline made a strangled noise and pushed past him, running across the street. Nicholas bolted after her.

There were people in the alley, pointing up and discussing it in hushed tones, milling around. There were constables and men from the fire brigade going in and out of the entrance.

Madeline pushed through a pair of constables and plunged up the stairs. Nicholas would have been right behind her but someone stepped into his way. It was Cusard, having materialized out of the crowd of spectators like a wraith. He said, "Something you got to know."

Nicholas paused and Reynard fetched up behind them. "What?"

Cusard's shoulders were stooped and he looked very old in the gray morning light. He said, "Ronsarde and Halle was in there too."

Reynard said, "No," and looked up at the rent in the building, his face aghast. Another brick fell, sending the front edge of the crowd scattering.

Nicholas's throat was tight. "How?"

"The Parscian sent a telegram for you, saying for you to come at once, that Arisilde was going to wake up. The Inspector told me to look for you and he and the doctor went off to here." Cusard hesitated, his face guilty. "I should've stopped 'em."

Nicholas shook his head. *If I had been there. . . .* "Go on."

"I had to go to the warehouse to find a boy to send, but by that time Verack—he was watchin' here last night—come for me, to tell me what had happened."

"They're dead?" Reynard asked.

Cusard shook his head and gestured in frustration. "They wouldn't let nobody in. And I didn't want to give notice to the constables—but they ain't carried nobody out."

"They let Madeline in." Reynard looked at Nicholas.

"Her grandmother was in there." Nicholas caught

Reynard's arm when he would have pushed on toward the building. "No, stay out here."

The constables tried to stop him but he told them that he was Madeline's husband and they let him pass. There were frightened tenants on the stairwell, crying children and people in various states of undress, and constables trying unsuccessfully to get them out of the building or at least out of the way. Nicholas wove his way past them until he reached the landing that was just below Arisilde's apartment. The skylight over the stairs had been shattered and part of the ceiling had come down. The concierge was standing on the landing, resisting all attempts to move him. He was arguing with a constable and an official-looking person in a frock coat.

"No," the concierge was saying stubbornly, his Aderassi accent thickening in his distress. "Do I look drunk nor mad? There was more than that—" He saw Nicholas and winced. "Ah, sir. The old woman, they got her in there."

Nicholas turned to the indicated doorway. It was the apartment below Arisilde's. The door had been knocked off the hinges and stood to one side and the floor in the hall and front parlor was littered with plaster dust and pieces of molding. A frowsy-haired woman wrapped in a dressing gown appeared and gestured him through a pile of broken crockery to a back room.

A single lamp revealed a bedroom in tumbled disorder, with old furniture and blue flowered damask. Madele had been laid out on the bed, her hands folded neatly, and Madeline sat next to her. Nicholas's first reaction was relief. Even though he knew there hadn't been time, he had been irrationally afraid that her body would have been used for necromancy. There wasn't a mark on her and except for the dust in her clothes and hair, she might have died in her sleep.

Madeline's face was utterly still.

The concierge stepped into the doorway behind Nicholas and touched his sleeve. He whispered, "Tell the lady we found her all curled up at the top of the stairs, like she was asleep. It took her so quick, whatever it was, that she didn't feel a thing. I don't want to say it to her now, but later, when she wants to hear it.''

"Yes, thank you.'' Nicholas nodded. *It would have had to take her quickly, a battle would have drawn too much attention.* And there were other sorcerers who lived in the Philosopher's Cross, though not powerful ones. If she had had a chance to fight, they might have come to help her. "Did you see it?''

"I heard it. An explosion, like a bomb, very loud, very sharp.'' The man glanced warily over his shoulder. "They think it was a gas explosion, but it was nothing like one and they don't know the wizard lives here. Wizards got enemies, everybody knows that.''

The constable and the official in the frock coat were making their way through the shattered apartment toward them. "They were all killed?'' Nicholas asked the concierge, speaking in Aderassi.

"That's just it!'' The man switched to his native language automatically. "We found the old Parscian man alive, but not a sign of the others, and these bastards don't believe—''

The official interrupted, "Excuse me, what connection do you have to this affair?'' If he knew he had just been called a bastard in Aderassi he gave no sign of it.

"My wife's grandmother was killed and I'm a friend of the tenant in that apartment,'' Nicholas answered, stepping back out of the bedroom so the man would focus on him and leave Madeline alone. To the concierge he said urgently, "Where's Isham?''

The man turned back down the hall and led him to another small, disordered room, the official and the constable still trailing them. Isham lay on the bed there, blood in his hair and on his face from multiple cuts on his forehead. The woman in the dressing gown was trying to bathe the cuts but the old man was moaning, barely conscious, and trying to push her hand away. Nicholas forgot about their audience and went hastily to his side.

"Isham, it's Nicholas,'' he said. The old man's face was badly bruised, there were other cuts and scrapes, and the colors of his Parscian robes were muted by plaster dust. "Can you hear me?"

Isham's hand came up, grabbed his coat with surprising strength. Nicholas leaned down, his ear close to the injured man's lips. His voice a weak rasp, Isham whispered, "Madele freed Arisilde. It was a corpse ring, hidden by a spell. I thought . . . there might be danger—But she removed it and nothing happened so I sent for you. But he must have known when the spell failed and he came . . . He came for Arisilde. . . ."

Isham tried to manage more but he started to cough, a racking, pain-filled sound, and Nicholas said, "That's enough, you've told me all I need to know." That was anything but true but he didn't want the man to kill himself with the effort. He probed at one of the cuts gently, trying to determine the extent of the injury.

"Careful, there's glass," the woman cautioned him.

She was right. Doctor Brile's surgery wasn't far from here. He would have to make arrangements to have Isham moved there immediately. And he would have to claim Madele's body so it wouldn't be sent to the city morgue.

"Sir," an impatient voice behind him said. Nicholas twisted around and the official took a step backward, startled and wary. Nicholas made an effort to school his features into an expression less threatening. He realized the man had been trying to get his attention for some moments. He said, "Yes?"

The official regained his composure and said, "This person," he indicated the concierge, "Has said there were three others in the apartment but we can find no sign of them. Can you confirm this?"

No sign of them. "Yes," Nicholas said. "This man and the woman were caring for the tenant, who was an invalid. Two of our friends were coming here early this morning." He looked at the concierge, who was standing at the foot of the bed, his arms folded, frustrated and highly affronted at having his veracity questioned. "Did they arrive before . . . ?"

"Yes, the two men, gray-haired, one with a doctor

bag, one with a cane? Doctors come all the time lately, I hardly notice.''

"How long before?'' Nicholas asked sharply, interrupting whatever pronouncement the official had been trying to make.

"Not long.'' The concierge narrowed his eyes, lips pursed in thought, anticipating the demand for a more specific answer. "I heard them go up the stairs, a door open and close. Then Cesar, from the market, came to argue about rent, but that was only for a moment and boom! It knocked us both down from fear. Things fell, dust came down the stairs in a great cloud. I thought the whole place would come down on our heads.''

It was a trap, then. If Nicholas had correctly understood Isham, then the removal of whatever spell had imprisoned Arisilde had alerted their opponent, but instead of acting immediately he had waited to see who would come to Arisilde's side. But if Arisilde was waking, why hadn't he tried to defend himself? *I have to get into that apartment.*

"And what relation was the tenant to you?'' the official asked.

Nicholas was glad he hadn't brought a pistol with him; he would've been tempted to shoot the man. But before he could answer, Madeline shouldered the bulky constable out of the doorway and shoved into the room. She stood, breathing hard, looking down at Isham. Nicholas saw the official look askance at her coat and trousers and he told the man, in a cold voice, "She's on the stage.''

"Ahh.'' The official pretended to understand that statement and persisted, "I understand the shock of the situation but—''

Madeline lifted her gaze to Nicholas. "How is he?'' she demanded.

Her eyes glittered and not from unshed tears. It was a dangerous light, uncertain and with an edge to it. Nicholas answered, "Not good. He needs to go to Doctor Brile immediately.''

The concierge abruptly remembered his duty and said,

"I get you a carriage," and pushed his way out past the constable.

Nicholas hesitated for a heartbeat, then put his faith in Madeline's quick wits. He stood and caught her hand, saying urgently, "You look faint!"

Her expression didn't change but she blinked and raised a suddenly trembling hand to her brow. Then she fell backwards, boneless and apparently completely unconscious, right into the arms of the surprised official. He staggered under her sudden and unexpected weight and the constable leapt forward to help support her. The woman who had been tending Isham yelped in sympathy and scrambled around the bed to help.

Nicholas shouted something about going for help and slipped past them and out the door. He reached the landing again, saw the other tenants still milling below, and hurried up the stairs.

The doorframe in Arisilde's apartment was cracked and splintered and the door hung on its hinges, revealing the familiar hall choked with rubble and debris. He stepped through it carefully, making his way into the long parlor at the back of the apartment. The hole was between the two windows that had looked down into the alley, the edges ragged with broken stone and shattered wood. The floor was buried under plaster from the ceiling and broken glass from the windows and the skylights and the remnants of the curtains were stirring gently in the cool breeze. Nicholas moved around the room, noting the familiar objects strewn about, the furniture broken or overturned, the scattered books and smashed plant pots.

A gas explosion, Nicholas thought in contempt. *Whoever came to that conclusion was delusional.* From the look of it all, it was immediately obvious that whatever had burst through the wall had done it from the outside coming in.

He left the wreck of the parlor and searched the rest of the apartment swiftly. The other rooms were not as badly disturbed, except for objects knocked off the walls and the cracks in the plaster. There was no sign of Ronsarde or Halle, no sign that anyone had been here.

Arisilde's bedroom was oddly undisturbed, as if it had been at the still center of a violent and destructive storm. The coverlet on the bed was thrown back and the impression in the soft mattress where Arisilde had lain was still visible.

He heard voices from below and knew he had run out of time. He moved quickly toward the door but a glint of white wedged into the bottom of the splintered doorframe caught his eye. He knelt and worked it free.

It was a piece of ivory, carved into the shape of a Parscian hunting cat's head. It was the ornament from atop the ebony cane Reynard had loaned to Inspector Ronsarde.

The concierge had found a carriage to take Isham to Doctor Brile's surgery and Nicholas used that confusion to get down the stairs to the lower landing without anyone noticing. In the ensuing effort to get the injured man down the stairs without hurting him further, Nicholas managed to give some coins to the woman who had let her rooms be used as hospital and morgue and to ask the concierge to send for an undertaker to take charge of Madele's body. He escaped into the street without further interrogation by constables or anyone else.

As he gave the coachman instructions and a note for Doctor Brile, he saw Madeline waiting across the street with Reynard and Cusard. He checked that Isham was settled as comfortably as possible, then sent the coach off and joined the others.

"Are you all right?" he asked Madeline.

"Of course," she snapped.

"Do we know anything of what happened?" Reynard asked, as if he didn't have much hope of an answer.

Nicholas shook his head. "From what Isham was able to tell me, Madele discovered what was wrong with Arisilde. It was a spell, not drugs or illness. But when she removed it, it somehow alerted the sorcerer. He waited long enough to draw a few of us into the trap." He stopped, compressing his lips, then looked at Madeline.

"Why didn't she tell me she had discovered what was wrong with Arisilde?"

"She never told anyone anything. She probably didn't want to get your hopes up if she was wrong." Madeline knotted her fists and paced angrily. "Damn stupid old woman."

Reynard was looking up at the ruin of the tenement's top floor. He said softly, "Now what?"

That wasn't a question Nicholas wanted to answer at the moment, even though he knew exactly what he had to do now. He looked around, struck by the sudden notion that he was missing something important. "Wait. Where's Crack?"

Reynard turned back and Madeline looked up. Cusard blanched and said, "He was with Ronsarde and Halle when I left. . . ."

Nicholas cursed and started back down the alley toward their coach. He would check the apartment but he knew he would find no one there. He had told Crack to "watch the others" and Crack would not have let Ronsarde and Halle leave the apartment alone.

19

Nicholas read the telegram one more time in disbelief, then crumpled it into a tight little ball. The struggle to control rage took all his concentration for a moment, but then he was able to turn to Reynard and say tightly, "I'm informed that any messages I send will not be delivered to Captain Giarde."

Reynard stared in disbelief. "Fallier?"

Nicholas considered it, then shook his head. The Court Sorcerer couldn't affect the delivery of private messages to the palace. No, that was the Prefecture's realm. "Albier. He thinks I'm trying to undermine him on Ronsarde's behalf. He has probably given orders to block messages from Ronsarde and Halle, as well." No one in the Prefecture knew that the two men had been in the shattered apartment in the Philosopher's Cross. Nicholas had sent his message from the telegraph office on the Boulevard of Flowers and then returned with the others to the Panzan apartment to find the place chill and empty, the fires gone out from lack of tending. As he had feared, Crack was nowhere to be found. Nicholas had sent Lamane over to check the warehouse, hoping against hope, but he knew Crack must have followed Ronsarde and Halle to Arisilde's apartment.

He threw the telegram into the hearth. Madeline was sitting on the divan near the window with her knees drawn up. She lifted her head and regarded him with a dark unflinching gaze, but said nothing. Cusard was pacing anxiously.

"But Albier's honest, or enough so for this purpose," Reynard said, looking thoughtful. "We could go to him and explain, ask for help."

Nicholas grimaced at the thought but as much as he disliked the idea of an appeal to Albier, it was the quickest way to get Captain Giarde's assistance. "Madeline will go to Albier." He hesitated, not wanting to drag Reynard into this. He had lost enough people to this sorcerer. *But I can't do it alone.* "You and I will go after the others."

Reynard stared hard at him. "You know where they've been taken?"

"It's only speculation." Nicholas found the folder of maps he had tossed into a chair and dug out the one he needed. He spread it on the table. "This is the key. The Monde Street sewer."

"He's hiding in a sewer?" Cusard said, coming over to look, his doubt evident.

"For the past few days the Monde Street sewer syphon has been subject to blockages, caused by bone. Human bone," Nicholas explained. At their expressions he said, "No, it's not what you're thinking. These bones were years old, that was apparent from even a cursory examination. That was why the sewermen were not alarmed."

"Better start from the beginning," Reynard said, exchanging a dubious look with Cusard.

"From experience I know how difficult it is to find a reliable, safe hiding place in this city," Nicholas said patiently. "Considering that our sorcerer chose Valent House the first time, I found it unlikely that he would have tried to purchase or acquire property, and the Prefecture would be investigating any deserted buildings that were possibilities. So before extending the search outside the city walls, I wanted to see if he had gone underground."

"The Sending. Isham said it could have been the remains of a long dead fay, buried somewhere, didn't

he?'' Reynard tapped the map thoughtfully. "A catacomb?''

"Exactly. After speaking to the sewermen and looking over the maps from the Public Works office, it became apparent that a catacomb was being cleared, the
bones dumped into the sewer somewhere above Monde
where they were flowing down into the syphon.''

"But what if there's been a collapse somewhere, and
the bones washed out of a catacomb naturally?''

"The sewer level would have dropped since there
hasn't been rain for days." Nicholas hesitated. It was all
a tissue of suppositions, but he still thought his reasoning
was sound. "It's only a theory. But I've thought hard
about it and it's the most likely option.''

Reynard eyed him thoughtfully. "How long have you
known this?''

Nicholas glanced at Madeline, but though she was
watching alertly she still betrayed no reaction. "Since I
looked at the maps I received from a clerk at the Prefect
of Public Works office last night, before we went to
meet you. I wanted to be sure it was possible for a catacomb to exist in the location it would have to occupy
for this to work. There's been so much building in the
past few decades and none of the original catacombs that
are still accessible are very deep.''

Reynard was nodding. There were catacombs that
were still in use under the cathedral and others in the
older parts of Vienne that were opened occasionally for
tours. "But this was a catacomb only our sorcerer knew
about? The same way he knew about everything else, I
suppose.''

Nicholas nodded, distractedly. "Once we know for
certain that this is the sorcerer's hiding place, we can
return and direct Fallier and Giarde and his men to the
exact location." He glanced at Cusard. "I'll need some
things from the warehouse.''

Cusard nodded and let out his breath in resignation.
"Sewers. Ghouls. I'm glad I'm old.''

"Let me be clear on one point," Reynard said. "The
idea is to locate the sorcerer so he can be dealt with by

Fallier and the other resources the palace can command, not take care of him ourselves.''

"Correct. The situation doesn't call for suicide," Nicholas said, a brow lifting ironically. "But should we be cornered, there can't be that much difficulty. After all, I am related to the man who killed the sorcerer Urbain Grandier.''

"As I remember the story Alsene shot him in the back, from a distance," Reynard said dryly, folding his arms.

"That would be my preference as well.''

"Hmm.'' Reynard stroked his mustache and said consideringly, "How does one dress for the sewer?''

Nicholas started to answer but Madeline stood suddenly, saying, "Nicholas, I'm going with you, not Reynard.''

They both turned to stare at her.

She seemed to realize she would at least have to clarify her position. "There are a number of reasons. One of which is that we know Edouard's sphere works for me and we don't know that it will work for anyone else, and there's no time to make a suitable test. I assume there will still be ghouls in the sewers.''

She paused, as if to give him leave to interrupt at this point, but Nicholas kept silent. He had never been spoken to in this tone by anyone not holding a pistol trained on him and he found himself unwillingly fascinated. He wondered if she would mention Madele.

After a polite interval, Madeline continued, showing no sign of being disconcerted by his silence, "I could threaten, I could shout. I could follow you or delay you if you try to stop me. But I'm not going to do any of those things. I'm just going with you.''

Nicholas waited but that seemed to be all. He cleared his throat. "That would mean Reynard would have to attempt to contact Albier and Captain Giarde.''

Her mouth tightened. She must know Reynard had been acquainted with Giarde from his days as a cavalry officer and Nicholas had to admit it was a low blow.

Dryly, she said, "I don't think Reynard's sensibilities are as delicate as yours."

Reynard and Nicholas exchanged another look. *I know she just insulted both of us but I'm not sure how*, Nicholas thought. He said, "You almost fainted from the stench when we went into the sewer from the prison." He was aware he sounded accusing. And ineffectual.

"You were ill when you saw the carnage in Valent House," she retorted. "I'd say that makes us even."

Nicholas took a deep breath for calm, then looked at Reynard, who said immediately, "This is your decision. I'm not in the middle of this."

The problem was that she was right about the sphere. Once they found the sorcerer's hiding place they would certainly be pursued; it could mean the difference between getting out alive and perishing nobly. Nicholas wasn't fond of the idea of dying heroically, alone or in company.

"We're running out of time," Madeline said softly.

"There's something I need to tell you both first." Nicholas folded the map slowly. Regardless of which of them went, he wanted them to know what they might be facing. "I don't think this sorcerer is a man pretending, to himself and everyone else, to be Constant Macob."

Madeline frowned. Reynard looked confused. He said, "But I thought that was the conclusion indicated by everything we'd discovered."

"It is," Nicholas assured him. "But I think he actually is Constant Macob."

There was a moment of silence, then Reynard said, "He is Macob, but not in the flesh, you mean?"

Cusard groaned and covered his face.

"Not in the flesh," Nicholas agreed. "Not anymore."

"You mean Edouard's device brought him back to life?" Madeline asked. She shook her head doubtfully.

"Good. We'll all need it later," Cusard muttered.

"No, I don't think Edouard's device did that. Or at least, not yet." There was an uncomfortable silence as that sank in. "I think Octave must have been in contact with Macob before he obtained the sphere and the notes on Edouard's work from Ilamires Rohan. I think Octave contacted, or was contacted by, Macob in one of Octave's earlier attempts at spiritualism. Macob used his sorcery to discover things of benefit to Octave. Necromancy is, after all, primarily concerned with divination and the discovery of secret knowledge. One of the things Macob discovered for Octave was that Ilamires Rohan still had one of Edouard's spheres. Octave blackmailed Rohan to get it then must have used the sphere to strengthen Macob's connection with the living world." He paced away from the table. "Macob must be planning some way to make that connection permanent, to bring himself back to life. To do this he apparently needed to get his body, or whatever was left of it, out of that room below what used to be Ventarin House. He sent Octave to contact the Duchess of Mondollot, but he didn't quite trust his accomplice. It was after all in Octave's best interest to keep the business of holding circles and discovering hidden treasures going as long as possible. Macob must have realized that Octave never meant him to succeed. So Macob sent the ghouls he had made with his necromancy and they located and stole the corpse for him. But it must have startled Macob that we arrived in Mondollot's cellars almost in time to witness the retrieval of the body, because he sent the golem of Octave to question my motives. He was afraid I had discovered that Octave was using Edouard's sphere." He shook his head. "No, he didn't want Octave to know what he really wanted, not at that point. He was playing at helping Octave with the spiritualism confidence game. I think it wasn't until that night after the circle at Gabrill House that Octave began to suspect the truth. He wanted to tell Macob that someone had tried to follow his coach, so he went unexpectedly to Valent House. Perhaps he truly didn't know the extent to which Macob had returned to his old practices until then. I only know that when I saw Octave at Lusaude's the next night, he was very frightened."

"But Macob's had his body back for days," Madeline said, gesturing in frustration. "That can't have been all he needed."

"No, there is some other element still missing. Something that is presently in the palace."

"The palace?" Reynard said, frowning. "What does the—Wait, you said Fontainon House was inside the palace wards. So Macob wanted Octave to hold a circle there and that would let Macob inside the wards and into the palace?"

"I suggested as much to Captain Giarde," Nicholas agreed. "But there was no proof."

"But what does Macob want there?"

Nicholas shrugged. "I don't have the slightest idea. The palace has been a home for sorcerers for hundreds of years. It could be anything. It might be something no one knows is there. No one except Macob." He looked at Madeline. "Do you still want to go?"

"You shouldn't have phrased it as a challenge," she said dryly.

Reynard had already departed for the Prefecture and hopefully a meeting with Lord Albier. If he couldn't convince Albier of the urgency of his errand, and if he avoided being thrown into a Prefecture cell, he would try an audience with Giarde directly. Nicholas had to admit that Reynard would be far more adept than Madeline at tackling the issue of Albier's bullheaded stupidity without infuriating the official to the point where he had him arrested.

After some hasty preparations, Cusard drove them in his wagon to the sewer entrance Nicholas wanted to start from. It was on a street with little traffic, lined with tenement apartments that were quiet during the day, with broad walks and potted trees that kept passersby at a distance. It was also very near to the Monde Street syphon.

The wagon was drawn up in such a way as to block the view of the manhole and Nicholas checked through the waterproofed knapsack he had quickly packed, enduring Cusard's doleful inquiries about extra candle stubs and matches.

Madeline stood nearby, with the sphere wrapped in sacking and tucked under her arm. She looked more impatient to get started than anything else.

Cusard followed his gaze, and muttered, "Take care of her ladyship there. And find Crack. I didn't realize I'd gotten so used to the bloody bastard."

"I will," Nicholas told him. "And don't worry; if everything goes well, we shouldn't be in much danger."

"Don't say that," Cusard demanded. "You're tempting fate."

They pried up the heavy metal cover and Nicholas went down first to get the lamp lit in the shaft of mild sunlight from the opening. Madeline climbed down after him and he motioned for Cusard to slide the cover closed.

As their eyes grew used to the darkness Nicholas could see this was one of the newest galleries. Their lantern revealed high brick-lined walls and a wide channel of dark flowing water. The walkway was clean and almost dry and there was only a faint trace of unpleasant odor.

The sluice cart was tied to a ring set into the walkway, the current tugging at it. It was a small boat with metal plates mounted behind it that could be raised or lowered to control water flow around the craft and a pierced metal shield in front to flush the sewer channel. This cart was one used for inspections and had had its shield removed so it would travel faster. Nicholas had bribed one of his recent sewermen acquaintances to provide it and his explanation that he was an investigator assigned to discover information detrimental to the Prefect of Public Works had insured enthusiastic cooperation.

He held it steady for Madeline, who climbed into the front and immediately unwrapped the sphere. "Anything?" he asked her.

"No." She shook her head, studying the sphere carefully. "It's still and cold."

As Nicholas retrieved the broad paddle from the walkway and stepped in behind her, he noted she hadn't asked, "What if you're wrong?" *If I'm wrong, our friends are dead, and we're wasting time here.* But he didn't think he was wrong.

Besides, there was more to worry about if he was right.

He untied the line anchoring the cart to the walkway and braced his feet as the flow jolted the little craft forward. "Ho," Madeline commented, startled at the speed. "We don't know what we're going into but at least we'll get there quickly."

"Isn't that always the case?" Nicholas said, keeping his tone light. He was relieved that she sounded more like herself, then silently cursed himself for allowing it to distract him. He knew she blamed him for Madele's death and justifiably so; if not for him the old woman would still be in peaceful retirement outside Lodun. But there was nothing he could do about it now. After a few false starts he used the paddle to direct the cart toward the gallery exit and into the main sewer.

The cart slid into a channel that was only slightly larger than the metal plates mounted behind it. Their speed increased somewhat, but there was no need to steer and Nicholas laid the paddle down and crouched on the narrow shelf at the stern of the cart. The ceiling was much lower here and the walkways narrower and the lamplight reflected off the water pipes in the curved roof. It bore a strong resemblance to the sewer channel they had entered from the prison, but it was still far cleaner. Nicholas knew that would change as they reached the older areas.

The cart carried them rapidly down the Piscard Street channel where they passed through another high-ceilinged gallery and exited into Orean Street. The walls and walkways grew dark with slime, the odor rising from the water grew more noxious, and their cart encountered solid objects that Nicholas preferred not to look at too closely. Madeline dug in the knapsack for the dark-colored rags Nicholas had brought and they each tied one around their nose and mouth. The rags had been soaked in a strong Parscian perfume oil; the scent was cloying, but it warded off the sewer stink admirably.

The new sewers were all long and straight, orderly channels with their flow controlled by syphons and galleries, though even these broad tunnels could be dangerous. They were lucky there had been little rain lately; sudden torrential downpours sometimes drowned sewermen. The older sewer, begun with the birth of the city and altered over hundreds of years, would be much harder to traverse. Nicholas said, "We're not far now." Orean Street would cross Monde, just below the syphon.

The lapping water made very little sound and Nicholas clearly heard voices echoing down the tunnel. "The lamp," he whispered urgently. Madeline hastily shut the cover on the dark lantern and lowered it to the bottom of the cart. Nicholas slowed their progress by stepping forward to the front of the cart and thrusting the broad flat of the paddle down into the muck at the bottom of the channel.

They were drifting toward the end where an archway opened into the collector near the syphon. Nicholas could see the glow of lamplight ahead, hear voices. There must be men on the walkway above the syphon, conducting an inspection. He handed the paddle to Madeline, who took it with only a little fumbling in the dark. Nicholas stood, bracing his feet apart against the cart's motion. As they neared the arch more light became visible, illuminating the rounded wall of a high-ceilinged chamber, and a breeze moved the stale damp air in the tunnel. He raised his arms and a moment later felt the slimy stone of the arch strike his hands. He grabbed the lip of it and the cart jerked forward, almost knocking him off his feet. Madeline rose to a crouch and jammed the paddle harder into the accumulated muck at the bottom of the channel. The cart stopped, the water gurgling as it rushed past.

Straining to hold on, Nicholas was surprised they could stop the cart at all. The Monde syphon must be blocked again and the water level dropping.

The men on the platform in the next gallery were discussing a drainage problem. Shadows were flung on the wall opposite the archway as their lamps bobbed and Nicholas caught the words "silt," "clogged," and "dynamite." He hoped that last was indicative of someone's exasperation and not something they had to worry about immediately. He heard Madeline grunt from effort and felt the cart shift as she resettled the paddle.

The voices faded and the light died away. Nicholas waited another few moments, then whispered, "All right."

Madeline lifted the paddle with a gasp of relief and he let go of the arch, grabbing the sides of the cart to steady himself. They drifted into the collector, Madeline using the paddle to guide them in a wide circle.

Without the lamp they were in a vast dark pit, echoing and silent except for the lapping of water and a distant rushing from the other tunnels. Nicholas found the dark lantern in the bottom of the cart and raised its cover again.

The light revealed the high walls of the collector and the walkway around the edge. Nicholas could see from the marks on the walls that the water level was normally several feet higher. At the far side of the collector on a broad stone platform was the end of the syphon, a long pipe that drew water from one end of the sewer system to the other. All that was visible of it was a gaping hole in the platform, surrounded by an iron guardrail. Suspended above the pit was what looked like the top half of a circular cage. It was actually the holder for the wooden ball that was used to clean the syphon of obstacles. Nicholas took the paddle back from Madeline and guided the cart over to bump up against the stone footing of the platform.

Cold, fetid air streamed up from the pipe, making Nicholas shiver even in his greatcoat. The surface around it was covered with stinking lumps of silt and sand. Nicholas leaned on the paddle to hold the cart steady and picked up one of the lumps, scraping the silt off it. He handed it to Madeline, who crouched down to examine it in the light of the lantern. She had to break it and look at the inside before she could make sure what it was. "Yes, it's bone," she said quietly. "Old and stained but brittle, as if it hasn't been in the water long."

Nicholas pushed off with the paddle and guided them toward the exit into the next sewer.

They were well into the older tunnels now and the stench would have been overpowering except for the cloths treated with Parscian oil. The lamplight caught furtive movement on the filth-choked walkways as rats travelled busily along and there was an occasional plop, as a spider or centipede dropped from the rounded ceiling into the stream. The sphere remained quiescent under Madeline's hands and Nicholas didn't know whether to be relieved or discouraged. They had had no time or means to test the sphere's range of influence but if the necromancer was really down here he thought it should have detected something before now. *But if we're attacked by a ghoul while we're stuck in this cart, it will go badly*, he reminded himself grimly.

Finally an archway sealed by a rusted grating appeared at the limit of the light. "That's it," Nicholas said, dragging the paddle along the bottom to slow the cart. "We'll walk from now on."

Madeline grabbed the stone lip of the walkway and helped him swing the cart against it. "I could feign delight but I think I'll save that for when we encounter something really horrible."

"Then it won't be long," Nicholas told her. He wasn't looking forward to this part of the journey, either. "This is the Great Sewer. It hasn't been drained in six hundred years."

Madeline muttered under her breath but made no other comment.

Nicholas tied the cart off to one of the metal rings sunk into the stone for the purpose and climbed up on the walkway to examine the grating. There was a lock which the Prefect of Public Works probably possessed the key for, but it was badly rusted. He pulled the prybar out of the knapsack and set to work separating the grating from the stone at the weak points along the side.

As they had discussed already, Madeline didn't offer to assist but stood by with the lamp and the sphere, keeping watch. The ghouls couldn't be running rampant in the newer channels or the sewermen would have seen them. But Nicholas was aware that sewermen died all the time, from falls, from noxious vapors that built up in the lesser-used tunnels, from sudden deluges of rain-water; if more sewermen had been killed in the past months than usual it would be put down to bad luck and no one would think to search for some other cause.

The grating broke away from the stone in pieces and soon Nicholas had cleared enough of an opening for them to squeeze through. He slung the knapsack over his shoulder, collected the lamp from Madeline and worked his way past the broken metal. On the other side he waited for Madeline to follow, holding the lamp up to get a look at the passage before them.

The ceiling was lower, the channel and the walkway narrower. The masonry was crumbled and cracked or coated with layers of filth and festooned with bizarre shapes of fungi. Ghost-lichen mixed in with the other growth threw sparkles of light back at the lamp.

Madeline squeezed through the opening behind him, clamping her hat down tight on her head and clutching the sphere against her side. "Anything?" Nicholas asked her.

She held the metal up against her cheek to make sure, then shook her head. "Not the slightest twitch. But there are water pipes all around us, aren't there? Maybe that's confusing it."

"Why would that confuse it?" Nicholas noted that she spoke of the sphere as if it were alive, as most sorcerers spoke of the Great Spells. He wondered if it was a habit picked up from Madele.

"Some complicated reason having to do with natural philosophy—how should I know? But the sphere is so light, it can't be made out of anything but copper or bronze or other metals that weigh hardly anything. Iron has magical properties; maybe it interferes with the sphere."

"Maybe," Nicholas said, grudgingly. There could be something in what she said. "That would be just our luck to haul the damn thing down here confident that it would protect us and then discover that it won't work." He started down the narrow walkway, choosing his path carefully.

"Though it did work in the other sewer," Madeline pointed out, following him.

"We're much deeper underground now." And this was one of the oldest sewers under Vienne, that anyone knew of, anyway. The fay had been much more virulent in the past. What if it had been imbued with forgotten magical protections that were interfering with Edouard's work? What if the old bones clogging the syphon had gotten into the water by a natural phenomenon and they were heading in the wrong direction entirely? *What if, what if, what if,* Nicholas thought, disgusted with himself. *Why don't we just give the hell up?*

Because he knew he was right. "Would you have followed me down here if you thought I was wrong?" he asked Madeline, out of perverse curiosity.

She snorted in disbelief at the idiocy of the question. "Of course not. What do you take me for?"

The channels here were almost choked at points with stinking mud and when the walkway disappeared for long sections into masses of broken stone, they had to stumble through the muck. Nicholas was glad he had bothered to get them both stout rubber-soled boots that laced up past the knee and that their gloves were thick.

Branchements led off to both sides and Nicholas used the compass to find the first two turns they needed to take, but then the arches overhead became even more cracked and dilapidated and they encountered several blocked or abbreviated galleries that weren't marked on the map. After taking the wrong turning down one of these blocked passages Nicholas had to stop, cursing, and look at the map.

"We should be close, almost too close," he muttered, kneeling on a relatively dry stretch of rock as Madeline stood over him with the lamp.

"We're somewhere," she said suddenly. "Look at that."

He looked up. There was a cavity hollowed out of the wall of the passage. Nicholas had thought it a partial collapse, but a closer look showed him that the walls were too regular. He stood and saw what had caught Madeline's attention. There were chains, heavily corroded but still clearly visible, mounted on the wall. He stepped closer and realized they weren't the remnants of some method to raise and lower dams in an ancient drainage system; they were shackles. He looked around but any other clues were hidden under years of filth. "This was a cell. They cut the sewer right through it."

Madeline held up the lamp and squinted at the other side of the passage. There were regular hollows in that wall as well. "I bet that's another. And that. Was there anything about an old prison on the map?"

"No, but. . . ." He turned in a slow circle, visualizing the map, the streets above. "If we're under Daine Street, then this could be part of the old rampart. It was demolished two hundred years ago." It wasn't on the maps anymore, but neither was the catacomb they were looking for.

"Nicholas," Madeline whispered suddenly. He looked around and saw she was gazing down at the sphere, her eyes intent. He stepped up and took the lamp so she could hold the sphere with both hands.

"Close, closer." Her brows drew together, then she shook her head. "No, it's fading, as if—It's stopped now." She looked up and studied the walls around them thoughtfully. "It was as if something it didn't like moved through a tunnel adjacent to this one."

Nicholas nodded to himself. That settled all doubts on the sphere's area of influence. "Back this way."

They made their way back to the last branchement and Nicholas hesitated, remembering that Monde Street ran roughly east-west and would have hit the rampart, if the old structure had still been there when the much younger street was cut, at an angle. It was difficult to visualize and he didn't want to examine the map again;

the sewers paralleled the streets they serviced, and it wasn't those streets he wanted to see, but the narrow, barely-passable roads and alleys they had replaced. "It has to be here. The catacomb must have been behind the rampart." He held up the lamp, studying the filthy, fungi-covered surface of the branchement wall.

Madeline probed the stone beneath the spongy growth with one gloved finger. "There could be any sort of hole or door under this stuff," she said thoughtfully. "Do we know which side of the channel it's on?"

Nicholas shook his head. The builders could have cut a sewer right through the catacomb the same way they had cut it through the cells beneath the old rampart. "You check that side, I'll take this one."

Nicholas kept the lamp since she had the sphere, and though this channel wasn't wide the light was inadequate and they had to search mostly by feel anyway. They had moved perhaps twenty feet down the wall, groping along it, when Nicholas stumbled. He felt the surface of the wall give and realized it was rotted wood, not stone. He tried to pull his arm back and felt a tug on his sleeve. He frantically flung his weight back, thinking something had caught hold of him, but his arm came free so readily he sat down hard on the walkway. His coat sleeve had been torn and as he got to his feet he realized it must have been caught on the metal frame still holding the rotten wood in place. *Idiot*, he thought. *But having a limb torn off by a ghoul would be most inconvenient at the moment.*

"Are you all right?" Madeline demanded, struggling toward him through the muck of the channel.

"Yes, just startled myself." He gave her a hand up onto the walkway. He hesitated a moment, holding her gloved hand and looking at her. Her boots, trousers, and the skirts of her coat were covered in unspeakable filth and with her hat pulled low and the rags tied around her mouth and nose, she looked like a graverobber. He knew he looked worse. He said, "If the ghouls hunt by sense of smell, we're in luck."

"Hmm." She recaptured her hand and cradled the sphere. "It's shaking again."

"Then we're on the right track," Nicholas said. He turned to the door. There wasn't much of it left. It was low, only about five feet tall, rotted to matchstick consistency and held together only by the rusted metal frame. Nicholas widened the hole he had inadvertently made so they could peer through and found a narrow passage, the walls slick with moisture from the sewer.

They broke away enough of the door to climb through and began to make their way down the passage. Scraping away some of the thick muck coating one of the walls, Nicholas could see it had been constructed with large cut stone blocks. The surface overhead seemed to be natural rock and the narrow corridor had been dug through it.

"Do you think this is a section of that battlement?" Madeline whispered. "It doesn't look like part of the sewer."

"Yes, I think this is all that's left of the lower course and we're in the passage that originally led to those cells."

"This sphere is about to shake itself apart," she said, sounding uneasy.

"Then we're close."

"Nicholas." Now she sounded exasperated. "This nonchalant attitude is beginning to wear."

"Would you prefer me to twitch hysterically?"

"If you could bring yourself to express such an honest and genuine sentiment as hysteria then—" She stopped and caught his coat sleeve. "Wait."

He waited, then heard it himself. A sharp knock, echoing from somewhere up ahead. It was repeated once, then silence. Nicholas moved forward a few steps, listening. He glanced back at Madeline, motioning that he was going to shut the lamp. She nodded and he pushed the shade down.

After a few moments he could see the distinct glow of light ahead, a whitish, green-tinged glow, not natural daylight. He looked back toward Madeline and realized he could see her outline against the wall. "There must be ghost-lichen all through this muck," he said, quietly. "Come on."

The light was growing—not brighter, Nicholas decided, but more defined. He could see an irregularly shaped opening ahead and there seemed to be more light beyond it.

They drew closer and Nicholas could see this passage dead-ended into a larger chamber. As he reached the opening he heard a rustle, as if old dry paper had been brushed against rock. He motioned Madeline to come forward and as she stepped up, he accidentally brushed his fingers against the sphere.

The metal was warm, an impossibility in the dank chill of the underground, and he felt a strange tingle in his fingertips, as if he had touched one of the electrical experiments displayed at the Exposition. He jerked his hand back and realized he had felt the contact through his gloves. *At least it's doing . . . something.* He wished they had some notion of how to control it.

He edged up to the opening, drawing the pistol out of his pocket. The passage dropped off into a large cavernous chamber, more than twenty feet high, and the ghost-lichen clustering thickly everywhere revealed pillars and the openings of crypts hollowed out of the walls. A great many life-sized statues of saints with gloomy expressions gazed down forbiddingly from niches above the crypt entrances. Nicholas thought the winged Saint Gathre, its face like something out of a hellish nightmare, was a particularly appropriate companion with whom to view the scene.

They had found the catacomb. The floor was about a ten-foot drop from where the passage broke off, but there was a broken section of pillar just below that might be stable enough to climb. Nicholas started to step down to it when Madeline urgently thumped his shoulder and pointed.

Something moved on the floor of the grotto, a dark form drawing back into shadow. Nicholas squinted in the dimness and saw the tattered cloth and ragged hair, the glint of bone.

There was at least one ghoul, maybe two, moving in and out of the open crypts and darting under the collapsed arches. One of them crept around a fallen slab propped up on a broken column, poking at the dark area beneath it, as if trying to flush something. *They're hunting*, Nicholas thought, watching that surreptitious motion. *For us?* That didn't seem likely. *If they knew to look for us they would know we hadn't reached the catacomb yet and they would be searching the sewer and the tunnel.* That meant—

The ghoul snarled suddenly and darted back from the slab, shielding its head. Nicholas saw the flying rock and the human arm that had thrown it and without stopping to think he leapt down onto the pillar and then to the catacomb floor.

The ghoul whirled on him, jaws gaping, its face little more than a bare skull. He raised the pistol before he realized he didn't even know if bullets would hurt the thing. Madeline leapt down after him just as the ghoul darted forward. Light flared suddenly, a glow that washed out the dim radiance of the ghost-lichen and rendered the chamber in stark shadowless glare.

The last time the sphere had demonstrated its power the event had been too quick and violent for Nicholas to really see what had happened. This time he saw it all, outlined in a white haze of light. The ghoul scrabbled at the ground, its claws throwing up dust, trying to turn and flee. Before it got more than a step it seemed to fold in on itself, then it burst apart and dropped to the floor as a pile of yellowed bone and rags.

The bright light was abruptly gone, leaving pitch darkness in its wake. Nicholas, caught in the act of stepping forward, stumbled and cursed and behind him he heard Madeline yelp. "Are you all right?" he asked in a tense whisper.

"Yes, dammit." She sounded more annoyed than frightened. "I hope it didn't kill the ghost-lichen too."

He found her arm and pulled her close. There had

been more than one ghoul in here. If the sphere hadn't disposed of all of the creatures he and Madeline were at their most vulnerable.

Time stretched agonizingly but it was probably only a minute or so until the ghost-lichen's glow began to return. Nicholas blinked hard, staring around, gradually able to discern the shapes of the fallen pillars and the crypt openings again. Something stirred under the propped slab and he stooped immediately to look under it.

The face peering out at him was Crack's. He was bruised and filthy, but alive. Nicholas caught his arm and drew him out, demanding, "Are you hurt?"

"Not much," Crack admitted. His voice was weak and hoarse.

"Ronsarde and Halle? Arisilde?" Nicholas asked urgently.

"I ain't seen none of them, not since the wall broke open."

Madeline took his other arm and helped him sit back against the slab. "His wrist is broken," she reported, her expression grim. "How did you get here?"

"I don't know." Crack shook his head, his face tense with pain. "Something came through the wall from outside." He looked at Nicholas. "It was like the house in Lethe Square, that thing that came through the floor."

Nicholas nodded. He thought this was all more than Crack's powers of description could handle and knew he would have to ask better questions. "Did you see what happened to the others?"

"No, I got knocked in the head and I thought the ceiling come down on top of me, then the next thing I know I was here," Crack answered. Madeline had dug a relatively clean scarf out from under her coat and was trying to fashion a sling for his injured wrist. With his good hand he gestured helplessly. "Where the hell is here?"

"A series of old tunnels and catacombs off the Great Sewer," Nicholas said. "Were you here when you woke?"

"I was down there." Crack turned awkwardly and pointed down the length of the catacomb. "I came this way, away from the ghouls and those other things."

"What other things?" Madeline asked, with a worried glance at Nicholas.

"They look like people but they come at you like animals. I think they're those things our sorcerer talked about, that come when the ghouls are made."

"Revenants?" Nicholas frowned. He remembered Arisilde telling them how the necromancer would have made the ghouls, using a ritual murder to give life to the bones of some long-dead corpse. He had said the victim would still have a kind of life, but would only be a soulless remnant of the person it had once been.

"You can kill 'em," Crack said, rubbing his forehead wearily. "I used a rock."

Nicholas stood to look down the length of the catacomb. From this vantage point he could tell it went on for some distance, winding through the depths with the ghost-lichen throwing light on the fallen statues and broken crypts. "Was Arisilde awake when you got to his rooms?"

Crack looked up at him worriedly. "No, but the Parscian said he would be soon."

Nicholas nodded to himself. They should take Crack and return now, while they could. If the ghouls were here the necromancer was not far behind and he knew enough now to find the location of this place from the surface. But if the others were here, perhaps injured and stranded only a little further up the catacomb. . . . He looked down at Madeline. "Well?"

She was watching him and had no difficulty following his train of thought. She nodded.

Crack was too injured to accompany them but it wasn't that great a distance through the tunnel and back to the sewer. Nicholas sat on his heels next to him and pulled out the map. He found a stub of pencil in his pocket and wrote a series of directions in the margin. "If Reynard has been successful, he should be waiting at the top of Monde Street for me with Captain Giarde and a guard detachment.'' *If he isn't, at least Crack is well out of this.* "This will tell them where to look for the necromancer."

Crack took the map but shook his head. "You can't stay here. There's more of them things, a lot more."

"We've got to," Nicholas told him. "And right now you are a liability and will better serve us by taking yourself to safety so I don't have to worry about you."

"That ain't fair," Crack said, through gritted teeth.

"I feel no obligation to be fair," Nicholas said, hauling Crack to his feet and ignoring his snarl. "You should know that by now."

It took both of them to get him up to the tunnel opening and by the end of it Crack was almost ready to admit that he wouldn't be much help in his current state. He collapsed, panting from exertion and pain, at the mouth of the tunnel, and tried to convince them to come with him. "You shouldn't stay. There's more of them things, I tell you."

"No." Nicholas handed him the lamp. He and Madeline both had candle stubs and matches in their pockets, enough to see them back through the sewer. "Now get moving."

"I can't walk no more," Crack said, not convincingly.

"I need you to take the message to Reynard or it will get a damn sight worse for us," Nicholas told him patiently.

Crack looked at Madeline in appeal. She shook her head. "I'm no help, I'm afraid."

Cursing both of them, Crack managed to stand. They watched him make his way down the tunnel and when he was out of earshot, Madeline jumped back down to the catacomb floor, commenting, "He's right."

"Of course he is," Nicholas said, following her.

"You really think we'll find the others in here somewhere?" she asked. "Alive?"

Nicholas stopped and looked at her. "It's a trap, Madeline, obviously. If you don't like it, go with Crack."

She swore in exasperation. "I know it's a trap, that's

the only reason to leave Crack alive. If we don't walk into it, you think Macob will kill the others?''

Nicholas pushed on ahead, finding a path through the ruined crypts. ''I know he will.''

''Of course, stupid thing to ask,'' Madeline muttered, following him.

Further down the tombs they passed were less elaborate, some mere hollows sealed with mortar. Many had been broken open over time and the floor was littered with smashed bones, moldering rags, and verdigrised metal. They had seen no more of the ghouls and none of the revenants who had attacked Crack, neither of which was a good sign. ''I thought there would be some sign of them before now,'' Nicholas admitted.

''Maybe it isn't a trap, though that seems unlikely.''

Nicholas paused to give her a hand over a rockfall that half-blocked the path. Water was seeping up through the cracks in the floor, he noted. ''Yes. I hoped he would be incautious enough to leave one or two more of our friends along the way, but that doesn't appear to be the case.'' Nicholas hesitated again. The debris underfoot was becoming more varied and they were tripping over rusted metal and rotted wood. There was even something crammed up against one of the tombs that looked like the rusted skeleton of a siege engine. The catacomb was getting narrower too and the ceiling was much lower overhead. He didn't like the look of it. *Could there have been another passage along the way, that we missed in the dark?* No, surely not. Surely the idea was to lure them into the sorcerer's stronghold, not decoy them off down some dead end.

''Look at that wall,'' Madeline said, pointing toward a projection that seemed to be breaking through the rocky side of the catacomb. It was made of cut stone and had a blocked-up gateway large enough to pass a carriage through. ''Are we running into the lower part of the rampart again?''

''Possibly.'' He moved toward it for a closer look. There was something dripping down the wall that didn't quite have the consistency of water. Pulling the perfume-soaked scarf away from his nose and mouth, he dabbed his fingers into the dark substance streaming down the wall and sniffed them cautiously. "It's a good thing we gave Crack the lamp." There was no telling how thickly the fumes had penetrated the air in this passage.

"Oil?"

"Paraffin." He glanced up at the ancient stonework woven in with the rock overhead. "If I'm right, we're somewhere below the Bowles and Viard Cokeworks. One of their storage tanks must be leaking."

"It's frightening that you know that," Madeline grumbled.

"It means we're where I think we are. The directions I gave Crack will be accurate."

They worked their way past the wall and almost stumbled on a set of broad steps, broken and chipped, leading down through an archway with elaborate scrolled carving. The angle of the steps and the slope of the ceiling made it impossible to see what lay beyond.

"There's light down there," Madeline said, low-voiced. "Torchlight."

They exchanged a look, then she sighed. "Well, we've come all this way."

Nicholas went down the steps first. Past the archway was a wide stone balcony with a broken balustrade, looking down on a bowl-shaped cave, almost twenty feet below the present level. It held a small city of free-standing crypts and mausoleums, many of fantastic design, with statues, small towers, and much ornamentation. The ghost-lichen hanging heavily from the stalactited roof gave it an otherworldly glow, as if they were looking down on a city of fayre. But Madeline was right, there were torches.

The largest crypt was the round one in the center. It had a domed roof and had been made to look like a small-scale keep, with towers with miniature turrets. Smoky torches were jammed between some of the stones of its crenelations, casting flickering firelight on the bizarre scene. In front of it there was a broad, round stone dais, several feet high. It looked like the platforms followers of the Old Faith often built in their holy places in deep forest clearings or high in the hills.

Nicholas moved forward, almost to the broken balustrade. "Careful," Madeline breathed. He acknowledged the warning with a distracted nod. The air was staler than that in the upper catacomb and there was a sweetish, foul smell under it. He could see there was a walkway or gallery, badly ruined in places, running from the balcony and along the walls on both sides, entirely encompassing the cave and ending in a set of stone stairs that were covered with rocks and debris from some earlier collapse. The stairs had led down to an open space in front of the dais and the keep crypt. *Like a processional way*, Nicholas thought. *Did they hold funerals there? Make offerings?* He knew very little about the Old Faith.

There was no telling how old the place was. It might go back to the founding of the first keep that had marked the original site of Vienne. From the martial nature of the statues, these could be the tombs of the first knights and warlords of Ile-Rien.

There was a clink from somewhere behind and above them, as if a rock had fallen. Nicholas looked back, frowning; since they had left the ghouls behind, the only sounds they had heard had been of their own making.

Madeline had heard something too. She moved a step or two away, looking at the shadows and hollows in the cave wall above them warily.

Nicholas motioned her back toward the stairs. He had his pistol and the sphere had been proof against the ghouls up to now, but he had the feeling they had come just a few steps too far.

He saw something luminously white on the edge of the balcony and for an instant thought it was a lichenous growth or some underground parasite. Then it moved and he realized it was a hand.

He shouted a warning to Madeline but it was already too late. They were coming up over the balcony in a silent wave. People—*no, not people*, Nicholas had time to think. Their faces were characterless, the features slack, the skin pallid and dull. Their clothes were ragged remnants but their bodies were so bloated as to make them nearly sexless and there was nothing in their eyes at all.

Light flared brighter and cleaner than the ghost-lichen's pale glow as the sphere reacted to them, but there were too many. Nicholas fired into the thick of them, again and again, but the bullets hardly seemed to slow them. The two nearest went down finally, their wounds bloodless, but there were still at least ten of them, more like twenty; moving with inhuman determination they pressed toward him, stumbling over the bodies of the fallen, and he had to back away. He had lost sight of Madeline but the sphere flared again, telling him she was near the base of the stairs. He shouted at her to run.

Then something crashed into him from behind, knocking his feet out from under him, and the last thing he saw was one of the revenants leaning over him before the light vanished.

20

Madeline was lost. **Utterly, irretrievably,** *she thought.
I will wander down here forever.* No, forever was unlikely. She would surely be killed by something long before forever arrived.

She had been driven back by the weight of the revenants. The sphere had accounted for a number of them but they seemed less self-aware than the ghouls and they hadn't fled. She had heard Nicholas firing at them and hoped that meant he had been able to get away. No, she was sure of that. He had been closer to the stairs than she had. She would have made it herself if she hadn't slipped and fallen down through that damn crevice at the edge of the stairs. Between the bad light and the dark color of the stone she hadn't seen it until it was too late. Now she was bruised all over and hopelessly lost.

She had found her way into a wide passage, the blocks in its walls regular and obviously shaped and set by human hands, the remains of a curving, dressed stone ceiling overhead. Whether it was part of the catacomb or some long forgotten underground level of the old fortifications, she couldn't tell. *And since I don't have the damn map of Vienne, underground and above, memorized, like Nicholas does, small good it would do me if I did know.*

Hopefully he had been able to get back to the relative safety of the sewers. Hopefully. It infuriated her that she was stuck down here, uselessly.

The ghost-lichen's light was just enough that she hadn't had to resort to her candle yet. She hadn't been attacked again but the ghouls couldn't be too far away; the sphere was trembling, its insides spinning like a top.

She drew near the end of the passage and saw the regular walls deteriorated into tumbled rockfalls, though the opening still seemed to continue. She could tell the floor had a distinct slant downward which was not encouraging. Madeline peered suspiciously into the shadows and the gaps in the rock at the end of the passage. She thought she could see the gleam of eyes and a surreptitious movement there. No, the ghouls weren't gone. She hoped they were only ghouls; she had reloaded her pistol from the box of spare ammunition in her coat pocket but it hadn't been too effective against them before.

Suddenly in the silence she heard footsteps. One person walking at a deliberate, heavy pace; the sound seemed to come from all around her. She hugged the sphere tightly, looking up and down the apparently empty passage. Her mouth was dry and she couldn't swallow past the lump in her throat. It wasn't Nicholas; she would have known the sound of his walk.

Out of the shadows at the far end of the tunnel a figure appeared. Madeline stared, too overcome with shock and sudden relief to react. It was Arisilde.

She made a motion to step forward but from the sphere in her arms came a sudden vibration, a pulse that she felt deep in her chest. She stopped in her tracks. That had been a warning.

Arisilde came toward her. He looked as she would expect him to, very pale and thin, wearing a dressing gown of faded blue and gold. He smiled at her as he drew near and said, "Madeline, you're here. How very good of you."

"Yes, I'm here, Arisilde," she managed to say. The sphere felt like it was going to fly apart in her arms, its wheels clicking in furious motion.

"And you brought the sphere." A breath of air moving down the passage lifted his wispy silver hair. He held out his arms to her. "Give it to me."

She could feel sweat running down her back despite the cold. She said, "Come and take it, Arisilde."

There was a hesitation but his expression of slightly daffy goodwill didn't change. He said, "It would be better if you were to give it to me, Madeline."

She felt that strong vibration of warning from the sphere again, as if it had reached a tendril into her heart and touched her soul in fear. She drew a deep breath. *Maybe it is alive.* But how could a thing of metal, even imbued with magic, be alive? How could it think? *Something that was alive and powerful wouldn't sit on a shelf in the attic at Coldcourt all this time and do nothing.* Not unless it needed a person, a living being, someone who could sense magic, to live. Maybe it used the consciousness of the person who held it to think with. *Maybe that's why this sphere works for me, and the one Octave had worked for him. And if I give this one to a real sorcerer....* "You built this sphere with Edouard, Arisilde. Why can't you take it from me?" *Why doesn't it know you? Why does it tell me to be afraid of you?*

He hesitated again, then shook his head and spread his hands helplessly. "It's because I was the one who did all these things, Madeline. I was only pretending to be unconscious all that time. I called the Sending and transformed the gargoyles in the Courts Plaza, and sent the creature into the prison. But I would never have hurt anyone. I was trying to get revenge on the men who killed Edouard, but it didn't work." The violet eyes were distressed. "I think I've gone mad, I'm afraid. A little mad. But if I could hold the sphere, I think that would help me. There's a part of myself in it, a part of me from before I went mad. If I could take that part back.... But you have to give me the sphere."

Madeline watched him for a long moment, then her brows lifted and she said dryly, "Do you think all women are fools, or just me?" He looked like Arisilde and he had Arisilde's sweet smile, but he was never Arisilde. Even if one included Isham in the plot, Madele had examined Arisilde and the notion that her grandmother could have been deceived in such a way was ridiculous. That Nicholas could have been fooled in such a way was unthinkable. Nicholas was suspicious of everyone. She wouldn't have been surprised if he had considered Arisilde as the possible culprit already and discarded the idea as simply not feasible. He had said their opponent was Constant Macob and Madeline had had to admit there was every sign in favor of it.

He stood there, expressionless, then her eyes blurred for an instant and she was looking at another man. She had never seen him before. He was young and very thin, with lank blond hair and a weak chin, his expression vacant. His coat and trousers were muddy and his waistcoat was torn open.

Madeline's brow furrowed. *Who the hell is this?* It might be one of Macob's victims, abducted off the street, but under the dirt his suit was a little too fine and Macob had preyed on the poor and street people he thought would not be readily missed. Then she remembered that Octave had had two other companions who had never been accounted for. Octave's driver had mentioned them before he had been killed. This man could very well be one of them. "I take it the driver was lucky," she said to herself.

He stepped forward and she moved back out of reach. Behind her she heard a frantic skittering among the rocks as the ghouls scrambled to get out of the sphere's range. There was no expression at all on the man's face; he might have been as mindless as one of the revenants. He took a sudden swing at her with his fist and she ducked away from it. She considered drawing her pistol, but she wasn't sure she wanted to fire it down here; there was no telling what else the sound would attract.

Watching him warily, she shifted the sphere to her right side, tucking it under her arm. His dead eyes followed it. He lurched forward and she let him grab her arm, then slammed the heel of her free hand up into his chin. His head snapped back and he staggered back a pace, tearing the sleeve of her coat. She kicked out, striking him solidly between the legs. He fell, collapsing onto the floor of the passage, obviously in pain but making no sound.

She moved away cautiously, making sure he wasn't about to jump back up again with inhuman strength. It didn't look like it. That maneuver had always worked well to discourage the attentions of importunate stagehands and actors; she was glad it worked on men ensorcelled to serve necromancers.

He rolled on the floor, making an attempt to stand and failing badly. She turned and ran up the passage, hearing the ghouls flee before her.

Nicholas realized first that he lay sprawled on his back on a damp, dirty surface, that the dampness smelled foul, that it was cold and firelight was casting flickering reflections over stone walls. He drew a shaky breath and lifted a hand to push the hair out of his eyes. There was a clink and a tug on his wrist. *Not good*, he thought. He leaned his head back and saw both his wrists were manacled to a short length of chain attached to a ring sunk deeply into a stone flag. The chains were old but not rusty. *Not disastrous, but definitely not good.* He tried to roll onto his side, but stopped abruptly as a splitting pain shot through his head. He cautiously probed the tender knot at the back of his skull. His fingers came away bloody.

The chains were loose enough to allow for some freedom of movement and he sat up on one elbow, slowly. He was inside one of the crypts; from the domed ceiling, it was the one shaped to resemble a miniature keep that stood in the center of the cave. It was lit by smoky torches shoved into gaps between the stones and some unhealthy radiance from the ghost-lichen came in through the large crack in the roof. The walls were covered with carving and inscriptions, obscured by layers of mold. It was not a family crypt; there was only one vault, a large, ornate, free-standing one in the center of the chamber. Atop it, carefully laid out as if for a wake, was a very old corpse.

Time had shrunken it to bare bones, held together by

withered strips of skin and muscle, festooned with the rotten remnants of leather and cloth. Nicholas thought he must be gazing on all that remained of Macob's physical body. Except. . . . *The skull is missing.* Either it had been removed for some purpose of Macob's or. . . . *Or it wasn't in the room with the corpse when the ghouls broke in. That's what Octave wanted to question the old Duke about.* On the bier next to it lay Nicholas's pistol.

He squinted and sat up a little more, wincing at the pain in his shoulder and head. The missing skull was not the only oddity. There was a woven webbing or net hung from the ceiling of the chamber and suspended in it was something small and round, of dull-colored metal. For one bad moment he was afraid it was Arisilde's sphere, which meant Madeline had been caught as well, but then he realized it was far too small. *No, it's the other sphere*, he thought with relief. The one Rohan had constructed with Edouard, that Octave had obtained by blackmail.

Except for himself and the corpse, the crypt was ostensibly empty. Madeline was nowhere to be seen. *She escaped*, he told himself. There was no point in speculating on anything else. As long as she had the sphere, she was in far better case than he was.

The crypt might appear to be deserted but Nicholas didn't think he was unobserved. He pretended to test the strength of the chains, tugging on them and trying to work the links loose, while actually examining the locks. Someone had searched his pockets, but they hadn't found the picks sewn into the cuff of his shirt. He didn't want to risk using them now and betraying their existence to a hypothetical watcher. One mistake and he was dead. He was most likely dead anyway, but the tension engendered by pretending there was still hope would keep him alert.

After a few moments he noticed the quality of light in the chamber was changing, the shadows sharpening, the torches becoming dimmer and the sick glow of the ghost-lichen correspondingly brighter and more defined. Turning his head to look at the doorway, Nicholas caught a growing radiance out of the corner of his eye. It was in the darkest corner of the crypt. He continued to watch the doorway expectantly.

He had time to notice that the damp chill in the air was becoming more concentrated as well, the cold intensifying until his bones ached and he could feel the bite of it in his fingers. There was a slight sound like a boot sliding over stone; a deliberate betrayal. Nicholas flinched as if startled and jerked his head toward the corner.

A figure was standing there in the shadows. It was a tall man, dressed in an old-fashioned caped and skirted greatcoat and a broad-brimmed hat. His face was gaunt almost to the point of appearing a death's head and it was hard to get a sense of his features. His eyes were dark pits under the shadow of his hat brim, impossible to read.

He stepped forward deliberately and said, "You needn't introduce yourself, I assure you I know who you are."

The voice was an old man's, hoarse and raw, as if he had long suffered from throat afflictions. *Or been hanged*, Nicholas thought suddenly. That was how Macob had been executed. This was fascinating. Terrifying, but fascinating. The accent was a little off too. It was still recognizably of Ile-Rien and particularly Vienne, but with odd twists in the pronunciation of some of the words. Nicholas hadn't decided what tack to take, but something in the man's confident manner made him answer, "Of course. You're Constant Macob. You know everything."

Macob took another step forward, the iron gray brows drawing together. He hadn't expected that response.

For a shade he was terribly real, his wrinkled face and rheumy eyes that of a living person. *You would think he would have made himself appear young*, Nicholas mused, *he has either no imagination, or no vanity*. The former was a disadvantage for Macob, the latter a disadvantage for Nicholas and in direct contradiction to his theories. Surely only an infinitely vain, self-obsessed man would try to hold on to life like Macob had. But sorcerers had to be artists as well as scholars; Macob couldn't lack for creativity or he would never have managed to take himself so far.

An indulgent tone in his rusty voice, the necromancer said, "I suppose you want to know my plans."

"I already know them, thank you."

The eyes narrowed, momentarily becoming dark pits, then Macob decided to be amused. "Gabard Ventarin wanted to know."

"Gabard Ventarin has been dust for two hundred years," Nicholas said, politely. "His name is known only to historians."

"A fitting end for him," Macob said, pleased. But there was something unconvincing about the manner in which he said it. Macob couldn't be too aware of the passage of time. Did he even really believe his executioner was dead?

What could it be like to cling to the world of the living this way? To refuse to move on, to remain chained to vengeance and old hates? *You might be lucky if you don't find out for yourself,* a traitor voice whispered, and Nicholas brushed it aside. Macob must live in the ever present now, all past and no future, never changing, never altering in the slightest degree. *Never learning from his mistakes.* He saw Macob was about to turn away and said quickly, "Why did you kill Doctor Octave?" He already knew the answer but he didn't intend to ask any questions to which he didn't already know the answers; this was no time to court surprises.

Macob's smile was slow and self-satisfied. "He . . ." faltered. He became infirm in my purpose so I destroyed him."

It didn't change Nicholas's opinion on what had occurred. He still thought the initial scheme had been Octave's quest for an ideal confidence game and that the spiritualist had participated in Macob's murders only because he had been forced to it. But it didn't surprise him that Macob's perception of events differed from this. He said, "Very wise of you."

Macob's eyes glinted. "And why shouldn't I destroy you?"

Ah, now we get to it. Causing terror could be addictive. Nicholas had seen that before in a number of men who had considered themselves masters of Vienne's criminal underworld. It was a ridiculously exploitable weakness and one Nicholas could diagnose from the first exchange of fake pleasantries. Macob liked to terrify his victims. For all Nicholas knew terror might be necessary to necromantic spells, but he thought the main motive was that Macob had learned to enjoy it. "Since you destroyed Doctor Octave, I would think you in need of more mortal assistance."

"Which you could provide." Macob said it without much evidence of interest.

"For a price." Macob seemed to have an air of pre-occupation that Nicholas didn't like. Not only was it not terribly complimentary to himself but it made him wonder what else was happening in Macob's little kingdom. Was it Madeline that was drawing the necromancer's attention, or Ronsarde and Halle, or Arisilde? He needed to do something to regain Macob's interest. "Despite all your sorcery, essentially you're just a criminal. A criminal who has been caught. I'm a criminal who has never been caught."

Macob's head lifted and his eyes returned to Nicholas. "I've caught you."

Give him that one or not? Nicholas made a swift mental calculation. *I think not.* "After I walked into your trap."

There was anger in Macob's eyes and something of frustration. "I wanted to bring you down here. I wanted to see what you were."

"And you wanted the other sphere."

Macob hesitated, then nodded to Rohan's sphere, suspended above the corpse. "That one is dying. It was never any good to me. Octave made it work for his ghost talking but it was never good to me." He gave Nicholas a sidelong look. "Not as I am."

As an attempt to elicit information, it was fairly transparent. *Not as he is? Not while he's dead, he means. And is that state likely to change?* Nicholas obligingly said, "It must have been one of the first constructed. And Rohan is powerful, but not as powerful as Arisilde." That was as close as he wanted to come to mentioning the others. If they were dead he couldn't help them, but if they lived, the last thing he wanted to do was direct Macob's attention toward them.

"You know much of the spheres?"

"No." Macob would know if he made anything up.

"The woman." Macob hesitated. He knew he was betraying himself and it was making him angry. Dangerously angry. His voice was a low ominous growl. "Does she know of the spheres?"

So Madeline was free and causing great consternation. Nicholas smiled. "She knows all that she needs to." *Or at least she thinks she does.* He added, "I could engage to obtain the missing skull for you. That is the item you're in need of, isn't it? The one Octave wanted to question the late Duke of Mondollot concerning? I doubt the Duke's information would have been helpful; it was surely removed by Gabard Ventarin at the time of your death as a further precaution." He paused. He had Macob's rapt attention. "It was removed to the palace, was it not?"

"Yes. A trophy." Macob stared at him, the malevolent eyes narrowed. "I know where it is. I can obtain it myself. I would not engage you to do so. I would sooner engage a viper."

Nicholas's mouth quirked. Constant Macob, necromancer and murderer a hundred times over, thought he was a viper. He was not quite light-headed enough to thank him for the compliment, but said, "That's a rather unjust assessment in light of your activities, isn't it?"

"I continued my work," Macob said, but he wasn't much interested in defending himself, to Nicholas or to anyone else. He was looking at the corpse again, his attention leaving his prisoner. "That is the only thing of importance."

Nicholas frowned. Vanity might not be the key to Macob's character after all. Was it obsession, instead? With his family dead from a swift and violent plague he had not been able to stop, had he thrown himself into his work until it had achieved such an overwhelming importance that every other consideration fell by the wayside? It would explain a great deal. *And it makes him far more difficult to manipulate.*

Macob turned back to Nicholas and started to speak, but the necromancer froze suddenly, all motion arrested, his head cocked in a listening attitude. Without another word, he strode toward the door. As he reached the shadow across the opening his form seemed to dissolve and it was impossible to say if he had walked out or vanished into the darkness. Nicholas sat up and awkwardly rolled his torn coat sleeve back to get to the shirt cuff and the lock picks. He tore open the seam of the cuff with his teeth and shook out the picks. This explained Macob's preoccupation at least. Nicholas might have preferred that Madeline had sought the safety of the surface instead of taking the sphere on some sort of rampage through Macob's hiding place but he also preferred not to become the central element of the next necromantic spell.

Working the lock picks on his own manacled wrists was difficult, but he had gotten himself out of handcuffs before and the manacles came off with only the sacrifice of some scraped skin. Nicholas stood too quickly and had to steady himself on the crypt wall as the floor swayed and his sight narrowed to a dark tunnel. He rubbed his temples as his vision cleared, thinking *this could present a problem.*

As soon as he could see he stumbled to the plinth and leaned on it. He checked his pistol but it was empty and the extra ammunition he had had in his coat had been removed along with his clasp-knife and anything else that might serve as a weapon. They had left his matches and other articles that might possibly be of use, just not at the moment. He shoved the pistol into his pocket with a muttered oath, then looked up at the sphere, suspended in the net above the corpse. Destroying it would probably be a great disservice to the furtherance of human knowledge, but he wouldn't leave it for Macob.

There was a sound from the door of the crypt, a soft footstep. Nicholas looked up and saw a man standing in the doorway, pointing a pistol at him. He was a large man, about Nicholas's age, with greasy dark hair and a ruddy, rough-featured face, his once good frock coat ragged and dirty. *One of Doctor Octave's colleagues*, Nicholas thought. There had been two other men besides the driver. Perhaps Macob had taken the rest of the ghouls with him and left only this last human servant to guard his prisoner. He had to be running out of ghouls; there had been a limited number to start with and Arisilde's sphere seemed to go through them rather quickly.

The man's eyes were lifeless, dull, but the pistol didn't waver. Nicholas said, "I'm no good to him dead." That wasn't quite true, but this man didn't look as if he had access to all his faculties.

He motioned with the pistol, indicating that Nicholas move away from the bier. The corpse was obviously important to Macob; he had gone to a deal of trouble to obtain it and the missing skull still obviously worried him. While there was madness in the necromancer's method, it didn't rule him. He had reasons for everything he did. *Not what one would call "good" reasons, perhaps, but reasons nonetheless*, Nicholas thought, obeying the man's gesture and backing away toward the wall.

Nicholas reached the wall and turning suddenly, stretched up and grabbed one of the torches. The man's reflexes were slow, doubtless the result of whatever Macob had done to him to secure his obedience; he was just raising the pistol to fire when the torch landed on the corpse. The rags of rotted clothing caught immediately.

There was an instant of hesitation, then the man ran for the bier. He dragged the torch out, dropping it on the ground, then beat at the burning clothing, oblivious to anything else. Moving forward, Nicholas picked up a broken paving stone from the floor. The man turned just as he was within reach and brought up the pistol. Nicholas grabbed his wrist to turn the weapon away from him and they grappled.

Nicholas lost his grip on the stone, trying to keep the pistol from pointing toward his head. The man wasn't inhumanly strong but he fought like an automaton with no concern for his own safety. Nicholas managed to swing him around, driving him back against the wall of the crypt, when there was a shriek of rage from somewhere above their heads.

No, Macob hadn't taken all the ghouls with him. A quick glance upward showed Nicholas two of the creatures were climbing through the crack in the dome and scrabbling headfirst down the wall. He wrenched an arm free and punched the man in the jaw, knocking his head sharply back and sending him sprawling. He heard the pistol strike the floor somewhere but the ghouls were almost on him and there was no time to look for it. He bolted for the door out of the crypt.

Once out in the half-light he ran past the dais and plunged into the maze of passages between the crypts, with no time to get his bearings. The ghouls moved too fast and he only had a few moments head start at best.

He could hear them behind him, careening into walls, screaming in high unearthly voices with all too human rage. He ran down between a row of crypts and saw an open passage into the rock wall. It wasn't until he had plunged into it and found himself in near total darkness that he realized he was too far down in the cave for this to be part of the catacomb and that he had hared off into totally unknown territory.

He couldn't go back now. He kept running, stumbling over half-seen obstructions along the ground, bouncing into walls, knowing that if he fell they would be on him in seconds. He saw a darker pool of shadow across the passage in front of him and knew it might be a hole in the ground. There were claws scrabbling on the rock behind him and he jumped wildly, not pausing to judge the distance or gather himself.

He hit the far side, lost his grip on slick stone and slid down. He caught the edge of the fissure, his feet finding purchase on a slope littered with loose pebbles and rock chips. The suddenness of it took his breath away; he hadn't really believed it was a hole until he felt the empty cold air beneath him instead of solid earth. The ghouls were screaming almost directly over his head, so he released his tenuous hold on the edge and let himself slide down.

The ghouls had tried to attack Madeline again and the sphere had destroyed them. The things had come after her only reluctantly, as if they had been driven to it. Since then she had had no sensation of being followed.

She was almost ready to sob with relief when she found a tunnel that led upward. The slope was steep so she made a sling for the sphere out of her scarf and tied it around her neck. Makeshift and none too secure, it still freed both her arms and made climbing the upward passage much easier.

She came out above the cave with the standing crypts again on a reasonably whole section of the walkway, her legs sore from the steep climb. The entrance to the catacomb should be over to the right, above the balcony, if she had her bearings. She could see flickering firelight, greasy in the bad air, showing between the cracks in the walls of the large crypt in the center. *What is Macob doing in there?* she wondered. *No, don't think of it, just go while you can.* The sphere didn't make her invulnerable.

She crept along the broken remains of the walkway, ducking to stay below what was left of the balustrade and moving slowly, despite her fear. As she drew closer to the place where she was certain the walkway met the catacomb, she saw something strange in the quality of light. After a moment her eyes found the glow of another torch, burning at the entrance of a crypt on this side of the cave.

She kept moving but that torch worried her. She reached the ruined balcony and saw with relief the entrance to the catacomb appeared unguarded by revenants. A few steps up and she would be in it and running back toward the sewer. She hesitated. The ghouls didn't need torchlight. In fact, she rather thought they were afraid of fire, from what Nicholas had said. Firelight meant people.

Her hands were clammy and her back hurt from the fall and she didn't particularly want to die down here. But if Nicholas hadn't gotten away it might be him. Muttering under her breath, she carefully found her way past the broken arch that lay across the balcony and back onto the walkway.

The crypt with the torch was closer but there was an impediment. Part of the walkway had collapsed entirely, leaving a gap of a few feet. She was able to get a hand-hold on an overhang and step easily across, but it would not make for a quick getaway.

The walkway curved and she pressed herself as closely against the wall as she could. She could see the front of the crypt now. A large part of the pitched roof had collapsed but there were still statues of helmeted pikemen on either side of the intact doorway. The torch was jammed into a loose chink above the door and she could see the mortar and stones had been knocked out of it, leaving an opening into the crypt. More evidence: if the ghouls had wanted in they could have climbed the wall; they had no need to open the crypt's door.

Speaking of ghouls. . . . There were at least three of them, like bundles of dry rags and bones, seated in front of that gaping doorway. They weren't moving or making any sound and she would have missed them entirely if she hadn't been certain they were there somewhere. They looked like unstrung puppets, cast aside until they were wanted again.

She edged along the wall, cautiously. She could see down into the crypt itself now, but it was deep in shadow and the torch had dazzled her eyes somewhat, so the ghost-lichen's light was negligible. Staring hard, she thought she could discern movement inside. Then a form leaned across the shaft of firelight falling through the open door and Madeline's heart leapt. It was Doctor Halle.

That's all I needed to know. Moving back until she was above the doorway and the guardian ghouls, she studied the edge of the walkway. The wall had crumbled here so if she was quick and sure-footed she could leap down to the flat spot there, and then to the floor of the cave. Not so hard. Not as hard as hanging in that flying harness in *The Nymphs*. She moved to the edge and readied herself, then hesitated.

What if she got them killed? Would it be more sensible to flee up the catacomb and bring help? Before she could decide, her foot dislodged a pebble and it struck the rocks below with a loud crack. All three of the ghouls reacted as one, their heads whipping around and the glazed, glaring eyes staring straight at her.

To hell with it, Madeline thought. She clutched the sphere tightly and leapt.

Being more used to humans who fled from them, her attack caught them by surprise. As she landed on the cave floor they started back from her but she could already feel the sphere shaking. When the light burst from it an instant later, she turned her head away and shut her eyes tightly to keep from losing her night-sight.

The light faded and she looked back to see three heaps of bones, scattered as the ghouls had started to flee. No, four heaps of bones; there had been a fourth one against the wall of the adjoining crypt that she hadn't seen.

She stepped forward into the doorway, whispering, "Doctor Halle?"

"Good God, it's you," his voice answered reassuringly.

She stepped back and pulled the torch free, holding it so she could see the inside of the crypt.

Ronsarde lay on the ground, his head pillowed on a folded coat. His face was still and sallow, his eyes sunken back in his head. The wrinkles and age lines were brought out in high relief; she hadn't realized before that he was so old. Halle was kneeling next to him. Their clothes were torn and filthy and Halle's face was bruised but he didn't look as badly injured as Ronsarde.

"You'll have to carry him alone," Madeline told him. "I've got to hold on to this thing."

Halle was already lifting Ronsarde, dragging one limp arm across his shoulders and pulling him upright. It was only the two of them, she saw. No Nicholas, no Arisilde. "Have you seen the others?" she asked.

Halle half-carried, half-dragged Ronsarde to the doorway and Madeline stepped back out of his way and cast the torch aside. They didn't need it and she didn't have any spare hands. Halle said, "Your man Crack was with us—"

"We found Crack; there's a catacomb above here and he was in it. We sent him back for help. I hope he's found his way out by now." *I hope Nicholas isn't dead. And what did Macob do with Arisilde?* There was no time for speculation. She climbed up onto her rock step and took Ronsarde's free arm.

With Halle pushing and her pulling, they managed to get him up onto the first ledge. Madeline looked up at the walkway unhappily. She could make it and Halle could on his own, but. . . . *But we're not giving up now.* She grabbed one of the balusters and swung up, ignoring the ominous crack from the stone and the wrenching pain in her arm. She reached down for the Inspector and caught movement out of the corner of her eye. Ghouls, several of them, leaping from roof to roof across the sea of crypts. And something else behind them, something dark, its form impossible to discern in the half-light.

Halle followed her arrested gaze and swore, loudly. Ronsarde picked that moment to come back to consciousness. He straightened in Halle's grasp and said, "What the devil?"

"Climb," Halle ordered succinctly. "Then run."

Ronsarde didn't argue, only reached up for Madeline's hand. She braced her feet and leaned back and in another moment he was scrambling up beside her. His breathing sounded labored and harsh but there was nothing they could do for him now. Madeline got to her feet and helped him stand as Halle climbed up beside them.

"That way." She pointed toward the catacomb. "Hurry."

Halle caught Ronsarde's arm and hurried. Madeline followed, not taking her eyes off the approaching ghouls.

The creatures had stopped on the roof of the nearest crypt, watching them with those staring eyes but not coming any closer. Their terror of the sphere was gratifying but the dark thing that her eyes just couldn't seem to focus on was still coming, flowing over the rooftops toward her, sometimes like an airy mist, sometimes like something far more solid and ominous.

They reached the gap in the walkway and Halle got Ronsarde across with difficulty. Madeline almost stepped backward into it, but her boot caught the edge and she recovered with effort, then turned and jumped across.

It had slowed them down but it didn't stop their pursuer. The dark thing was on the walkway now. A glimpse back showed Madeline its motion was more halting and jerky now, more like a man running. The sphere under her arm was ominously quiet. *If it can't stop that thing we're dead*, she thought desperately.

They reached the entrance to the catacomb. Madeline caught Ronsarde's other arm and helped Halle pull him up the broken steps. She stumbled, barking her shins on the stone and barely noticing. The thing was almost on them; its proximity made her skin itch. She gave Halle a shove and shouted, "Keep going."

She swung around in time to watch it cross the balcony and start up the steps toward her. It was a man now, she could see his shape in the obscuring cloud of shadow and firefly flickers of light. The sphere was silent in her arms. It wasn't going to help them. He was on the top step a hand's breadth away and she could see his face. An old man's face, but hideous with greed and somehow inhuman, like a death mask.

Then Madeline felt a concussion, and there was a searing white light. She blinked and found herself sitting on the step, staring at the cave of crypts, and everything was rippling like a hot stone-paved street on an intense summer day.

The man was nowhere to be seen. Then an instant later her eyes found that unnaturally dark blot of shadow and mist, tumbling back across the crypts, a leaf in a windstorm.

The sphere in her hands was hot and trembling a little.

Sense returned to her and she staggered to her feet and ran after Halle and Ronsarde.

The slope was steeper than Nicholas thought and he couldn't control his descent. He half-tumbled to land hard on a shelf of rock. He blinked dirt out of his eyes and managed to push himself up, feeling bruised and battered muscles protest. He squinted up the slope toward the narrow opening at the top but the ghouls didn't seem to be pitching down after him.

He was on a ledge hanging above a deep, shadowed pit with sloped sides. There was ghost-lichen here, just enough to see by. The walls were rough stone, pocked with irregular cracks and fissures, and a pool of foul-smelling water had collected in the bottom. It was either the dim, unnatural quality of the ghost-light or his blurry vision, but the dimensions of the pit were hard to judge and a fold in the rock cut off his view of a section of it. There was a crack in the wall nearby that seemed to open into a deeper fissure. He kept an eye on it warily as he staggered to his feet. It was the perfect lurking spot for ghouls or revenants.

The wall just above him was too steep to climb and he started to make his way along the ledge to where the slope wasn't so dramatic. There seemed to be an inordinate amount of debris from the catacomb down here. He stumbled on a pile of bones and disturbed a ragged heap of detritus that gave off an odor so sickly sweet it made him gag.

There was a scrabbling above him, then a shower of pebbles rained down the slope as a revenant burst out of a crack and barrelled straight for him. Nicholas reached for his pistol before he remembered it was empty. He flung himself back against the wall and grabbed up a rock. He had time to see the creature was an old revenant, its features distorted until they were barely recognizable as human, its clothing in rags, then it raced straight past him and flung itself into the deeper crevice he had noted earlier.

Nicholas stared after it, his brows drawing together. *That . . . was not a good sign.*

Down in the pit below he heard a shifting, something heavy moving and grating against the stone. Nicholas hesitated, but an awkward scramble across the ledge would just make him more of a target. It was better to face whatever it was here with the wall at his back. Then it growled.

It was a low rumble, sounding more like rock grinding but with an animal tone to it that was unmistakable. The sound reverberated throughout the pit like a distant underground train. *That isn't a ghoul, or a revenant.* Nicholas sank back against the wall and held his breath.

Something stirred below, creeping out of the deep shadow. At first it blended in against the mottled surface of the rock, then he made out something vaguely like a human head with patchy gray-green flesh. There was a scrambling in the rocks above him and Nicholas twitched minutely before he caught himself. He stayed motionless even when chips of rock and bone rained down on him. Then he saw a revenant burst from cover on the ledge above and skitter down the slope.

The thing below moved in a blur, suddenly resolving into a recognizably human shape. Its skin was horribly discolored and gaped open in places to reveal bare yellowed bone. Nicholas thought it was a larger version of the revenants until it started to climb the slope toward the one that was trying desperately to escape.

Seen in perspective it was far larger than any human, perhaps twenty feet tall. Moving with an uncanny swiftness, it climbed the rocky slope and snatched the revenant. What Nicholas had seen before was the bare crown of its head and it had been standing further down in the pit than he had thought. Its skull still bore ragged remnants of hair and it wore rusted chains wrapped around its upper body. The revenant had barely time for one shriek of terror before the thing tore it apart.

Slowly, Nicholas started to edge backward toward the fissure in the rock wall. It might be a dead end and teeming with revenants but it was too small for that thing to fit into. It had to be another dead fay, like the one Macob had used for the Sending. Perhaps buried in the catacomb, long forgotten beneath the present-day city's foundations.

It was eating the revenant, or trying to. *It doesn't realize it's dead*, Nicholas thought. The sight would sicken him if fear hadn't already overridden every other emotion. He reached the end of the ledge and eased himself carefully to his feet.

It turned suddenly as if it had heard him. The one remaining eye seemed to be staring directly at him, though it was covered with a heavy white film; the other eye was an empty socket surrounded by bare skull. The mouth was open, revealing jagged teeth and the decaying lips were curled in a snarl. Nicholas leapt for the next ledge.

He heard it behind him as he landed and he swarmed up the jagged rocks. He felt a tug at his coat just as he reached the lip of the crevice and threw himself forward. The coat ripped and he rolled down over rough rock and foul-smelling debris. The thwarted roar of rage echoed down the narrow passage.

Nicholas crawled several yards further down before he looked back.

It was digging at the edges of the fissure and pounding the stone, furious at losing its prey. The thing's face was even worse at close view, the dead tattered flesh revealing the bone beneath and the teeth jagged yellowed daggers. He could see the wound that must have killed it the first time, a gaping hole in the side of the skull that looked as if it had been made by a cannonball or a ballista.

That would have been an ignominious end to a checkered career, Nicholas thought, taking a deep breath to try to calm his pounding heart. His hand was burning and he realized he had ripped his glove and torn his palm open climbing the rocks and not even noticed. He found a handkerchief in an inner coat pocket and stanched the blood, then stood carefully, trying to ignore the fact that his knees were still shaking. Keeping his head down to avoid the low ceiling of the passage, he made his way deeper into it, stumbling a little on the bones and other unspeakable debris that littered the floor.

It was so dark, with only small patches of the ghost-lichen to light the way, that there could have been any number of revenants hiding in the crevices and gaps in the rock, but nothing attacked him. Nicholas thought he would be safe until the fay stopped clawing at the entrance and snarling its frustration. The revenants still active down here must have survived by learning when to go to ground; they would stay silent and still until the creature left.

There was a brighter patch of dimness ahead and Nicholas headed for it. The passage was growing more narrow and he had to climb fallen chunks of stone and navigate narrow gaps. He struggled through the last crevice and almost fell out of it onto a paved floor. There was just enough light from the opening in the wall ahead to show him that this was a room built of regular shaped blocks and not just a hollow carved in the rock. *Another part of the old fortification, perhaps.* The opening had been a square window but a chunk knocked out of the corner gave it an irregular shape. It was high on the wall and Nicholas had to look for hand- and foot-holds in the ancient mortar before he could pull himself up high enough to look out.

Outside lay another section of the pit about half the size of the area haunted by the fay. There was a gap in the side that must lead back to the other section and a round, regular opening overhead. Nicholas could still hear the creature growling and scratching at the other entrance to the crevice, so he was at least temporarily safe here. There were bones scattered on the ledges below and several corpses in a much more recent state of decay, still clad in rags of clothing. Nicholas squinted at a pallid form on the ledge several yards below and stiffened suddenly. The body lay face down but the hair was almost shoulder-length and entirely white.

Nicholas had scrambled up onto the flat stone sill of the window before he realized what he was doing. He hesitated, listening for the fay, and heard another low rumbling growl echo through the crevice. He lowered himself as far down as he could, then let go and dropped to the ledge immediately below. Trying to move as silently as possible, he climbed down the rocky slope, cursing the small avalanches of pebbles his boots touched off. Closer he could see the body was the right size, that it wore a dull-colored dressing gown. *If he's not dead*, Nicholas thought. If the fall down here or the old dampness of the place hadn't killed him yet. He reached the outcropping and crouched near the motionless form, brushing the loose hair back from the face.

It was Arisilde. His face was white and there were dark bruises under his eyes, that was all Nicholas could tell in the light from the ghost-lichen. He looked dead. *But he looked dead before.* Nicholas rolled him over, gently lowering his head to the ground. There was dirt in his hair and his robe was stained and torn from contact with the damp stone, but Nicholas couldn't see any new injuries. If he was breathing it was shallowly and Nicholas's own pulse was pounding too hard for him to detect Arisilde's. *Damn it, we're both going to be dead for certain in a moment.* But Isham had said Arisilde was waking.

Nicholas patted Arisilde's face and chafed his freezing hands while trying to think. Isham had also said something about a ''corpse ring'' which Madele had removed. Nicholas hadn't heard the term before but he remembered Madele's interest in the ring that had charred the flesh around the dead woman's finger at Chaldome House. Arisilde didn't appear to be wearing any kind of a ring now but he hadn't before either, when they had first found him in this condition in his apartment.

Nicholas felt each of Arisilde's fingers, wary of illusions or avoidance spells, then checked his feet. He felt a hard metal band around the smallest toe and almost didn't believe he had found it. He worked the band off and sat back on his heels, watching Arisilde hopefully.

There was no change, or at least no visible one. Nicholas looked at the ring he had removed. It was a plain cheap metal band, no odd inscriptions or glyphs inscribed on it, but he was careful to keep from inadvertently slipping it onto one of his own fingers.

Arisilde still showed no sign of waking and in the silence of the place. . . . Silence. *I can't hear the fay*, Nicholas thought. He shoved the ring into his pocket and grabbed Arisilde's arms, hauling him up and managing to sling him over one shoulder. He didn't know how long the creature had been silent; if he had any luck at all, it had been distracted by another fleeing revenant.

He managed to get Arisilde up the slope and to the ledge just below the window but it was slow and awkward going. Nicholas let him down, propping him up against the wall, and took a deep breath. He was going to have to climb the rock face to the opening with Arisilde a dead weight over his shoulder.

He started to lift Arisilde again but froze when he heard a skitter of pebbles from the other side of the pit. Nicholas lowered Arisilde and glanced around frantically. There was a small crevice where the rock had broken through the old stone wall with an overhang that provided some shelter. Nicholas found the pitiful and far too recent remains of the last creature to take shelter there and hastily flung it out, then worked his way as far back into the corner as he could. He dragged Arisilde in after him, pulling the limp body half into his lap and letting the head rest on his shoulder. They were in deep shadow here and it gave them more of a chance than being caught in the open did.

There was another rush of disturbed rock chips, then stealthy movement at the far end of the pit. Nicholas stopped breathing, stopped thinking when the huge fay crept into sight. Its head swung back and forth, a seeking motion. It knew there was something alive in here or at least something that moved, and it hadn't given up yet.

Nicholas's hold on Arisilde had unconsciously tightened. Suddenly the sorcerer drew a deeper breath. *He's waking*, Nicholas thought, stunned. *What a time to prove Isham right.* He leaned his head down to Arisilde's ear and in an almost voiceless whisper said, ''Don't move.''

The fay crossed the floor of the pit, the stumps that had been its feet stirring up a small cloud of dirt and debris. Arisilde gave no sign he had heard or understood him but he didn't betray them with a quick movement. Nicholas could feel him breathing now, deep regular breaths, as if he was in a natural sleep. That might be some intermediate stage before real consciousness. There was no telling how long it would take Arisilde to wake or if he would be capable of performing sorcery when he did. *Think*, Nicholas told himself. *Come up with a clever way to kill that thing because it's not going to leave until it finds us.*

He watched it hunt for them along the lower reaches of the pit, kicking at piles of ancient bone, poking behind rockfalls, casting its hideous head back and forth like a hunting dog on the scent. *Cold iron and magic kill fay*, Nicholas thought, his mind racing. *And we have rocks and nothing.* He might try to cause a rockfall to crush it but he didn't see how; the loose stones were all far too small to hurt it and the large ones too heavy for him to shift. And it was so fast it might well duck out of the way. His pistol was empty and useless. . . . And made of steel, which was still iron, as far as sorcery was concerned. Except if he tried to throw the pistol at the thing it would do nothing but further enrage it. *When it eats us perhaps it will accidentally swallow it and that will cause some discomfort. . . . Now there's a thought.*

He looked at the revenant who had been the last occupant of their shelter. Its legs had been torn away but most of the torso was left. The fay was on the far side of the pit digging at a pile of filth, stirring up a cloud of dust. Now or never.

Nicholas shifted Arisilde over, propping him against

the wall. He squeezed out past him and knelt next to the revenant, searching around for a fragment of rock with a relatively sharp edge. The fay whirled around, alerted by some faint sound. Nicholas froze, gritting his teeth, cursing the persistence of the damn thing.

It growled low but couldn't seem to pinpoint his location. After a moment it turned back to digging at the side of the pit, slinging a small boulder out of the way in its annoyance.

The noise of the fall masked the slight sound as Nicholas rolled the revenant over. He used the fragment to tear the belly open and had to swallow hard to keep from gagging at the stench released.

The fay turned and came back toward this side of the pit, its head cocked, as if certain it heard or sensed movement. Nicholas slipped the empty pistol out of his pocket and forced it into the revenant's body cavity.

The fay moved closer, the low growl rising again. Nicholas waited until it was almost just below, then tipped the revenant off the ledge.

The fay dove for it instantly, clawing at the rock as the revenant bounced down the slope. Nicholas scrambled back into the shelter of the crevice thinking, *Come on, you greedy bastard, go after it.*

The fay pounced as the revenant rolled to the end of the lowest ledge and crammed the battered corpse into its maw.

Nicholas crouched against the wall next to Arisilde's limp body. *There now.* If it worked at all. If it worked in time.

Madeline caught up with Ronsarde and Halle only a little further into the catacomb. The Inspector was leaning heavily against one of the crypts. His eyes were closed but the lids fluttered as he fought to return to consciousness.

"He keeps blacking out," Halle explained as she climbed over some broken steps to join them. "He's had a bad knock on the head."

"We're all right for the moment but we've got to keep

moving.'' Madeline was trembling so hard from fear and their precipitate flight that her teeth were chattering. She was relieved Halle was too occupied to take notice of it. She lifted Ronsarde's other arm and stretched it across her shoulders to get them moving again. This was going to be difficult. She was strong for a woman but she couldn't carry Ronsarde all the way out of here, even with Halle's help.

''The sphere destroyed that thing that was coming after us?'' Halle asked as they made their way forward.

''It stopped it. I don't think it destroyed it.'' Madeline was still having difficulty believing what she had seen with her own eyes. The sphere must be alive to some extent. She certainly hadn't told it to lay a trap for Macob, if Macob that thing had been, luring him close enough and then letting go full blast. That had been no accident; this little metal ball had exhibited human cunning. ''Nicholas should be up ahead of us here somewhere,'' she added. She only hoped he was still searching for her in the catacomb or the tunnel and hadn't decided to turn around and look for her back in the cave. ''I've been lost for a bit.''

''How did you know where to look for us?''

''Nicholas deduced it.'' Even in the bad light, she could tell Halle's face was strained and ill. ''How were you brought here?''

''I'm not entirely certain,'' he admitted. ''We were in the sorcerer Damal's apartment in the Philosopher's Cross and I had just started to examine him. He still appeared to be unconscious though it seemed to be a natural sleep and not the state he was in before. Then something struck the outer wall of the building. I was knocked unconscious. We woke as prisoners where you found us and we've seen no one except the ghouls. Wait. Your grandmother and the Parscian Isham, they were in the apartment,'' Halle said suddenly. He stopped, as if ready to turn back to search for them. ''Were they—''

''My grandmother's dead.'' The dim light had given her a wonderful headache; she wanted to rub her eyes but with the sphere to hold onto and Ronsarde to support, she had no free hand. She didn't want to think about Madele's death. "Isham was badly injured but Nicholas had him taken to a physician, that was a few hours ago." At least she thought so; her watch had been pinned inside a coat pocket and been torn loose in one of the near-misses. She had lost it and all track of time.

"I'm sorry. Your grandmother—"

She shook her head, warning him off. "Nicholas thinks this sorcerer, this man who's doing this to us, is actually Constant Macob himself, or his ghost or shade or something."

"Can that be possible?" Halle muttered, then shook his head, annoyed at himself. "What am I saying? Of course it's possible."

"Damn sorcery," Ronsarde said suddenly, in a weak voice. "Didn't consider that as a valid hypothesis. Tell Valiarde—"

"Sebastion, save your strength," Halle said urgently. "You can't tell him anything until we get out of here."

"Tell Valiarde," Ronsarde continued stubbornly, ignoring the interruption, "that Macob isn't mad. Conclusion I came to, studying the historical accounts. Halle, you know—"

"No, I don't agree, and you know it," Halle said, exasperated. "I think he is mad, but it's a strange sort of madness. Madmen are often cunning, but not so deliberate. Macob's madness didn't—that is, hasn't hampered his intelligence."

"And he's dead already, so killing him is problematical anyway," Madeline said. "It's all right, Inspector, we'll tell Nicholas."

Ronsarde stopped suddenly, let go of Halle, and with startling strength grabbed the collar of Madeline's coat. Ferocity lending force to his voice, he said, "Tell Valiarde that in my study in my apartment on Avenue Fount, under the loose tile on the right side of the hearth, there is a packet of documents. He must see them."

Halle recaptured Ronsarde's arm and urged him to move. The Inspector seemed to be losing consciousness again. He added, "I wanted him to see. . . . Not pertinent to this matter but he must know after this is over. . . ."

"Do you know what he means?" Madeline asked Halle.

"No." Halle shook his head. "I just hope we last long enough to find out."

They made their way back through the catacomb with what seemed painful slowness, but fear kept them moving. There were three ghouls waiting for them at the entrance to the tunnel that led to the sewers but the sphere disposed of them almost desultorily, as if it had faced a greater challenge and now found ghouls rather passé. *Next you'll be talking to it*, Madeline thought wearily.

The tunnel was difficult until Ronsarde woke abruptly again. He was able to lean on Halle, allowing Madeline to light one of the candle stubs she had in her pocket so they could see past the point where the ghost-lichen died out. As they made their way closer to the sewers the rising stench, fetid and familiar, was a welcome sign that they were almost home.

They reached the rotted door into the old sewer channel and Madeline was about to help Ronsarde through when they heard voices.

She and Halle stared at each other in the dim candlelight. "Crack got through," she whispered hopefully. But she didn't hear Nicholas's voice.

"I'll make certain," Halle said. "You wait here with Sebastion."

"All right." They eased Ronsarde down so he could sit against the wall and she handed Halle the candle. "Don't go too far. There are branchements and turns and you'll get lost."

Halle made his way up the broken path toward the voices and she sat next to Ronsarde. After a moment, she thought that was a mistake. Her legs ached from climbing and running in the damp chill, her muscles were strained from lifting Ronsarde and her arms were sore from holding the sphere so tightly. She leaned her head back against the filthy wall and closed her eyes; she wasn't sure she could get up again.

The candlelight faded as Halle moved further away and they sat for a moment in the pitch dark. Then the sphere began to emit a dim, golden glow. Madeline stared down at it. The color of the light was very like flame, as if it was imitating the departed candle. She glanced up to meet Ronsarde's eyes. He was still conscious and his gaze was sharper. He smiled and said, "Clever gadget."

She heard the voices again then, louder this time. She recognized Doctor Halle, who sounded relieved, and the person replying to him was. . . . "That's Reynard!" she said to Ronsarde.

"Doctor, is the Inspector with you?" someone called out.

"And Captain Giarde," Ronsarde said, identifying the voice and sounding pleased. "Success may be at hand."

But where's Nicholas, Madeline wondered. *He must have been far ahead of us.* If he had realized she was behind him he would have turned back to look for her and they would have encountered him in the catacomb or the tunnel. If he was ahead of her, she realized coldly. *But if he was behind me. . . .*

The voices came closer as Halle led the rescuers toward them. "Yes, Crack told us," Reynard was saying. "Nicholas and Madeline are with you?"

Halle's answer was inaudible but she heard Reynard reply, "No, he's not with us, are you sure—"

More confused answers, then Halle saying distinctly, "But Arisilde Damal, the injured sorcerer, was taken prisoner also. He and Valiarde must still be down there."

The man Ronsarde had identified as Captain Giarde said, "Fallier and the other sorcerers are planning to collapse the underground chambers. If there's anyone left down there—"

"You can't leave them there," Reynard said, sounding furious. "You wouldn't know where the bastard was without Nic's help. I'll go down after him."

"I'll show you the way," Halle said.

"No." That was Giarde again. "We'd just lose the

lot of you. I can hold Fallier off, give them time to get out, but if we wait too long this necromancer will escape—"

More protests. It sounded as if Giarde had a great many men with him and Reynard and Halle were trapped among them. Madeline looked at Ronsarde.

The Inspector's expression was tired and vexed. He said, "I wish I could accompany you, my dear. You are a resourceful woman but a little assistance never hurts." He let out his breath. "I can contrive, however, to delay any possible pursuit."

"Thank you," she whispered. She leaned over and kissed him on the cheek, then got to her feet. "I'll be back."

As she stepped back through the door and into the tunnel, she heard Ronsarde whisper, "I hope to God you will."

21

Nicholas watched the fay stalk back and forth, clawing at its belly. It had lost interest in searching for them but refused to go away and perish somewhere else. The lost time was grating; he only hoped Crack or Madeline had reached the surface by this point to carry the word of Macob's whereabouts to the help that was, theoretically at least, waiting for them.

Crushed back into the crevice as they both were, it was hard to tell if Arisilde was showing any more signs of returning consciousness. If he didn't wake soon, Nicholas had no idea what to do with him. He couldn't leave him here in this condition. With the giant fay eliminated there was no telling what other inhabitants of this place would emerge and if Arisilde wasn't conscious enough to defend himself, it would be murder to leave him here. "What am I going to do with you?" Nicholas muttered to himself.

"Might I move now?"

The voice was a weak whisper and plaintive, but as the first time Arisilde had spoken in days, it was entirely welcome. Nicholas could have shouted in relief but he confined himself to saying, "Yes, but slowly. It's still down there." He pressed back against the wall to give him room. "How do you feel?"

"Rather . . . horrid, actually." Arisilde managed to sit up a little. He blinked as if even the dim light of the ghost-lichen was too much for him. His face was terribly drawn and gaunt, but he was alive. "Rather confused, too."

"Do you know where you are?"

"I thought I was at home." Arisilde peered at the fay pacing below. It gave a high-pitched shriek of anger and clawed at its belly again, leaving wide tears in the putrid flesh. "Oh, my. That's awful, isn't it?"

"Mildly, yes," Nicholas agreed. "It's a fay or what's left of one. I tried to poison it but since the creature is already dead it's taking much longer than I thought."

Arisilde greeted this speech, which must have sounded quite mad, with a complacent nod. "I see, yes. Most inconvenient. Now, why are we here again?"

"The necromancer I was searching for enspelled you with a corpse ring, do you remember that?"

Arisilde's vague gaze suddenly sharpened. "Someone came to the door. Isham was out so I went to open it. There was a man, he handed me something. . . . Oh, I'm a fool. That's the oldest trick in the world." He shook his head, his expression rueful. "He handed me a ring and said he wanted me to tell him where the person who had owned it was now. I said I'd work on it. He even paid me. People around the neighborhood bring me those sorts of commissions all the time. The ring probably had a charm, a simple, subtle one, that suggested I put it on. Where was I wearing it?"

"On your foot, oddly enough," Nicholas said. Arisilde's opium habit must have left him open to this. His power was proof against open assaults but his failing senses left him vulnerable to more subtle, indirect attacks.

"That's quite a good idea, actually; Isham would have checked my hands. I don't remember putting it on at all. But if I was under the influence of a charm, I wouldn't." He sighed. "I failed you, Nicholas."

"We can assign blame later, Ari." Nicholas was thinking hard. Macob must have put the ring back on Arisilde and simply dumped his body down here with the unwanted revenants. Well, it was hardly surprising. He knew Macob had no respect for life.

Nicholas considered the fay again. It seemed increasingly distracted and was staying at the far end of the pit. They might be able to make it back up to the opening into the fissure and from there get through to the other side of the pit and reach the way out. "Can you stand?"

Arisilde frowned in concentration and tried to pull his legs up. With some effort he managed to bend his knees, wincing in pain. "Not yet. I'll keep trying. Is there a time constraint?"

"We can't afford to wait long." Nicholas drew a sharp breath. With so much time in an unconscious state Arisilde must be unbelievably stiff. He said, "Listen: this necromancer is Constant Macob and he's been dead nearly two hundred years. He has what's left of his corpse and he seems to be using one of the spheres—"

"Macob, the Necromancer, himself? That's not good," Arisilde interrupted, startled. Then his gaze suddenly sharpened. "Is the corpse intact?"

"No, he's missing the skull," Nicholas answered. The expression on Arisilde's face was not encouraging. "What does it mean?"

"He's trying to bring himself back to life, that much is obvious. But how?" Arisilde frowned into the distance. "The planets are in entirely the wrong configuration for that sort of—Wait, I wasn't unconscious for months, was I?"

"No, no. Only a few days."

"That's all right, then." Arisilde paused in thought again, then asked urgently, "You said he had one of the spheres? That Edouard made? Which one?"

"One that Ilamires Rohan helped him with. Doctor Octave blackmailed Rohan for it."

"Rohan helped Edouard? I didn't even realize. . . ." As the knowledge sank in, Arisilde swore incredulously. "That bastard Rohan. He didn't even offer to testify in Edouard's behalf. I knew he was a hypocrite but—"

"I know," Nicholas said, his mouth set in a grim line.

Arisilde ran a trembling hand through his hair, as if trying to get his thoughts in order. "What does the sphere do?"

"I don't know, Ari. I was hoping you could tell me." Nicholas's voice rose a bit in exasperation and he lowered it hastily, glancing at the fay to make sure he hadn't drawn its attention. It didn't look in their direction, entirely occupied with the iron in its belly.

"No, I haven't the faintest idea," Arisilde assured him. "I suppose it was an early effort. Rohan, hmm? Well, as long as it isn't that last one that Edouard made, the one I helped with. Even he thought that one was a bit much." Arisilde nodded to himself. "Now if this necromancer had that one, we would be in a real difficulty." He looked up and saw the expression on Nicholas's face. "Oh."

"It was the largest of the three at Coldcourt, with the copper-colored metal case?" Nicholas asked, reluctantly.

"Yes, that's it." Arisilde looked worried. "He does have it?"

"No, Madeline has it. She came down here with me but we were separated and she escaped. At least, I hope she did." Frustrated, Nicholas looked back at the fay. "I haven't had any chance to search for her."

"As long as this Macob doesn't have it. I don't suppose we should ever have made that one in the first place, but it's a trifle late for regrets, isn't it?"

"What does it do?" Nicholas demanded. He was glad Arisilde wasn't dead but he was also ready to bang the sorcerer's head against the nearest rock.

"It's hard to say." Arisilde gestured earnestly. "A little bit of everything, I should think, from the spells Edouard wanted me to cast for it. At the time I think he knew more about sorcery than I did, for all he was never able to perform it. The spheres were meant to allow anyone to cast spells, even a person with no talent and no ability for magic. It was all based on Edouard's theories about how the etheric plane worked. He thought everyone had some ability to sense the presence of magical phenomena—"

"Even if it wasn't on a conscious level. Yes, he told me." Nicholas had heard it all at length before Edouard died. Edouard had believed that it was only the people who had a heightened perception of magic, who could consciously sense it, who could learn to become sorcerers, but that everyone had some awareness of it. "And Rohan said the spheres will only work for someone who has some talent for magic, despite what Edouard wanted."

"Yes, Edouard was disappointed. They never turned out quite right. But Madeline has some talent, she should be able to control it. If she can give it some direction, it can do the rest." Arisilde looked thoughtful. "This Macob—he's dead, you say? He couldn't possibly remain on the plane of the living and use his powers without some sort of assistance. If there's no other sorcerer in the matter, then it must be the sphere he has that's keeping him here. If Macob used it the way it was meant to be used, it would be as if he had another living sorcerer performing spells but completely under his domination. If he manages to force his spirit to reinhabit his body, he won't need the sphere anymore but it would make him . . . well, terribly powerful." Arisilde said this apologetically, as if it was somehow his fault. "The spheres seem to give the bearer, in some measure at least, the power of the sorcerer who helped create it. I put all my best spells into that last one I helped Edouard with. Somehow, all that machinery inside it, those gears and things, remember the spells. Edouard explained it to me but I never fully understood."

"So if Macob brings himself back to life, the sphere he has now will give him all the same power of Ilamires Rohan, Master of Lodun, plus his own not inconsiderable abilities?"

"Well, yes."

"And if he gets his hands on the sphere Madeline has now, he will also have your power?"

"Well, yes, but not as I am now, you know. It will be as I was then, when I made the sphere. Before I had all my little difficulties, you know."

Nicholas was almost too distracted to notice that this was the first time Arisilde had ever referred, even obliquely, to his opium addiction. He said, "As you were then, at the height of your power?"

"Well, yes."

"But how can he possibly retrieve the skull from the palace? It's protected by the wards. Except. . . ."

"Yes?"

Nicholas shook his head, frustrated. "Macob was apparently a genius at creating new spells. With all these dead fay around—"

Arisilde was nodding. "Yes, I wouldn't put it past him to have thought of some way around the wards."

For a moment it was tempting to concentrate on finding the others and escaping, leaving Fallier and Giarde to deal with Macob. But that was a fool's choice; if Macob returned himself to life, he would not suffer anyone to live who had interfered with him. *And I'll be damned if I let him use Edouard's work to do it.* Nicholas swore under his breath. "Whatever he means to do I have to stop him." He had the germ of an idea but he wasn't sure if it was even remotely possible. He dug the corpse ring out of his pocket. "Just how subtle is this spell, Ari? Could it fool Macob?"

Ari studied the ring, eyes narrowed. "It might. It's a very good spell, meant to fool a strong sorcerer. And if Macob was distracted, perhaps by working other difficult spells. . . ."

Their eyes met. Arisilde's gaze was worried. He said, "You would have to be careful."

"Careful? You mean suicidally rash, don't you?" Nicholas asked, smiling lightly. "Will you be all right if I leave you here? There are ghouls and the revenants you told me about. Can you defend yourself?"

"Oh, I'll be fine." Arisilde gestured reassuringly, as if Nicholas was leaving him in a cafe on the Boulevard of Flowers and there might be some difficulty in securing a cab. "Do go on. I'll follow as soon as I can."

Nicholas eased out of the crevice and stood cautiously, keeping one eye on the fay. It was on the far side of the pit still, reeling drunkenly and snarling at shadows, well past taking notice of him.

"Nicholas," Arisilde said urgently. "Take care. He is a powerful sorcerer, but you know, I do think you're much better at scheming things than he is."

Nicholas had no time to sort that statement out. He nodded to Arisilde and started to climb the wall.

Nicholas had considered the possibility that the ghouls would still be waiting for him up in the tunnel, he just had no notion of what to do about it. With the giant fay still stalking distractedly around, it was impossible to search the pit for another exit.

He made it through the fissure into the other section of the pit and back to the ledge at the base of the slope. The crack at the top of it was visible as a darker patch in the rough stone above and there didn't seem to be any ghouls actually peering down at him from it. He started to climb.

His shoulders were aching by the time he reached the top and his fingers bleeding through what was left of his gloves. It was too dark in this tunnel to tell if there were ghouls lying in wait or not but he couldn't hear anything moving around. He dragged himself up over the lip of the crevice and collapsed onto the floor of the tunnel, breathing hard. If the ghouls came now, there wouldn't even be a struggle. It was a moment before Nicholas could roll over and get to his feet.

He had to cross the crevice again to get out of the tunnel, but after a little fumbling around in the dark he found the far side had a large enough lip that he could edge along it with only the minor danger of pitching head first back down into the pit. That accomplished, he felt along the wall until the relatively brighter light of the ghost-lichen in the main cave became visible through the tunnel entrance. There he paused, concealing himself in a fold of the wall and trying to get his bearings.

He was on the wrong side of the cave for the catacomb entirely, he realized. The mold-covered walls of the nearest crypts blocked his view of the rest of the cave, but he could tell by the light reflecting off the roof overhead that more torches had been lit, probably around the central crypt. Macob must be preparing himself to act. *I need a view of what's happening over there.*

He worked his way around the edge of the cave back toward the catacomb entrance, climbing over the tumbled remains of broken statues. Reaching the other side, he found a low crypt near the wall where he could get a vantage point. He jumped until he caught hold of the stone coping along the roof and hauled himself up. From there he could see the central crypt.

Torchlight lit the miniature battlement and the delicate turrets, threw oddly shaped shadows on the great cracked dome. The dais was empty except for an odd pattern of shadow. *No, not shadow*, Nicholas thought. He felt through his pockets until he found his small spyglass. Looking through it, he could see Octave's servant standing near the doorway into the crypt and on the dais itself. . . . There were dark markings on the light-colored stone, perhaps of soot. Most of the pattern was lost in shadow but he could see enough to know that Macob was preparing for the working of a spell.

Displaced pebbles struck rock behind him and Nicholas twisted around, violently startled. There was a dark form on the ledge above just below the walkway, but it was gesturing agitatedly at him. "Madeline," he breathed. He didn't know whether to be relieved that she was all right or angry that she hadn't gotten herself out of here yet. He stood and made his way to the edge of the roof.

Madeline jumped and he steadied her as she landed, pulling them both down into a crouch. Their embrace was cut short when something hard and metallic thumped Nicholas in the ribs. He held her at arm's length and saw she had the sphere in a makeshift sling around her neck.

"We've been looking for you," she said breathlessly.

"We?"

Madeline glanced down at the sphere and shook her head in distraction. "I mean, I've been looking for you. I found Ronsarde and Halle and led them out."

"Good. What are you doing back here?"

"I came to look for you, what do you think? We have to get out of here now. Fallier is going to collapse the cave."

Nicholas shook his head impatiently. "That won't work. Macob knows we sent Crack for help, he knows what Fallier will do. He probably wants them to destroy this place. Then everyone will assume that he's dead and he will be free to do whatever he wants."

"Nicholas, we have to leave now," Madeline persisted.

"I found Arisilde." He told her about the pit and the corpse ring. "He's said that Macob can bring himself back to life. With the sphere Macob already has, he could be more powerful than ever before."

"Dammit, Nicholas." Madeline swept her hair back angrily. Her face was badly bruised, he could tell that even in this light. She let out her breath in resignation. "And Macob will just come after us again, won't he? We know too much about him."

"He won't take all this interference kindly, no."

"I saw him, when I found Ronsarde and Halle and we were escaping," she said, sounding as if the memory wasn't pleasant. "No, he's not going to give up on us. Well then, just what are we supposed to do?"

"I have a plan." This was true. "I just don't know whether it will actually work or not." This, unfortunately, was also true.

"What is it?"

"Arisilde said you should be able to control the sphere if you try. He said if you give it the direction, it would do the rest. I need you to make it hide you with an illusion, one so strong Macob can't see through it or even know that it's there."

"But—"

"No, listen to the rest. Get inside that large crypt, where Macob has his body. Put the corpse ring on it, but not on a finger, on a rib." He only hoped Arisilde was right and that Macob would fail to detect his own spell until it was too late. "Then when he reinhabits his body—"

"The spell on the ring will take effect and he'll be a living corpse, like Arisilde was." She nodded impatiently. "And it will be inside him so a surgeon would have to remove it. But Nicholas, any sorcerer can see through an illusion. Even a layman can see through one if they know it's there, and Macob is going to be on the lookout for something like that."

"I know. I'll distract him."

"How? By getting yourself killed?"

"There are some things up in the catacomb I can use to make a very suitable distraction."

"That paraffin that was leaking down the wall?"

"Yes." It was hard to read her expression in the dim light, but she didn't sound very happy. "Can you make the sphere hide you with an illusion?"

"I know the spell. Madele taught it to me years ago. If the sphere works like Arisilde says. . . ." She looked away. "I think so." She let out her breath. "But I don't like it."

"It's only the once," Nicholas said, and felt like a traitor. How many days ago had he said he would never ask her to use her magic if she didn't want?

"Just don't get killed and make it for nothing," she said dryly. "Here, take the pistol. I won't have a free hand for it."

While she was digging the spare bullets out of her pockets, Nicholas considered telling her not to linger here if his trick didn't work. He wanted her to run and not wait for Arisilde or himself. But he knew it would only be so much wasted breath since she would do whatever she liked, anyway. Annoyed at the truth of this realization, he said, "Let's just get it over with, then."

Madeline nodded, but as Nicholas started to stand, she grabbed a handful of his hair and kissed him. It was a hasty embrace and Nicholas lost his balance and sat down hard. Madeline let him go and crawled to the edge of the roof, swung over and dropped to the ground with agile ease. Nicholas whispered after her, "Don't move until the distraction starts. And don't be so damn sentimental."

* * *

Madeline crouched behind a crypt, near the dais but out of sight of it. She leaned back against the mold- and filth-encrusted stone and pulled the sphere free of the sling. She held it in her lap and felt it hum gently. *All right, here we go*, she thought. She closed her eyes and began the spell of avoidance. She felt nothing. The incantation ran through her mind with no rush of power, no sense of gathering forces. *It's been too long*, she thought, as she finished the spell and there was nothing in her head but her own thoughts. *Too long for me.* Madele had been right of course, when she had told her that if Madeline didn't use her skills she would lose what little power she had. She opened her eyes and started to stand.

She froze when dust moved on the floor around her, pushed outward as if by some unfelt breeze. *Holy.* . . . Spells of avoidance wouldn't cause physical displacement. She concentrated, trying to get some hint as to what the sphere had done. For an instant she had it. She was surrounded by not just a spell of avoidance, but by obscura major and minor and various nothing-to-see-here charms, a complex mesh of them. *Damn, I wish we had known to try this before. It would have come in handy. Madele would have loved this.* . . .

Standing in that maze of power, feeling it under her control even though it was only through the sphere, she understood suddenly that Madele must have cared about magic with the same intensity as she herself cared about acting. Madeline had always seen power as a means to an end and it had been an end she was not particularly interested in achieving; she had never thought of it as an art in itself.

She stepped carefully out of the shelter of the crypt, moving to a better vantage point. If she was lucky, Macob would never know what hit him.

Nicholas found a place to climb back up to the walkway and from there found the entrance to the catacomb again. After searching through the layers of stinking debris, he dug out two wheels that he had noticed earlier, half-buried under rusted metal and rotten wood. He was in luck and they were mostly intact. While they wouldn't support a wagon's weight anymore, they would do well enough for what he had in mind.

He filled the bottle he had used to hold the Parscian perfume oil with the paraffin leaking down the wall and then quickly lashed the two wheels together with a length of rusted chain. His outer coat was too sodden with sewer water to be of use, so he wound his jacket through the spokes of the wheel, along with some fragments of wood and rags from one of the open crypts. After the spare bullets Madeline had given him were inserted into it at intervals and it was soaked with more of the paraffin, it was ready.

Nicholas dragged the wheel down the steps and back to the balcony. Crouching in the shelter of its broken balustrade, he checked the revolver one last time. He had saved back enough bullets to reload it once, but no more. The diversion needed to be as diverting as possible and if it didn't work, he doubted there would be time for him to reload.

He took a cautious look over the balustrade and saw there was more activity on the dais. The remaining ghouls were collected on the crypt roof, like a brooding flock of particularly ugly doves. Down on the dais were two men, the one he had fought with earlier and a slighter, blond man, who must be Octave's second missing servant. The larger man was simply standing near the circle drawn on the stone like the will-less automaton he had become. The blond servant disappeared into one of the pockets of shadow near the wall of the central crypt, then limped back into the light, carrying what appeared to be an old metal urn. He climbed the steps of the dais and set it down just inside the boundary of the outer circle, then backed away.

So Macob was making his preparations though there was no obvious sign of the necromancer's presence. This would be easier if Arisilde was here, but there was no sign of him, either. Nicholas felt a pang of worry, wondering if the sorcerer had been struck ill again or attacked by something in the pit, but there was no time to look for him now.

Staying in a crouch, he rolled his wheel down the walkway until he reached the point in the gallery where it curved around and the balustrade dropped away. From here it led straight along the wall to the top of the pile of rubble that had been the stairs leading down to the dais. He crouched, bracing the wheel against the last steady baluster, and fished in his pocket for his matchbox.

Below on the dais, the torches flickered and almost died. The blond servant flinched and stared around but the other man didn't react; he simply stood there, numb and motionless. When the torches surged back to life, Constant Macob was at the head of the dais.

The shadows seemed to cling to the necromancer's coat like a living cloak of darkness and his hat brim concealed his features. He took two carefully measured paces forward and stood before the circle. The blond man made a sudden run for the edge of the dais as if he meant to bolt for safety through the ruined crypts. Macob lifted a hand and three of the ghouls leapt off the roof of the crypt and bounded after him.

They caught the fleeing man at the bottom of the dais steps and dragged him back up, struggling and shouting. Macob pointed at him without turning his head and the man's cries choked off to silence. The ghouls dropped him and retreated back to the roof, leaving their captive to lie in an unmoving heap on the dais.

This ceremony, whatever it was, was obviously going to require a sacrifice. *I suppose it's poetic justice*, Nicholas thought, bracing his wheel in the middle of the walkway and squinting along its path. If the man had helped Macob trap his earlier victims, then he surely knew what was in store for himself. Nicholas jammed the perfume bottle containing the paraffin between one of the spokes and the chain and removed the stopper. Madeline must be moving around down there somewhere, but Macob hadn't reacted to her presence. But to reach the inside of the main crypt she would have to cross the torchlit area between the entrance to it and the dais and no matter how powerful Arisilde's sphere, this was her first time to do such a thing and she would need help.

The other servant, who had remained as unmoved throughout all this as one of the statues, now stepped forward. He moved across the dais toward the edge of the circle and stooped to pick something up. Nicholas caught the gleam of light on edged metal and knew it was a knife. It must have been one of the objects the other servant had carried up in preparation for the spell. *Nicely ironic touch*, Nicholas thought, *to force the man to lay out the preparations for his own murder*. But he doubted Macob had even considered that aspect, or at least not consciously; the necromancer would maintain a façade of indifference over his enjoyment of his violence.

Macob didn't appear to be doing anything but the casting of a spell like this might not appear like much to a layman's eyes. Most of the work would be taking place in Macob's mind. The large servant had reached the other man and bent over him and Nicholas judged Madeline had had enough time to get into position.

He stood and gave the wheel a push.

The two wheels lashed together gave the contraption some stability and it rolled down the walkway without wobbling overmuch. Before it reached the slope and gained speed, Nicholas struck a match and tossed it into the paraffin trail left by the open bottle. The oil caught readily and the flames travelled swiftly along it to the source.

The oily rags caught and the whole mass went up just as the wheel reached the part of the gallery where it sloped down to the wrecked stairs.

The sound must have caught Macob's attention. His head jerked toward the gallery. The ghouls ran along the roof of the crypt, leaping down from it, but the wheel bounced down the stairs and landed on the dais near the edge of the circle. It spun and fell on its side and the ghouls scattered back from the flames. Behind them, Nicholas thought he glimpsed a dark figure run across the lighted face of the crypt toward the door. Macob stood rigidly, fists clenched, glaring at the burning wheel and the shrieking ghouls. The servant who had been about to kill his comrade started back, shaking his head, looking around in bewilderment.

Nicholas was already running back along to the nearest break in the balustrade. He scrambled down over the rock pile to the cave floor. He had thought about firing at the dais to increase the confusion but the last thing he needed to do at this point was accidentally shoot Madeline; she was going to have enough trouble when the flames reached the bullets embedded in the packing in the wheel.

Nicholas ran down past the crypts, coming out in the open area before the dais just as the first bullet went off. With another nice touch of irony it almost struck him, tearing through his coat sleeve and ricochetting off the stone wall behind him. Nicholas dived away as other bullets struck the crypts, the floor, the dais. Ghouls shrieked louder, scattering at the onslaught.

It should only take Madeline a moment to slip into the crypt, put the ring on the corpse's rib, and slip out and back into the shadows. Nicholas got to his feet and bolted down one of the paths between the crypts, hoping the ghouls would chase him now that they had seen him, leaving the way clear for Madeline.

The ghouls were running all right, but in all directions, confused and terrified by the fire and the popping explosions. Nicholas laughed and ducked down another pathway. Then something grabbed him by the back of the neck. He tried to wrench away but he was caught in the grip of an irresistible force. The scene in the street near Fontainon house flashed through his mind: Octave in the grip of that towering, terrifying figure, shaken and cast down like a child's toy puppet. Then he saw the nearest wall coming toward him and the blow was like being struck by a train.

He didn't lose consciousness though the world fluttered in and out of existence and everything seemed set at an odd angle. Some snatches of reality were more real than others: the roughness of the stone he tried to grab onto as he was dragged past, the bruising impact on the bottom step of the dais.

At the top he came back to himself enough to recognize the large servant leaning over him. He took a wild swing at him, landing a blow on the man's jaw, but the return punch knocked him over backward. He struggled to push himself up but the man grabbed his shoulder and shoved him down and he met the rough surface of the dais face first. He had a confused view of Macob looking down at him and struggled to sit up. He was pushed down and held with a knee in his back and despite struggling and cursing he couldn't prevent his wrists being tightly bound.

The weight left his back and Nicholas rolled over and managed to sit up. The ropes were rough and felt new and strong; he might work his hands loose eventually but not soon enough.

Macob was looking down at him, his hat brim shadowing his expression. The necromancer seemed more solid than he had before and there was an air about him like the breath from an open grave, detectable even in this place of damp and cold and fetid odors. He said, "It wouldn't have mattered if you had run away. I would have found you."

"I know," Nicholas assured him. "You're predictable that way."

Macob was already turning away, his form wavering, drifting like smoke, then rematerializing into solidity as he stepped back to the edge of the circle. Nicholas worked at the ropes though he knew it was hopeless. *This is damnably embarrassing.* He looked at the servant who was standing nearby, staring off into space, his eyes red-rimmed and empty. The other man still lay on the dais, motionless except for the rise and fall of his breath.

Macob must have the two men completely under his control though how, Nicholas had no idea. He had never heard of a spell that could enslave the human mind in such a way. But Macob had used drugs to help render his victims suggestible; this might be any combination of drugs, mental suggestion, and spells.

Macob lifted a hand. The servant retrieved the knife where it had fallen and moved woodenly to where his comrade still lay insensible on the stone. No, not insensible, Nicholas saw. The man's eyelids were fluttering. He must be aware of exactly what was happening.

From this close an observation point, Nicholas could see dust stirring within the circle, moved by the invisible forces Macob was drawing into it. The movement centered on the urn and from the dust pattern it was as if the currents of power were spiralling down into it.

Macob gave no outward signal but there was a sudden strangled cry. Nicholas twisted around to see the servant grab his former comrade by the shoulder and stab him in the chest. Blood welled and the man clutched helplessly at the protruding blade. The other servant straightened, still no expression on his face. In the circle the urn was trembling. It shook violently, fell on its side, and started to spin.

Over the clatter of the metal urn, Nicholas realized he was hearing something else. Something familiar. He turned his head, pretending to be wincing away from the sight of the man bleeding to death, trying to hear it more clearly. It was the humming, clicking whir the sphere made when it was in the presence of inimical magic. Nicholas swore under his breath. Madeline must be close, only a few steps away.

The urn was still spinning but now a dark gray substance was pouring out of it. It wasn't dust or ash or at least not anymore; it streamed out in a solid mass, spiralling up until it made a spinning column almost five feet high. Now there was a shape forming out of it, as if a statue was buried in the center and the gray sand was streaming away to reveal it.

The sound of the sphere was closer and Nicholas watched Macob carefully for any sign of awareness. The necromancer was staring at the circle and the thing forming out of the gray sand, all his attention apparently caught by it. One of the ghouls crouched near Nicholas sidled away, its mad eyes empty of anything like thought, as if some unseen force had gently nudged it aside. Nicholas took a relieved breath. He had been afraid the sphere would give itself and Madeline away if it came within striking range of one of the creatures, but either she had managed to restrain it or it knew what it was about. Nicholas sat up a little more, holding his bound hands out from his back. She must be almost there.

Then Macob turned toward him and he saw the gleam in his eye and the cold smile. Nicholas snapped, "He knows, dammit, run."

He heard boots scrape on the stone behind him but it was too late. Macob lifted a hand and light flashed and Nicholas fell away from a searing heat that singed his face. He twisted around to look, heart frozen in fear, but Madeline stood unhurt in the open space below the dais, still holding the sphere. He shouted, "Strike back at him, hurry!"

Madeline's head twitched. He had disturbed her concentration and Nicholas cursed himself for distracting her. Of course, that was what she was trying to do.

Deliberately, Macob moved to the edge of the dais. He was still smiling. He said, "She cannot strike me. The device was only meant for defense."

Madeline and Nicholas exchanged a look. It might be a guess but it explained too much of the sphere's behavior. *And it would be just like Edouard to build in such a stipulation*, Nicholas thought grimly. "He can't attack you either," Nicholas told her. "If he does you can turn his own power against him. Just walk away." Macob could, however, threaten to kill him, but he was rather hoping that aspect of the situation would slip the necromancer's mind.

Madeline must have realized the other point that Nicholas hadn't dared voice aloud. That if she could bring the sphere within range of him, then Macob could hurt neither of them. She leapt forward, made it almost to the last step of the dais before she staggered back as if she had run into an invisible wall. She recovered her balance, swearing loudly.

Macob said, "The barrier is around us." He gestured, indicating Nicholas, the circle and the thing now crouched inside it, the nervous ghouls and the castle crypt, the enslaved servant standing motionless and the man who lay dead in a pool of blood. "It is also purely a work of defense. The sphere will not react."

He turned back to the creature inside the circle. It was a gray, wizened figure, its body human except for clawed hands and three-toed feet. Its head was a triangular wedge with predatory eyes buried in deep sockets. Macob gestured again and the creature disappeared.

"You sent it to the palace," Nicholas said. He was aware of Madeline storming up and down at the bottom of the dais, trying to find a way past the sorcerous barrier. *I'm going to have to do this the hard way,* Nicholas thought. He met Macob's eyes. *You don't think I'm capable of it, do you? You won't suspect anything until it's too late.* "It's a fay but it's already dead, so the wards won't stop it."

"Correct," Macob said. His expression was sane and quiet, almost peaceful. "I will have my life and my work. Everything that was taken from me. You have lost."

"You could say that," Nicholas said. *But you would be wrong. Even the best go wrong. The trick is to be there when it happens.*

In the circle the dead fay winked back into existence with a suddenness that the eye almost refused to accept. Nicholas didn't realize he was actually seeing it until it stepped forward and handed Macob an ivory casket.

Macob opened it, not even bothering to watch as his messenger dissolved back into dust and ashes. The necromancer tossed the casket away and lifted up the object it contained, a yellowed skull with crystals set into the eye sockets. Macob lifted a brow and said, in the first thing close to humor Nicholas had heard from him, "His Majesty Rogere always did have execrable taste."

He turned and Nicholas's heart almost stopped. *God,*

*no, he has to put it with the rest of his bones. He'll see
the ring*, he thought. Then the servant stepped forward
and took the skull from Macob and turned to carry it
into the crypt.

As the man passed inside the dark doorway of the
crypt, Macob looked at Nicholas and said, "I meant to
use him for my final effort but I think it would be better
with both of you."

"Yes, I gathered that, thank you," Nicholas said bit-
ingly, to cover his relief.

The servant returned, climbed the dais again and stood
ready.

Macob turned back toward the circle. He seemed to
be using it as a focus, an anchoring point for the forces
he was mustering. He made no gesture but the servant
moved stiffly toward the body of his late companion,
put his foot on the chest and removed the knife with a
jerk.

Nicholas realized then what had struck him when he
had last looked at Madeline. She had been standing with
her hands in front of her as if she was holding the
sphere, clutching it protectively to her chest. But her
hands were empty.

She had handed it to someone. Someone who had approached the dais unseen, passed through Macob's barrier without alerting him and now crouched nearby,
aided by the relic created by the lost powers of his youth.
Nicholas was never more sure of anything in his life.

A faint whisper, barely a breath in his ear, said,
"When he strikes at you, fall down as if you've been
hit. I'll take care of the rest."

Arisilde's voice. Nicholas whispered, just as softly,
"No."

There was no answer but he felt something brush
against the back of his coat. Arisilde had shifted position. Nicholas drew a deep breath. The last thing he
wanted to do was startle Arisilde, who must be at the
center of a complex web of spells. One strand pulled at
the wrong time and the whole structure might collapse,
even with the sphere's help. He whispered, "If we're to

be rid of him he has to complete this spell.''

Again there was no answer from Arisilde. *If I were him, I'd kill Macob's servant as Macob obviously intended to do before I conveniently turned up, and complete the spell for him that way,* Nicholas thought. *But then, it's a good thing I'm not Arisilde.*

The servant was coming toward him with the knife and everything seemed to happen far more rapidly than it should. Nicholas had no time to brace himself, no time for anything except to flinch back when the blade struck home. He fell backward, a roaring in his ears, a tearing pain in his gut.

A wave of darkness swept over him, then just as abruptly it gave way to bright sunlight. He was in the garden of the house they had lived in when Edouard was working at Lodun, sitting on the bench near the wisteria. Sitting next to him was Edouard himself.

Nicholas looked into his foster father's eyes and for a moment saw the same distance and determination that had marked Macob's gaze.

Edouard smiled, a little ruefully, and said, ''Two sides of the same coin.''

''No,'' Nicholas said. He didn't even have to think about it. ''If you can see the trap, you're not likely to fall into it.''

''Ah.'' Edouard nodded. ''Remember that.''

Somewhere far away there was a scream, compounded of thwarted rage and heartbreaking loss.

''That's done it,'' Nicholas told Edouard, though he couldn't have said what ''it'' was at the moment.

A cloud passed over the sun and the light started to die. Edouard leaned forward and said something else, but the words were hard to hear and his sight was blurred and. . . .

Nicholas opened his eyes. The reality of the cave, the cold, the stink of death, hard stone under his back, was like a blow. His head was in Madeline's lap and Arisilde was leaning over him. There was blood everywhere and his chest ached horribly. He took a breath and it was like being stabbed again.

Arisilde sat back on his heels. "That'll do," he said brightly. "Close, though, wasn't it?"

Madeline's face was bruised and pale, streaked with tears and dirt, her eyes huge and reddened from the smoke. He said, "Madeline?"

She shoved him off her lap. "You bastard! I could kill you."

She sounded serious. After a couple of tries, Nicholas managed to roll into a sitting position. "You're welcome," he said. His voice was hoarse and he cleared his throat. "Help me up."

It took both of them, since Madeline was more overcome than she appeared and Arisilde was scarcely in better case than Nicholas. The body of Macob's last servant lay nearby in a pool of his own blood, his throat slit. He must have done it to himself on Macob's command to increase the power of the spell.

Once Nicholas could stand, he started toward the crypt, Madeline following him.

Macob's body lay on the slab, still wrapped in the rags of its clothing and winding sheet. It had been restored to an appearance of recent death and the flesh, though bloodless and a little withered, was unmarked by time. The eyelids were open, revealing the crystals King Rogere had had embedded in Macob's skull.

Nicholas leaned on the slab and pointed up at the sphere suspended above it. "Get that down, can you?"

One hand on his shoulder to steady herself, Madeline found footholds in the side of the slab and got enough height to reach the hanging sphere. She tore the net open on the second try, managed to catch it, and leapt down.

She handed it to him and Nicholas hefted it thoughtfully. It felt dead like the other two spheres that had been stored in Coldcourt's attic. Cold and silent and motionless. But he would have to make sure.

He put it down and found a loose chunk of stone from the plinth. He hefted the stone thoughtfully, checking its weight, then knelt and steadied the sphere with his free hand. He thought it would take at least several blows; he might not have been surprised if it had proved impossible. But the sphere shattered on the first impact.

Nicholas started back as odd fragments of colored metal scattered everywhere. Sparks of red and blue light splattered across the floor, rolling like marbles until they disappeared into the cracks between the stone flags. He realized there was a white light on his hand, clinging to it like a thick fluid. He was too startled to be worried and it wasn't painful. He shook his hand and the light dissolved into tiny sparks that vanished in the damp air. He thought he heard voices whispering, almost familiar voices. Rohan's? Edouard's? But the sound swelled and died away before he could identify them.

Nicholas stood slowly, looking at the remains of the sphere. It was only so much junk now.

Then he realized he was hearing something, a deep, rumbling reverberation echoing down from one of the tunnels. He looked back at Madeline, frowning, puzzled. He could tell by her expression she had heard it too. She shook her head, baffled.

Then the ground started to shake. They stared at each other, both coming to the same realization at once.

Madeline said, "Dammit, it's—"

"Fallier," Nicholas finished for her. He started toward the door, staggered as the ground suddenly rolled under his feet. Madeline stumbled into him and they caught each other and almost tumbled out the doorway.

Arisilde had been kneeling beside the smudged circle and was just standing up as they came out. He swayed as the ground shuddered again and the last of the pediment cherubs on the crypt across the dais crashed to pieces against the rocks. Madeline paused to grab up their sphere, left forgotten on the dais. Nicholas steadied her as she stood and they plunged toward Arisilde.

He caught them, bracing them against the continuous jolts. His eyes were distant and he was muttering, "The structure is still here, yes, the dissipation hasn't been too great, I think I might. . . ."

Nicholas grabbed the sorcerer's shoulder to steady himself, keeping an arm around Madeline's waist. There was a great crash as the balcony and most of the walkway cracked and folded away from the cave wall, smashing down onto the outermost ring of crypts. With forced patience, he said, "Ari, if you would. . . ."

Madeline tried to comment and choked on the cloud of dust that was rolling over them from the passages that had already collapsed.

"Yes," Arisilde was saying, "I think I might—" A portion of the roof went, striking the crypt with the armored knight and smashing it to pieces. "I think I'd better," Arisilde finished. "Madeline, the sphere, please."

She passed it to him. "Can it stop what Fallier is doing?"

"No." Arisilde held it out, one-handed. "But if this works, it won't have to."

The sphere was reacting as it always did, the wheels inside spinning rapidly. *You would think after holding off Macob that long, it would be tired*, Nicholas thought, foolishly. Obviously the thing didn't get tired. If Macob had managed to take it. . . .

Dust and small fragments of rock rained down on them. Arisilde tossed the sphere into the circle. Madeline cried out in protest but instead of smashing on the stone, the sphere hung in midair, buoyed up by the power gathered there.

It spun faster, inside and out, until Arisilde muttered, "It's not enough."

There was a crack loud enough to be audible over the shaking and crumbling of the walls around them. The sphere exploded, fragments of hot copper showering over them. Nicholas ducked, pulling Madeline closer. Even as the copper fragments struck them and the blue light flared, he felt an iron grip on his arm and Arisilde suddenly dragged them both over the boundary and into the circle.

Nicholas was seized by a sudden vertigo and then the sickening sensation of falling. An instant later he realized he was falling, just as he landed hard on a smooth stone surface. *It didn't work*, he thought. *We're still here*. But the rumble of the collapsing warren was distant, a barely audible echo, and the shaking of the ground had become a mere tremble.

Nicholas pushed himself up on his elbows. It was pitch dark and he could hear water running. He said, "Madeline?"

There was a heartbeat of silence that stretched into eons, then he heard her say, "Unh," or something like it.

A warm white glow sparked and grew, revealing the rounded brick roof and flowing channel of black water of one of the newer sewers. Nicholas was sprawled on the walkway and Madeline was only a few feet away, sitting up and rubbing her head. Arisilde was steadying himself against the wall and the light was coming from a jewel-like orb of spell-light suspended in the air over his head. He looked down at Nicholas and said, "That was close. Two feet to the left and we would have materialized inside the wall."

"Thank you for the precipitate exit, Ari," Nicholas said. His head ached and when he tried to sit up his stomach lurched threateningly. He was thinking he might have to lose consciousness now.

There were voices down the length of the sewer, the yellow glare of lanterns. "Now who's that, I wonder?" Arisilde said, mildly curious.

It was too late, anyway. *Arisilde and Madeline will just have to handle it*, Nicholas thought, and then he did pass out.

22

Nicholas drifted back to awareness believing he was in his own bed. He rolled over under the tangle of blankets and reached out for Madeline. It was her absence that really woke him.

He sat bolt upright. The room was opulent. Heavy oak panelling inlaid with rare woods, a garden scene tapestry old enough to have been hung when Rogere was on the throne, equally antique and priceless Parscian carpets spread casually before the marble mantel as if they were rag rugs. He was in the palace, obviously.

Cursing, he slung the heavy coverlet aside and struggled out of the bed. He was dressed only in a linen nightshirt. As he looked around for his clothes he caught sight of himself in the mirror above the mantel and gave a startled exclamation, thinking it was someone else. Bruises had turned the side of his face a dull green-black and his right eye was puffy and swollen. Yes, he remembered that. *This is bloody wonderful*, Nicholas thought sourly, continuing the search for his clothes. It was going to make assuming a disguise damned awkward.

As he was opening and shutting the array of carved and inlaid cabinets in futile search the door opened to allow in a very correct and disapproving upper servant, attended in turn by a very correct and expressionless footman. "Can I assist you, sir?"

Nicholas straightened up. "My clothes."

"We had to destroy most of them, sir. They were . . . not salvageable."

This was what he should have expected but at the moment it only increased Nicholas's fury. Making sure to enunciate each word clearly, he said, "Then I suggest you get me something to wear."

The servant cleared his throat. He had obviously expected his charge to be somewhat more overawed by his surroundings. "The physicians felt it would not be wise—"

"Bugger the physicians."

They brought him clothes.

Nicholas dressed hastily in the plain dark suit that mostly fit and boots that were a little too small. He wasn't sure if the consternation of the servants was due to his refusal to accept his status as a prisoner, or that they had simply expected him to spend most of the day in bed, moaning. The place in his chest where he had been stabbed felt, and looked like, he had been kicked by a horse.

The servants didn't try to stop him but the majordomo hovered conspicuously as Nicholas stalked through the antechamber and salon and out into a high-ceilinged, pillared corridor. He paused there, noting the presence of two palace Guards who appeared startled to see him.

This might be the King's Bastion or possibly the Queen's. The carved panelling on the walls was certainly old enough and the marble at the base of some of the columns bore cracks and discolorations from age. He started to turn to the majordomo to ask where the hell he was when he saw Reynard coming down the corridor.

Reynard looked in far better shape than Nicholas but his brow was creased in a worried frown. They must have sent for him in the hope that he could exercise some sort of restraint over Nicholas.

"Where's Madeline?" Nicholas asked as soon as he was within earshot.

"She's all right, I've had word from her." Reynard took his arm and drew him behind a pillar where they could speak in comparative privacy, much to the consternation of the majordomo and the Guards. Lowering his voice, Reynard said, ''She left before you and Arisilde were found by the Prefecture. She wasn't sure what our status was with the palace and thought at least one of us should be on the outside.''

Nicholas nodded. ''Good.'' A little of the tightness in his chest eased. *She's alive and she's well out of this.* He tried to get his thoughts together. ''Is Crack here as well?''

''No, I thought it better if no one in authority got too curious about him. Once he gave us the map and told us where you were, I had him hauled off to Doctor Brile's surgery. Fortunately for the men who did the hauling, he was too exhausted to put up much of a struggle. I received word this morning that he's patched up and recovering nicely.''

''And Isham?''

''He was well enough to sit up in bed and demand to know where we were and what had happened Brile said, so he should be all right in a few days. He's a tough old man.'' Reynard hesitated. ''It's too bad Madeline's grandmother—''

''Yes, it is.'' Nicholas looked away; he didn't want to discuss Madele. ''Did Madeline say where she would be?''

''No, but there was something else she wanted me to tell you. This note was in our code, by the way, so it's not as if half the palace knows our business.'' Reynard glanced idly around, unobtrusively noted the location of the Guards and lowered his voice a little more. ''When you were down in the sewer and Ronsarde thought he wouldn't make it out, he told her he had some papers hidden under the floor in his apartment and that she was to make sure you got them. It can't be about Macob or he would have told us before this, surely.''

Nicholas started to reply then stopped, arrested by a sudden memory. A memory of a moment that had never taken place. The garden at the old house at Lodun, and speaking to Edouard while he listened to Macob's scream of rage. The last thing Edouard had said was *if*

I had known it would worry you so much I would have told you about the letter. He said, ''No, I think I know what it's about.''

''Oh.'' Reynard was a little nonplussed. ''Well that's good, anyway, because she went to Ronsarde's apartment last night to retrieve the papers and found the place had been ransacked. Whatever it was, it's gone now.''

Of course it is. Nicholas closed his eyes briefly and swore. *Montesq runs true to type, as usual*. ''Is Ronsarde here?''

''Yes, I was just over there, though I couldn't get in to see him. He's going to recover according to the physicians.''

Nicholas thought hard. An idea was beginning to form, though there were some things he had to make sure of first. He looked at the guards loitering nearby, then turned back to Reynard. ''Are you free to leave or are they watching you as well?''

Reynard hesitated, his expression hard to read. ''Nic, Giarde has offered me a colonel's commission in a cavalry regiment, the Queen's First. As a reward for sounding the alarm over Macob, I suppose.''

''That's a very prestigious regiment,'' Nicholas said. His throat was suddenly dry. He had known Reynard had never wanted to leave the cavalry. He was a military man at heart and would still have been in the service if he hadn't been unfairly driven out.

''Yes, service to the Crown and all that. Ronsarde apparently said some complimentary things, too.'' Reynard cleared his throat.

''Have you accepted it?''

Their eyes met and Reynard's mouth quirked in a smile. ''Not yet.''

''How coy of you.'' Nicholas paused, and suggested cautiously, ''Before you do, can you get some messages out of the palace for me, without anyone knowing?''

''Well, I'm not a Queen's officer yet.''

Ronsarde was ensconced in a suite of rooms in the King's Bastion and there were a number of physicians, upper level palace servants, and officials of the Prefecture in attendance. Nicholas talked his way through the anteroom just as the inner doors opened and the Queen emerged with her train of attendants. Nicholas tried to duck behind a pedestal bearing a bust of some late bishop, but she spotted him and cornered him against a cabinet when he tried to retreat.

"You're awake," she said. She eyed him with that startling directness, then turned to study the china ornaments in the cabinet. "Did you know where it was?" she demanded.

Nicholas was aware he hadn't properly bowed to her but it was impossible now as she had him backed into a corner. At least, he decided, she was armed with neither the cat nor Captain Giarde. "Did I know where what was, your majesty?"

"It was buried back in some salon, in a box no one had looked in for years." She glanced at him to see how he was taking it, and added, "That's odd, isn't it?"

He deduced that she was talking about Macob's skull and that she was not accusing him of knowing its location, but trying to impart it as an intriguing curiosity. "It wasn't as odd as some things that happened, your majesty."

She considered that judiciously, then nodded to herself. "Are you going to see Inspector Ronsarde?"

"Yes, I was."

She looked up at the large and well-armed Queen's Guard who had been standing at her elbow throughout the conversation. He turned and suddenly a path opened through the crowd to the door into the inner chambers of the suite. The Queen stepped back so Nicholas could get past and he made his escape gratefully.

It wasn't until he walked into the bedchamber that Nicholas realized that Ronsarde had been housed in a set of state apartments. The room was about the size of a modest ballroom, with two large hearths with intricately arabesqued marble chimneypieces. The enormous bed, hung with indigo curtains, was set up on a dais and had a daybed at its foot. Ronsarde lay in it, propped up by a mass of pillows with Doctor Halle and another physician standing nearby. Halle was pale and had a large bruise on his forehead but otherwise appeared none the worse for his experience. The Inspector, however, was too red-faced for real health. "I don't want to rest," Ronsarde was saying in a querulous tone. "It's ridiculous that—Ah!" He saw Nicholas and sat up straight. "There you are, my boy."

Nicholas walked to the foot of the dais. He wondered which Kings of Ile-Rien had slept in this chamber. No recent ones, since the furnishings were too far out of date. *Rogere, perhaps?* With the current Queen's sense of humor that was all too possible. He said, "If I could speak to you alone. . . ."

Ronsarde looked at Halle, who sighed and reached for his medical bag. "I suppose it would do more harm to argue with you," Halle said. He gestured the other doctor ahead of him and clapped Nicholas on the shoulder as he passed.

Nicholas stepped up to the bed and as the door shut behind the two physicians, he said, "Your apartment has been vandalized."

"Yes, I know." Ronsarde's welcoming expression faded a little. He said, "It was discovered when Halle sent for some of my things this morning. I knew it wasn't you, since your men would have known where to look." He paused, worried. "Madeline did escape the sewers, did she not?"

"Yes, but she didn't fancy palace hospitality."

Ronsarde let out his breath. "Sit down, at least, and don't stand there like an executioner. I can tell you what was in those documents."

Nicholas sat down on the edge of the bed, aware of the tension in his muscles and a headache like a stabbing needle in his left temple. Ronsarde said, "I never stopped investigating the case surrounding your foster father. I say the case 'surrounding' him, because in some ways I now believe he was incidental to it."

Nicholas nodded. "It was always difficult to keep sight of the fact that necromancy is a magic of divination and of the revealing of secret information.''

"Yes," Ronsarde said, gently. "Count Rive Montesq was Edouard Viller's patron. Count Rive Montesq has been linked, through various circumstantial reports, to blackmail and illicit financial dealings. Two fields of endeavor in which the revelation of secret information would be of great benefit.''

"And Edouard had a device, invented with Arisilde Damal, the most powerful sorcerer at Lodun at that time, that would allow a layman to perform magic.''

"That was intended to allow a layman to perform magic," Ronsarde corrected. "As we know, and as Viller and Damal must have discovered almost immediately, the device did not function quite as anticipated and the wielder had to have some small gift of magic before it would work.''

Nicholas looked down at his hands, avoiding Ronsarde's perceptive gaze. "Montesq must have asked Edouard to use the sphere for necromancy, to discover secrets.''

"Viller refused, not only because it was a violation of law, but because he couldn't use it. He was not a sorcerer. Montesq, being a liar himself, did not believe Viller was telling him the truth. But Montesq wanted the power of the sphere. He is a man who craves power. It must rankle that he has to depend on hired sorcerers for magic." Ronsarde ran his fingers along the edge of the quilt thoughtfully. "He was Viller's patron and it would have been easy for him to obtain keys to the rooms Viller was using for his work. He entered them one night after Viller had gone and he tried to use the sphere.''

"And it didn't work," Nicholas said.

"The failing could not be his, of course, so he tried again. He brought a hired thug, who took a beggar woman off the street for him, and he tried the necromantic spell in Macob's time-honored fashion. And it did not work. So he left and allowed Viller to take the blame.''

Nicholas said nothing.

Ronsarde hesitated, then added carefully, "It helps to

know why something occurred, when one is reconstructing a chain of events, but it can also cloud the issue. You can't be faulted for suspecting that your foster father had actually committed the crime he was executed for. The evidence was overwhelming and he was the only one directly associated with the situation who had a motive to use necromancy. His desire to speak to his dead wife was well documented during the trial. And he wouldn't talk. He wouldn't tell you what had happened. And you knew he was keeping something from you. The power of the 'why' obscured the 'how.' '' His mouth twisted ruefully. ''It can happen to anyone. It has certainly happened to me.''

Nicholas shifted. His shoulders ached from tension. ''What was in the missing documents?''

''They were sent to me a month ago. I was pursuing the matter from the only direction that was left to me: that Edouard Viller knew something detrimental to Montesq and that he did reveal this information to someone before he was executed. To that end I was tracing and contacting his correspondents. I had had no luck. Then I was sent a package of letters from Bukarin, from the daughter of a man Viller had corresponded with for some time, a doctor of philosophy at the Scholars' Guild in Bukarin. The man had died before Viller was executed. The daughter had received my request for information that was directed to her late father and sent me all Viller's letters that she could find among his papers. One was unopened. It had been sent only two days before the dead woman was discovered in Viller's workroom, but had arrived after the man it was addressed to had passed away. In it Viller describes the curious incident of Count Rive Montesq's request that Viller use his device for necromancy.''

''Why didn't he tell me?'' Nicholas said. The words sounded oddly hollow.

''Montesq must have threatened your life to insure Edouard's silence.'' Ronsarde spread his hands. ''It doesn't matter. We have all that we need. Montesq will suffer for his crime.''

"You don't have the letters anymore." Nicholas shook his head. "Montesq knows. He's been preparing all this time while we were pursuing Macob."

Ronsarde's brows drew together.

"He sent Fallier after me and directed Lord Diero of the Prefecture to arrange your arrest," Nicholas explained. "He has known all along. He is well prepared by now to deal with a public accusation."

"It doesn't matter how well he has prepared. It won't help him."

"Don't be naive."

Ronsarde glared at him, but his expression turned worried when Nicholas got to his feet and said, "I assume I'm to be detained here."

"For your own good," Ronsarde said, watching him carefully. "Only until Montesq is formally charged."

Nicholas nodded. "I'm going abroad and my man Crack will be looking for a new position shortly. You need someone to watch your back, who could help with your work. Would you consider taking him on?"

"Crack would certainly be adept at frightening away any old enemies in search of revenge," Ronsarde admitted. "I assume he was innocent of the murder charges against him?"

Nicholas smiled, a trifle ironically. So Crack's real identity hadn't escaped Ronsarde's notice either. "Any in-depth investigation of the extortion branch of Montesq's little empire will reveal that Crack was framed for those charges."

"All right." Ronsarde nodded, then asked sharply, "Where are you going?"

"You're the greatest detective in Ile-Rien," Nicholas said. He put his hands in his pockets and strolled to the door. "Figure it out."

His next visit was to Arisilde, who had been given a smaller suite of rooms on the same floor as Inspector Ronsarde. It was less difficult to obtain entry and Nicholas was soon sitting in the chair next to his bed. "How are you?" he asked.

"Oh, better, I suppose." Arisilde's long pale hands plucked anxiously at the coverlet. "Have you heard anything about Isham? No one here seems to know."

"He's at Doctor Brile's house, awake and recovering." He told Arisilde what Reynard had heard about the Parscian that morning.

"Good." Arisilde sat back against the pillows, more at ease. "I hope he's well soon enough that he can come and see me here. It would be terrible if we all visited the palace and he missed it." His violet eyes turned pensive and he added, "The Queen was here. She's very sweet, but she asked me if I wanted to be Court Sorcerer. I don't think she's very fond of Rahene Fallier. I told her I'd have to think about it. I'm not very reliable, you know."

"You were there when it counted, Ari."

"Well, yes, but. . . . I remembered what I had been going to tell you, you know. That night I went so mad and charged all over the room."

"What was it?"

"I'd looked at those things you brought me. The fabric with the ghost-lichen on it and the remnants of that golem. There was the mark of an unfamiliar sorcerer on them. A very powerful sorcerer. But it went right out of my head until now."

"It wouldn't have mattered, even at the time." Nicholas hesitated a long moment. "I came to tell you that I'm going away for a while."

Arisilde brightened, interested. "Really? Where?"

"Abroad. I'll write you when I get there and let you know. If you like, you and Isham can move into Coldcourt while I'm gone."

"Ah, yes. They told me that Macob didn't leave much of the garret. That would be very nice. And you'd better write Isham instead of me. He'll keep track of the letter better than I would." Arisilde watched him a moment, his gaze sharpening. "Take care of yourself, Nicholas. I don't think I could manage to bring you back from the dead twice."

Nicholas stood, an ironic edge to his smile. "Ari, I hope you won't have to."

They were watching him, of course.

Nicholas sent two messages, one to Madeline and one to Cusard, both in code. Reynard got them out for him easily enough under the cover of an innocuous note to Nicholas's butler Sarasate at Coldcourt, asking him to send one of the footmen with some clothes proper for court attire.

Ronsarde demanded to see him again but Nicholas dodged the Inspector's questions and refused to elaborate on his future plans. He had to endure a court luncheon where the others in attendance all seemed to know his Alsene antecedents and to be present only to get a look at him. It did however provide Reynard, who now had the Queen's favor and Captain Giarde's powerful patronage, with an opportunity to be rude to a number of highly placed courtiers.

Rahene Fallier was also there, with a dour expression somewhat at odds with his usual implacable visage.

After the luncheon, Nicholas slipped away from the men assigned to watch him and followed Fallier. The sorcerer went through the wing that held the galleries and grand ballrooms and into the main hall of the Old Palace, which adjoined the newer, open sections of the structure with the older defensive bastions. At the top of the massive stone spiral stair that led to the King's Bastion, Fallier stopped, turned back, and said, "What do you want?"

Nicholas climbed the last few steps. Fallier's eyes were cold and not encouraging. "We need to talk."

"I think not." Fallier took his gloves out of his pocket and began to pull them on.

"I know you didn't do Rive Montesq's bidding of your own will."

Fallier hesitated, all motion arrested, then finished tugging on his glove. He looked at Nicholas and the expression in those opaque eyes was deadly.

Nicholas leaned one hand on the balustrade. "No, you

don't want to kill me," he said, easily. "I have friends who wouldn't take it kindly. Especially Arisilde Damal, who is ordinarily the mildest of creatures. But he is suffering the effects of many years overindulgence in opium and his temperament could be uncertain."

Fallier considered that. "Damal would be a worthy opponent," he said. "Perhaps . . . too worthy. What do you want?"

"I don't care what Montesq is holding over your head. I studied at Lodun myself, at the medical college. I know many student sorcerers dabble with the harmless minor divinatory spells of necromancy. Of course, with your position at court—"

"I understand you. Go on."

"You don't know what Montesq will ask for next."

"I can imagine," Fallier said dryly.

From his tone, Nicholas suspected Fallier had already been approached to aid Montesq in eluding Ronsarde's charges. But if he read Fallier right, that wouldn't be a problem. He said, "Then you wouldn't be adverse to helping me put Montesq in a position where he couldn't act against you."

Fallier actually unbent enough to sneer mildly and say, "If it was only a matter of giving testimony—"

"It isn't, and we both know it." Nicholas smiled. "I'm speaking of a way to stop Montesq from acting against anyone—permanently."

Fallier eyed him a moment thoughtfully, and nodded. "Then I think we need to speak in private."

With Reynard's help, Nicholas received permission to visit Doctor Brile's surgery to see how Crack and Isham were recovering. It was Ronsarde from whom the permission had come, he knew. He thought the Queen would have let him wander as he pleased and Captain Giarde, though always a dark horse, didn't have anything against him. It was Ronsarde who thought he needed watching.

He was transported in one of the palace coaches and delivered to the door of Doctor Brile's surgery. The doctor appeared bemused by the liveried Royal Guards who posted themselves on his stoop, but conducted Nicholas upstairs to where his patients were housed.

Nicholas saw Isham first, who was sitting up in bed though unable to talk for long without tiring himself. He reassured the old man as to everyone's safety and told him that Arisilde wanted to see him as soon as possible. But as he was taking his leave, Isham gestured him back with some firmness and said, "About Madele—"

Nicholas shook his head abruptly. "I don't want to—"

"She was not an old woman," Isham continued, ignoring the interruption. "She was a witch, from the time when witches were warriors. She had done everything from curing plague to crawling behind the lines in border skirmishes with Bisra to assassinate their priest-magicians. She was very old and she knew she would die soon, and she preferred a death in battle. Do not look doubtfully at me. When you are my age you will know what I say is true."

"All right, all right," Nicholas said placatingly. Isham was looking gray about the mouth again. "I believe you."

"No, you don't," Isham said stubbornly, but allowed himself to be laid back in bed. "But you will, eventually."

Nicholas went next door to see Crack, who greeted him with an impatient demand for information. Nicholas spent more time than he meant, telling Crack what had happened in the caves and how they had defeated Macob.

He hadn't alluded to Madeline's current whereabouts, but Crack wasn't fooled. He said, "She was here."

"She was?" Nicholas tried to look mildly interested, but knew he wasn't fooling his henchman.

"The doctor don't know it—she climbed in through the window. Isham don't know it either, since he was asleep and she didn't want to wake him."

Nicholas gave in. "What did she say?" he demanded.

"Some things," Crack said. It would have been evasive, except Crack never was. He added, "She's worried at you."

Nicholas put it out of his mind firmly. He had too much to do now and he would know if she had received his message when he went to Coldcourt. "Never mind that now," he said. "I've spoken to Inspector Ronsarde about you working for him while I'm gone." He explained further.

Crack didn't like the idea and expressed his displeasure volubly. Patiently, Nicholas said, "It would only be until I returned, then you could decide if you wanted to continue with the Inspector or come back with me. You'll get your normal retainer from me, anyway. Sarasate will see to that."

"It ain't the money," Crack grumbled. "What about Montesq?"

Nicholas glanced at the door of the room, making sure Brile was out of earshot. "Montesq won't be a consideration anymore."

"He won't?" Crack sounded hopeful.

"No."

"Then I'll think on it."

And that was the most he could get out of Crack. Nicholas went out to the consulting room where Doctor Brile was sitting at his desk in his shirtsleeves, writing. The physician stood and put on his coat when Nicholas came into the room. "You saw both of them?" he asked.

"Yes." Nicholas hesitated. He had brought money to pay Brile for his services but in light of his next request, it would look unpleasantly like a bribe, and he knew the physician wouldn't respond well to that. "Make sure they have whatever they want and send the bill to Coldcourt. I won't be there but my butler has instructions to arrange payment."

"I wasn't worried," Brile said mildly. "Are you going now?"

"Yes. Do you have a trapdoor to the roof?"

It was Brile's turn to hesitate. Nicholas saw him considering the presence of the Royal Guards at his door, perhaps weighing it with what he had seen of Nicholas's concern for his patients. He said finally, "There's a back door to the court behind the house."

"There is probably someone watching it."

Brile sighed. "I knew it would lead to this when Morane turned up at my door in the middle of the night. Will I be arrested if I help you?"

"I doubt it, but if you are, ask to speak to Inspector Ronsarde or Doctor Halle. They know all about it."

"Then I'll show you the roof door."

It was later that night, long after the streetlights were lit. Pompiene, Count Rive Montesq's Great House, looked down on the empty street, towering over the more modest town houses that clustered around it. Its original fortress-like façade had been modernized to make it current with fashion and a number of generous windows and a second floor terrace gave it an airy, fanciful appearance.

Across the street a figure stood in the shadows, muffled in a dark shabby coat and a hat with the brim pulled low. It wasn't raining but a damp mist hung heavy in the air and the flickering light of the gas lamps gleamed off the slick paving stones.

He crossed the street, moving toward the arcaded carriage alley at the side of the house. He avoided the pool of light from the single oil lamp that hung over the carriage doors and went instead to an inconspicuous portal further down the alley. It was a servants' door and though it was heavy and well-made, the inside bolts hadn't been shot and after some moments' work, the lock yielded to the picks.

Everything there was to know about this house, from its original floorplan to its furnishings to the habits of its servants, he already knew. The door opened into a narrow dark hall, with the servants' stairs on one side and the entrances to the pantries and servery on the other. He slipped past these doorways, hearing muted voices from the kitchens, and out the curtained door at the end and into the main foyer of the house.

The gas sconces and the chandelier were lit, revealing the house's main entrance, a carved set of double doors framed by multi-paned windows and a grand sweep of double staircase that led up into the public and private rooms. He took the right branch of the stairs, moved soundlessly down the carpeted gallery at the top and paused at a door that stood partway open.

It was a room made familiar by long hours of watching, spying. It was dark but a fall of light from the hallway revealed bookcases and a beautifully carved marble mantel and glinted off the frame of the watercolor and the marble bust by Bargentere. Across the room, above the large desk of mottled gold satinwood, was the painting *The Scribe* by Emile Avenne, the large canvas taking up a good portion of the wall above the wainscotting. He crossed the room swiftly, stepped around the desk and began to open drawers. Locating the one where Count Montesq kept correspondence, he took a packet of letters out of an inside coat pocket and placed it within. Shutting the drawer, he paused, listening to a quiet step out in the stairwell. He smiled to himself and stepped to the other side of the desk and opened another drawer, pretending to search it.

That was how the light caught him when the library door swung fully open. Two men stood there and a voice said, "Don't move."

He stayed where he was, knowing at least one firearm was directed his way. A figure stepped into the room and lit the gas sconce on the wall. The light revealed a burly, rough-featured man standing in the doorway, pointing a pistol at him. Count Montesq adjusted the height of the flame in the sconce, then turned unhurriedly to light the candle lamp on the nearby table. He said, "You were foolish to come here." His voice was warm and rich and he was smiling faintly.

The man he knew as Nicholas Valiarde said, "Not foolish."

Montesq finished with the lamp and stepped back to take the gun from the wary guard, motioning him to step out into the hall. The Count pushed the door closed behind the man and said, "After you dropped out of sight, I thought you were dead."

"Oh, why the pretense?" Nicholas said, showing no evidence of discomfiture at being caught. "I'm sure Rahene Fallier told you that Inspector Ronsarde had surfaced again and that he extricated me from Fallier's clutches and used the episode as a chance to solicit Captain Giarde's assistance."

Montesq's eyes narrowed. "You know about Fallier."

"I know everything, now."

"Not quite everything."

"Fallier also told you that I approached him today and asked for his help to circumvent the wards on this house, so I could enter it tonight."

The smile on the Count's lips died. He didn't try to deny the charge. "But you came anyway? Why? What could you possibly hope to accomplish?"

"It was the only way."

Montesq had observed that something in the quality of his guest's voice was not quite normal, that there was a flatness in his dark eyes. "How disappointing," Montesq drawled, coming to the wrong conclusion. "I was hoping you weren't mad."

"It is a little tawdry, isn't it?" Nicholas agreed, watching him with an odd intensity. "Ending like this. There was one thing I wanted to ask you."

"Yes?"

"You did realize that Edouard was telling you the truth. The spheres never worked for just anyone; they had to be wielded by a sorcerer, or someone with at least a minor magical talent."

Montesq hesitated, but there was no harm in admitting such things to a dead man. "I realized it, after I killed the woman."

Nicholas nodded to himself, satisfied. "I'm glad you said that."

Montesq smiled, one brow lifted in a quizzical expression. "You don't think I'll shoot, do you?"

"No, I know you will," Nicholas said, quietly. "I'm counting on it."

They both heard the crash and a surprised shout as a downstairs door was flung open. Montesq's head jerked involuntarily toward the sound and Nicholas leapt at him, making a wild grab for the pistol. Montesq stumbled back and as footsteps pounded up the stairs, he fired.

Two burly constables of the Prefecture were first into the room but Inspector Ronsarde was right behind them.

Ronsarde paused in the doorway, redfaced and breathing hard from the run up the stairs. The two constables had seized Montesq and taken possession of the pistol. The sight of the body on the carpet in front of the hearth broke the Inspector's temporary paralysis and he crossed over to it. He knelt and felt for a pulse at the throat, then jerked his hand back as if he had been burned. Ronsarde looked hard at the face, then slowly stood and turned to Montesq.

Their eyes met. Montesq's expression of bafflement turned to rage. In a grating voice, he said, "You bastard."

One of the constables reported, "When we came in, he was standing over him with the pistol, looking down at him, sir."

"Yes," Ronsarde said, nodding. "I'm sure he was."

Doctor Halle appeared in the doorway, more constables behind him. Taking in the scene, Halle swore and pushed past Ronsarde to the body. He knelt and ripped open his medical bag, then froze as he stared down at the face of the corpse.

The constables at the door made room for Lord Albier, who was trailed by his secretary Viarn and Captain Defanse. Albier summed up the situation with a swift glance and ordered Defanse to secure the house and arrest the servants.

Halle stood and turned a bewildered expression on Ronsarde. "This isn't—This man's been dead for—"

Ronsarde said, "Yes?" and stared hard at Halle.

After a moment, Halle cleared his throat and finished, "Moments, only. A few moments." He picked up his bag and retreated to a corner to gather his thoughts.

Albier stepped into the room now, glancing ruefully at Ronsarde. "Well, when you're right, you're right," he admitted gruffly.

Ronsarde's lips twitched. "Or vice versa," he murmured inaudibly.

Montesq had had a moment to recover himself. He said, "I was attacked by that man—"

"He's unarmed," Ronsarde interrupted. He hadn't bothered to search the body, but he was reasonably sure of his facts.

Albier nodded to Viarn, who went over and began to go through the corpse's pockets. "You won't find it easy to explain this away, sir," Albier said to Montesq with some satisfaction. "This wasn't a burglary. It's early evening, the lamps lit, your servants everywhere. You must have invited the man in."

Montesq almost bared his teeth in fury. "He entered without my knowledge, with sorcery."

Albier raised a skeptical brow. "If he was a sorcerer why did he let you shoot him? Besides, Inspector Ronsarde had information that you would have an interview with a man whom you would attempt to murder tonight."

"I'm sure he did." Montesq turned his cold gaze on Ronsarde and said contemptuously, "You violate your principles, sir."

"Do I?" Ronsarde said softly. "If you hadn't shot him, this would all have fallen to pieces. He laid the trap, but you didn't have to step into it."

Albier frowned. "What would have fallen to—"

"Sir!" The secretary Viarn was holding up a pocket watch with a jeweled fob. "Sir, he has several documents that should identify him but they all seem to be in different names, and he has this!" He stood and handed the watch to Albier. "Look at the inscription on the back of the setting for that opal."

Albier squinted down at the jewel in his palm, half turning so the lamplight would fall on it. "Romele," he breathed. "This is one of the pieces stolen in the Romele jewel robbery." He and Viarn exchanged a significant look. "That man is Donatien."

From his corner, Doctor Halle made a muffled noise and Ronsarde rolled his eyes in disgust. Montesq said, "Donatien . . . ?" Slow understanding dawned in his eyes and he swore bitterly under his breath. "If I had known. . . ."

Albier rounded on him. "If you had known? It looks a good deal like you did know, sir. That what we have here is a falling-out among thieves."

"No, does it really?" Montesq said acidly.

"There's something missing," Ronsarde said, his expression thoughtful.

"What?" Albier asked, startled.

"Direct evidence of the good Count's involvement with Donatien." Ronsarde looked around the room appraisingly. He moved behind the desk and studied the array of drawers. All were firmly shut except one, which had been left open a hair. Ronsarde let out his breath. Since he had seen the face of the dead man, he hadn't known whether to laugh hysterically or shout and stamp. He opened the drawer and lifted out a pack of letters. "What are the names on those documents, Viarn?"

The secretary sorted hastily through the papers he had retrieved from the body. "Ordenon, Ferrar, Ringard Alscen—"

"Ah, yes." Ronsarde nodded to himself. "Here are letters from men of those names to Count Montesq. I'm sure this will provide the confirmation of your theory, Albier."

Albier was surprised and a little uncomfortable. "My theory? You told me to come here, Ronsarde, and you've been pursuing Donatien for years. I'm sure it was your work that led to this."

A muscle jumped in Inspector Ronsarde's cheek. "Oh, no," he said. "I can't take credit for this."

*   *   *

Later, as the Prefecture moved into Count Montesq's Great House in force, questioning servants, confiscating documents, collecting evidence, Ronsarde and Halle escaped outside and moved across the street to where a gas lamp lit a circle of wrought iron benches with a small fountain in the center. It was a damp cold night and a mist was beginning to rise.

Doctor Halle stood with shoulders hunched and hands jammed into the pockets of his greatcoat. He said, "There's just one thing I'd like to make certain of—"

"I will check with the authorities at the city morgue tomorrow and discover that sometime yesterday afternoon a person answering to our friend Cusard's description claimed the body of an unidentified and recently deceased young man. That he perused all the available male corpses before making his choice, rejecting the ones that had been dead too long or been killed by some obvious means, such as stabbings or disfiguring blows to the head," Ronsarde said. "I will wager you the price of a dinner at Lusaude's grill room that this is so."

"I won't take that wager," Halle said. After a moment, he chuckled.

"It's not funny," Ronsarde said stiffly.

"Of course you're right." Halle stopped smiling but he didn't give the impression of suffering any sensation of guilt. He noticed that further down the street the colored lamps outside the cafe in the ground floor of the promenade were lit, signifying that it was still open for business. Halle knew Ronsarde shouldn't be out in this weather and steered their steps toward it, the Inspector following him by habit. After a moment, Halle said, "I understand it must have been a golem constructed in some fashion out of the corpse, and when Montesq destroyed the spell by firing the pistol into it, the rest of the thing dissolved, and left only the body. But who made the golem? Was it Arisilde Damal? He's been at the palace all day inside the wards. Could he control the creature from there?"

"It wasn't Damal," Ronsarde said, his mouth thinning. "It was Rahene Fallier, who had every reason to silence Montesq."

"Good God, Fallier," Halle said in wonder. He shook his head and chuckled again, then glanced at Ronsarde's face. "Sorry."

Ronsarde continued, "If the Count tries to reveal any of the information he was using to blackmail Fallier now, it will simply be more proof against him."

"Masterful," Halle said, admiringly. He caught Ronsarde's glare, and said, "Oh, come now. Valiarde played you expertly."

"Thank you for mentioning it. But he also counts on me not to expose him."

Halle stopped in his tracks. "You wouldn't."

"I could," Ronsarde said, grimly. "Damn that boy. He could have been a brilliant investigator." Then he relented and allowed himself a slight smile. "But I won't expose him. Did you see the look on Montesq's face?"

"Did I? When I first walked in I thought you'd struck him, he looked so shocked."

Laughing, the two men walked down the dark street toward the lights of the cafe.

The port city of Chaire smelled of dead fish and salt sea, or at least this portion of it did. It was long after midnight but the lower level of the old stone docks still bustled with activity when Cusard's wagon pulled in. The shoremen and carters were hauling last minute cargos to and from the steamers preparing to leave the next morning. Nicholas jumped down from the wagon seat, dressed in work clothes and an old greatcoat, a battered leather knapsack slung over one shoulder. He usually preferred to travel light but the trunk weighing down the bed of Cusard's wagon had to accompany him on this trip.

Cusard dropped the tail of the wagon and as they waited for the shoremen to get around to them, he sniffed and said, "You got all your papers and tickets?"

Nicholas rolled his eyes. Cusard was going to get maudlin. "Yes, poppa. I'll remember to stay away from fallen women, too."

"Like my own son, you was." Cusard let out his breath in a gusty sigh. "Should of beat you more when you was a boy."

"Probably." Nicholas leaned back against the wagon. "For the love of God, Cusard, I'm going to Adera for a few months, not Hell."

"Foreigners," Cusard commented succinctly. He eyed Nicholas thoughtfully. "You'll miss the trial."

"That's for the best. Montesq is going to be convicted of murdering Donatien, his partner in crime. I don't want him to have the opportunity to prove that Donatien is alive and well and living under the name Nicholas Valiarde."

Cusard grunted. "I'll save the penny sheets for you."

"Just stay away from the warehouse or any of the other places I had to give them."

"No, I was going to walk around 'em with a sign on my back saying 'Arrest Me.' " Cusard sighed again. "That's like a son to me all right, leaving me to fend for myself—"

"Your share is enough to buy a villa on the March—"

"High living will do you in every time," Cusard interrupted sententiously. Then he grinned. "Did the Count in, didn't it? High living and being too clever by half."

Nicholas tried to maintain a stony façade, but his lips twitched in a smile. "Yes, it did, didn't it?"

The shoremen came for the trunk then, grunting at its unexpected weight as they lifted it down from the wagon bed.

As Nicholas was signing the bill of lading one of them, with the forthrightness characteristic of tradesmen in Ile-Rien, demanded, "What have you got in here, bricks?"

"Almost," Nicholas said, truthfully. Small, highly

valuable bricks. He added, not so truthfully, "It's sculpture actually, busts and small figures."

That was dull stuff for men who unloaded cargos from Parscia and Bukarin and they showed no further interest in the trunk's contents.

"You'd better be going," Nicholas told Cusard. "It's a long drive back and you're so damnably old."

"You and your mouth," Cusard said, and cuffed him on the side of the head. "Tell her ladyship to take care of herself."

"I will," Nicholas said, as the old man climbed back aboard the wagon and lifted the reins. *At least I hope I'll have the opportunity.*

Once the trunk was loaded and the shoremen tipped, Nicholas could have boarded the ship and sought the comfort of the first class cabin he had booked. Instead he climbed the stairs to the upper level of the dock and sat down on one of the stone benches.

It was very late and in the chill night there were few people venturing to take the air. The bustle of last minute loading and passengers arriving to board the ships was all taking place on the lower dock and this broad walk seemed very isolated. Hundreds of lamps still burned in the great hotels and the amusement pavilion at the opposite end, but that was far away.

He knew Madeline had gotten his message. He had gone to Coldcourt after escaping Brile's surgery to give Sarasate instructions to expect Arisilde and Isham. There had been a host of telegrams to send too, warnings and instructions to different parts of his organization. Sarasate had reported that Madeline had been there earlier to pack a few of her things and had told him that Nicholas would be there soon with further instructions. She hadn't said where she was going.

Alone he had watched the scene enacted in Montesq's library through Arisilde's enspelled copy of *The Scribe*. *So all the books are right*, he thought, *revenge is bitter*. Then he smiled to himself. *But I'll get over it.*

Seated on the bench, he waited long enough to get thoroughly chilled and very afraid when he saw a lone figure making its way down the promenade, moving into one of the pools of light from the wrought iron lamps.

Nicholas drew a deep breath in relief. He would recognize that walk anywhere.

It took her long enough to reach him that he had managed to school his features into a mild expression of welcome, instead of grinning at her like an idiot. Madeline sat down on the bench next to him, dropping a carpetbag near his feet. She was dressed in a conservative travelling costume under a new gray paletot. She looked at him a moment, her face bemused, then said, "I thought about making you wait and catching the pilot boat at the last minute tomorrow morning, but I couldn't be sure you wouldn't do something dramatic."

This time he couldn't help the grin. "Me? Do something dramatic?"

"Idiot," she said, and busied herself with adjusting her hat. "Now tell me how it was done. Where did you get the body?"

Nicholas let out his breath. "This afternoon I sent Cusard to the city morgue to look for a fresh, unclaimed male corpse, of about the right age, with no obvious wounds. It didn't even have to resemble me. Fallier would take care of that when he made the golem and afterward, well, the Prefecture knows that Donatien is—was—a master of disguise."

"Couldn't Montesq claim that he shot Donatien in self-defense?"

"Oh, I'm sure he will. But before he arrived the golem placed a packet of letters in Montesq's desk. Some of them date back to the beginning of Donatien's rather checkered career and make it clear that Montesq planned most if not all of Donatien's activities."

"That must have been difficult."

She was right about that but the blow to his ego had been a sacrifice Nicholas was willing to make. "It did give me a twinge or two." He pulled off his black leather riding glove and shoved her the brown stains on his fingers. "I was more worried by what would happen if Ronsarde saw the stains from the tea I used to age the paper for the older letters. He would have known immediately I was up to something more than a simple murder. I'm lucky correct court attire demands gloves.''

Madeline frowned. ''That was terribly cruel to make poor Ronsarde think you were bent on shooting Montesq in some grand self-destructive gesture. He must have been very worried about you.''

''It will teach him not to be overconfident.'' Nicholas continued, ''My observations of Montesq through Arisilde's portrait made it possible to salt the letters with realistic and verifiable details. The later ones implicate the solicitor Batherat, who is a nervous sort and will probably break down under the first questioning session and volunteer information about Montesq's own indiscretions.''

''Well, it turned out better than I hoped, I'll tell you that.''

They sat in silence for a few moments, Nicholas watching the way the cold breeze off the ocean lifted the loose strands of hair that had escaped from her hat. ''The theater rehearsal season will be just starting when we get to Adera. You can look for a part in something.''

''A leading role, you mean,'' she said, in perfect Aderassi. ''And what will you do?''

He shrugged. ''There's the university in the capital. I could finish my medical degree. A letter from Doctor Uberque should help me gain admittance.''

Madeline snorted. ''That'll last a week.''

''Probably,'' he said, grinning again. Sobering, he decided there was something else he needed to ask, and finally managed, ''Do you blame me for Madele's death?''

Madeline shook her head slowly. ''I did, at first. But it's more accurate, and more characteristic of me, to blame Madele for Madele's death. She knew what she was risking. And it probably maddens her, wherever she is, that she missed the whole fight against Macob. That's probably punishment enough.'' She gave him a sideways glance. "If you're going to get sentimental, let's get on the damn boat before I change my mind."

"Yes," he said, satisfied with that answer. "Let's go."

acknowledgments

Thanks to Nancy Buchanan, for reading the manuscript in bits and pieces of very rough draft and for invaluable help with the research, including locating a copy of *The Lighter Side of My Official Life*, out of print since the 1920s. Thanks also to Z.P. Florian, for the story of the Hungarian fighting the Turks, and to Timothy John Cowden, for the story of his aunt, Lillian Saxe, who really did write a note in a book she left to him like Edouard did in Chapter 7. And finally, thanks to Troyce Wilson for ideas, support, and most of all, patience.

We hope you've enjoyed this Avon Eos book. As part of our mission to give readers the best science fiction and fantasy being written today, the following pages contain a glimpse into the fascinating worlds of a select group of Avon Eos authors.

In the following pages experience the latest in cutting-edge sf from Eric S. Nylund, Maureen F. McHugh, and Susan R. Matthews, and experience the wondrous fantasy realms of Martha Wells, Andre Norton, Dave Duncan, and Raymond E. Feist.

SIGNAL TO NOISE

Eric S. Nylund

Jack watched his office walls sputter malfunctioning mathematical symbols and release a flock of passenger pigeons; his nose was tickled with the odor of eucalyptus. Inside, the air rippled with synthetic pleasure and the taste of vanilla.

"I need to get in there," he told the government agent who blocked the doorway.

"No admittance," the agent said, "until we've completed our investigation on the break-in."

Puzzles, illegalities, and dilemmas stuck to Jack— from which he then, usually, extracted himself. That gave him the dual reputation of a troubleshooter and a troublemaker. But the only thing he was dead sure about today was the "troublemaking and sticking" part of that assessment.

The agent stepped in front of Jack, obscuring what the others were doing in there. National Security Office agents: goons with big guns bulging under their bullet-proof suits. And no arguing with them.

Today's trouble was the stuff you saw coming, but couldn't do a thing about. Like standing in front of a tidal wave.

Jack hoped his office *had* been broken into, that this wasn't an NSO fishing trip. There were secrets in the bubble circuitry of his office that had to stay hidden. Things that could make his troubles multiply.

"I'll wait until you're done then."

The agent glanced at his notepad and a face materialized: Jack's with his sandy hair pulled into a ponytail and his hazel eyes bloodshot. You have an immediate interview with Mr. DeMitri. Bell Communications Center, sublevel three.''

Jack's stomach curdled. ''Interview'' was a polite word that meant they'd use invasive probes and mnemonic shadows to pry open his mind. Jack had worked with DeMitri and the NSO before. He knew all their nasty tricks.

''Thanks,'' Jack lied, turned from the illusions in his office, and walked down the hallway.

From the fourth floor of the mathematics building, he took the arched bridge path that linked to the island's outer seawall. Not the most direct route, but he needed time to figure a way out of this jam.

Cold night air and salt spray whipped around him. Electromagnetic pollution filtered through the hardware in his skull: a hundred conversations on the cell networks, and a patchwork of thermal images from the West-AgCo satellite overhead.

Past the surf and across the San Joaquin Sea, the horizon glowed with fluorescent light. Jack regretted that he'd stepped on other people to get where he was. Maybe that's why trouble always came looking for him. Because he had it coming. Or because he was soft enough to let little things get to him. Like guilt.

Not that there was any other way to escape the mainland. Everyone there competed for lousy jobs and stabbed each other in the back, sometimes literally, to get ahead. He had clawed his way out with an education—then cheated his way into Santa Sierra's Academé of Pure and Applied Sciences.

But it wasn't perfect here, either. There were cutthroat maneuvers for grants, and Jack had bent the law working both for corporations *and* the government. All of which had helped his financial position, but hadn't improved his conscience.

He had to get tenure so he could relax and pursue his

own projects. There had to be more to life than chasing money and grabbing power.

Now those dreams were on hold.

His office had been ransacked, and the NSO had got too curious, too fast, for his liking. Had they been keeping an eye on him all along?

He took the stairs off the seawall and descended into a red-tiled courtyard.

In the center of the square stood Coit Tower. The structure was sixty meters of fluted concrete that had been hoisted off the ocean floor. It had survived the San Francisco quake in the early twenty-first century, then lay underwater for fifty years—yet was still in one piece.

Jack hoped he was as tough.

The whitewashed turret was lit from beneath with halogen light, harsh and brilliant against the night sky. Undeniably real.

Jack preferred the illusions of his office; sometimes reality was too much for him to stomach.

No way out of this interview sprang to mind, and he had stalled as long as he could. The crystal-and-steel geodesic dome of the Bell Communications Center was across the courtyard. Jack marched into the building, took the elevator to sublevel three, and entered the concert amphitheater.

On the stage between gathered velvet curtains, the NSO had set up their bubble.

Normal bubbles simulated reality. Inside, a web of inductive signals and asynchronous quantum imagers tapped the operator's neuralware. It allowed access to a world of data, it teased hunches from your subconscious, and solidified your guesses into theories. They made you think faster. Maybe think better.

But this wasn't a normal bubble. And it was never meant to help Jack think. It was designed for tricks.

THE DEATH OF THE NECROMANCER

Martha Wells

She was in the old wing of the house now. The long hall became a bridge over cold silent rooms thirty feet down and the heavy stone walls were covered by tapestry or thin veneers of exotic wood instead of lathe and plaster. There were banners and weapons from long-ago wars, still stained with rust and blood, and ancient family portraits dark with the accumulation of years of smoke and dust. Other halls branched off, some leading to even older sections of the house, others to odd little cul-de-sacs lit by windows with an unexpected view of the street or the surrounding buildings. Music and voices from the ballroom grew further and further away, as if she was at the bottom of a great cavern, hearing echoes from the living surface.

She chose the third staircase she passed, knowing the servants would still be busy toward the front of the house. She caught up her skirts—black gauze with dull gold striped over black satin and ideal for melding into shadows—and quietly ascended. She gained the third floor without trouble but going up to the fourth passed a footman on his way down. He stepped to the wall to let her have the railing, his head bowed in respect and an effort not to see who she was, ghosting about Mondollot House and obviously on her way to an indiscreet meeting. He would remember her later, but there was no help for it.

The hall at the landing was high and narrower than the others, barely ten feet across. There were more twists and turns to find her way through, stairways that only went up half a floor, and dead ends, but she had committed a map of the house to memory in preparation for this and so far it seemed accurate.

Madeline found the door she wanted and carefully tested the handle. It was unlocked. She frowned. One of Nicholas Valiarde's rules was that if one was handed good fortune one should first stop to ask the price, because there usually was a price. She eased the door open, saw the room beyond lit only by reflected moonlight from undraped windows. With a cautious glance up and down the corridor, she pushed it open enough to see the whole room. Book-filled cases, chimney piece of carved marble with a caryatid-supported mantle, tapestry-back chairs, pier glasses, and old sideboard heavy with family plate. A deal table supporting a metal strongbox. *Now we'll see,* she thought. She took a candle from the holder on the nearest table, lit it from the gas sconce in the hall, then slipped inside and closed the door behind her.

The undraped windows worried her. This side of the house faced Ducal Court Street and anyone below could see the room was occupied. Madeline hoped none of the Duchess's more alert servants stepped outside for a pipe or a breath of air and happened to look up. She went to the table and upended her reticule next to the solid square shape of the strongbox. Selecting the items she needed out of the litter of scent vials, jewelry she had decided not to wear, and a faded string of Aderassi luck-beads, she set aside snippers of chicory and thistle, a toadstone, and a paper screw containing salt.

Their sorcerer-advisor had said that the ward that protected Mondollot House from intrusion was an old and powerful one. Destroying it would take much effort and be a waste of a good spell. Circumventing it temporarily would be easier and far less likely to attract notice, since wards were invisible to anyone except a sorcerer using gascoign powder in his eyes or the new Aether-Glasses invented by the Parscian wizard Negretti. The toadstone itself held the necessary spell, dormant and harmless, and in its current state invisible to the familiar who guarded the main doors. The salt sprinkled on it would act as a catalyst and the special properties of the herbs would fuel it. Once all were placed in the influence of the ward's key object, the ward would withdraw to the very top of the house. When the potency of the salt wore off, it would simply slip back into place, probably before their night's work had been discovered. Madeline took her lock picks out of their silken case and turned to the strongbox.

There was no lock. She felt the scratches on the hasp and knew there had been a lock here recently, a heavy one, but it was nowhere to be seen. *Damn. I have a not-so-good feeling about this.* She lifted the flat metal lid.

Inside should be the object that tied the incorporeal ward to the corporeal bulk of Mondollot House. Careful spying and a few bribes had led them to expect not a stone as was more common, but a ceramic object, perhaps a ball, of great delicacy and age.

On a velvet cushion in the bottom of the strongbox were the crushed remnants of something once delicate and beautiful as well as powerful, nothing left now but fine white powder and fragments of cerulean blue. Madeline gave vent to an unladylike curse and slammed the lid down. *Some bastard's been here before us.*

SCENT OF MAGIC

Andre Norton

That scent which made Willadene's flesh prickle was strong. But for a moment she had to blink to adjust her sight to the very dim light within the shop. The lamp which always burned all night at the other end of the room was the only glimmer here now, except for the sliver of daylight stretching out from the half-open door.

Willadene's sandaled foot nearly nudged a huddled shape on the floor—Halwice? Her hands flew to her lips, but she did not utter that scream which filled her throat. Why, she could not tell, but that it was necessary to be quiet now was like an order laid upon her.

Her eyes were drawn beyond that huddled body to a chair which did not belong in the shop at all but had been pulled from the inner room. In that sat the Herb-mistress, unmoving and silent. Dead—?

Willadene's hands were shaking, but somehow she pulled herself around that other body on the floor toward where one of the strong lamps, used when one was mixing powders, sat. Luckily the strike light was also there, and after two attempts she managed to set spark to the wick.

With the lamp still in hands which quivered, the girl swung around to face that silent presence in the chair. Eyes stared back at her, demanding eyes. No, Halwice lived but something held her in thrall and helpless. There were herbs which could do that in forbidden mixture, but Halwice never dealt with such.

Those eyes— Willadene somehow found a voice which was only a whisper.

"What—?" she began.

The eyes were urgent as if sight could write a message on the very air between them. They moved—from the girl to the half-open door and then back with an urgency Willadene knew she must answer. But how— Did Halwice want her to summon help?

"Can you"—she was reaching now for the only solution she could think of—"answer? Close your eyes once—"

Instantly the lids dropped and then rose again. Willadene drew a deep breath, almost of relief. By so much, then, she knew they could still communicate.

"Do I go for Doctor Raymonda?" He was the nearest of the medical practitioners who depended upon Halwice for their drugs.

The eyelids snapped down, arose, and fell again.

"No?" Willadene tried to hold the lamps steady. She had near forgotten the body on the floor.

She stared so intensely as if she could force the answer she needed out of the Herbmistress. Now she noted that the other's gaze had swept beyond her and was on the floor. Once more the silent woman blinked twice with almost the authority of an order. Willadene made a guess.

"Close the door?" That quick, single affirmative blink was her answer. She carefully edged about the body to do just that. Halwice did not want help from outside—but what evil had happened here? And was the silent form on the floor responsible for the Herbmistress's present plight?

With the door shut some instinct made the girl also, one-handedly as she held the lamp high, slide the bolt bar across it, turning again to find Halwice's gaze fierce and intent on her. The Herbmistress blinked. Yes, she had been right—Halwice wanted no one else here.

Then that gaze turned floorward, as far as nature would let the eyes move, to fasten on the body. Willadene carefully set the lamp down beside the inert stranger and then knelt.

It was a man lying facedown. His clothing was traveler's leather and wool as if he were just in from some traders' caravan. Halwice dealt often with traders, spices, and strange roots; even crushed clays of one sort or another arrived regularly here. But what had happened—?

Willadene's years of shifting iron pots and pans and dealing with Jacoba's oversize aids to cooking had made her stronger than her small, thin body looked. She was able to roll the stranger over.

Under his hand his flesh was cool, and she could see no wound or hurt. It was as if he had been struck down instantly by one of those weird powers which were a part of stories told to children.

THE GILDED CHAIN
A Tale of the King's Blades

Dave Duncan

Durendal closed the heavy door silently and went to stand beside Prime, carefully not looking at the other chair.

"You sent for us, Grand Master?" Harvest's voice warbled slightly, although he was rigid as a pike, staring straight at the bookshelves.

"I did, Prime. His Majesty has need of a Blade. Are you ready to serve?"

Harvest spoke at last, almost inaudibly. "I am ready, Grand Master."

Soon Durendal would be saying those words. And who would be sitting in the second chair?

Who was there now? He had not looked. The edge of his eye hinted it was seeing a youngish man, too young to be the King himself.

"My lord," Grand Master said, "I have the honor to present Prime Candidate Harvest, who will serve you as your Blade."

As the two young men turned to him, the anonymous noble drawled, "The other one looks much more impressive. Do I have a choice?"

"You do not!" barked Grand Master, color pouring into his craggy face. "The King himself takes whoever is Prime."

"Oh, so sorry! Didn't mean to twist your dewlaps, Grand Master." He smiled vacuously. He was a weedy, soft-faced man in his early twenties, a courtier to the core, resplendent in crimson and vermilion silks trimmed with fur and gold chain. If the white cloak was truly ermine, it must be worth a fortune. His fairish beard came to a needle point and his mustache was a work of art. A fop. Who?

"Prime, this is the Marquis of Nutting, your future ward."

"Ward?" The Marquis sniggered. "You make me sound like a debutante, Grand Master. *Ward* indeed!"

Harvest bowed, his face ashen as he contemplated a lifetime guarding . . . whom? Not the King himself, not his heir, not a prince of the blood, not an ambassador traveling in exotic lands, not an important landowner out on the marches, not a senior minister, nor even—at worst—the head of one of the great conjuring orders. Here was no ward worth dying for, just a court dandy, a parasite. Trash.

Seniors spent more time studying politics than anything else except fencing. Wasn't the Marquis of Nutting the brother of the Countess Mornicade, the King's latest mistress? If so, then six months ago he had been the Honorable Tab Nillway, a younger son of a penniless baronet, and his only claim to importance was that he had been expelled from the same womb as one of the greatest beauties of the age. No report reaching Ironhall had ever hinted that he might have talent or ability.

"I am deeply honored to be assigned to your lordship," Harvest said hoarsely, but the spirits did not strike him dead for perjury.

Grand Master's displeasure was now explained. One of his precious charges was being thrown away to no purpose. Nutting was not important enough to have enemies, even at court. No man of honor would lower his standards enough to call out an upstart pimp—certainly not one who had a Blade prepared to die for him. But Grand Master had no choice. The King's will was paramount.

"We shall hold the binding tomorrow midnight,

Prime," the old man snapped. "Make the arrangements, Second."

"Yes, Grand Master."

"Tomorrow?" protested the Marquis querulously. "There's a ball at court tomorrow. Can't we just run through the rigmarole quickly now and be done with it?"

Grand Master's face was already dangerously inflamed, and that remark made the veins swell even more. "Not unless you wish to kill a man, my lord. You have to learn your part in the ritual. Both you and Prime must be purified by ritual and fasting."

Nutting curled his lip. "Fasting? How barbaric!"

"Binding is a major conjuration. You will be in some danger yourself."

If the plan was to frighten the court parasite into withdrawing, it failed miserably. He merely muttered, "Oh, I'm sure you exaggerate."

Grand Master gave the two candidates a curt nod of dismissal. They bowed in unison and left.

KRONDOR
The Betrayal

Raymond E. Feist

The fire crackled.

Owyn Belefote sat alone in the night before the flames, wallowing in his personal misery. The youngest son of the Baron of Timons, he was a long way from home and wishing he was even farther away. His youthful features were set in a portrait of dejection.

The night was cold and the food scant, especially after having just left the abundance of his aunt's home in Yabon City. He had been hosted by relatives ignorant of his falling-out with his father, people who had reacquainted him over a week's visit with what he had forgotten about his home life: the companionship of brothers and sisters, the warmth of a night spent before the fire, conversation with his mother, and even the arguments with his father.

"Father," Owyn muttered. It had been less than two years since the young man had defied his father and made his way to Stardock, the island of magicians located in the southern reaches of the Kingdom. His father had forbidden him his choice, to study magic, demanding Owyn should at least become a cleric of one of the more socially acceptable orders of priests. After all, they did magic as well, his father had insisted.

Owyn sighed and gathered his cloak around him. He had been so certain he would someday return home to visit his family, revealing himself as a great magician,

perhaps a confidant of the legendary Pug, who had created the Academy at Stardock. Instead he found himself
ill suited for the study required. He also had no love for
the burgeoning politics of the place, with factions of
students rallying around this teacher or that, attempting
to turn the study of magic into another religion. He now
knew he was, at best, a mediocre magician and would
never amount to more, and no matter how much he
wished to study magic, he lacked sufficient talent.

After slightly more than one year of study, Owyn had
left Stardock, conceding to himself that he had made a
mistake. Admitting such to his father would prove a far
more daunting task—which was why he had decided to
visit family in the distant province of Yabon before mustering the courage to return to the East and confront his
sire.

A rustle in the bushes caused Owyn to clutch a heavy
wooden staff and jump to his feet. He had little skill
with weapons, having neglected that portion of his education as a child, but had developed enough skill with
his quarterstaff to defend himself.

"Who's there?" he demanded.

From out of the gloom came a voice, saying, "Hello,
the camp. We're coming in."

Owyn relaxed slightly, as bandits would be unlikely
to warn him they were coming. Also, he was obviously
not worth attacking, as he looked little more than a ragged beggar these days. Still, it never hurt to be wary.

Two figures appeared out of the gloom, one roughly
Owyn's height, the other a head taller. Both were covered in heavy cloaks, the smaller of the two limping
obviously.

The limping man looked over his shoulder, as if being
followed, then asked, "Who are you?"

Owyn said, "Me? Who are you?"

The smaller man pulled back his hood, and said,
"Locklear, I'm a squire to Prince Arutha."

Owyn nodded, "Sir, I'm Owyn, son of Baron Belefote."

"From Timons, yes, I know who your father is," said

Locklear, squatting before the fire, opening his hands to warm them. He glanced up at Owyn. "You're a long way from home, aren't you?"

"I was visiting my aunt in Yabon," said the blond youth. "I'm now on my way home."

"Long journey," said the muffled figure.

"I'll work my way down to Krondor, then see if I can travel with a caravan or someone else to Salador. From there I'll catch a boat to Timons."

"Well, we could do worse than stick together until we reach LaMut," said Locklear, sitting down heavily on the ground. His cloak fell open, and Owyn saw blood on the young man's clothing.

"You're hurt," he said.

"Just a bit," admitted Locklear.

"What happened?"

"We were jumped a few miles north of here," said Locklear.

Owyn started rummaging through his travel bag. "I have something in here for wounds," he said. "Strip off your tunic."

Locklear removed his cloak and tunic, while Owyn took bandages and powder from his bag. "My aunt insisted I take this just in case. I thought it an old lady's foolishness, but apparently it wasn't."

Locklear endured the boy's ministrations as he washed the wound, obviously a sword cut to the ribs, and winced when the powder was sprinkled upon it. Then as he bandaged the squire's ribs, Owyn said, "Your friend doesn't talk much, does he?"

"I am not his friend," answered Gorath. He held out his manacles for inspection. "I am his prisoner."

MISSION CHILD

Maureen F. McHugh

"Listen," Aslak said, touching my arm.

I didn't hear it at first, then I did. It was a skimmer.

It was far away. Skimmers didn't land at night. They didn't even come at night. It had come to my message, I guessed.

Aslak got up and we ran out to the edge of the field behind the schoolhouse. Dogs started barking.

Finally we saw lights from the skimmer, strange green and red stars. They moved against the sky as if they had been shaken loose.

The lights came toward us for a long time. They got bigger and brighter, more than any star. It seemed as if they stopped, but the lights kept getting brighter. I finally decided that they were coming straight toward us.

Then we could see the skimmer in its own lights.

I shouted, and Aslak shouted, too, but the skimmer didn't seem to hear us. But then it turned and slowly curved around, the sound of it going farther away and then just hanging in the air. It got to where it had been before and came back. This time it came even lower and it dropped red lights. One. Two. Three.

Then a third time it came around and I wondered what it would do now. But this time it landed, the sound of it so loud that I could feel as well as hear it. It was a different skimmer than the one we always saw. It was bigger, with a belly like it was pregnant. It was white and red. It settled easily on the snow. Its engines,

534

pointed down, melted snow underneath them.

And then it sat. Lights blinked. The red lights on the ground flickered. The dogs barked.

The door opened and a man called out to watch something but I didn't understand. My English is pretty good, one of the best in school, but I couldn't understand him.

Finally a man jumped down, and then two more men and two women.

I couldn't understand what anyone was saying in English. They asked me questions, but I just kept shaking my head. I was tired and now, finally, I wanted to cry.

"You called us. Did you call us?" one man said over and over until I understood.

I nodded.

"How?"

"Wanji give me . . . in my head . . ." I had no idea how to explain. I pointed to my ear. "Ayudesh is, is bad."

"Ask if he will die," Aslak said.

"Um, the teacher," I said, "um, it is bad?"

The woman nodded. She said something, but I didn't understand. "Smoke," she said. "Do you understand? Smoke?"

"Smoke," I said. "Yes." To Aslak I said, "He had a lot of smoke in him."

Aslak shook his head.

The men went to the skimmer and came back with a litter. They put it next to Ayudesh and lifted him on, but then they stood up and nearly fell, trying to carry him. They tried to walk, but I couldn't stand watching, so I took the handles from the man by Ayudesh's feet, and Aslak, nodding, took the ones at the head. We carried Ayudesh to the skimmer.

We walked right up to the door of the skimmer, and I could look in. It was big inside. Hollow. It was dark in the back. I had thought it would be all lights inside and I was disappointed. There were things hanging on the walls, but mostly it was empty. One of the offworld men jumped up into the skimmer, and then he was not clumsy at all. He pulled the teacher and the litter into the back of the skimmer.

One of the men brought us something hot and bitter and sweet to drink. The drink was in blue plastic cups, the same color as the jackets that they all wore except for one man whose jacket was red with blue writing. Pretty things. I made myself drink mine. Anything this black and bitter must have been medicine. Aslak just held his.

"Where is everyone else?" the red-jacket man asked slowly.

"Dead," I said.

"Everyone?" he said.

"Yes," I said.

AVALANCHE SOLDIER

Susan R. Matthews

It lacked several minutes yet before actual sunbreak, early as the sun rose in the summer. Salli eased her shoulder into a braced position against the papery bark of the highpalm tree that sheltered her and tapped the focus on the field glasses that she wore, frowning down in concentration at the small Wayfarer's camp below. They would have to come out of the dormitory to reach the washhouse, and they'd have to do it soon. Morning prayers was one of the things that heterodox and orthodox—Wayfarer and Pilgrims—had in common, and no faithful child of Revelation would think of opening his mouth to praise the Awakening with the taint of sleep still upon him.

The door to the long low sleeping house swung open. Salli tensed. *Come on, Meeka,* she whispered to herself, her breath so still it didn't so much as stir the layered mat of fallen palm fronds on which she lay. *I know you're in there. Come out. I have things I want to say to you.*

The camp below was an artifact from olden days, two hundred years old by the thatching of the steeply sloped roofs with their overhanging eaves. Not a Pilgrim camp by any means. No, this was a Shadene camp built by the interlopers that had occupied the holy land in the years after the Pilgrims had fled—centuries ago. A leftover, an anachronism, part of the heritage of Shadene and its long history of welcoming Pilgrims from all over the world to the Revelation Mountains, where the Awakening had begun. Where heterodoxy flourished, and had stolen Meeka away from her. And before the Awakened One she had a thing or two to tell him about that—just as soon as she could find him by himself, and get him away from these people . . .

Older people first. Three men and two women, heading off in different directions. The men's wash house was little more than an open shed, though there wasn't anything for her to see from her vantage point halfway up the slope to the hillcrest. The women's wash house was more fully enclosed. That was where the hotsprings would be, then.

Where was Meeka?

The sun would clear the east ridge within moments, and yet no man of Meeka's size or shape had left the sleeping house. In fact the younger people were hurrying out to wash, now, and there were no adults whatever between old folks and the young, so what was going on here?

Then even as Salli realized that she knew the answer, she heard the little friction of fabric moving against fabric behind her. Felt rather than heard the footfall in the heavy mat of fallen palm fronds that cushioned her prone body like a feather-bed. Well, of course there weren't any of the camp's men there below. They were out here already, on the hillside.

Looking for her.

"Good morning Pilgrim, and it's a beautiful morning. Even if it is only a Dream."

She heard the voice behind her: careful and wary. But a little amused. Yes, they had her, no question about it. She could have kicked the cushioning greenfall into a flurry in frustration. But she was at the disadvantage; she had to be circumspect.

"How much more beautiful the Day we Wake." And what did she have to worry about, really? Nothing. These were Wayfarers, true, or if they weren't she was very much mistaken. But there were rules of civility. She had meant to get Meeka by himself, without betraying her presence; but she had every right to come here on the errand that had brought her. "Say, I imagine you're wondering what this is all about."